The *Girl* from the Sugar Plantation

SHARON MAAS

Bookouture

Published by Bookouture
An imprint of StoryFire Ltd.
23 Sussex Road, Ickenham, UB10 8PN
United Kingdom
www.bookouture.com

ISBN: 978-1-78681-296-4
eBook ISBN: 978-1-78681-295-7

This book is a work of fiction. Names, characters, businesses,
organizations, places and events other than those clearly in the
public domain, are either the product of the author's imagination
or are used fictitiously. Any resemblance to actual persons, living or
dead, events or locales is entirely coincidental.

'I believe that there should be values other than money in a civilised society. I believe that truth, beauty and goodness have a place. Moreover, I believe that if businessmen put money, profit, greed and acquisition among the highest virtues, they cannot be surprised if, for instance, nurses, teachers and ambulance men are inclined to do the same.'

John 'Jock' Middleton Campbell, Baron Campbell of Eskan (8 August 1912–26 December 1994)

Chapter 1

1934, British Guiana, South America

When I was sixteen I made a pact with the devil. He came in the form of a fawning, red-faced and rather plump middle-aged man by the name of Mr Foot; but I was too innocent, too inexperienced in the ways of men, to guess his unsavoury intentions. Oh, I had an inkling, certainly. A twinge of intuition, a sense that his offer came with a price. But I was too excited to care. I ignored the undertones, so obvious in retrospect.

It was a pact born of my need for validation; my need, I suppose, for love: for isn't love the foundation of all other needs? But I only realised this in hindsight. At the time I craved applause, and that's what Mr Foot offered. Naive as I was, I had little clue as to what this agreement would eventually involve, but Mr Foot wasn't to know that; in his eyes I was easy pickings. He made the offer, opened a door and blindly I leapt through it. That door was my escape route: from a prison without walls or bars or boundaries, a prison consisting of infinite skies and endless green fields. But I'm getting ahead of myself. Let me explain.

I was born with a sugar spoon in my mouth, heiress to one of the great sugar dynasties of British Guiana, a remote colony perched on South America's eastern shoulder, tucked neatly between Brazil, Venezuela and two other Guianas. A land of great rivers and far-stretching seas, its arms wrapped around you as a mother. We called it BeeGee, a diminutive so much warmer and intimate

than the stern formal title, a name spoken like a luscious secret
among those of us who knew and loved her.

BeeGee. I miss it so much. The very word conjures up memories
of sunshine and flowers, butterflies and birdsong, beautiful white
wooden houses on stilts against a backdrop of succulent green. I
tend to forget the ugly parts. I tend to forget that it wasn't like that
for us all; that unhappy as I was, still I was born to privilege, that
within the dark underbelly of our little dynasty lay great suffering. I tend to forget that my little private prison was child's play
compared to that of so many of my brothers and sisters; that in
fact I was one of the lucky ones, despite my perceived misfortune.

Nevertheless, I *was* miserable. Our particular dynasty was in
danger of falling apart, with only me – female and half-blood,
the worst combination possible – as the final twitching limb and
potential saviour. The stalwart Englishmen who had wrestled our
sugar-gold from the earth (or rather, ensured it was wrestled; lowlier
beings did the actual work) were all long gone, leaving behind just
the two of us: Mama and me.

Promised Land, our crumbling kingdom, was a hundred-acre
estate in the county of Berbice on BeeGee's Corentyne coast, east
of the capital city of Georgetown. It was the only home I've ever
known, the foundation stone of my identity. From my bedroom
window on the upper storey of the estate mansion – rebuilt by
Mama after the Great Fire of 1921 – I looked out over a veritable
ocean of cane, green as far as the eye could see, reaching out to the
horizon, to the Atlantic in the distance, green ocean merging into
brown ocean. All my life I had absorbed the sights, the sounds,
the smells of the sugar year. The flood fallowing, when the ratoons,
the baby canes, have been planted, when water from the irrigation canals is let into the fields; the planting, the manuring, the
weeding: coolie women in once-bright, now faded saris bent low
in the muddy fields. The burning of the cane when the air would
be filled with the aroma of scalded cane-juice, rich, evocative,

unforgettable. The cane growing higher, higher, above my head, even when I sat on horseback – ten feet tall and more.

Then the harvest; swarms of coolies in the fields with their cutlasses, hacking down the giant cane-stalks; blackened by ash and burnt cane-juice, they would carry their bundles of cane on their backs and load the punts waiting on the navigation canals, swearing and shouting as they worked. Then the punts, pulled by mules, slowly making their way along the gridwork of canals to the factory, perched on the edge of the estate, as far away from the house as possible, a groaning monster devouring those canes, sucking them into its bowels, chewing them and grinding them with huge black metallic teeth and belching great black billows of smoke up through its tall chimneys.

A sugar plantation has a spirit of its own, and Promised Land was part of my identity. I had absorbed that spirit and knew it as intimately as I knew the rooms and hallways of our mansion and the paths through the splendid garden Mama had planted around the house, a riot of colour and birdsong.

And yet…

I might be a princess, but I was a deeply flawed one, a princess unworthy of the throne. Not in Mama's eyes, but in the eyes of the outside world, and they never missed a chance to let me know how imperfect I was. Not blatantly, you understand; but with subtle half-glances, frowns, awkward silences when I appeared, they placed an invisible glass wall between them and me to let me know my place. I never needed it spelled out in so many words; I had eyes. The hierarchy was plain to see, the layers that dictated and defined your place in society, ordained, it seemed by God. Black the bottom, white the top and a multitude of shades in between, with me floating precariously somewhere in the middle. Half-blood. Mixed-breed. Brown. The collective noun was 'coloured'. A status of its own, containing within itself a wealth of unstated derogatory adjectives.

While adults managed to conceal their contempt beneath a thin veneer of civility, children were not so subtle, nor so polite; children speak out the truth as learned from their parents and called me those names to my face: mongrel, mule, monkey and worse.

Up here in the Corentyne, far away from the incestuous and intricately layered social hierarchy that is Georgetown society, Mama had etched out a status for me. I was her daughter, adopted or not, and that spoke volumes. Mama, as the only female plantation owner in the colony, as a member of the board of the Sugar Producers' Association, was highly respected. She had a sharp tongue and feared no man. Indeed, men feared her. Everyone did. Mama always got her way; that's what they all said. Many hated her, even; but she was inviolable. I, on the other hand, was an open target: a child, a girl, a lightning rod. A pariah.

My status as princess pertained only within the narrow confines of our own plantation; beyond the plantation, beyond the Corentyne, I was nothing.

And so I fled. I fled from the sense of wretchedness and nothingness, from the sense that I did not belong, the knowledge that not all the plantations in the colony could rectify the error of my blood. I fled into the arms of music.

For more than all of this, more than the Atlantic reaching to the horizon, the endless fields of green, that vast Corentyne sky, as wide as it was high, everywhere space and more space, more than the air I breathed and the sun on my back and the birds and the flowers, it was music that gave wings to my soul. It was the piano I loved. My fingers longed to dance along the keys of a piano, fashioning such wings, wings of music, wings to let me soar. Most of all, music brought healing to that deep wound invisible to all but myself.

And that's where Mr Foot came in. Mr Foot held out a hand of opportunity, and I grasped it as a drowning man grasps at a floating branch.

It all began at the traditional Christmas ball at Promised Land. The usual crowd, the Bees and the Crawfords and the Wrights and the Feet (as everyone called Mr and Mrs Foot), from the neighbouring estates of Albion and Dieu Merci, Port Mourant, Rose Hall and Waterloo, Sophia's Lot and Monkey Jump, had gathered at our house. After dinner came the entertainment, and I played the piano accompaniment to the usual Christmas carols: 'Joy to the World', 'O Little Town of Bethlehem', 'Silent Night' and the rest, and even a little solo at the end. The applause was enthusiastic and, for once, I earned words of praise from those thin-lipped, pale-faced denizens of the plantocracy.

I dare say much of the tribute I earned was to flatter Mama, whom, her being a member of the board of the Sugar Producers' Association, everyone wanted to sweeten. Yet, I hoped behind the applause also lay genuine appreciation. Because I was good. I knew I was good, and I say this without vanity.

I first learned to play at the age of five, when Oma Ruth was still living with Aunt Winnie in Georgetown. Mama and I had been in town, staying at the Park Hotel – Mama had some business with the Sugar Producers' Association that would keep her there for a month, and she left me with Aunt Winnie and Oma Ruth during the day. That's when Oma taught me to play.

'She's a natural,' Oma had said, and that was the beginning of it all. 'She must have piano lessons when you go home!' Oma insisted, and though Mama wasn't keen on the idea – Mama always joked she didn't have a single musical bone in her body – I begged and cajoled and, in the end, she arranged for me to visit a teacher once a week in New Amsterdam. I'd always been able to wrap Mama around my little finger, and the next thing I begged for was a piano of my own. From the day the piano was delivered I was a child obsessed. I practised for hours on end, before school in the morning, after school in the afternoon. When I was fourteen my piano teacher said, 'I can't teach her any more. She's better than me.' And that was the end of that.

It was frustrating, as I knew there was still room for improvement, but BeeGee was a barren desert when it came to musical education; Georgetown was bad enough, but out here in the country? There was no one to teach me, and all I could do was play and play and play. 'You're worse than your grandmother,' Mama would complain, and I took that as a compliment.

That Christmas concert was the start of it all; the first time I'd played in public, the first time Mr Foot, the administrative manager of Albion plantation, heard me play. Afterwards he drew me aside for a private word. Even that was an extraordinary occurrence; white people, adults, never spoke to me beyond the cursory obligatory murmurings of polite society: *How do you do? Merry Christmas! What a pretty dress!* I was flattered from the start.

'Miss Smedley-Cox,' said Mr Foot, 'What a magnificent performance! Such a talented young lady – as talented as you are beautiful. You know, while you were playing I had an idea. I wonder if…'

He hesitated. And then, with much hemming and hawing, he continued:

'I was wondering if you would like to play at the reception at the Georgetown Club in a month's time? It's being held as a welcome party for the young lad who is coming to be trained in estate management – the heir to the Campbell throne, if you will. It will be quite a big do – everyone will be there – and I've been scratching my head trying to pull together the entertainment. It's going to be a splendid evening, and to have you play for us, as enthrallingly as you did just now – why, I'm sure we'd all be delighted.'

'You – you want me to play? At the Georgetown Club?'

I could not believe my ears. I had never set foot in the Georgetown Club, the Buckingham Palace of the colony. Everyone knew it was barred to coloureds. Mama, of course, was a regular there; due to her position on the Sugar Producers' Association, she often had to attend this function or that, and somehow to date she had managed to circumvent my exclusion with a modicum of dignity.

Even she was not willing to break such a time-honoured taboo, not even to pamper my pride.

But to play there? To actually play at the exclusive Georgetown Club? To play for a real English audience beyond the paltry groups of neighbours and estate staff? To play in public, to be heard and, hopefully, appreciated and applauded by the planter aristocracy, the Booker snobs, the white upper class? I couldn't believe it. I gaped and stuttered, and Mr Foot coughed and continued.

'I'll have to ask the SPA's permission, of course; but seeing as your mother is on the board, and knowing of her persuasiveness – she brings such a feminine touch to all our meetings! – I have no doubt that it will be approved. After all, you aren't coming as a guest, exactly—'

At the word 'guest' he turned lobster-red and hesitated, and I understood. As part of the entertainment I would be an employee at the function, not an invitee, and so convention could be sustained. My status there would be clear, as clear as that of the coloured maids who would be serving the sandwiches and the black barman who would be mixing the cocktails and pouring the rum punch. The only difference was that I would not be in a starched maid's uniform.

I understood, and he understood that I understood. I was to know my place. I was not an invitee; I was not to mingle, talk to the guests, behave in any way that would compromise myself – or him. I was to come, play and go.

'You will be paid accordingly, of course,' he added. 'Quite deservedly. Of course, there are other musicians – there's a rather good calypso fellow coming, Doctor Jangles, and we have a steel band lined up as well. Just to give it all a local touch. You know, the exotic element.'

He paused at this point.

'You do understand, don't you, that this is as a special favour from me? You do understand that it's a great' – he coughed ' – privilege for you to be invited. An unusual – ah – kindness. There are several other more experienced pianists in Georgetown, after all. And that I hope – er – would be delighted – well. No need to be indelicate. We do have an understanding, don't we, my dear?' And he looked at me, and winked. It was that wink I chose to ignore.

Though young, I was not a complete newcomer to the ways of men. I had already endured my portion of advances and intentions, advances that would certainly have been scandalous had I been of higher status; that is, white like them, like Mama. On more than one occasion I had been pinched; once, a young man had swept me behind a curtain and tried to kiss me. I had shoved him away. Men perfected the art of placing hands on knees beneath the dining table, or playing with feet, or, when they danced with me, of letting fingers wander where they shouldn't. That wink should have been easy to interpret, and at some unseen level I *did* understand. But I was not listening at that level, I was listening only to the fever of unrealised ambition. Ignoring the wink, I nodded vigorously and I'm sure my eyes must have radiated all kinds of acquiescence, as did my eager smile.

Encouraged, Mr Foot continued:

'As I was saying we do have the usual local entertainers but it would be rather wonderful to have some European music as well. I'm sure young Mr Campbell would appreciate it. And you, Miss Cox – well, you really are – for your age – the best such musician the colony has to offer. A very gifted young lady, and so beautiful as well, your golden skin, that magnificent mane of yours…'

He actually reached out, now, to touch my hair. Our housemaid Katie had done it for me and had managed to tame it so much that it cascaded over my shoulders and down my back in a tumble of curls and ringlets while my crown remained demure, kept obediently in place by a complicated arrangement of plaits and pleats and velvet ribbons. My hair was the bane of my existence. It refused to be restrained in any way. It kinked and curled and flew away when I would prefer it to fall neatly into place. It tangled and teased, refusing to bend to my will. If it were not for Katie I don't know what I would have done – cut it all off, most probably, and run around like a darkie boy with a close-cropped cap. That would certainly have suited me. But I did have Katie, and she did have magical hands where hair was concerned.

I drew back from Mr Foot's eagerly grasping hand, but not from him. I was interested; of course I was! I knew just one thing: this was my big chance. My debut. Yes, I would play for them; I would stun them with the beauty of music. Because my hands too were magical, on the keys of a piano.

'Mr Foot,' I said, 'I should be delighted to play at the Georgetown Club!'

With those words I sealed our little pact.

'What about your mother?' he asked, rather nervously. 'You'll need her cooperation. Her permission.'

'Don't worry about Mama,' I said, with more confidence than I felt. 'I'll persuade her.'

Chapter 2

Mama, as I'd feared, was not in favour. 'As an employee?' she exclaimed when I told her the following day. 'How can you play as an employee? You are my daughter! It's an insult, I hope you haven't agreed?'

'Oh Mama! Of course, I agreed! Don't you see? This is my chance!'

'Darling, I'm sorry, but you can't agree to this sort of thing without my consent. You're still a child.'

'I'm not, Mama, I'm not! I'm sixteen, almost adult! And I'm the best pianist in the country, Mr Foot himself said so. And I really want to; I really, really want to. Please let me? Please, please, please!'

I danced around her with clasped hands and pleading eyes; this was the best way to melt any objections she might raise. I knew this from past arguments. Mama might have a heart of steel to others, but not to me. I knew how to melt her. But this time she narrowed her eyes and glared at me.

'Mary Grace! Have you no pride? No shame? Can't you feel the insult?'

'No! It's not an insult, it's an honour! It really is, Mama! Everyone will be there, Mr Foot said; even the Governor himself! It's my chance, Mama, my first chance and maybe my last! Please let me… It means so much to me!'

Her eyes softened at that. She took my hands in hers and squeezed them, then let go and placed them over my ears and gave my head a jiggle as if trying to shake sense into me. Then she let go and took my hand and led me into the gallery. 'Darling, we need to talk,' she said. She picked up the cushion on one of the cane chairs, shook it out to free it of lizards or insects, puffed it up, replaced it and gestured for me to sit. My heart sank. Another lecture was coming on, and all I wanted was a simple yes. This 'we need to talk' was always a signal for an embarrassing and awkward mother-to-daughter conversation. I didn't want to hear it.

'Mama…' I began. 'Please, just—'

'No. You need to hear this,' she said firmly, and I knew then that there was no avoiding it.

'Look at me,' she said then, and I looked up and met her eyes. Mine were moist; I could feel it. I hated these little talks. They were like fingernails scratching at a soreness, and instead of alleviating it, only made it worse. It was a soreness that would not go away, however much I tried; a soreness that tore away every sense of value I could muster on my own, every notion of my own self-worth.

Even the belief that I was the country's best pianist – according to Mr Foot – could not heal that soreness.

'Darling, this is a cruel world we live in.' It was a hollow statement, and so I nodded. It meant nothing. I kept my eyes lowered, now: I did not want to meet hers.

'And we all have our burdens to bear. British Guiana is a world that belongs to the British. We have to accept that. They set the standards. They lay the rules.'

I looked up then. 'Why do you say *they*?' I cried. 'You are one of them! Look at you, white as any of them!'

She chuckled then, and glanced at her bare forearm. 'Well – apart from the sun's attempts to turn me brown as a berry, that's true!'

'So if you're British and I'm – I'm your daughter, that makes me British too!'

I met her gaze square on, challenging her to deny it.

The smile vanished from her lips. 'It's not as easy as that,' she said. 'It's not easy at all. Darling, you know the problem. You know the difference! You've been dealing with it all your life, but now it's time to grow up and face some ugly truths.'

That's what she thought. Just because a child hides away the wound, has learned to smile and laugh it all away, doesn't mean she's dealt with it. It just means she can act well. I'd never told Mama about the taunts and the jibes I'd parried all my life. As a young child, I'd attended the plantation's senior staff primary school, where all the children were British, and white, except me. I'd never told her about the name-calling. I'd never told her the reason why I never entered the senior staff compound to play tennis with my peers, or use the pool. I'd never told her of the mothers, and the teachers; they might not call me names, but I had learned to gauge an adult's response to me by the look in their eyes and the tone of their voice as much as through their actual words. Some relief had come when I moved to New Amsterdam High School, for the pupils there were mixed, and I found friends who looked like me. But the hurt had lodged itself into my consciousness and there it had stuck: not visible to anyone, least of all to Mama, and only felt by me when someone scratched at it. As she was doing now.

Now, Mama said: 'Darling, Georgetown is no place for you. The Georgetown Club – you can't go there. You can't play there. I never told you – but – well—'

She stopped. 'Don't make this difficult for me!' she cried then. 'You must know. You must feel it? Those people, they'll be hateful to you. They'll be rude. They'll – they'll tell you things – lies – insult you – me. The very fact that Mr Foot has invited you as an employee, an entertainer, should tell you all you need to know. You could never go there as a guest. It's whites only. You need to know that. You'd be little more than a servant. And yet you're my daughter. My daughter! They won't accept my daughter!'

The more words she uttered, the more loaded those words became. Loaded with anger, and loathing, and spite. And the more I understood.

'This isn't about me at all, is it, Mama?' I said then. 'It's about you. The insult to *you*. When they reject me, they reject you.'

I sprang to my feet. Tears stung my eyes. Mama, I knew, would never relent. Mama was proud, and vain, and adamant. She would rather see me miss this chance than accept the insult inherent in the invitation. I made to rush away, but as I passed she grabbed my wrist and pulled me back.

'Wait – no. Mary Grace, don't go. We still need to talk. It's not about the Georgetown Club, it's about – something else.'

I glared at her. 'About what?'

She lowered her eyes. 'About – us. You and me. You asked… you wanted to know – I said I'd tell you one day…'

'Oh.' I stopped, and looked down at her, and then retraced my steps, and sat myself down.

'You always wanted to know…' she began. And, all of a sudden, I knew what was coming. This was to be the day of truth. Finally.

Mama, usually so confident, so forceful, so dominant in all matters, had an Achilles heel. I had discovered it years ago, when I first started asking why.

Why, when both my parents were white – I had seen photos of my father – was I only a few shades lighter than the labourers who worked our fields and our factory? Obviously, I was adopted. But who were my birth parents? What happened to them? Were they still alive? Did they abandon me? Did they ever love me? Why had Mama and Papa taken me in? Had they chosen me or were they somehow forced to take me? Did Mama love me in spite of my skin colour? I knew she didn't like dark-skinned people. She cursed them every day. Was I the exception? Did she really love me, or was she just pretending? As much as she'd have loved a white child of her own?

I wanted, I needed, to hear it from her. I wanted to hear her say she had chosen me and loved me and it didn't matter about my skin colour or my blood or my birth: that she loved me all the same. That I was her real daughter, even if only adopted.

I must have been seven or eight when I first asked. Mama had hedged and hawed. 'It's a little bit hard for you to understand, darling,' she'd said. 'I'll tell you later.'

But I had not dropped the questions. I pestered Mama with these questions, and always she pushed me away, referred me to a time when I was older and she would tell all. 'You're too young to understand,' she'd say.

But I needed to know. I badgered and bothered her until one day – I must have been about ten – flustered beyond anything I'd ever seen, she cried out: 'All right, if you must know! If you must know, I'll tell you but you won't like it. Do you still want to know?'

So I nodded. 'Yes,' I said.

'Very well then. Your mother was a servant on one of the plantations. A black woman. Your father was – a white man from Georgetown. I don't know him. Your birth mother – she died – she died of – in childbirth. Are you happy now?'

I looked at her, straight in the eye. She looked away. That's when I knew there was more to the story, a lot more; but that's all I would be getting that day.

So all I said was: 'Thank you for telling me.' And I ran away to my secret place in the garden and cried my eyes out. But the next day, more questions came. What was my birth mother's name? Did she have brothers and sisters? Parents? They'd be my relatives, after all. Could I go and visit them? Were they in Georgetown? Perhaps they'd love me, and I'd love them back. And so my questions did not cease; indeed, they became yet more detailed. I was curious, too, about my father. Unsure about the facts of life, I wondered why Mama didn't know who he was. Had he been married to my mother? Could white men marry black women? Was it possible? She must know! Why didn't he want me? Where was he?

Mama meant well, but outspoken in all other circumstances, on this topic she became evasive. She told me lies. I could see right through those lies; that he had disappeared, left the country, all kinds of things. I wished she'd stop. Stop dangling the truth before my eyes in thinly veiled obscurities, in mysterious ambiguities that only made me more curious. Mama was no prude; I wished she'd just come out with it. Might as well try to squeeze blood from a stone.

'These are difficult questions. It's a long story. You're a child – you can't really grasp it all. When you grow up, I'll tell you everything.'

'You promise? Cross your heart and hope to die?'

She smiled then, and had taken me on her lap, and whispered it: 'Cross my heart and hope to die. I'll tell you the whole story when you grow up.'

But I wanted exact dates. 'When will I be grown up?'

'When you're – twenty-one.'

'Twenty-one! That's ages away!'

'That's the age when people are adults, though.'

'I can't wait that long! Please, Mama – please! Don't make me wait that long! I need to know!'

I pulled away from her, tried to ease myself off her lap, but she pulled me back.

'All right then. I'll tell you when you're – eighteen.'

'That's still too old! Fourteen!'

She laughed a mocking laugh. 'Fourteen? Why, at fourteen you're still a child. I said you need to be adult to understand certain things. I won't tell you a day before you're… you're—'

'Sixteen!' I cried. 'If you say sixteen I promise never to ask again, I promise to wait.'

She mulled for a while, thinking it over, and then she said, reluctantly, 'Very well, then. Sixteen it is.'

'You promise?'

'I promise. But you must promise not to ask again.'

I promised.

And now I was sixteen. The day had, it seemed, arrived.

Chapter 3

I'd promised never to ask again, but I had not promised not to find out on my own. The more Mama played hide-and-seek, the more I'd been driven to pry.

Because of course Mama's hint of a long story had only made me all the more curious. I had long been making my own investigations. That's why, when I finally did turn sixteen, I did not even bother to ask.

And that's why Mama's overly dramatic 'You always wanted to know…', with its promise of deep secrets to be revealed, now came as an anticlimax.

'Oh, that!' I exclaimed. 'About my birth parents, you mean? I already know, Mama. I found out.'

She visibly paled. 'You found out? How? Did someone tell you? How…? Darling, if you've heard rumours…'

I'd never seen her this flustered, hot and red. She picked up a fan from the glass-topped gallery table and began to fan herself vigorously. I sat back in my wicker chair and laughed and reached out and took her hand.

'Nobody told me, Mama. I searched and I found. I found out all on my own.'

'But how? Where?' She pulled her hand away and started to scratch her temples. Her face had turned red as a lobster, so I laughed again.

'I'm clever, aren't I? You should have hidden the documents better. I found the documents and I put two and two together. I figured out the secret.'

'What documents?'

'Why, the ones in that big file in the cabinet in your office. I was looking for my birth certificate and I found it.'

'But – that file is locked up!'

'And I found the key. And found the file, and read it. It says you and Papa are my parents. Clarence and Johanna Smedley. But that's not true, is it? It can't be true because you're white and so was he. So I kept looking through that file, to find out who my real parents were, and you know what else is in it. You know, don't you?'

Her eyes narrowed as she looked at me. She stopped that nervous scratching.

'What did you find?'

'You must know what's in that file! Five other birth certificates. Five! Five children born to four different mothers! Three of them with long Indian names and then another one with an English name – Emily. Emily Smith. Five different mothers but only one father: Clarence Smedley – Papa!'

'Darling, I—'

'I mean, I had heard the rumours before. That Papa was terribly unfaithful and used to have affairs with coolie women. I already knew that. Everybody knows that. It's no secret. So I wasn't really surprised.'

'Darling, I…' Mama rang the little bell on the table and Verbena, the kitchen maid, bustled out of the kitchen. Mama made the sign of drinking. Verbena nodded and hurried into the kitchen. Mama didn't finish whatever it was she was going to say. Not often lost for words, she now muttered something incoherent and fanned herself vigorously. I waited for her to speak and when she didn't, I continued.

'And then there was also that letter signed by Papa acknowledging fatherhood of the children, and then a letter from the lawyer, representing all those women jointly, and claiming child support. And from Papa's lawyer agreeing to support them. So you see,

I know everything. I know that I was just another mistake… I suppose my real mother must have really died, like you said, and so Papa and you took me on and you adopted me and that's why I'm your child.'

Verbena reappeared with a tray on which stood a jug of lime water and two glasses. She poured us each a glass. Mama drank; I didn't.

Mama had, miraculously, visibly relaxed by now, and nodded vigorously.

'Yes, darling. You see now why I couldn't tell you before. Such a scandal your father caused, fathering all those children! Although it wasn't really a scandal – for some reason it's accepted that estate owners will run around seducing labourer women, their own employees, and all they have to do is pay them off when they have children. I have the feeling some of these women do it deliberately even. Yes, they lose their reputation and they can't marry, but they get such a fine pay-off, they don't care. They are far better off than if they were to marry some poor rice farmer. They get a cottage of their own and their children are of course lighter-skinned and even if they are called bastard for a few years, once they grow up they get better jobs and the mothers have far more independence. Anyway, yes. That's the kind of trouble Clarence got himself into.'

'And then I came along.'

'Yes! And he adored you, darling. Really he did.'

Mama replaced her glass on the table, leaned forward and took both my hands in hers. She looked directly into my eyes, holding my gaze. Mama always did this when she wanted to re-establish our very close connection, our inviolable mother–daughter link. It always worked. Yet now, somehow, it seemed strained, overwrought, as if she were too eager, too zealous in her persuasion.

'He was a really good father, I promise you. And I… I couldn't have children. We had tried for so long but there's something wrong with me. Either I didn't conceive or else I miscarried. So when – when you came along, and your birth mother couldn't—'

'Who was she, Mama? Did she really die in childbirth? Or did she not want me?'

This was the part I had been unable to discover among Mama's papers. It had been a relief to know that Papa really was my father, but my mother – who was she? Why did she give me up? Or was it true that she'd died in childbirth? Had Mama told the truth, or did she just want me to stop asking? Was she perhaps still alive, somewhere? There was no paper trail leading to her, no trace of her at all, no mention. Mama was named as mother on my birth certificate, Clarence Smedley as father. My real mother's name had been completely obliterated. Mama, meanwhile, had let go of me and poured herself another glass of lime water. She sipped at it as she spoke.

Mama drained the glass, set it down and reached out again over the table, reaching for my hands. I hesitated before complying.

'I told you, darling. Why won't you believe me? She died in childbirth – I told you long ago! So, of course, Clarence, your father – well, he brought you home to me, a tiny baby, and begged me to take you in, and I fell in love with you immediately. And that's the whole story. You see why I couldn't tell you earlier? A child can't understand. About men and women and having affairs and all of that. I was only trying to protect you, darling.'

'What was her name?'

'What? Whose name?'

'My birth mother's.'

'Oh! I've forgotten. Let me think…' She paused, taking time to sip at her drink before continuing, frowning as if scouring her brain. 'I think it was – yes, it was Martha. Martha Jones. A coloured woman, not an East Indian. That's why we called you Mary. In her honour. Martha and Mary – from the Bible! And later I added the name Grace. Mary Grace. Such a lovely name! Anyway, you have been Mary Grace ever since.'

'Oh, I see. So you had me from the start – since I was a baby? A newborn?'

'Yes. And loved you from the start. I don't care about your skin colour, darling. I don't care that you aren't white like me. That doesn't matter in the least. Look at your Aunt Winnie, and the boys! They're not white either, are they, and you know how Winnie adores them!'

Mama's sister, Aunt Winnie, lived in Georgetown with her eight sons. I loved them all – the boys were like brothers to me, and I often wished I had grown up with them all, because it was such fun being the only girl in a household of boisterous boys. When I was younger I used to visit them regularly, or else they came up to visit – a few at a time. Oh, those times! Those boys! Never a dull moment. They could pull adventures out of their ears, and they spoiled me rotten. When I was with them I became a different person, a different girl, running and jumping and doing the things boys do, play-wrestling on the ground and catching tadpoles in the trench. Humphrey taught me the tricks of crossword puzzles, Charlie to play tennis, Freddy to ride a bicycle, Gordon to climb trees and watch lizards, birds and ants. As I grew older, they warned me of the ways of adolescent boys, and how to defend myself against straying male hands; they taught me the secret weapons of a woman. Returning to Promised Land after a stay with my cousins would always seem dull at first. Alone there in the vast spaces of the Corentyne, I had only music and reading for entertainment, my only escape from myself. And so the two halves of my being emerged, and I moved from one to the other with ease: the sensitive, introspective, artistic me of the plantation, she who could fly to the stars with music; and the wild, outgoing, daring me of the city, she who loved the rough-and-tumble of Quint masculinity.

But a scandal surrounded my cousins: they were all dark-skinned – various shades of dark, from the almost-white of Leo to the deep mahogany of Freddy. This was because Aunt Winnie had married George Quint, a black man. Aunt Winnie in her youth had caused the outrage of the century when she turned her back on upper-class British society to marry a poor black postman.

The result was uproar. Snooty British society had thrown Auntie out onto the street and – sometimes literally – spat upon her. She had told me bits of her story in the past, to comfort me when I cried out my sorrow over my own rejection. 'You can't let others determine your worth,' she told me. 'If they throw you out, stand up again and go your own way. As long as you know your way is right and good – and you must make sure it is so – do it. Your value is intrinsically yours, bound up in your very humanity; believe in it, and hold your head up high.'

That's what she had done; while raising eight boys she had clawed her way out of rejection. She had held up her head, rolled her eyes at the snobbish ignorance of others, risen to her feet and marched on with never a vicious word of retaliation: she was now not only accepted but a highly respected icon of society. After all, only an idiot or a bigoted fool could reject a person of such overwhelming presence as Aunt Winnie. You didn't just see her, you felt her, and it was a good feeling. She had literally charmed her way back into the English fold, never bowing to arrogance or slight, never angry, always self-assured and never compromising herself. Since Uncle George's death, I'm told, she had truly come into her own, a pillar of strength just by being who she was. Ma Quint, everyone called her, a name she had truly earned as the matriarch of a huge and diverse family.

I loved Aunt Winnie, almost as much as I loved Mama, and I loved staying with her and the boys. But Mama wouldn't visit; she never did, and I didn't know why. Mama and Auntie had the most strained relationship imaginable. When asked why they each gave a different reason.

'Yoyo and I have a different opinon on how Promised Land should be run,' was Aunt Winnie's explanation of the discord between her sister and herself. 'Your mother is a bit of a tyrant,

Grace. She exploits her workers. Your Oma tried to change her but couldn't. I'm quite happy to call a truce but Yoyo doesn't believe in truces; you're either friend or foe.'

'It has to do with your Oma,' Mama said. 'It's not right when a mother prefers one child above the other. Your Oma always preferred Winnie and that of course led to tensions. We can't help it; we don't like each other.'

But I knew for sure that the 'not liking' part was entirely on Mama's shoulders. Aunt Winnie was a lady who calmed troubled waters, who couldn't harbour a grudge against a single soul. Perhaps it was true, that Oma favoured Aunt Winnie; but surely that wasn't Auntie's fault? Surely, now that Oma was safely back in Austria and out of the way, the path was clear for them to make amends?

Sometimes I wished Auntie was my mother, not Mama. I would have loved to grow up with eight brothers. In town. My life would have been so very different. But I couldn't entertain such thoughts. They were unfair to Mama; they were disloyal. But oh – how lonely my life was out here! There was nothing to do, except play the piano and read books. I had never been to a proper ball. Never been escorted to the cinema by a young man. The young men I met from our neighbouring estates were British, and white, and I knew without words that I could never aspire to a romance with one of them, much less marriage. Mama had warned me early enough; when it came to marriage, she said, my prospects were limited. No British family of any standing would allow me in as a bride. British Guiana society was carefully layered; there was a real danger that I would have to marry down: a Portuguese businessman, for instance, or a man from the coloured upper-middle class.

'That's just the way it is,' she said. 'But there's still hope. What you must do is this: ensnare a wealthy white man of independent means, even if he's a bit older. Make him fall desperately for you. Other women have done it so why can't you? You're beautiful enough; men can't resist beauty. And those older men, they aren't so fussy. They do marry coloured women; they're considered particularly exotic. You can get one of those. Never marry down, Mary Grace. Your Aunt Winnie did, and see where it got her.'

In my eyes, it had got her far: she had a lovely big house in a nice part of town and eight bright and handsome sons. Uncle George had died before I could get to know him, but I knew from the way the way everyone spoke of him that he had been a good father and husband, loved by all, who had risen above his ordained place in society. I opened my mouth to tell Mama all this, but she cut me off and said, 'Anyway, to get back to the subject, darling: this is the reason why I can't let you play piano to entertain guests at the Georgetown Club. It's awfully impertinent – downright rude – of Mr Foot to even suggest such a thing. An insult to me! He wouldn't dare ask one of the young daughters of the other board members to do such a thing. Who does he think you are, some Parisian chorus girl kicking up her legs at the Moulin Rouge?'

'Mama! It's not a bit like that!'

'It certainly is! It's paid entertainment. It is what it is. Who else is entertaining?'

'Well – he said a calypsonian, and a steel band.'

'There! See? That's exactly the insult.'

I realised that we had reached a stalemate. Mama had dug in her heels. Mama's pride was inviolable: offend her once and that was the end of all negotiations. I had only one weapon left in my arsenal. I burst into tears.

'You're so mean!' I sobbed. 'This is my only chance! I'll never get to play in public again, never!'

She reached out for me, tried to embrace me, comfort me. Mama could never abide my tears. 'Oh darling!' she said. 'You play in public all the time! Look at Christmas – everyone loved your playing. You brought our carol singing to life! And I'm sure you'll get other invitations, at Albion and Dieu Merci, when they have dinner parties and so on. People love musicians, and—'

I wrestled myself from her grasp, and continued to bawl.

'It's not the same! I don't want to play these stupid little songs. "Oh My Darling Clementine" and "Daisy Daisy" – I'm sick of it! I want to play Bach, and Mozart, and Chopin! I want to play for people who would appreciate it. The Governor! And – and this new fellow from England. I want to make my mark!'

Between sobs I managed to get it all out. I had to show her how serious this was. How important to my life. All the hours I had spent at that piano, perfecting my art: they had to pay out at some point. Mama didn't understand music, and didn't appreciate it: more often than not, she told me to stop because she couldn't stand the din. The din! She called Mozart a din! 'I need earplugs!' she'd complain when I played in the evening, and request that I sing 'She'll be Coming Round the Mountain' or some other nonsense instead.

'I don't have a musical bone in my body,' she'd laugh, as if it were something to be proud of, and those were the times I most longed for Auntie Winnie and Oma Ruth. Mama even acknowledged that I'd have been better off with them. 'You get your musicality from the Birnbaums,' she once said. 'The Austrian side of the family.' Oma, Ruth Birnbaum, was originally from Austria, from Salzburg. She had fallen desperately in love with my grandfather and married him and come out here to be with him. She had returned to Austria when I was twelve, to care for her ageing father.

'Except that I'm adopted – so no relation!' I reminded her.

'Well… these things aren't necessarily genetic,' she then said, 'it's also programming. Oma Ruth taught you when you were a young child. All the modern psychologists say that nurture is more important than nature. Oma Ruth gave you the impulse, and the rest was your own hard work.'

Now, as I sobbed my heart out, hands over my eyes, I could see between my fingers that she was softening. Mama could not bear to see me in pain, and though my disappointment now was genuine, I exaggerated my distress. She was helpless against tears if they came from me.

'Darling…' she said, reaching for me; but again I wriggled away.

'Please, Mama. Please, please, please! Let me go. I don't care if they insult me, I truly don't care. I'll play so well they'll only have admiration afterwards. They'll applaud me, and you as well. I promise you, Mama. I'm good, I really am!'

'Well, I wouldn't know what good was if it screamed into my ear!' she said. 'But at least it's piano and not violin. When Winnie used to play that screechy thing, I would run out of the house – it was like a donkey braying!'

I wanted to defend Auntie Winnie, who played the most beautiful violin music, but I thought better of it. Mama was on the verge of capitulating. I gave one more heartbreaking sob.

'It's the most important thing in my life!' I bawled.

She sighed then, and I knew I'd won.

'Oh well, all right then. But—' I leapt from my chair and threw my arms around her. 'Thank you, Mama! Thank you, thank you! I love you so much!' And I showered her with so many kisses that now she was the one pushing me away, trying not to smile and failing.

'But that means I'll have to come as well. I can't let you go on your own, to face those hyenas at the Georgetown Club. They won't dare insult you to your face if I'm with you.'

'Oh yes, Mama – I want you there! Please come. And then you'll see how good I am!'

'Well, I don't know about that. I can't tell the difference between dulcet and discord, but I suppose you'll need some support.'

She sighed again. 'I suppose you'll need a new dress too. I can't let you go in rags.'

Chapter 4

The following week, Mr Foot came over from Albion to discuss the repertoire. He explained that, having given the matter some thought, he had decided that I was to be the star musician of the evening; that I was to offer a whole hour of playing. The others – the calypso singer and the steel band – would act as an introduction.

'Has the SPA board agreed yet?' I asked, quite suspicious; suspicious, not of him, but the board.

'Not yet,' replied Mr Foot. 'But I'll explain it all to them. You see, I don't want to overwhelm Mr Campbell with local music. I'm sure his taste is far more sophisticated than that. The calypsonian and the steel band – they are just a taster, a bit of exotic native culture. If you can even call that kind of music culture. If you can even call it music.'

'Oh, I adore good steel band music!' I cried. 'It can be rousing at times, but also so soothing – and isn't it wonderful how they can extract such beautiful sounds out of old steel drums? I've even heard them play Bach – it was really good!'

Mr Foot shrugged. 'If you say so; you're the musician. But let's get around to the repertoire. It should be appropriate. Nothing too demanding – we don't want you making mistakes, do we? Let's keep it simple. A few pretty, feminine pieces; perhaps some evening tunes to delight the company. What do you suggest? Perhaps you can give me a few examples of pieces you are most competent at.'

I duly obliged and offered a few suggestions, playing them for him: Beethoven's 'Moonlight Sonata' and 'Für Elise', Mozart's *Eine Kleine Nachtmusik*, a few Chopin nocturnes. He found them all delightful. Bending down close to my face, he tra-la-laed merrily along with the Mozart, and hummed with the Chopin, and generally made a brave attempt to show off his appreciation.

'It's all perfectly wonderful, my dear!' he exclaimed. 'I am unable to choose – you make your choice, and let me know in a week's time, and I'll have a programme printed. Such a gifted girl you are! And beautiful, too! I'm sure many men have told you you're beautiful…'

We were standing by this time and he took a step closer to me; I feared he'd kiss my cheek, and took a step back. And that was the moment I first opened my eyes, and realised what I had really agreed to, and what I had missed in my eagerness for applause. I remembered the warnings of my cousins: beware of flattery, they'd said. Beware; be wary. But I hadn't.

A feeling of disgust, like a spider crawling down my spine, overcame me, and I stepped back even further. But he took my hands in his and pulled me close again, and squeezed them slightly. 'My dear, this has been such a pleasure. I do feel it has brought us closer together, and perhaps you like me a little better now… just a little?'

He squeezed my hands even tighter. His were moist, and clammy, and I pulled mine from his clasp. My cousins here would have recommended a sharp word of reproach, but all I did was to stutter out a lame response:

'Mr Foot, I-I don't think—'

'I was actually wondering, my dear, if you would call me Harold, and I can call you Mary Grace? Just between us, of course; not when we're in public.'

I tried to conjure up all the advice my cousins had given me for just such situations. *Pull away, stand up straight, glare at him. If he insults you, give him a slap. Never show weakness.* But all that emerged from my lips were more weak stutterings.

'Mr Foot, I-I don't think that would be appropriate. I-I-I'm so grateful to you, b-b-but—'

'It's all right, my dear, no need to explain. I do understand; I have daughters myself, after all, and I do know how delicate you females are in such matters. I won't insist for the time being. I am content to be patient. And one must always be aware of etiquette. But maybe you could *think* of me as Harold; and I shall think of you as Mary Grace. Is that a possibility?'

'Please, Mr Foot – I don't want—' I said. Mama entered the music room just then, and Mr Foot quickly dropped my hands and spoke in a jovial voice.

'Then it's all agreed, Miss Smedley-Cox. I'm so pleased, and I look forward to the reception. I can see it's going to be a proper little concert. Mrs Smedley-Cox, your daughter will be the star of the night!'

'I should hope so,' said Mama, and immediately began a conversation on plantation business. That was Mama: nothing but business in her mind. I slipped away unobtrusively. And, much as I looked forward to my debut concert – because Mr Foot had called it that and so would I – from now on, I knew for certain that I had bitten off more than I could chew. And I wondered if it was worth it.

'You must have a beautiful dress!' said Mama. 'You must be the most sensationally gorgeous female in the room. You must outshine all those insipid plantation daughters. You must demonstrate to that chinless new chap that you might be not quite of his class but you have class of a different calibre. Because you do.'

'Mama, it's not about my looks, it's about my playing!'

But Mama was incapable of understanding. For her, the concert, as with life itself, was all about competition, and as she was no judge of music, it was to be about feminine wiles, female attraction, a matter with which she was well acquainted. Mama, in her mid-thirties, was still a beauty: her hair dark blonde, her skin golden, her eyes blue, she was well aware of how to use her appearance as a weapon. Men admired her, and she basked in their admiration, and flirted. However, she was securely married, to an American, Geoffrey Burton, who chose to spend most of his time in Louisiana, where he owned a sugar plantation. Sometimes he came to visit her, visit us, and at those times Mama truly blossomed; but she refused to live in America – because of me, she said. Racism there was even worse than in BeeGee. I loved her all the more for that decision. And so she lived in a long-distance marriage, for my sake. She even kept the name of her first husband, Smedley, after marriage, for me, so that we would both have the same name, Smedley-Cox. I did not like Uncle Geoff, as I called him, at all. And it was mutual. We tolerated each other, though; always polite, we survived our times as a pretend family.

But I could see that Mama used both her beauty and her dominating personality to forge her path; men tended to capitulate at such a combination. I saw with my own eyes how she with singular force edged herself not only into a position as a sugar planter but to her place on the board of the SPA and how men melted before her. And it was Mama's great disappointment that I would never be considered in the same way. How could I be, touched by the tarbrush as I was?

'You're too docile!' Mama complained again and again. 'All this music and reading and walks in the garden, floating up on cloud nine – it's turning you into a jellyfish. At your age I was riding out into the fields and showing the labourers that I was the new boss. I carried a whip, even if I never used it. You need some of that spirit. You need *Haare auf die Zähne* – hair on your teeth!'

Hair on your teeth – a German expression, apparently, for toughness, one of the few expressions Mama had decided to memorise from the language taught her by her Austrian mother. Alas, my teeth were still smooth and white, and I knew for sure I'd never wield a whip, not even for show. But Mama's demands on my character did nothing to improve my sense of worth. She did not hesitate to call me names: cream puff, and milksop, and, her favourite, jellyfish. I never bothered to remind her that a jellyfish was hardly a pushover – they might often lie on the seashore, seemingly innocuous in their transparent stillness, but step on one and the sting could lame you for days. Mama, however, was oblivious to such fine arguments and I often wondered how a woman as intelligent as she could be so ignorant as to believe that calling a child names could ever encourage that child to switch character. She wanted to turn me into a version of herself, and her failure to do so was her biggest frustration. And this concert, it seemed, now that she had acquiesced to it, was to be turned into the battlefield on which I would finally triumph.

'We'll show them!' she said now. 'A combination of your playing and your beauty and this dress – they'll know who they are dealing with, even if they'll never admit it!'

'Mama, I just want the opportunity to play in public, that's all. It's all very well to play for myself; music makes me so happy. But I want to make others happy too.'

'Even the people who insult you? Who reject and disdain you?'

'Yes, Mama, *especially* them. I want to show them they are wrong. I want to show them it's what inside that counts, and the only way is through music. Music is my very soul, Mama. It's the only way I can make myself heard. It's the only way I can actually be myself.'

Mama shrugged. 'I'll never understand this music business. It's a foreign language to me, like Chinese or something. I blame your grandmother – she's the one who put music into your head. A useless hobby, but she and Winnie – well, you take after them. I remember when we were children: your Oma Ruth filled the house with music. That piano we had then; her parents sent it all the way from Salzburg. And she and Papa used to roll back the carpets and dance, and we would all dance with them. Those were the days – so innocent. I suppose childhood days are always pure. And then…'

She shrugged, as if to shake off the past. I knew a little of that past; how the rot had set in and it all went downhill, ending with the fire that destroyed the Promised Land plantation house as well as Oma's precious piano.

'I should have put my foot down. Music is weakness, and she encouraged it. I should have taken control, taken you out into the fields with me more, raised you to be a planter. Really, I should be putting my foot down. I don't understand it, but if it's what you want, my darling…'

'Yes, Mama. It's all I want.'

Mama decided that I should wear a dress of emerald green silk to the concert. Green, after all, was her favourite colour, and though I had little sense of fashion, style was Mama's forte, so green it had to be. She and I chose the material together at an East Indian fabric shop in New Amsterdam; we bought a whole skein of Indian silk, because the dress was to have a full skirt and puffed half-sleeves and be simply stunning.

'It sets off perfectly the gold of your skin,' Mama said at the fitting, stroking my arm. It was such a strange thing; I was always being praised for the colour of my skin (So golden! As if it has trapped the sunlight!) and yet it was exactly this that made of me an outcast. This was the strange English reasoning. How could a thing – skin – be beautiful and enviable, and simultaneously the very thing for which one is rejected? It made no sense. But so little did in the world I lived in.

Mama whipped out a tape measure and she and Katie and the private dressmaker she had engaged began their prodding and poking and pinning all over again. We were in a bit of a hurry – the concert was the following weekend, and we would be travelling to Georgetown on Thursday. Mama and I were to stay at the Park Hotel, as usual. I had begged to be allowed to stay at Aunt

Winnie's, but Mama had, once again, refused. I never understood why we could not both stay there – after all, they were sisters – but we never did. Even so, why could not I, who loved them all and was loved in return, stay there, and Mama stay at the hotel? Why didn't they get on, anyway? But that seemed just another secret I was too young to understand.

When I was a child it had been different. Mama had allowed me to live with them once for a month, and visit for weekends; but the older I grew, the more questions I asked, the more she restricted those visits. Now, I had not been to town for over a year, and my cousins had not come up to visit for longer than that. It's said that every family has its secrets, and we are no exception: the Coxes, the Smedleys, the Quints. One day, I would know the whole truth. But right now, I had a performance to prepare for; the performance of my life, and at least I would be seeing them all again when we were in Georgetown, my aunt and my cousins – what remained of them. A couple of Aunt Winnie's eight sons had gone off to England to study. I had lost track of who was where; but I was almost as excited about seeing them all again as I was about the concert.

Chapter 5

Mama's best friend, Margaret Smythe-Collingsworth, came up to visit that Saturday; she would stay the week, and we would all travel down to Georgetown together. By that time Mama had made a complete turnabout on the matter of my performance. Now, she was all in favour of it; however, I was a little peeved at the amount of self-delusion she continued to indulge in.

'Mary Grace is just like me,' she said to Aunt Margaret as we retired to the gallery after dinner. 'She may appear timid but that's just on the surface. She is strong; she does not care what others think. Snubs and sneers do not affect her, and that's why she's determined to show off her brilliance. This was her decision, not mine – she persuaded me. See what a strong will she has! Apart from that, she is by far the most beautiful girl in the colony, and she knows it. I am so proud of her.'

Really? Couldn't she see that deep inside I was quaking with apprehension and nerves? Did Mama so overestimate me that she truly believed I was a replica of herself, a butterfly in a cocoon just waiting to spread her wings, and that this concert would be the stage? The more she expressed this version of my future, the more fear grew inside me. I would never, ever, be able to live up to her expectations. I would never, ever be that social butterfly, admired and courted by all those who mattered. Most of all, I would never, ever be good enough to be chosen as a bride by the kind of man Mama saw as my equal.

And that was the core of my problem: even now, the more I considered this invitation by Mr Foot, his inappropriate hints and advances, the more I realised my predicament. I knew I would never give in to his unsuitable proposals – I did not even like him, much less love him; in fact, he repulsed me. But what had I let myself in for? How far would he go? And how dare he even suggest such a thing? Mr Foot could only dare to do as he did because of my unconventional breeding. He knew, as we all did, that my marriage prospects were, at least as far as men of equal standing were concerned, non-existent. That most likely I would never find a husband among the eligible bachelors of society – those sugar princes who, were I of worthy stock, would have fallen over themselves backwards to win my hand. Because, even if one of them should by some miracle fall for me and ask for my hand, their families would never allow it. Mr Foot, in other words, thought I was desperate: easy pickings.

'Really proud,' Mama continued. 'Come here, darling, let me give you a hug.' She pulled me to her and embraced me. We took our seats; the maid followed with our cocktails. Margaret liked her alcohol, and never visited without an ample supply of El Dorado rum. I, of course, was not allowed to drink. This was to be their little gossip hour.

'See, Margaret? She and I, we're a team. She's a real little princess. Run along now, my sweet, and finish packing. We'll be leaving early tomorrow morning; you need to be ready when you get up. Come on, Margaret, here's your glass. I do loathe these Booker events but one can't avoid them, can one? You know the saying, keep your friends close, but your enemies closer. I need to see this new fellow up close, and the earlier the better. He's going to be owner-manager of Albion; we'll be neighbours. The sooner we meet, the better.'

I pricked my ears; if this new chap was going to be our neighbour, I wanted to hear more. Life stands still on the Corentyne coast; a new neighbour is always an interesting event. So I remained seated; if anyone knew anything about him, it would be Aunt Margaret. Indeed, I wasn't disappointed.

'There are all sorts of rumours about him,' said Aunt Margaret. 'Marjorie Baldwin received a letter from her people in London the other day – a real louche, he is. Fast cars and loose women are his main forte. His family have packed him off to BeeGee in the hope it'll knock some sense into him. There are rumours of some girl he was courting – entirely inappropriate. They had to get him out of the country.'

Mama laughed. 'Oh, that's so typical! These young men, sent off to the colonies because their fathers can't cope. I remember so well the letter Papa received from Uncle Percy, about just such a young man gone off the rails. They sent him to us, to give him some spine and a bit of chin. The result being that he ended up as my dearly beloved husband. Now, Margaret, don't snicker. It's not respectful of the dead. May he rest in peace, dear Clarence.'

But Aunt Margaret continued to snicker. 'Yes, dear departed Clarence. We all know how that went, don't we, Yoyo?'

Mama immediately made a face at Aunt Margaret, a face with a frown that said *Say No More*, because I was present and I wasn't supposed to know too much. But I did, by now.

Aunt Margaret ignored Mama's warning. She loved nothing more than a good gossip, and any mention of my father loosened her tongue.

'BeeGee seems to be the last dumping ground for all those black sheep making themselves a nuisance in England,' she continued. 'I suppose this new chappy is another one of them, sent to the back of beyond to make a man out of him and drive some sense into an empty head, as with Clarence. I did warn you, Yoyo, at the time. Everyone could see at a glance how that little folly of yours would end up.'

'Clarence was a very fine man and a dear husband and a devoted father.' Mama straightened her back and raised her chin, and her nostrils flared as she spoke; another lie, for my sake. Everyone knew that Clarence Smedley had been a drunkard, and had died by falling into an irrigation trench when I was just a toddler. Mama knew that I knew but she liked to keep up the pretence. 'Mary Grace, are you still here? Do run along now, dear. You need to finish packing. Katie will help you.'

This time I did say goodnight and take my leave.

The next morning, we were up at dawn for an early breakfast. Half an hour before we were due to leave for the ferry a ferocious jangling of the doorbell caused us all to rush into the main hallway. Samson, our houseboy, opened the door, and in fell Mr Bond, Mama's estate manager.

'Trouble!' he gasped, snatching off his pith helmet. 'Another protest. It's bad this time, Ma'am.'

Mama groaned. 'Not another one! What do the little buggers want this time?'

I cringed at Mama's language. I didn't know much about plantation business and how to run it, but I hated the way she spoke of our East Indian labourers. Surely they were humans too, just like us. Why use such dreadful language? Mama could be so crude at times.

'It's schooling, again,' said Mr Bond. 'They won't let it go, Ma'am. They're insisting on a proper primary school for the little ones.'

'What will they want next? How bad is it?'

'Well, see for yourself!' He gestured to the window and we all walked over. The double metal gate to the compound was a good distance away, down an alleyway of glorious bougainvillea bushes, but the house had been deliberately built so that the gate was in full view of the gallery window. And now we saw it: a clamouring crowd behind it, men, half-naked, fists raised or clinging to the bars of the gate, rattling it. Our coolie labourers. We could hear them, too, a faint chant in the distance. We couldn't understand the words but the tone was clear: these men were angry. Furious. And they were many, a host, maybe a hundred, or more. It was quite frightening.

'Look, Mr Bond, can't you deal with them this time? Tell them we'll employ a teacher for an hour a day, and build a shed against the sun. Or something. I can't be bothering with this nonsense right now; we're just about to leave for Georgetown.'

'No, Ma'am, I don't think they'll accept that, and I can't handle it on my own. I've already had lengthy discussions with Mahmoud, their leader. They're serious about it this time. They've threatened another strike.'

Mama paled. 'A strike? Good lord! We can't have that. Harvest starts next week!'

'Exactly,' said Mr Bond. 'That's why you're needed. You'll need to make a decision and reach an acceptable compromise. It is, after all, a reasonable demand. Parents do want the best for their children.'

'The worst thing in the world for a planter is educated coolies,' grumbled Mama. 'I do suppose you're right, though; I can't allow this to escalate just before the harvest. I'll have to deal with it. Sorry, darling,' she continued, turning to me, 'trip cancelled. But I'm sure you—'

'No, Mama, please, no! You can't cancel. I have to play, I have to! Please, Mama, let me go alone. I beg you, please!'

'She can come down with me,' interjected Margaret. 'I'm still going. She can stay with me, too. Obviously, she can't stay alone at the Park.'

'I should think not!' said Mama. 'But, if you're sure…'

'I could stay with Aunt Winnie!' I cried. 'Oh Mama, please let me, I should love to!'

'Certainly not!' said Mama firmly. 'Very well, you may go; Margaret will be your chaperone, and you will stay at her place. I'll remain here and deal with these hooligans. What a bother!'

'Thank you, Mama; oh, thank you!'

'Gilbert will already be waiting with the car, but he won't be able to use the main entrance. Tell him to slip out through the back, Margaret. You'd better go now. Come and give me a kiss, darling. I do wish you all the best on Saturday night. Show them what you can do. Show them you're my daughter!'

'I will, Mama; I will.'

Aunt Margaret and I made our escape through the backlands, and as we drove away, leaving behind Mama and the plantation and all the troubles, I felt as if I were leaving a world behind, and entering another. I was on the brink of something new, something big. I sank into the back seat as we drove off in a cloud of dust, and as I breathed out I knew, deep inside, in my bones, in my blood, in my breath: a new era was about to dawn.

Chapter 6

Gilbert, as instructed, drove us first along an unpaved track on the backdam, finally turning north towards the main road shortly before Albion estate. Along that main road it was a further two hours to New Amsterdam; there, we arrived in time for the 2 p.m. ferry across the Berbice River to Rosignol.

The Rosignol dock was teeming with people. Stout market women from the villages and farmlands of the East Coast Demerara waited to cross over into the Corentyne, their baskets bulging with produce, from plantains and avocados to the long strips of bora beans and leafy callaloo. Donkey carts laden with huge branches of bananas, regular sized as well as the miniature spice bananas and small but plump apple bananas. Coconuts, green-fleshed and brown-shelled. Mangoes galore; breadfruit, pineapples, green pawpaws. There were longer dray carts loaded with planks from one of the Demerara sawmills – somebody was building a new house on the Corentyne. Heavy machinery; imported, perhaps, from America. And just people, swarming the streets so that the car had to creep slowly between them, now and then interrupting a lively mid-road chat with a blast of the horn.

But soon we were free, heading west along the coast road towards the capital, rolling through the countryside. Guiana's coastal plain is six feet below sea level and the land is flat; but it had been conquered by the Dutch, who, experts at sea management, had rescued it from the floods, tamed it, brought the water under control, built dams and *kokers* – sluices – drained and irrigated it, and made it suitable for farming. Now, it was farmed mostly by East Indians, those

fortunate or enterprising ones who had managed to negotiate their
freedom from indenture. Flooded fields of emerald green paddy
with coolie women bent double in the water, weeding. Of course,
the ubiquitous cane fields, endless miles of cane at various stages
of growth: fields burnt black, or sprouting with new shoots, or at
half- or full-height, towering up into the vast sky. We passed fishing
villages, where fishermen had spread their black nets over the bare
ground, while the shore to our right was lined with fishing boats,
upside-down beside the Sea Wall. And then the Sea Wall itself –
that long brick structure stretching from Georgetown to Rosignol
as a barricade against the ocean, the most vital gift of the Dutch.
Most of the plantations along this coast had once been in Dutch
hands, thus some of the names: Beterverwagting, Vreed en Hoop,
Kyk-Over-Al. The French, too, had come and gone, and left their
mark in the village names: Non Pareil, La Bonne Intention and
Mon Repos, and of course our own neighbour in the Corentyne,
Dieu Merci. But it was the British who stayed, giving their villages
quintessentially British or biblical names: Adventure, Land of
Canaan, Fort Wellington, Enterprise, Promised Land.

Finally, the outskirts of Georgetown, Plaisance, and then Kitty,
and then, finally, Kingston, where Gilbert delivered us to Aunt
Margaret's mansion and, job done, departed. He would stay with
relatives in another part of town, and pick me up on Sunday for the
return drive. Aunt Margaret showed me up to my room, where I
unpacked. Soon after that, dinner was served, and we were joined by
Uncle Carl at the table. I liked Uncle Carl; he too was musical, and he
seemed genuinely pleased for me, and the evening passed pleasantly
enough. I was so excited I was sure I would not sleep a wink – but I
did, and woke up the following morning a bundle of nerves.

All my exhilaration had fled overnight. All I could think of now
was the audience I'd be playing to. There I'd be at the grand piano.

Already I could feel the beady eyes of the elite on me, judging me, condemning me, hating me. I would falter, and play the wrong notes; I'd be making a fool of myself! Who did I think I was, to play to such a distinguished audience? All of British Guiana's high society would be there, including this new fellow, fresh off the boat from England, distinguished as they come, one of the few owner-managers in the colony. Albion was an important plantation, big as Promised Land; not as important as Bookers, of course, but then, Bookers owned every one of the other plantations. Promised Land and Albion were the only privately owned ones left on the Corentyne coast. The snooty board of the Sugar Producers' Association – except Mama – would be there.

And their wives: it was the wives I feared the most. When I was a child, it was the wives who had prevented me from having a friend, a female friend, one to share all the joys and perils of growing up a girl; their mothers, the wives, looked down their noses at me. And so I had chosen friends outside the ranks, sons and daughters of the plantation workers; I had run wild, as Mama called it, swimming in the canals and catching fish and coming home covered in mud. Which, of course, made everything much worse as far as the English society ladies were concerned. I might claim I didn't give a hoot, but it hurt. Rejection always hurts. Being looked down upon as unworthy stings in a place inaccessible to the rational voice in my head that tells me it doesn't matter; that as long as I have Mama and Aunt Winnie and my cousins, all of whom love me unconditionally, all is well with the world.

I woke up with all these nagging doubts and inhibitions. It was Friday; the concert was tomorrow night. I felt I needed a further month of practice to be as good as I needed to be. I felt like telephoning Mr Foot right now, to tell him I couldn't do it; that he should get one of the established older pianists instead, stiff-backed Mr Macintosh or grey-haired Miss Jackson; that I was not up to it. But I didn't. Instead, after breakfast I borrowed

Aunt Margaret's bicycle and sailed over to Aunt Winnie's home in Lamaha Street, bordering Kingston.

How I loved that house! Like most Georgetown houses, it was built in the Dutch Colonial style, of white-painted timber. It stood proud and high on thick white stone columns; you reached the front door via an outside staircase covered in a profusion of climbing bougainvillea. It had two storeys, and a jutting gallery along the front; along the gallery it was open to the Atlantic breeze with a frieze of sash windows, which were closed only when it rained. At the sides of the house, and in the upstairs bedrooms, were Demerara windows, intricately carved at the triangular sides, closed by louvred shutters that could be pushed open with a stick. The gallery gave way to a spacious drawing room, and behind that, the kitchen. Between the kitchen and the drawing room was a hallway, from which a staircase led up to the bedrooms and bathroom.

As the Quint boys grew older and taller, needing more space, extensions upwards and outwards had been added; a high tower topped by a cupola, and Bottom House rooms added on willy-nilly between the downstairs columns, and even an annexe, a separate cottage joined to the back of the house by a connecting passageway suspended in air, where Aunt Winnie's father-in-law, old Mr Quint, lived. An architectural monster was that house, yet intriguing, magical; I had always felt at home there. Our own house at Promised Land was more traditional in design, and more beautiful, but it held none of the vitality, the heart, of this house. Because that was provided by those who lived within: the eight boys and their mother, my beloved Aunt Winnie.

Aunt Winnie, of course, welcomed me now with open arms and a multitude of kisses. Busy as usual, explanations and congratulations over, she roped me into helping her prepare lunch for the family, and it wasn't long before, sitting at the kitchen table, picking weevils and pebbles out of a mountain of raw rice, I was pouring out my fears and doubts to her. I could tell her everything; unburden my heart. It had always been like that. She was like my second mother, and once again I wished she was my real mother, that I had grown up with her and her bunch of boisterous boys instead of as a single child on Promised Land; hers was a home brimming with energy and love, with her as its backbone, its beating heart. But I never allowed such thoughts to take root. No, I loved Mama. She was the best mother in the world, and Promised Land was a little piece of paradise she had created just for me.

I even told Aunt Winnie about Mr Foot. She only laughed. 'Oh, that dirty old man! He's always had an eye for the girls. If he gets too close, give him a slap. Don't let him intimidate you, Grace – his bark is worse than his bite. Take it from me.'

I nodded, relieved; my main worry, right now, was nerves. What if they attacked me, just as I was about to play, and left me paralysed?

'Well, Grace, dear, there's only one remedy for self-doubt and fears,' said Aunt Winnie firmly after I had finished complaining. Auntie had always called me Grace, not Mary Grace, for some reason I didn't understand. I'd once asked her why, and all she said was, 'Because you are Grace to me.'

Now she said: 'Come with me, right now. Let me just...' She adjusted the flame on the kerosene stove so that the beef stew she was cooking would bubble away mildly for a while, put the rice in a huge pot with salted water to boil, took me by the hand and led me into the drawing room. In the corner stood the upright piano where I had first learned to play, sitting beside Oma or alone, practising scales for hours on end.

'Don't think of yourself, dear, just be with the music. BE the music,' she told me as I sat down at the piano seat. 'Let the music speak for itself.'

She drew up a chair and sat beside me to listen as I placed my hands on the keyboard, closed my eyes, took a deep breath – and began. A moment later my fingers were dancing over the keys: Bach, Mozart, Beethoven, Brahms, Chopin – magicians of the heart, every one of them. My soul soared up high, caught by the magic that is music, flying away from the mundane world on dulcet wings of sound. As if a charmed wand had passed over it, my heart was freed of all care or fear, let loose to soar and to rejoice and to bathe in music, washed clean. Merged with the music, I ceased to exist; I was one single stream of passion, enclosed in music; I *was* music, that needy little me taken up into something so grand, so magnificent, so monumental, it took my breath away. Yes – breathtaking was the word. Music breathed through me: it was my breath, my life. This was that elusive IT I sought, the panacea for all my private and personal pains, my needs, my thirst and hunger: music, my everything. Heart and hands connected in an intimate, exquisite bond of sheer beauty and joy.

Finally it was over and I turned to Auntie; but she was no longer there. At some point during my playing she had stood up and returned to the kitchen, and I hadn't even noticed. I went in search of her.

She was draining the rice, so I stood there and waited till she had placed the pot back on the wooden counter and wiped her hands on her apron, and then there were no words needed: she opened her arms and I moved into them; they closed around me and we stood there swaying for a silent moment. Then she drew away, looked me in the eye and said, with the half-smile she used when she needed to say something so obvious few words are necessary, 'See?' And there was no more to be said.

Chapter 7

'Never put yourself before your music,' Aunt Winnie said afterwards, as we laid the table. The twins and Freddy would be home from school soon, and Humphrey, the eldest, back from work. All my other cousins were learning different things in different places. Will was in London, studying medicine on a scholarship, and Leo in New York, studying business administration. Gordon was in the jungle somewhere, following jaguar tracks, and Charlie on a sugar estate in the Essequibo, learning the plantation business; obviously he should have been doing this apprenticeship at Promised Land, but family politics being what it was – well, Aunt Winnie had advised him to stay away: Mama could be difficult.

I couldn't wait to see them, especially Freddy, the youngest, my favourite.

'Are you coming to the conc— the reception?' I asked Aunt Winnie as I straightened the cutlery. Auntie didn't mix much with the English crowd. She was, of course, as much a part of high society as Mama, but it was different with her, because she had married Uncle George, a black man.

'Oh, no,' she said now in reply to my question. 'I never go to these functions. A lot of stuffy old English snobs, not my cup of tea at all!'

'Oh, but then I'll be there all on my own. Please come, Auntie! Just so I have some support there?'

'Your Aunt Margaret's going, isn't she?'

'Yes, yes. But you know Aunt Margaret…'

I need say no more. Aunt Margaret wasn't a real aunt, not a relative at all; but she was Mama's one true friend, and that said everything. She was my godmother, and yes, she was good to me. But I'd never really taken to her, and I knew that for some obscure reason Aunt Winnie and she were at secret loggerheads. Nothing so crude as enmity – Aunt Winnie had never, in my presence at least, said a negative word about her. But I could feel such things, and now it was left unsaid that Aunt Margaret's presence at the concert would be of no help to me.

Aunt Winnie took my hands in hers, looked deeply into my eyes. 'Grace, dear – you don't need support. Remember what you just did. Close your eyes, take a few deep breaths and simply dive into the music. Let music be your strength, your support. Don't depend on anyone for strength. I'm not coming, but I know, I just know, that you'll be wonderful. As wonderful as you were just now.'

She hugged me and let me go again, and we continued to set out the plates. I counted. 'That's you, me, Humphrey, the twins, Freddy – there's one plate too many, Auntie!' I said.

'Oh, no, that's fine,' came the reply. 'Dorothea is coming to lunch today.'

'Dorothea?' I frowned, trying to remember who Dorothea was. A friend of Auntie, most probably.

'Oh, you haven't met Dorothea yet, have you? She's Freddy's little friend, from around the corner – Parson Van Dam's daughter. You'll like her – you're both about the same age. She and Freddy are inseparable.'

The moment she said the words I knew I'd hate this Dorothea. Freddy was mine! Born just a few months after me, he and I were almost as close as twins. That is, during the times we were able to be together, which were increasingly seldom the older we grew. I hadn't seen him for a year. I wouldn't have minded him having a boy friend, with whom to be inseparable – but a girl? That was *my* role in Freddy's life! Of all of Auntie's eight sons Freddy was the one most like me: at once dreamy, sensitive and adventurous, full of exuberance, yet caring and kind – and musical, though Freddy's instrument was the mouth organ, not the piano. Unlike me, Freddy simply pulsed with confidence and was so gregarious nobody could resist him – he'd simply charm them into liking him. He was the darkest of his brothers, and like them had experienced prejudice in his life, but he had never allowed that to stop him, was never hurt by slights, as I was, and never offended even by insults to his face. I longed for that nonchalance to brush off on me. Freddy was also my advisor on matters of the heart, a subject I simply couldn't bring myself to discuss with Auntie, much less with Mama. He was the perfect counsellor. I had so looked forward to seeing him; now I'd have to tolerate this Dorothea, claiming his attention, his heart.

'Darling, don't worry about it! You'll like her, you really will. She's had her problems, just as you have. I'm sure you'll like each other.'

Aunt Winnie had always been able to read me like a book, so it didn't surprise me now that she could see right into me and see the weed of jealousy and meanness sprouting there. Pull it out, I heard the voice of my conscience say, pull it out, and don't nourish it.

So I did. It would be hard to share Freddy with another girl – would she sit with us up in the tree-house, eating mango or pineapple slices or spitting out genip seeds and talking about a hundred different things; would the three of us ride bikes up to the Sea Wall and play cricket on the beach? Well, I would give her a chance. I had no choice.

Yet I couldn't stop the jealousy. I had one day with Freddy. One day only. She had him all the time – every day! Couldn't she stay away just this one day, so I could have him to myself? I longed to tell him about the concert and my fears and Mr Foot and my pact with the devil – find out his thoughts on all these matters – but I couldn't if Dorothea was there. What a nuisance. I just hoped that Freddy came home first, so that I at least had him first today.

But of course, Dorothea came first. She just walked in without knocking – Auntie never locked the front door – swinging her school bag and ripping her Bishops' High School hat from her head.

'Hello, Ma!' she called. 'I'm here!'

Ma! She called Auntie Ma! I couldn't believe it. Stop it! I reprimanded myself. Everyone calls Auntie Ma. That's her name: Ma Quint. It doesn't mean anything, her calling her Ma.

But of course, it did. Ma after all, means Mother, and Auntie was the mother of my heart. Dorothea calling her Ma as casually as that, as if this was her home, could only mean one thing: that Auntie was the mother of her heart too. I had to share not only Freddy, but Auntie. And I couldn't even call Auntie Ma – that was one privilege denied to me. No – I could never like this usurper.

But then Ma came bustling out of the kitchen with a steaming pot of rice in her hands, placed it on the central mat on the dining table, gave Dorothea a bear hug and then turned to me.

'Grace – Dorothea. Dorothea – Grace. I just know that you two will be great friends.'

And she bustled back into the kitchen, leaving the two of us staring at each other.

Dorothea spoke first. 'Hello, Grace,' she said, and held out her hand for me to shake. I took it, still gazing into her eyes. And something happened in that moment. My jealousy melted; my fear of having to share the people I loved with a stranger simply dissolved into empty space. I liked her; I couldn't help myself. And I knew that once again, Auntie had been right. Dorothea and I could be friends, would be friends. It was as simple as that. I just knew it.

She was a little shy, and so was I; that was maybe the bonding element. Had she been just slightly haughty, or proud, or condescending – well, I don't think I could have borne it. I detected the same tongue-tiedness in her as I felt myself, but she had saved the situation by speaking first.

'Hello,' she continued, in a soft and pleasant voice, 'I've heard so much about you – from Freddy. I'm so pleased to meet you.'

I just didn't know what to reply. All I knew was that I liked her, and so I smiled as I held out my hand, which she clasped as if

I really was a long-lost friend. I liked her all the more for that. It helped, too, that she was physically not much different from me. Her complexion was of the same caramel colour as mine – I had assumed she was white, so that was a pleasant surprise. She, too, was of mixed race. Her hair, though, was scraped back across her scalp and pulled into two tight braids that fell over her shoulders – it must be rather painful, I thought. No doubt someone, her mother, most likely, was trying to straighten out her 'bad' hair – bad meaning frizzy, like mine. I was glad that I was allowed to wear mine simply, tied back in a loose bun. But hair and skin was something we had in common, and I looked forward to hearing of her particular experience in growing up between two races.

'Come along, you girls – the boys will be in any minute now. Help me to bring out the rest of the food,' cried Auntie, interrupting our session of breaking the ice. We both immediately dropped our hands and almost bumped into each other as we hurried to the kitchen, and we both giggled as we both tried to make way for the other, but then all that came to an end as Freddy bounced in the front door.

Bounced, and bounded – over to me, and then he flung his arms around me and swung me up into the air – Freddy's customary way of greeting me – and twirled me around while I laughed and struggled to free myself.

'Grace, Grace, Grace – how I've missed you! Why'd you stay away so long? Are you trying to avoid me? Have you got a young man up there in the Corentyne? If you have, well, you can't just forget me like that! And you've met Dorothea. See, I'm just as busy! You'll love her – just like I do. I'm going to marry her one day.'

'Oh, Freddy!' was all I could manage, because I was all giggles and all joy. Freddy was sunshine on a gloomy day. Once I had finished giggling I said:

'It's your fault, Freddy. You never reply to my letters.'

'Oh, I never write letters. You know that. I never write anything – I'm every teacher's nightmare – my handwriting's so bad, and my spelling. I'll never make it to university, but who cares! I like to see people face to face. You look marvellous – and you've grown, too. A real young lady! Now tell me – is there someone? You didn't say anything in your last letter. Is it a secret? You know you can't keep secrets from me, and I can't keep secrets from anyone, so you might as well tell us all now. Who is it? Who's put the shine on you?'

'It's not so much a who as a what,' said Aunt Winnie, coming in from the kitchen with a bowl of steaming fried plantain. 'Grace is going to play tomorrow at the Georgetown Club, in front of the entire English community. And she's all excited about that. That's what gives her the glow.'

'What? That pack of bloody high-nosed pampered chumps? Say it's not so!'

My spirits sank.

'It's true, Freddy. It's such an honour, such a great opportunity to play in public!'

'To play in public? Is that all you want? Why, I could have organised a concert for you in no time – you'd get half of Georgetown cheering for you! Why bother with the English? They're just a tiny layer on top of everyone else. Why do you want their approval? Brown skin not good enough for you?'

I must have reddened and my face must have fallen, because he took me in his arms. 'Sorry, Gracie, I didn't mean to be mean. Is that a rhyme or a pun? I don't know. I didn't mean to hurt you. But I hate to see you kowtowing to that crowd. They're not worthy of you.'

That was Freddy all over – straight talking, and yet sensitive and caring, and not ever bowing to the hierarchy of race that ruled our country. I wished, suddenly, that I had his courage, his confidence. Why was it so important to me to play before BeeGee's English aristocracy? Why couldn't I be satisfied with an audience of Africans and East Indians and coloureds? With his critique Freddy had thrown up into the air, into my consciousness, the deep need of social approval that still lurked within my depths, derived from the scathing rejection I had received from that very elite. A need to show them – and by showing them, to gain my own self-worth.

But surely self-worth is at its purest when it is self-sustaining, not needing anyone's applause? But there was no time for such anguished self-searching right then, because the twins, Percy and Rudolph, came charging through the front door and they too were greeting and hugging me, and I realised with a pang once again how much a part of this family I was. These were the siblings I'd never had, and being with them all made me feel complete. Percy and Rudolph, a year older than me, were especially delightful, but I missed the four that were absent: Gordon, Charlie, Will and Leo. They pampered and protected me, teased and tortured me, the sister they'd never had, and almost the youngest of them, apart from Freddy. What girl would not relish such a position?

'I'm starving!' said Rudolph, loosening his Queen's College tie and pulling out a chair. 'What's for lunch?'

Percy was busy opening pots and sniffing them all. 'Metagee, rice, fried plantain, callaloo, potato balls…' he recited.

'No eating yet!' said Auntie in her strictest voice. 'We're going to wait for Humphrey.'

A collective groan went around the table. By now we had all taken our seats, except Auntie, and just two chairs were empty – Humphrey's at the foot of the table and Ma's, opposite at the head. But at last Humphrey strode through the door and we were complete.

Humphrey, dear old Humphrey, the adult among my cousins: shy and sparse of word, socially awkward. With his limp and his stutter and his thick glasses, he was perhaps the kindest and most generous man I'd ever known. When I married, I hoped it would be to someone like Humphrey; he was my model of what a good man should be. He too greeted me with a hug and a few warm words of welcome, and took his seat. The three younger boys wolfed down their food, with Auntie constantly calling on them to watch their manners and eat slowly and chew properly and not eat with their mouths full. Humphrey ate slowly and chewed thoroughly, and Dorothea and I tried our hand at conversation. I found out that she was defying her parents by being here; that they were so strict they would never, ever have allowed her to mingle with the Quints, who, for the Van Dams, were, quite literally, beyond the pale.

'No pun intended,' she said with a rueful smile. 'They really are the most dreadful snobs. Mum in particular, even though she's the darkest of us all. But she's a social climber, and wants me to mix only with the English. Marry a white man, just as she did. Snag a white man, I should say. But Freddy and I…' Freddy, in the midst of his banter with his brothers, must have heard his name; their eyes met across the table and a look of such tenderness passed between them that I shuddered, and felt ashamed of my previous condemnation of her, sight unseen. I took her hand on the table and squeezed it, and she turned to me and squeezed mine back.

'How come you're able to come here for lunch?' I asked.

She blushed. 'I lie to them,' she said. 'I have to. Otherwise—'

'Otherwise she gets licks,' Freddy said. 'They gave you licks a few times, right?'

'Yes, I get bad licks. And so I find ways and means. I tell them I'm going to a friend – an English friend, of course – for lunch and to do homework together. I hate lying, but I have to.'

She didn't look like the kind of person who'd lie to her parents, and though lying is obviously wrong, I understood why she did it and respected her for it. I didn't know if I could do it – lie to Mama about sneaking around, visiting a suitor. But then, I had never loved anyone the way she obviously loved Freddy. I wasn't sure I ever would. I had my music; for the time being, at least, that was enough for me.

And obviously Aunt Winnie condoned this lie, otherwise Dorothea would not be here; and if Aunt Winnie condoned something, I knew it had to be right. She was the personification of ethical behaviour as far as I was concerned, the gold standard of right and wrong. In everything I did, I measured myself against her: would Aunt Winnie do that, say that? What would she do or say? Sadly, I couldn't say the same for Mama. So much she did was obviously wrong, and I knew that was the bone of contention between her and Auntie.

'So, Grace, how's your mother?' Auntie asked me now, changing a subject that was obviously awkward for Dorothea. 'Why didn't she come with you? Surely she'd want to be present at her daughter's grand debut!'

'She was going to come; she was all dressed and packed and ready for the trip. But at the last moment there was trouble on the plantation.'

'Another protest?'

'Yes. This time, the labourers want a school, a primary school for their children.'

'And get it they should!' exclaimed Auntie. 'For goodness' sake, what's wrong with her? Why does she deny them such a basic right? Every child should have the benefit of education, labourer or not, brown skin or white. I suppose Yoyo doesn't agree?'

'She says they're uppity. That educated labourers won't want to work on the fields.'

'So she deliberately keeps them ignorant. That's so – that's so…'

Auntie struggled for words until she gave in and said, in a calmer voice, 'Sorry, Grace, I shouldn't be criticising your mother to you but I do hope you understand that this is very, very wrong. But I won't say anything more on the subject. Let's talk about your music.'

And that's what we did for the rest of the meal, after which the boys helped her to clear up and wash the wares, and Freddy, Dorothea and I escaped with a plate of pineapple tarts and a jug of freshly-made mauby to Freddy's tree-house, where we spent several pleasant hours chatting about this and that, and we sealed the establishment of our trio with a hearty chink of Auntie's best cocktail glasses.

Chapter 8

Since the reception was not till Saturday evening, and I dreaded spending the day moping around Aunt Margaret's house, Auntie decided to take us to the beach – me, Freddy and the twins. Dorothea couldn't get away from home and Humphrey couldn't get away from work, but the rest of us piled into the car with a picnic basket, some blankets and a large parasol. I didn't have a bathing suit, but Auntie had kept one from when she was a girl and it fitted me perfectly. Off we chugged, up the coast to Buxton, where many years ago the Quints had put up a small beach cottage.

We had a wonderful time, as always, and Auntie took the opportunity to talk to me about my future. It was a painful subject. We all knew my problem: finding a suitable husband. Here in British Guiana there were no other prospects for a girl such as me. Mama would have loved me to follow in her footsteps, but once it became clear that I had neither the talent nor the inclination for plantation management even she had abandoned that idea. So the next best thing was for me to marry a suitable man who could do the job.

Suitable, of course, meant English. Mama wanted me to marry up, but past experience had taught us both how unlikely, if not impossible, that would be. And she'd done her best. She'd tried to coach me in the art of making myself appealing to men; but I was bad at it, too shy to apply the feminine tricks she said would cause young men to fall at my feet, hopelessly in love. A year ago she had initiated some introductions with appropriate young Englishmen but all had fallen flat due to the problem of my blood. They might be suitable, but I was eminently unsuitable, even with the lure of a prosperous plantation. It seemed my race trumped every other card I held. Not that men weren't attracted to me – they were, and showed it, but in inappropriate ways, as evidenced by the attentions of Mr Foot. I could catch ther eye, but never hold their heart.

Once, a year ago, I had met a charming young man at a Glasgow Christmas party; his name was Frank Carter. We had danced, and he, in the throes of a sudden and overwhelming passion, had taken me out to the veranda and clumsily proposed marriage, leaving me stuttering and finally speechless. Possibly he was drunk. Yet he had written the very next day to emphasise that he meant every word; that he was serious, loved me for all eternity and wished to marry me. I allowed myself to feel an emotion I chose to tentatively call love; a sort of swelling in the heart, similar to what I felt when I played a beautiful piece of music. I started to hope; yes, I was young, only fifteen, but we all knew that one must start young in these matters. I even showed the letter to Mama, who ecstatically began investigations as to his background, his family, his wealth. But only a week later Frank wrote to retract his proposal: his family would not allow it. Mama was furious. She blamed me for not trying hard enough, at failing in the art of enticement; but quickly found a solution.

'You must aim for an older man,' she said over and over again, 'a man who doesn't need his parents' approval. Old, rich and white. They love exotic coloured maidens like you. They're easy to ensnare.'

Mama, it must be said, did not believe in love or romance; sentimental nonsense, she called it. For her, marriage was a business contract. She had entered into it twice and was in fact still married, to Geoffrey Burton, who lived in far-off Lousiana. It was an alliance I never fully understood, based as it seemed to be on the merging of property.

But the experience with Frank had sorely undermined my confidence. I became acutely aware of my limitations. If even a young man of Frank Carter's modest standing deemed me unsuitable, who would ever accept me? An ageing widower of forty, was that my lot? And I became wary of the word 'love'. Unlike Mama, I believed in love. But if love can vanish so quickly from the heart, as it had with Frank, if it is not worth fighting for, then it cannot be love. From that day on I guarded my heart carefully. I wanted to be loved, to marry for love, but if no suitable husband could be found, what would become of me?

'You should just marry someone unsuitable,' was Freddy's advice, and by that he meant a black or a coloured man or an East Indian. I had no objection myself, but I knew without asking that Mama would be devastated. For me to marry down – well, it would break her heart, and I couldn't possibly do that. A further dilemma was my lack of opportunity – when and where would I meet appropriate suitors, suitable as well as unsuitable, hidden away as I was in the Corentyne?

'You should come and stay with us here in Georgetown,' Freddy said. 'I'll show you a good time and you'll meet some spiffing fellows.' There was nothing I'd love better, but again, I knew without asking that Mama would object. Indeed, it was a constant balancing act for me between the things I longed to do and Mama's approval. She and Auntie were like fire and water: the only way to make things worse would have been to move in with the Quints.

In the past year I had gone off the idea of marriage altogether – it was just too depressing to think about. Instead I had concentrated on my music, but that too led to a dead end. I could see myself growing up to become that dear old spinster aunt who would play at the birthday parties of my cousins' children. Musical chairs would become my forte, and that would be it.

'Leave it be,' said Aunt Winnie when she dropped me off at Aunt Margaret's later in the afternoon. 'Something will turn up. I believe that there is a path drawn up for us, a good path – we only have to be open, and it will find us. And I have an idea.'

'What?'

'Well, I won't tell you yet – it's just an infant of an idea. If it comes to anything, I'll let you know.'

And I had to be satisfied with that. My future looked entirely dismal. Musical chairs, it would be. But at least I had tonight's reception to look forward to, so once I was back at Aunt Margaret's, I went through my repertoire once more and then it was time to get ready. The maid had ironed the creases out of my beautiful dress, and there it hung, ready and waiting for me to slip into. I had a new pair of shiny new shoes, which Mama and I had chosen in New Amsterdam, and all that needed to be done was my hair – but Aunt Margaret's personal hairdresser was coming in to do that. She wasn't nearly as good as Katie, but once I was dressed and coiffed and my face powdered and I had a smidgen of colour on my lips – well, I looked in the mirror and couldn't believe what I saw. For the first time ever I really believed I was beautiful. That mirror did not lie. A truth that was confirmed when I came downstairs and Aunt Margaret's husband laid eyes on me. He whistled.

'A dream in green,' he said, offered his arm and led me down to the car, Aunt Margaret following behind. She didn't mind; Uncle Carl flirted with all the young ladies and she was used to it. But his approval lifted my flailing spirits just a little higher. Yet, I was nervous. This was my big night, I had to succeed! But if I didn't, if I made a fool of myself? The mortification! And worse yet, Mama's anger!

But being beautiful gives a girl a sense of confidence; I felt that confidence right up to the moment the valet opened the car door outside the Georgetown Club and I stepped out into the milling throng of guests. Heads turned to look at me and I felt, rather than heard, the gasp of affront that floated through them as we stepped towards the stairwell that led up to the main hall. Though I kept my eyes lowered, I still heard and felt the sniffs of disapproval, the frowns on the ladies' foreheads, the pursed lips of disdain, the whispers of cloaked outrage. And every last smidgen of confidence fled. I would have bolted back to the safety of the car; indeed, I would have run down Main Street and all the way back to Kingston and the sanctuary of Aunt Margaret's home, or even back to Lamaha Street and Aunt Winnie's comforting arms, had not Uncle Carl once again grasped me firmly by the arm and led me up the stairs. I wanted to face them, to speak to them, to explain that I was not gatecrashing; I was here not as a guest but only as a paid entertainer; I wanted to grovel, to ask them to give me a chance, to just let me be. But I let myself be led away without a word.

There, to my great relief, Mr Foot was waiting.

'Ah, my dear, there you are at last! I was beginning to worry – all the other entertainers are here already. Let me take you to them.' He looked me up and down, and his eyes bulged. 'My dear, you look splendid! Slightly overdressed. Perhaps you should have dressed more – modestly. You aren't in competition with the other ladies, you know! Never mind, come with me.'

And then he took my arm and led me through a corridor of silenced staring guests to a back room, where, he said, I was to wait with the calypso singer and the steel band members until I was called.

'It won't be too long,' he said. 'And a maid will bring you some snacks and drinks. Just a little bit of patience. I'll see you after the performance. Mr Campbell isn't here yet. Just relax; have a glass of punch, it will calm you. Don't worry, you'll be fine.'

And he was gone, and I was alone in a room of strangers. But it was better, better by far, than the Georgetown Club lounge with its crowd of outraged guests. Still, the damage to my confidence was done. Beauty is a fleeting prop, a scaffolding of fragile glass, and that prop had fallen by the wayside and lay there splintered.

At first I made halting conversation with the other musicians, but in the end I was simply too nervous to engage and fell silent. I wished it all away. I wanted to go home again, forget about it all.

Anything but face that sneering crowd waiting outside. I should not have worn a pretty dress. I should have come in a simple cotton frock appropriate to my status. It was all Mama's fault – Mama and her ambition for me. Mama and her pride and her sense of outrage on my behalf. 'You'll be the most beautiful woman there!' she'd said. 'My daughter is not to be treated as staff. You'll look like a princess. Believe me, their jaws will drop when they see you.' And their jaws had indeed dropped; not in admiration, but indignation. Now they'd never be impressed by my music. I wanted to get up and run to Aunt Winnie and weep. I wanted time to stand still; but of course it didn't.

The calypsonian was called in and we heard his rather bawdy songs playing from behind the closed door. Then it was the turn of the steel band. And then it was me.

I took a deep breath and forced myself to recall Auntie's encouraging words as I walked out towards the grand piano, but not only were my hands trembling, so was my mind; I had failed even before I'd begun. Something about taking deep breaths and giving myself to the music… But how could I do that, when I'd been so put to shame?

A stony silence greeted my walk to my instrument. I kept my eyes averted – I could not bear to see the mocking glares of those people, the ladies especially. And the guest of honour – this awful Mr Campbell himself. He'd be there, fresh from England, with all the prejudices that implied, looking down on me, a native girl pretending to be Somebody. I wanted to die. Run away. Anything except sit down at that piano and place my hands on the keys. But I did it anyway.

I closed my eyes, took a breath, raised my hands and let them fall. And then something happened: something strange, unexpected and utterly miraculous. Perhaps it was touching the piano that did it; perhaps it came from deep inside me: an uprising of sheer outrage, a flinging upwards of my true spirit. Whatever it was, I erupted.

And what emerged was – a miracle. Not the agreed repertoire, the lively and happy Mozart Mr Foot and I had decided would be my opening piece, and which would have required a little speech from me – something about my grandmother who hailed from Salzburg, as did Mozart, and my dedication of the evening to her as she was my very first teacher. No, I could not do it.

A power swept through me, took control of my entire being: mind, soul, hands. My fingers fell to the keys and took me along with them. What came from them as they danced and bounced across the keys was not something sweet and feminine and pretty and happy; it was not one of the delightful evening pieces Mr Foot and I had carefully selected together. What came out was an amalgamation of – well, of every emotion held back behind the veil of respectability and patience and shyness I presented to the world. Nothing shy about the 'Héroïque', Chopin's Polonaise in A-flat major. As its name implies, it's the heart-cry of a hero: *why, why, why*, the music cries out in the first thirty seconds of introduction, followed by the majestic response: *because, because, because…* No concrete answer to the why, the eternal why of humanity; the pounding octaves of the left hand, still asking why; the response, the majesty, the power, the glory. I ceased to exist; I ceased to exist and only the music existed: I became that music, fervent and fierce, the notes pouring out from the depths of my being; all the frustration, the anger, the desolation, the heroism. Yes, the heroism! In playing, I became that music, that heroine, climbing past the hurdle of my miserable faltering little self and into the sheer majesty of music.

Even at the first opening bars I heard a muted gasp from the audience, then a holding of breath, and then – oh, and then the glory of it, rising up from the depths of my soul and into my fingers. I was transported, resurrected, renewed; I was aflame with the glory of the music. I played not a single note wrong. My fingers found their assigned keys with ease. The music came from me in a single gush of ardour, of aching, reaching up and out and grasping the highest, grasping God, with every single thread of my being. I felt magnificent; it was magnificent.

It was exactly as Auntie had said: there was no more me. I ceased to exist, completely surrendered, united, absorbed in the music, in the magnificence of it, and thus was I made magnificent, my tiny fragile 'me-ness' dissolved, expanded into something beyond words, beyond will, beyond my person. I was that music; and anyone listening who cared to be equally surrendered, equally absorbed – well, we were all as one, one entity, one humankind. And I understood right then how and why music has the power to unite, to break down walls: because it speaks to a common soul, a common spirit, and brings us all back, if we are so willing, into that communality.

And then it was over. Silence, complete silence, as if the entire room was holding a single breath.

And then it came. Applause: from a single pair of hands. 'Brava!' cried a male voice, and I turned slightly, shy once again, to see who it was. It was a young man I'd never seen before, standing in front of his chair in the front row, clapping and crying out 'Brava!' again and again and again. Next to him and in the rows behind him the rest of the audience sat as if stunned; faces turning to glance at one another, as if seeking affirmation; and then, muted at first, one by one, the clapping started until applause filled the room like the gushing of a waterfall. I too was stunned, not fully believing what had just happened. And then I smiled, and curtseyed, blushing, and as the applause died I was finally able to give my little speech about Salzburg and Mama and I launched into the Mozart, followed by the beautiful and calming 'Moonlight' Sonata by Beethoven, a fitting end to my programme, like a goodnight lullaby.

Once again applause filled the room, and this time when I turned around everyone was standing and they were all smiling; and the young man strode forward and took my hands and kissed them both; he was followed quickly by a red-faced Mr Foot, who made a hasty introduction.

'Mr Campbell, this is Miss Smedley-Cox, Miss Mary Grace Smedley-Cox, the most talented daughter of one of our most esteemed sugar magnates, who sadly could not attend tonight – Miss Smedley-Cox, this is Mr John Middleton Campbell, of the Campbell Brothers, our guest of honour. Mr Campbell's grandfather was governor of the Bank of England – he comes from high aristocratic stock, Irish and Scottish; he's just down from Oxford – marvellous fellow. My dear, my dear, you outdid yourself; that was magnificent! Simply…' But I didn't hear what else he had to say because I was gazing into the warmest eyes I had ever seen; greeny-brown, they were, and seemed almost fluid, like an ocean inviting me to just plunge in. I could not pull my eyes away, nor my hands, which he continued to hold.

'Jock – call me Jock!' he said, and then, 'Miss Smedley-Cox, so pleased to meet you!' Again I blushed. 'That was simply – well, Mr Foot put it aptly, magnificent!'

'Thank you, dear, thank you,' said Mr Foot, his hand on my arm, trying to dislodge my hands from Mr Campbell's, which would not be dislodged. 'Now, Mr Campbell, if you would just lead the way, we shall all move into the dining room for dinner. Miss Smedley-Cox, once again I thank you – a wonderful performance. We must do this again, if you don't mind…'

He paused, and as neither of us made a move, he said, quite firmly this time, 'Mr Campbell, if you would now come along. I believe Miss Smedley-Cox's car is waiting outside.'

So I took the hint – I pulled my hands from his grasp and bent to pick up my silk shawl, which had fallen on the floor, and made to retreat. But Mr Campbell was there before me. He picked up my shawl, handed it to me and placed a possessive hand on my arm. 'Nonsense! How can you send her off like that? Not a bit of it! She's coming to have dinner with us. She's my guest – if you'd do me that honour, Miss Smedley-Cox?'

He smiled at me and I smiled back and nodded imperceptibly, boldly, knowing full well that I was flouting the rules.

'Perfect!' he said. 'Then let's all go through. Your playing has certainly given me an appetite! Come along then.' He held out an elbow to me and I took it, and he led me into the dining room, where long tables with white tablecloths and gleaming cutlery awaited us. There were name cards at the seats, and Mrs Foot, who seemed to be in charge of the seating, asked us to wait while she bad-temperedly made some rapid adjustments, shuffling the cards around; then the two of us came forward, and he took his place at the head of one of the tables with me to his right. And dinner was served.

Mr Campbell turned to me. 'I'm not a musical fellow, you know,' he said. 'Usually, I'm bored by classical music – a bit of a philistine in that respect. But what you played, Miss Smedley-Cox, it moved me. I felt something, something I've never felt before. It – it moved me.'

'Oh! But that's the most important thing about music, isn't it? It should move the heart – speak directly to the heart. It's a universal language, not needing an interpreter.'

'Well, that's exactly what happened – it spoke to my heart. What was it? It wasn't on the programme, as far as I can tell.'

'No,' I replied. 'It wasn't planned. It just sort of… burst out of me. I had to play it – it was like a compulsion. I can't explain it.'

'What was it? Was it Bach? Mozart? See, I do know the names of the composers but I can't tell one from the other!'

'Chopin,' I said. 'Polonaise in A-flat major. It's actually known as the "Héroïque". It's quite famous.'

'The "Héroïque" – the heroical. The perfect name for it. And you played it beautifully. You sounded like – well, a heroine.'

Our eyes met, but I could not hold his gaze, and looked away to dip my spoon in my soup and take a sip.

The rest of that night passed as if in a dream: I remember it all as a blur. White-gloved black waiters gliding around the table, serving the second course and the dessert. The chink of cutlery and crockery. The hum of muted conversation. Covert glances in our direction. And Mr Campbell, every word he said. He was so gracious, so kind and at the same time so commanding, but in an engaging way, not at all dominating as men are wont to be. He emitted a strength that was entirely mesmeric, hypnotic almost. He asked me questions about myself, and I answered them – about my age, and where I lived, and my family. I found out what I knew already, but had not properly registered: we would be almost neighbours. Mr Campbell – 'Call me Jock!' he said again, so I did – had come to take over his family plantation at Albion, just a few miles west of Promised Land.

'But I won't be going up there just yet,' he said. 'I'll be coming up to visit the place, but then it's back to Georgetown, to start work on the family wharf. After that, we'll see. But when I come to Albion, I'd love to visit Promised Land – just a friendly neighbourly visit – and meet your mother. She sounds fascinating.'

'You'd be very welcome,' I said. I wished I could stop blushing. 'Mama will be delighted to meet you. She was so sorry she couldn't be here tonight – there was some trouble on the plantation and she was held back.'

He frowned. 'Really? What trouble?'

'A labourer protest, we have them quite often. They are demanding a school for their children.'

'Well, of course they should have a school!' exclaimed Jock. 'One thing I know for certain is—'

He stopped. 'Oh, I'm sorry, Mary Grace. I may call you that, mayn't I? I shouldn't be talking politics or business tonight – this is just a friendly getting-to-know-you reception. So…'

He placed a hand over his mouth to indicate that he would talk no more about schools or plantations, and his eyes twinkled, and I hoped he could see the twinkle in mine as well. I remembered what Aunt Margaret had said about the chinless young rakes, sent by their aristocratic families to the West Indies to cure them of their libertine ways.

She had summarily dismissed Jock as of that ilk. Was he? I couldn't believe it. I had some experience of such charmers, but somehow Jock just felt different. His words seemed so sincere – but wasn't that the very modus operandi of rakes, feigning sincerity? Perhaps I was too naive to tell. Though it was his personality that so attracted me, I also liked his looks. He had a strong face, not conventionally handsome but striking, topped by a shock of surprisingly black hair.

One thing for certain: he was anything but chinless.

He sighed. 'You're so young, Mary Grace, and so talented. You must not let that talent go to waste. I see it so often – talented young women, and then they get married and forget to hone their skills, or haven't the time to do so, so wrapped up in them as they are in babies and domestic duties. Their gift gets rusty, and falters, and dies. You must not let that happen to you. How old are you, by the way?'

'Sixteen, nearly seventeen.'

'I thought so. Promise me, Mary Grace, promise me that you'll keep on playing. Promise me that you'll nourish and care for that gift – and it is a gift, you know – and not let it decay. Promise me you won't rush off and marry the first young man who crosses your path.'

'Ha! That's an easy promise to make!'

'All the most eligible young bachelors in town must be running after you! Surely you lack the fingers to count the proposals? You must be able to take your pick, talented and beautiful as you are.'

I blushed again at his compliment, but shook my head. 'Sadly, no. No candidates at all, I'm quite beyond the pale.'

He frowned. 'I don't understand – what do you mean?'

I swallowed, and took my courage into my hands.

'Mr Campbell—'

'Jock, do call me Jock.' It was the third time he'd said this.

'Jock, maybe you're colour-blind – but just look at me!'

I laid down my cutlery and stretched out my arms.

'You see? Beyond the pale – literally. This isn't a tan, Mr—Jock. No English young man of standing will approach me with a bargepole, much less propose.'

Emotions flickered across his face: sudden understanding, outrage, shock and then relief. He laughed.

'Well, then, no distractions. Just keep on playing, Mary Grace. I want to hear you play for me many, many times in future. Will you do that for me?'

His charm was so infectious, I laughed. 'Of course! Gladly!'

'Well then it's a pact. You'll keep it up, and play for me again.'

After dinner there were drinks and cigars for the men while the women retired to tinker with faces and hair and clothes. I felt the wrathful glances. Yes, I had made a grand entry into society, but I had earned no love for it – not among the females, at any rate. There were an unusual number of young women my age or slightly older among us, and I surmised that this Mr Jock Campbell must certainly be counted among Georgetown's very most eligible bachelors. He too would not have enough fingers to count his choice of wife – if, indeed, he was looking for a wife.

He probably wasn't. His reputation had come before him as a ladies' man, a charmer, a man who loved fast women and even faster cars. Yes, he had charmed me, but he had no doubt charmed many women in his past and would go on to charm many more. And, after all, it was my music he loved, not me. Nothing had really changed.

Up to this point I had carried with me a lingering soreness due to my rejection by the one young man I had purported to love, Frank

Carter. Frank had always been there at the back of my mind, an unappeased hope. From the moment I met Jock Campbell, however, that soreness was healed, but only to be replaced by something else, and something worse: a longing for the undeniably unattainable and the knowledge that it was just that: unattainable. That, once I stepped down from the heights of music, once I was earthbound again, I could never, ever be good enough.

I was standing in line waiting for the lavatory, alone with my thoughts, when Aunt Margaret bustled up and took my arm. 'Come, dear, you can do that at home. Let's go. Dear, you were spectacular! Wait till I tell your dear mother, she'll be delighted. You were the star of the evening. Nobody can ever ignore you again. You've made the debut of your life!'

Ha, I thought, if only you knew. For my part, I suspected I'd be lonelier than ever before.

Chapter 9

The following day, Sunday, I went to church, not with Aunt Margaret but with Aunt Winnie and the boys – she rang me bright and early to invite me, and came to pick me up with the car. Aunt Winnie, as usual, attended the Catholic Sacred Heart church on Main Street; the family she had married into was Catholic, and so she had changed denomination. 'What does it matter, which church or temple we attend?' she would say with a laugh. 'We all worship the same God anyway, just in different ways.'

So Humphrey drove, Aunt Winnie sat next to him in the passenger seat, while I sat in the back seat squeezed in with the twins and Freddy. I would have loved to go home with them after the service and enjoy one of Auntie's marvellous Sunday lunches, but I knew that Gilbert would be waiting for me with the car back at Aunt Margaret's, and that lunch today would consist of packed sandwiches and a flask of cold tea.

I felt empty that day, and church did nothing to relieve it, not even the wonderful organ music that introduced the service and accompanied the hymn singing. I suppose it is inevitable: when you soar, you must inevitably come down to earth again, and earth must seem so much more mundane once you have seen heaven. And I had seen heaven.

At breakfast I had told Auntie about my great success the night before, and she was delighted. 'I knew it!' she said. 'I just knew it, darling. All that is within you and it has to come out. And I'm pursuing my little idea and I'm going to be making some enquiries and no, I'm not going to tell you what it is just yet. You must be patient.'

I did not tell her much about Jock Campbell; just that he had been so gracious and had led the applause and invited me to dinner even though I had not been invited. She approved thoroughly of him. 'He sounds like a very fine young man,' she said. 'We could do with some more fine young Englishmen in the colony. Most of them are such spineless creatures when they come here. Well done him!'

Freddy snorted. 'They're a bunch of racist pigs, all of them!' he said. 'He won't be any different!'

'Oh, but he is. He is!' I cried, and immediately regretted my outburst, for they both stared at me.

'So that's where the wind blows,' said Aunt Winnie with a twinkle in her eye. 'Ah, Grace, you're just sixteen. I know what it's like, meeting someone wonderful at sixteen. But it's never easy, my dear, so don't get carried away. I did, at your age, and it wasn't pretty.'

I knew immediately what she was referring to – her own romance with Uncle George. Aunt Winnie always warned me about the excesses of emotion that could besiege a girl in the first flights of fancy. 'It's not yet love,' she always said, 'don't call it love – it might grow into love, but it's not there yet. It's just infatuation, wild emotion, without foundation. Love needs deeper roots than wild emotion; love needs time.'

I'd remembered her words while falling for Frank Carter, and had managed not to fall too deeply. Now, I would need stronger chains to hold me back. So with every thought of Jock Campbell that arose, I imagined a hand, a great open-palmed hand, pushing back that thought. And so I managed to keep those unruly emotions at bay. At church, I prayed for strength of heart, but when Humphrey dropped me at Aunt Margaret's a great sense of emptiness overcame me: it was all over. I'd had my much-anticipated debut – but what now?

On the trip back to Promised Land, I had hours and hours to wallow in this sad, sticky sense of anticlimax. My life lay before me now as a bleak and dry landscape, worse than ever before. What could possibly remain, now that I had seen the heights? Yes, I could continue to play glorious music, and perhaps now invitations to play publicly would start to trickle in. Perhaps Jock Campbell would facilitate such performances. But it could never be the same; and what then? There were scores and scores of glorious compositions and I would play them all, one by one, and perhaps gain applause and recognition for my skill. But it wasn't enough.

The joy of having soared to the heights, of being lifted on the wings of music, was already just a memory. And yes, I had for a few moments found the validation I so desperately yearned for, validation through the very people who had rejected me. I had shown them, as I had sworn to do. But what was the intrinsic value of that? It all seemed so trite, so worthless, compared to the genuine and authentic and so very, very satisfying respect that had been given to me by one single person.

Jock Campbell. Never had I met such a person before. Never had a human being caused me to glow simply by their presence, and their attention, and their genuine caring; and though the afterglow of that presence was fast fading, the very memory of it enabled me to be lifted up again and again and again in little moments of elation. This was a man! This was what a man should be! This was what a human being should be! This was the gold standard!

Up to this point Aunt Winnie had been the model against which I measured myself, my morals; my behaviour. She loved me with a selfless love, and she was such a caring person herself that it had been natural for me to aim to follow in her footsteps. But she was my aunt, she had known me from babyhood, loved me with a mother's love, as a daughter, and her love was self-evident.

Her words now only served to deflate me all the more.

What Jock Campbell had given me was the opposite of self-evident. He had raised me from the ditch and placed me on a mountain; a stranger stepping out of nowhere had given me a hand and pulled me up to my true height. The very presence of him caused me to tingle, gave me a sense of the unimaginable possibilities that lay before me, that lay within me.

This was the kind of man I wanted to marry. And that knowledge was what left me so bereft, so bleak as the car chugged eastwards, homewards: because there would not be a second Jock Campbell. There could not be a second Jock Campbell. He was one of a kind.

I did not for a moment deceive myself into thinking I could marry him, or that he would marry me. I knew my place well enough. How many girls far more beautiful than me, far cleverer than me in myriad ways, far more confident than me, would fall at his feet! Why, he could take his pick – a man like that had surely only to snap his fingers, should he wish to marry. Last night he had worked a bit of magic, raised up one little Cinderella and clothed her in glitter for a few hours, but already the glitter was fading. It had no substance; it was just that – glitter – while he was pure gold.

By the time we arrived home night had fallen, and not just literally: a darkness shrouded me. I had seen a glimpse of light, for one evening, but darkness had descended within me and it was all the darker due to the contrast with that glimpse. I knew my place, and it was right here on Promised Land, locked away from the world and separated from it by miles and miles of cane fields, with no one for company except an exacting, bad-tempered mother and a few servants, and only my music to comfort me. Here, I would bury myself and grow old. Only sixteen, and my life was already over – but now? After the glimpse of glory that had been mine for just one hour, it all felt flat; empty. I could see no perspective. Was I to spend the rest of my days here, alone with my piano? Yes, I continued to practise, to improve – but to what purpose? Was it enough to soar ever higher on the wings of music, alone, unloved, lonely? What did my future hold, except one day after the other, a string of days turning into years and years into decades, and me at the piano, playing and playing for non-existent ears? Jock Campbell had said he would visit, and one day he would surely be a neighbour – he had said so himself – but even that prospect rang hollow; what was the point? His showing up would only serve to make abundantly clear how hollow my own life was.

In the absence of sons, Mama had wanted me to grow up to take over the plantation, to learn the business of planting, but for years now I had known that not only did I have no interest in being a planter, I had no aptitude either. I had no understanding of making a profit, which was, after all, the aim of sugar production. This business of the school for labourer children, for instance – all I could think of was, why ever not? While I was away, it seemed, Mama had somehow reached a compromise with the labourers – a small schoolhouse was to be built and two primary schoolteach-ers employed, while older children would be transported to the secondary school down the coast at Rose Hall. The labourers had wanted more, but as Mama painstakingly tried to explain to me, it would have been uneconomical. Had I been in charge I would simply have built the school, if that made them happy, and never looked at the calculations. For Mama, it was all about the calcula-tions. I had attended secondary school in New Amsterdam, but my schooling had come to an end last term – no point in any more learning, Mama had said, you need to learn estate business. And I tried, but it all ran off my mind like rain from a rooftop. This angered Mama. 'You're all I have,' she said, 'you need to understand how sugar farming works.'

Sometimes she would speak of my marriage; after all, the next best thing would be for me to marry a planter's son, someone who would run the plantation while I gave him babies and played the piano, and gave her grandsons, who could be appropriately raised. But Mama knew the problems involved here: no one from the planter caste would have me. For my part, I wished I could move to Georgetown and live with the Quints. But Mama would have none of it. Now, she was running on a different tack. 'You know, Mary Grace,' she said. 'Perhaps you could interest a Portuguese fellow? There's another privately owned plantation run by a Portuguese family up on the east bank – they have a few sons of the right age, I believe.'

'Oh, Mama!' I sighed, 'no, and no, and no. Please, please, no more matchmaking! It's just so tiresome.'

'Very well, dear, but don't blame me if you end up a withered spinster, giving piano lessons to the spoilt daughters of the upper class! Because that's the way you're heading.'

'Well, so be it,' I said, and walked away to read a novel. Books and music, that was my entire life, all that was left to look forward to.

In the midst of this wallowing in the wilderness, Mr Foot showed up once more. How could I have forgotten the pact we had made? Obviously he hadn't. A few weeks after the reception, he paid me a call, at a time when he knew that Mama would be out on the fields. I had no choice but to let him in, show him to a chair in the gallery and ask Verbena to serve lime juice and biscuits.

'My dear, my dear, you were marvellous! Simply marvellous! Everyone in town is talking about you now.'

'Yes – but surely not in a good way!'

Oh yes, I had noticed the whispering ladies, the raised eyebrows; the pursed lips as I left the Georgetown Club that evening. I may have been a success with Jock Campbell, and Mr Foot may have been pleased that I had done well, for reasons of his own – but to have won Jock's undivided attention at dinner must surely have been hard for them to swallow. Why, the entire table had had to be rearranged, and carefully planned introductions postponed.

Now, he blustered, 'My dear, you must take no notice if you sense a certain – a certain spitefulness towards you. It comes of ignorance. I can assure you that you are in secret well admired. Some people are vindictive, I admit, and would rather see the back of you than the front' – at those words he stared at my bodice, eyes bulging – 'but it is only a result of jealousy, and you must ignore it. Now, as for me, you must know that I have nothing but the greatest admiration for you, a young lady of such accomplishment. And there's nothing I would like more than to show you that appreciation. Er—'

He stopped. And then he took my hand, raised it to his lips and kissed it. I pulled it away. He edged closer. 'Dear, I do so admire you! You must know – you must feel it too! How could such admiration not be felt, not be reciprocated – please, let me touch you, just once – your lips, so full – so lovely…'

We were sitting in two wicker chairs next to each other; he pulled his closer, reaching for me again, touching my arm, my face; pushing his own face up to mine.

I pulled away, scraped back my own chair.

'Mr Foot – please! This is most inappropriate! I am not – not some…'

His voice changed, hardened. 'Ah, but you are, my dear, you are! You must know that you are nothing. In the eyes of decent society, you are nothing. I am your doorway into being something, to gaining stature. Yes, Mr Campbell may have given you some attention, but he does that to all pretty ladies. You need not harbour any exalted ideas concerning him. You need not think you are anything special. Your piano playing? You may have enjoyed one evening in the spotlight but you can just as well sink back into obscurity. I can ease your way into a more elevated position. I am willing to help you up – I have the connections, I can arrange for you to play at some very exalted venues. Or I can leave you to sink back where you came from. Who are you? Your mother may be a respected figure, but you cannot erase that touch of the tarbrush; you are a child of low birth and you will never overcome that without my help. Take it or leave it, but I do expect some thanks from you. You know exactly what I mean. You have no hope of making a good marriage, but I have connections and I can help you find a perfectly respectable coloured man of good standing. There's a price for everything, my dear, and as a pianist, and as a woman, you will go nowhere without help. Now, just think about that. Remember that I can ruin you as well as I can raise you up. It only takes a word from me – I can do it. I shall now take my leave. Think about it, I'll be back.'

And without another word he stood up, walked over to the hat rack, took down his pith helmet and was out of the door.

I would have obsessed about his words for weeks on end had not, that very morning, not an hour after he had stormed off, a letter plopped through the letter box at the gate, brought to the house by the yardboy, Bono, and laid on the silver tray in the hallway. Addressed to me, it was from Aunt Winnie.

'My dear Grace,' it read. *I have not forgotten you; I've taken some steps, but it's taken some time for me to get a response, and it's exactly the response I was hoping for. Here's the background: when Humphrey was a baby I had to go to Caracas to get treatment for his clubfoot. I stayed with a nurse called Gabriella, and she and I became good friends. While I was there I noticed that there was an excellent school of music quite near to where she lived, the Escuela Nacional de Musica. We went to a few concerts there, and I did feel a bit of a pang – how wonderful it would have been, I thought at the time, to go to that school and become an accomplished violinist! Indeed, there was a very gifted female young violin soloist at one of the concerts, and I remember thinking, that could have been me.*

And I began thinking, even while you were here, that could be you, Grace! You're certainly gifted enough to attend that school. Why not, I thought, why not? And you know, dear – why not, indeed? So I wrote to Gabriella after you had left. I asked her to find out what it would take for you to attend that school. What you would have to do. How much it would cost. Where you could stay. And so on. I received her reply yesterday. All you need to attend the school is to be good enough. For them to ascertain that you need to go to Caracas and be auditioned. That's all. If you're good enough, they'll take you. As for where you could stay, Gabriella said the very thing I was hoping she'd say: you can stay with her! Her husband is a doctor and they have a large house. She also has two daughters a little older than you, and plenty of room in her home. 'Tell Grace she is most welcome,' she wrote. 'She will be like a third daughter to me.'

So that's the opportunity, Grace. I hope it makes your eyes shine and your heart race. You are much too young to be thinking about marriage anyway, much better to do something useful with your life. If you like the idea, all you have to do is persuade your mother to send you. Now, I know Yoyo and I know that she will object, mostly because it was my idea. But I also know that your mother is wrapped around your little finger, and I know your powers of persuasion; and if you like the idea, I don't think I need say another word. It's in your hands. The boys send their love, and so does Dorothea. We all hope to see you again soon – hopefully, on your way to Caracas! Gabriella says you can come at any time.

All my love,

Aunt Winnie

Even before I had finished reading the letter my hands were shaking and my heart was beating so loudly, I could almost hear it; and I could hardly breathe, hardly sit still. I stood up and paced the gallery as I finished reading, and then I ran to the kitchen and threw my arms around Doris, the cook, laughing and crying with joy; and then I ran upstairs to seek Katie, who was doing the mending, and I hugged her and flung her around in a jig, crying out with joy: 'I'm going to study music! I'm going to Caracas!'

And then I ran off to find Mama. She was out on the plantation, of course, busy as ever. So I went to the stables and saddled one of the horses and off I rode, out into the fields. I didn't stop until I had found Mama – she was at the factory – and breathlessly told her of the chance that had opened up to me.

'Not a bit of it!' was her immediate reaction, but I took no notice. I galloped back home and started packing.

It took a whole evening to persuade Mama, but I had my proven methods, and I did, as I knew I would; as Aunt Winnie knew I would. Once that was done there was no reason to spend another day in that wilderness. The very next day, Gilbert drove me back to town.

This time I stayed with Aunt Winnie, not with Aunt Margaret. I did not have any travel documents, but I had had enough forethought to bring my birth certificate with me, so I applied for a passport, and I was issued one in a matter of days. We booked my passage for the following week: I would be taking a ship from Georgetown to Port of Spain, Trinidad, and from there, a further ship to Caracas, just a short leap across the sea.

Chapter 10

Such joyful days, spent with Auntie and my cousins, and with Dorothea. But there was one thing missing; one thing I had to do, one person I had to see before I left: Jock Campbell.

I felt I owed him so much. Though my playing of the Chopin on the night of the reception had been entirely my own doing, it was he who had ensured it had received the right acknowledgement. Had he not led the applause, what would have happened? I was convinced that, had it not been for Jock, I would have been met with stony silence, or at most, a smattering of polite but reluctant clapping. I would have slunk away afterwards, out of the limelight, back to my little hidey-hole of self-abasement. By bringing me out into the light he had given me such a boost of confidence and hope. It's true that in the last few weeks much of the shine had fallen away yet it was always there, established within me, and had only to be retrieved and polished for the glow to be restored. Indeed, the very fact that I was off to the music conservatory in Caracas, and going with such joyful anticipation, was proof enough of the miracle Jock had worked within me. I had never thanked him. I needed to do so. As soon as possible.

Auntie made enquiries, and found out that Jock was staying at the Campbell family home in Georgetown, Colgrain House, which was just around the corner in Camp Street. So I wrote a little letter to him, telling him of my plans, and thanking him for all he had done.

'You may not be aware of it, Jock,' I wrote, *but it is your kindness that has buoyed me up these last few weeks and has given me the courage to take this new and marvellous step. Please accept my gratitude; you were exactly the right person at the right time, and you may well have changed my life.*

I walked around the corner and slipped the envelope into his letter box. I was hoping for a reply before I left. I received something better: Jock himself, at our door, the very next evening.

Aunt Winnie's house was built, typically of the Dutch Colonial style, on high stilts with an outside staircase. When visitors rapped at the front door whoever was nearby – and this time it was me – would first look out of the window to check who it was. And it was Jock. He saw me leaning out of the window, slightly stunned, and waved. I rushed to open the door.

'Jock! How wonderful – I mean, how kind of you to drop by! I didn't think…'

He removed his floppy-rimmed sun hat and shook my hand.

'Good evening, Mary Grace. May I come in?'

I was blocking the doorway, flustered as I was. I moved aside. 'Yes – yes, of course! Do come in! I'll go and fetch my aunt – do come into the gallery – take a seat – I'll get some refreshments – Auntie! Auntie!'

She came hurrying from the kitchen, wiping her hands on her apron.

'Yes, dear, what is it?'

'Auntie – this is – it's Jock, Jock Campbell. You remember? I told you. He's here!'

'Mr Campbell! How kind of you to drop in, do take a seat. I'll send in some refreshments.'

Jock and I sat down in the gallery overlooking Lamaha Street. The gallery was lined with windows, every one of them wide open as always, and since it faced north, and the street was the very last in Georgetown before the Atlantic, a permanent cool breeze blew through the house, cooling it during the day and keeping us free from mosquitos at night. It was already dusk; the frogs in the gutters outside the white picket fence were croaking their nightly anthem, a thousand crickets chirping their staccato accompaniment.

'My word, this is a lovely place you've got here,' said Jock. 'What an ideal location! Colgrain House is in rather a stuffy location – the garden is lovely, but it does tend to hold back the breeze.'

'Yes – I like it too. But Mama's house at Promised Land is just as breezy.'

'Ah, Promised Land. What a delightful name. So many of the plantations here have such delightful names. Land of Canaan, Garden of Eden – quite biblical.'

'I suppose for someone who came from Europe to settle it was a Promised Land. Some ancestor of mine.'

'And now you're off to find a Promised Land of your own!'

'No – no, I'll be back. I'll just be there for a few years, studying music. But it's not certain yet. I'm just going for an audition. I haven't actually been accepted. If they accept me I'll stay. If not—'

'But of course they'll accept you. How could they not? I'm not a particularly musical chap, but I can recognise genius when I hear it.'

'You flatter me, Jock. I'm not a genius. Maybe I have a talent for the piano but that's all. Mozart was a genius; I'm not. I don't compose anything, I just play it with a bit of virtuosity.'

'It's more than virtuosity – it's got heart, and that's what makes it special. To me, at least.'

I smiled. 'Well, I hope then whoever auditions me hears what you heard. I'm a bit nervous.'

'No need at all. Just play for them the way you played the other night, and you'll be fine.'

'I suppose so. Thank you for your encouragement.'

I decided to change the subject; enough of talking about me and my music. It embarrassed me, and besides, I felt that too much confidence would jinx the audition. There's something to that saying, pride goes before a fall, and I worried too much self-belief would make me stumble. A silence, awkward to me, fell between us. It was obviously not awkward to him; he was regarding some paintings hanging on the wall in the drawing room, and stood up to see them better, leaving the gallery. I stood up and followed him.

'My word – these are marvellous!' he exclaimed. 'Who's the artist?'

'My cousin, Charlie. He's a fantastic artist – just an amateur, but he's sold a few paintings. He's in the Essequibo right now, working on a farm of some sort. But his real love is art.'

'I dabble at a bit of oil painting myself, but I'm not nearly as good as this. The expressions on those faces!'

And it was true. Charlie painted people, local people at work and play, and he caught them just as they were. A group of market women, squabbling. Boys playing cricket on a village street. Fishermen bringing in their catch on the Buxton foreshore. Girls playing hopscotch. Charlie captured them all brilliantly, brought them to life on canvas.

Jock had been moving from painting to painting, and now stood before a simple portrait, the face of a man, high-browed, slightly smiling, brown skin shining like silk.

'Who's this?'

'My husband, George. Sadly no longer with us.'

Auntie had approached us silently from behind, and now she too stood gazing at the portrait. It invited one to gaze, to look into the dark eyes; they seemed to draw one in, invite one to join Uncle George in a happy place deep within his soul. I often stood there gazing, wishing I had known him better. I was five years old when he died, and had just the vaguest memory of him.

'My condolences,' said Jock. 'He was a good man, I can tell.'

'Indeed. Charlie was only twelve when he painted that,' said Auntie. 'He somehow captured the spirit.'

'You must miss him,' said Jock.

'We do. A lot.'

'How did your husband die, if you don't mind me asking? No, I'm sorry. That was an impertinent question.'

'Not at all. Death is a reality and there's no point in hiding from it or avoiding the subject – it will come to all of us one day, won't it? I don't mind you asking. The fact is he died as a consequence of a labour protest. But come along – I've brought some little snacks over to the gallery. And some ginger beer. Or would you prefer something a little stronger? Rum and ginger instead?'

'Ginger beer is fine,' said Jock as we returned to the gallery. 'But – tell me about this uprising. Mr Foot did mention there's occasional disruption on the plantations?'

'Occasional? Ha!'

Jock waited for Auntie to continue, and when she remained silent he prompted her.

'Go on – tell me more. What kind of disruption? Why? And how often?'

'I think that's for Mr Foot to tell you, not me,' Auntie replied. 'You're a planter after all, like my sister. My husband, and I myself, we're on the other side so it's not my place to discuss it with you. I'm not an argumentative person, Mr Campbell, and I detest quarrels. I'd rather we didn't have this conversation, it upsets me too much. Now, why don't you and Grace enjoy your snacks? I'll be off – work to do, as always! The kitchen won't clean itself.'

And she was off. Jock looked at me, puzzled. 'Strange,' he said. 'I'd have loved to hear more – she seemed almost afraid of discussing it.'

'Auntie isn't afraid of anything,' I replied. 'But she avoids plantation politics, always. It's the reason she and my mother don't get on; it's a contentious subject. I try to stay out of it myself. I hate politics. I hate taking sides. And on a plantation you're forced to take a side, you'll see. But your side is clear – you're a planter, after all. There are two very clear sides, a clear line drawn, and – well, you'll see. You haven't been up to Albion yet? What are you doing in town?'

It was a clumsy attempt to change the subject, but it worked – for the moment.

'I'm working on the company's wharfs, for the time being. But I'll be going up to Albion soon. I'm sorry you won't be at Promised Land – I'd have loved to drop by to meet you and your mother.'

'You can still go. My mother would be happy to meet you. You're neighbours, after all.'

'Yes, but you won't be there, and you're my main incentive!'

He chuckled, and so did I, and a little spark of flirtation flickered in his eye. What they said about him, that he was an inveterate ladies' man, was definitely true; though he had been nothing but utterly courteous towards me all this time, there was no disguising the practised charm of a man who knew his effect on a young and inexperienced girl. I was determined not to fall for it; I knew too well the dangers of falling for men beyond my station. I'm far too emotional; once I let go of my hold on my feelings they tend to gallop away with me, and I had learned, the hard way, to rein them in.

So I quickly dismissed that little flicker of a flirt and tried to deflect it by asking him about his first impressions of Georgetown, but he would have none of it. He brought the conversation right back to the thing I most wanted to avoid.

'So tell me, in a nutshell, about the politics of a plantation. What is it I need to know about the two sides you speak of?'

I took a deep breath and decided to answer him as succinctly as possible.

'On the one side, the planter side, maximisation of profit. On the other side, from the labourer standpoint, basic amenities; quality of life. That costs money. The two sides are irreconcilable, Jock, and you'll soon find that out. Planters are not usually very nice people. My mother is not a very nice woman. My aunt is, but she isn't a planter. You're about to become one. You're a nice man, but you might not be nice any more when you become a planter. I think it's called a conflict of interest. And I'm sorry about that.'

As the silence that followed these words lingered on I realised: I had left Jock Campbell utterly speechless.

Chapter 11

Winnie

Winnie was never so happy as when surrounded by all her boys, a pleasure that was now rare, but once again granted about a year after Grace's departure to Caracas. Will and Leo were permanently back from their studies, Gordon was back from the rainforest as the rainy season had set in, and Charlie was on a visit to town for some dental fillings. Humphrey, Percy, Rudi and Freddy were all at home as it was a Sunday, and a late Sunday lunch was followed by a relaxing afternoon in the gallery.

Leo, the first to rise from the table, immediately plonked himself into the Berbice chair next to the window: he felt it was his right. He closed his eyes, and it wasn't long before he was snoring. Humphrey and Freddy cleared the overladen dining table and ordered their mother to join Leo in the gallery, to get her off her feet, but she would have none of it; a cake was in the oven and had to be seen to. Gordon settled into a Morris chair with a fat book on rainforest animals he'd borrowed from the Public Free Library, while the four remaining boys – Rudi, Percy, Will and Charlie – changed chairs and gathered together around one end of the dining table for an after-dinner game of whist. Quenched, comfortable, collected: this was family life as it ought to be, and every one of them was content to the maximum. For Winnie, a rare moment of supreme serenity.

She plunged a knife into the cake and it came out dry; it was ready. She removed it from the oven and placed it on the kitchen table; they would eat it that evening. In the meantime, she removed a plate of sliced pineapple from the Frigidaire, another modern gadget she had recently acquired. Winnie loved nothing more than labour-saving devices and household appliances; she collected such things with the intention of freeing up some time for herself, but she never actually was free, for there was a new job for every free minute, which was the real reason she had stopped playing the violin. Winnie did not believe in wasting time.

Now, she handed round the plate of pineapple and each of her boys took a slice. Freddy and Humphrey, emerging from the kitchen having washed the wares, joined their brothers in the gallery. Freddy pinched Leo's nose; Leo squirmed and woke up. 'Hey!' he cried, 'What the hell…?'

But Freddy only laughed. 'Lazybones! Make way for Ma! Ma, come on. Get off your feet, Leo here's the gentleman incarnate.'

'I can't rest in that chair,' said Winnie. 'It's too half-half. You're not sleeping and you're not awake. If I want to sleep, I'll go to bed. At night. Stay where you are, Leo!'

'Thank you, Ma,' said Leo and immediately lay back again and closed his eyes.

Freddy shrugged. 'As you wish. But you shouldn't encourage old Leo.'

'Oh, let him rest, I've enough to do. Maybe we can all go for a drive later.'

'Or a walk,' said Gordon, looking up from the game, which he was losing. 'Wouldn't mind stretching my legs. Georgetown just gets me so lethargic.'

'Leo enjoys lethargy,' said Charlie. 'That's why he's getting so fat.'

'I'm not!' cried Leo, suddenly sitting up.

'What's this, then?' said Freddy, poking Leo in his rather flabby tummy. 'Too much of the good life! A walk would do you good.'

'Actually, no. I have other plans.'

'Hmmmm… female plans, I'd wager.'

'What's it to you? My business entirely.'

'So, Leo, when are you going to propose?' asked Will.

Leo had been courting a pretty girl by the name of Agnes for the last month. She was the daughter of a prominent Portuguese businessman – and since Leo was the businessman in the family, it was clear to all that such an alliance could only be to his advantage. Not that Agnes wasn't a perfectly lovely girl – not only in appearance, but also in character. But Leo's particularity was that he did nothing that wasn't in some way to his own advantage, which, in the case of Agnes, led to some jocular teasing on the part of his brothers. Agnes was surely much in demand; it would be entirely like Leo to put in his stake early. In spite of his excellent prospects as an up-and-coming new recruit at Bookers Shipping, coupled with high ambition and that certain *I'm in charge* attitude women seemed to fall for, Leo could not allow himself to grow complacent. He was one of the lightest-skinned of his brothers, a distinct advantage in British Guiana's extremely racially nuanced hierarchy, an advantage Leo could not afford to ignore. Agnes was Portuguese – not quite white, but white enough for Leo's aspirations.

While he couldn't change the racial mix of his family background, Leo could change his character: 'Try to be a bit nicer, dear,' was his mother's advice to him, while his brothers constantly teased him about his slowly expanding girth, not particularly attractive in a man not yet thirty. Unlike most of his brothers Leo had never taken to sports, and, in fact, avoided every opportunity for movement of any kind. As much as he was unrelenting in his ambition and hard-working in the office, at home he was, to put it frankly, downright lazy. Freddy in particular let him know it.

'Let him be!' said Winnie now. 'Leo, ignore them. Would you like to take the cake over to Agnes when you go? I can easily bake another.'

'Good idea!' said Leo. 'Thanks, Ma.'

'Ma, you spoil him!' said Freddy. 'It'd be better for him to run all the way to the Sea Wall and back.'

'Ma, can I borrow the car?' asked Leo.

'It depends,' said Winnie, 'on what the rest of us are doing. A drive, or a walk?'

'Well, seeing as we can't all fit in the car…' said Charlie.

'So I get the car.'

'Wait a minute. You have a bike! I need the car this evening. Joyce lives up at Diamond.'

Leo was not the only son presently courting; Charlie, too, was seeing a young lady, who lived on a sugar estate on the East Bank Demerara. Dental cavities were not the only reason he was in town; however, there was far less calculation involved in this case than in Leo's, for Charlie loved his Joyce and had already proposed. She had accepted; all that was left to do was to obtain her parents' approval.

'Charlie gets the car. Leo, Charlie's right, you can take the bike. So that's settled. The rest of us: a walk to the Sea Wall?'

'Y'all go – I'll come later,' said Freddy.

'Sorry, not me, either,' said Humphrey. 'I have this case… need to work on it.'

'I'll come,' said Rudi.

'Me too,' said Percy, his twin.

'Count me in,' said Gordon. 'Cricket on the beach, you two?'

'If the tide's out,' said Rudi. 'I'll get the cricket bag.'

Chapter 12

The tide was indeed out and the boys soon found enough young people on the beach to form two teams. Winnie watched for a while and then strolled away along the promenade, towards the mouth of the Demerara River and the groyne, the wide jetty where the river met the Atlantic. She loved coming here: it brought back memories of the old days, when George was alive; when Sunday afternoons meant an obligatory march with all eight boys up to the seafront, cricket on the beach; at Easter, kite flying, and sometimes, even, when the tide was in and the water just right, swimming. Those days were long gone and most of her boys were men now. Only the twins, Rudi and Percy, and Freddy, were still at Queen's College. Her duties towards them were almost done: she had raised a fine set of human beings, helped them find their footing and was sending them off, one by one, to make their way in the world; her contribution to society over and done with.

She sighed and smiled, and waved at a couple she knew walking towards her, arm in arm; nodded at two women she remembered from choir practice; and frowned as she tried to put a name to the face of the young man now approaching her at rather a fast pace.

'Mary Grace's aunt!' he said, holding out his hand. 'Sorry, I've forgotten your name – I don't think I ever knew it, actually – but I never forget a face. Jock Campbell.'

Winnie's eyes lit up in recognition. 'Ah! I thought I'd seen you before! I'm Winnie Quint.'

They shook hands, and Jock fell into step beside her. She continued: 'How time flies! It was just before Grace went off to Caracas, wasn't it?'

'Indeed! Over a year ago. How is she? Has she been back? Is it all working out? I remember she was a little nervous about the audition. I assume it went well?'

'She loves it! And you were so encouraging! The audition went so well they took her on immediately. She was back for Christmas and stayed with us for a week. After that she went back to her mother at Promised Land. Didn't she contact you? Did she never write to you?'

'No. What a pity! If I'd known, I'd have dropped in to visit her. Unfortunately, I don't have much contact with Mrs Smedley-Cox – your sister, I believe?'

'Neither do I,' said Winnie. 'We have our differences, to put it tactfully.'

Jock looked at her keenly, eyes narrowed. 'Yes, tact might be a good thing when speaking of such matters, but I rather prefer plain speaking. I do remember, when I met you that day, you hinted of such differences. You mentioned disruptions, and plantation politics, and were too upset to tell me more, because you assumed we'd take different sides. I remember that conversation well. In fact, I've thought about it several times over the last year. And I think you might be wrong.'

'Wrong about what?'

'About us taking different sides.'

Jock and Winnie gazed at each other as they walked towards the groyne side by side, each sizing up the other; Jock's eyes warm, inviting, Winnie's closed, mistrusting, probing.

'What are you trying to say, Mr Campbell?'

'I'm trying to say that my tendency is towards the other side.'

'The other side, Mr Campbell, is the side of the Indian labourers. They work for you. It's not in your interest to take their side. I've been through this very thoroughly with my sister and I understand plantation politics. And I'll tell you quite bluntly that I do not approve of the inhumane treatment of the workers. My husband fought on their side, and so did I. You're a planter, like Yoyo – my sister – like the whole Booker exploitation machinery. I'm on the other side. That's all I'm saying.'

'And you can't imagine that a planter might have some sympathy for the plight of the workers?'

'No, not at all. Because it's all about profit, isn't it? That's what Yoyo keeps reminding me. A sugar plantation isn't a charity, she says. There's no room for compassion. Because, you know, she felt compassion once. But the moment she got involved with the running of the estate, well, all of that flew out the window. Since then it's all been about maximisation of profit.'

'I see no reason on earth why maximisation of profit cannot go hand in hand with the humane treatment of the very people who enable such profit. I see no reason on earth why the workers who actually make the product – in this case, sugar – why they can't enjoy some of the benefits. The thing is, Mrs Quint, I believe that profit alone cannot determine the strength or the well-being of a business. I believe in such abstract things as beauty, truth, caring.'

Winnie stopped in her tracks. She stared at him.

'Mr Campbell – Mr Campbell! You can't speak like that! It's – why, it's treason!'

He chuckled. 'Please. Call me Jock.'

'Those are fighting words, Mr Campbell – Jock. But you're young – you've a lot to learn. You're only at the start of your career. You'll see. The sugar business is tough, it'll harden your heart. There's no room for softness on a plantation, that's what Yoyo says.'

'You don't know me at all, Mrs Quint.'

'Then tell me. Tell me about yourself. Tell me who you are.'

'If you really want to know…'

'I do. Let's sit down. Tell me all about yourself. Your family, where you're from; your hopes, your dreams.'

She indicated an empty bench, and they took their seats. Jock began.

'I feel I need to apologise for this, but I come from wealth and privilege. Born with a silver spoon heaped high with sugar in my mouth. My family – well, what can I say? I'm from strict Presbyterian Scottish stock. My great-great-grandfather had been a ship owner and merchant of Glasgow. Towards the end of the eighteenth century he established the Campbell family fortune in the West Indies. My family's been in British Guiana for generations. We grew wealthy through our holdings here. We kept slaves. We grew rich on the backs of slaves. I feel almost guilty—'

'No need,' said Winnie. He was almost like a little boy confessing he'd stolen the biscuits. She smiled to encourage him. 'Carry on. My family story is similar; I won't judge you or condemn you. The Coxes were just as bad. I remember the shock when I discovered that. I was just sixteen at the time.'

Jock smiled at her in gratitude, and continued.

'I'll give you a bit of background,' he said. 'Glasgow trading houses had already been long experienced in supplying the needs of North American slave plantations at the time. They were all too ready to capitalise on new markets in the sugar industry in the West Indies and British Guiana. We – that is, John Campbell and Company – were among the principal beneficiaries of that to "enjoy a booming trade". We – and I say "we" deliberately, I consider it personal – supplied merchandise to the slave plantations along the coast of Guiana, then in Dutch hands. Then we began to acquire plantations from planters facing bankruptcy.'

'Just like Bookers,' said Winnie.

'No better than Bookers,' Jock agreed. 'Plantation ownership was often a result of planters being indebted to merchant houses. Failing to liquidate debts in time resulted in foreclosure.'

'Again, just like Bookers.'

'Indeed. Ownership of these slave plantations made us mighty, Mrs Quint. By 1800 it – we – had become one of the leading Scottish companies trading in the West Indies. The Campbells became landowners in Scotland, people of stature. In the 1860s and 70s we moved from the Essequibo coast to the Corentyne coast. It was much more wholesome – not damp and malarial like Essequibo.'

'And that's how you ended up at Albion,' Winnie finished for him.

'Exactly. See, Winnie, I hardly knew any of this before I came here. I was a shallow pleasure seeker. Interested only in sport and cars and – well, in girls. I mean, I also loved literature and art, it wasn't just fun and games. But I wasn't serious about my future here. It was all so – theoretical. I knew nothing of the realities. I had no inkling of – of slavery. I enjoyed our wealth without wondering where it had all come from. I never questioned my privilege. And that was my mistake. I was a bit of a – well, what can I say? A wastrel. Not interested. I had no idea of the past, and no interest in the sugar industry. My family sent me here to – well, actually, it was about a girl. I wanted to marry her but she wasn't suitable, so the family sent me away. They sort of – caught us in a compromising situation.'

'Really! That sounds interesting. What on earth were you doing to her?'

He chuckled. 'Kissing her on a tennis court. My uncle found us. The family was deeply shocked.'

'So – you grew up with morals, did you?'

He nodded. 'I should say so! I was raised by the very strict, conscientious, upright ethics of my grandfather. Always meticulously prepared, always punctual. And ambitious! A Presbyterian mould that allowed for no half-measures.'

'That sounds… dire.'

He nodded. 'It certainly was – it was stifling. And somehow I felt… well, that's just one side of it, the Scottish side. See, the other side, my mother's, is Irish, and it's just the opposite. The Irish side was my emotional side, and that proved the stronger. I absorbed this gentler side of my nature from a young age.

'When I was three the family sent me to Glenstal Castle in southern Ireland, to be safe from the bombs of the German Zeppelins. It was a grand place, the traditional seat of my mother's family. And something happened there. You see I could never quite mesh with those strict and formal and stiff aristocratic ways. In Ireland I found a different world. From the start I felt completely at home in the world of our family's Catholic gamekeepers and farmhands. It was humble and chaotic and they were simple people, but so warm, so intimate; they took me into their fold. I felt love and caring and – well, I just felt at home with them. So I learned to dance at two weddings: on the surface, I adapted to the formal and stylised life within an upper-class family, because I had to. But it was with the lower classes, the "help", that I found my heart. I was charmed. I found a world formed more by instinct and intuition than by logic and protocol, a world of poetry and humour, of people who wore their hearts on their sleeves, people who could love, laugh, cry, hate openly, who didn't live controlled by manners and social taboos.'

Jock stopped for breath. He had spoken for a long time without stopping, as if fulfilling a need to speak his mind, to tell Winnie all. She often had that effect on people: she listened, asked questions, and they opened up to her.

'Am I talking too much?' he asked now. 'I don't usually go on about myself so much. Tell me if I'm boring you.'

'Not at all,' said Winnie, softly. 'Do go on.'

'Well, after the war I returned to the family home in Kent, only for everything to reinforce itself, because there, the differences between the worlds of privilege and the underclasses on whom that world was built were more obvious than ever. And again, I sided with the underdog. My parents were Christians, yet they treated their servants like chattels: they could not marry, they had hardly any holidays, they were underpaid. The maids had to rise at 4 a.m. to light the kitchen ranges and the fires in the rooms. I was admonished never to be rude to the servants, yet no one in my family knew the first names of the people who had worked for them thirty years or more. I was outraged.'

'I'm betting that you did know their first names.'

'Of course! I knew their first names, and addressed them accordingly. I was so uncomfortable with my position of great privilege, Mrs Quint, I felt terrible. So I turned to the servants just as I had turned to the gamekeepers and farmhands in Ireland. By the time I went to Eton I'd already absorbed notions of human equality that were distinctly subversive to the old elite order into which I'd been born and raised. Somehow, I achieved the art of straddling both worlds, of moving with ease among the anointed and among the oppressed.'

'That's fascinating,' said Winnie. 'Now tell me about your education. You mentioned Eton?'

'I did. But then a severe bout of polio meant that I couldn't take up the traditional place at Trinity College, Cambridge. Instead, I went to Exeter College, Oxford. That allowed me to escape the snooty Etonian world for a more liberal one. At Oxford, I found freedom: freedom to explore, in the world of literature, and subversive political ideas, and philosophy, and books. Freedom from my family's Presbyterian certainties and severe moral codes; from the Etonian mould of my heritage. I read omnivorously, widely, the classics, history, philosophy, politics… everything I could get my hands on. But I never got a degree; I was lazy in my studies. I preferred sports and the good life of frivolous pleasures. I realised I wouldn't pass my finals, so I came down from Oxford without sitting them. I refused to fail at anything I set my hand to, I had a tremendous will to win.

'And I did excel, and eventually win, at sports. I finally regained all the mobility I'd lost through polio. With one exception: I abhorred all blood sports, all violence; all killing of innocent animals. In that I once again defied the etiquette of my heritage.

After Oxford – well, that's when I became so frivolous. I was a fancy-free tearaway. I loved girls… Which brings us back to the lovely Olga Webb.'

He laughed, and so did Winnie.

'I was besotted with her, and would no doubt have married her. But the family deemed her suburban, beneath my station as a Campbell. A cooling-off period seemed the right thing at that juncture. They decided to pack me off to run the Campbell plantations in British Guiana. And so – well, here I am! I'm sorry for rambling on like that.'

'Not a bit of it,' said Winnie. 'It's remarkable story, and you're a remarkable person. Tell me more. Tell me what you think of British Guiana – or BeeGee, as we call it. Tell me what happened when you came here.'

'Well – it was a shock, a huge shock. When I first came, I had no interest in sugar and no idea what I wanted to do in life; I was just one of those spoilt sons of the upper class, spending money without having earned it. I'd been raised on romantic notions of life on the sugar plantations, a pleasant, easy-going life of striding about in a pith helmet and enjoying cocktails at sunset. So – it was a shock.'

'Tell me!' coaxed Winnie.

'You're sure?'

'Very sure.'

Chapter 13

Jock

The Campbells owned two sugar estates, Ogle, on the east coast of the county of Demerara, and the larger plantation, Albion, on the Corentyne coast further east, over the Berbice River. In Georgetown, they owned La Penitence Wharf on the Demerara River, and Jock's first job was there at the docks. He was tasked with the assessment and processing of claims by merchants whose merchandise had been broached, broken, lost or stolen, a rather mundane job in which he was himself rather a floundering ship at first.

One of the first claims he dealt with was from a certain B.G. Pawnbrokery. One of those East Indians with funny names, he assumed, and replied with a letter headed: 'Dear Mr Pawnbrokery…'

His supervisor brought the error to his attention, and explained to him how pawnbrokery works, for Jock had never heard of such an institution: a poor person pawned his personal belongings for a small sum of money, just to tide him over a financial crisis. The trouble being that poor people are constantly in financial crises, and never get their belongings back. He was outraged that such exploitation could exist, but that was just the beginning.

The next outrage was more of an ongoing one: the Georgetown Club was just next door to his family residence on Camp Street, and as a member of the elite plantocracy that ruled the colony, he received one invitation after another to the club. There he was initiated into the rules of his class.

'You can't trust a coolie, or an African.' He heard it again
and again, and it never failed to shock him. In fact, just about
everything anybody said shocked him. The plantocracy, of which
he was an honoured member, and the colonial rules shared an
intimacy, a common ethical code, a common sense of supremacy.
He already knew such attitudes from his background in the British
aristocracy; this was the first time, however, that he had encountered
such blatant and outspoken bigotry against entire swathes of the
population; such deep prejudice and hate-infused intolerance of
others, based only on the colour of their skin or their race. It was
his first encounter with racism. Jock found himself an outsider
in that select club of white, affluent colonial society, a world of
privilege and condescension and fusty old dogmatism.

He knew and loved a different world, the 'other'. Just as he had
befriended the farmhands in Ireland and the servants in Kent, he
proceeded to break established protocol by hobnobbing with the
African dock workers. These men, he found, were competent,
interesting and loyal; he got to know them by name – which he
would always be sure to get right, for he believed a man's name
was important to his dignity – and they would come to him with
their cares and their worries and unburden themselves to him,
trusting in him; and he helped them if he could, got them out
of scrapes. He was, in short, a renegade; and the plantocracy and
the colonial rulers and the white businessmen and their attorneys
did not like it one little bit. Jock Campbell was a thorn in the side
of the British Guiana ruling class; a bull in the legendary china
shop of carefully established rules of etiquette between the races
and classes of colonial society. He smashed the delicate porcelain
of white supremacy.

The third and most devastating shock to his system, however,
came at his first visit to Plantation Albion, where he was welcomed
enthusiastically by Mr Foot, who immediately offered to show
him around.

Jock removed his pith helmet and looked up at the big Corentyne sky and breathed in the fresh Atlantic breeze, cool and welcoming in the scorching heat. Its salty tang felt clean and invigorating; it nipped at his clothes and ruffled his hair like a playful girl, and its breath swept over the land, rippling the emerald-green ocean of cane around him, and swirled around him with cool light fingers, enticing him to dance. Mr Foot, the Albion estate manager, was talking, but Jock hardly heard; his heart was soaring, for he was falling in love with the land, and a man in love has no ear for mundane lectures on maximum yield and last year's profit. Jock smiled and opened his arms as if to embrace the world.

Since he was a small boy the names Corentyne, Essequibo and Demerara had been music to his ears; they held a certain magic, a lure. The tales his parents had told nourished the dream of an exotic country, a hot strange land across the ocean where English planters were kings, walking tall in knee-length trousers and white pith helmets, and sipped rum swizzlers of an evening on the breezy verandas of their pristine colonial mansions. A land where the living was good; and where he, too, would one day be king, and live a life of adventure, of romance. A sugar kingdom was a sweet and golden world, and Jock was the heir, the Crown Prince; and at last this world was his. He had come home. And here, in the midst of the rippling cane, he felt it in every cell of his body. Olga Webb faded into the past: this was his future.

They left the cane fields and walked out along the backdam, towards the factory; and as they walked, the fresh sea breeze seemed to carry stray strands of something less pleasant, more pervasive, and the further they walked the stronger became the smell. Finally Jock stopped, and stared, frowning. There in front of him stood several long, low ramshackle buildings, rough constructions made of coarse wooden planks haphazardly hammered together, black holes for windows and doors. No, not even buildings: they were more like piles of rotting wood set aside for burning, and they stood in what appeared to be a lake of stinking black mud. A miasma of wretched despair hung over the site, a cloud of squalor that wafted through the air and seeped into Jock's soul, along with the stench of human excreta and rotting refuse. It was a scene in sharp contrast to the clean crisp green of the cane fields behind them.

'What on earth are those?' he asked Mr Foot. 'Pigsties?' For indeed, pigs roamed the area, grunting in excitement at the dubious treasures they found in the mud.

Mr Foot replied dismissively, 'Oh, those are our coolies' logies.'

'You mean, people live there? The stench is appalling! How can they stand it?'

'They're used to it – they don't mind in the least. These people are not like you and me, you know. Basically they're brutes.'

Jock swallowed the words he wanted to say, and said instead, 'Why don't they have proper houses?'

'Well, we already had the logies when the slaves were freed so it was logical to put the coolies here. It saved money. Why build new houses when—'

'Slaves? We kept *slaves?*'

'Of course we did! All the plantations did. How do you think we built this colony?' Mr Foot frowned at Jock's naivety. 'Come along now,' he said. 'Let's move on. Over here we have…'

Jock followed Mr Foot, away from the logies towards the smoke-belching factory. He walked automatically, glancing back now and again at the hovels; he could hear Mr Foot's voice, telling him of world markets and decreased sugar production and declining profit, quoting figures; he could even manage the occasional grunt, punctuating Mr Foot's speech at the appropriate places, as if in approval; but his mind was elsewhere. He himself was speechless. He felt physically sick. The stench seemed to have soaked into his skin, his soul, and disgust rose in his gorge.

Finally leaving the hovels behind them, Jock and Mr Foot approached a freshly painted building, simple but palatial in comparison to the hovels they had just seen, and clean. Mr Foot pointed to it in passing and said: 'That's the stable for our mules.'

Jock finally found his voice. 'Why don't you let the coolies live here, and put the mules in the hovels?' he asked, almost flippantly.

Mr Foot looked at him as if he were mad. 'Mules cost money to replace, Mr Campbell. This is a business, not a charity.'

Jock's world crumbled apart. He had come to the colony with not the slightest inkling that his life of privilege had been built on the backs of African slaves and indentured Indian servants. He had come with no idea that cruelty and bloodshed and suppression of the most basic human rights, everything he loathed in life, was the foundation stone of his family fortune. That his life of plenty had a shadow side, a dark and ugly underbelly; that the Campbell work ethic, buy cheap and sell dear, meant abject misery and wretched poverty for thousands of labourers.

This was the work ethic of all the planters, but, as Jock would discover in the days and weeks to come, his family were among the worst. In British Guiana, the Campbell name was synonymous with great brutality. That, then, was his inheritance. The idyllic planter's life was an illusion, a rose-tinted dream.

Up above, indeed, the white gods lived in their heaven. But down below the black and brown workers, whose sweat made that heaven possible, lived in hell. His first instinct was to turn tail and run from the devastating truth, back to a perfect England of fast cars and pretty girls.

But Jock was neither a runner nor a quitter. Two things he knew with certainty.

First, that British Guiana was his spiritual home. He would stay.

Second, that he must spend the rest of his life expunging the stain of slavery from his family's history. He must break the mould; he must atone. He must right those ancient family wrongs.

It was almost a religious experience: Jock's Damascus. It was more than a vision: it was a knowledge, an insight. A calling.

Chapter 14

With every word Jock spoke, Winnie found herself melting more and more towards him; for his words resonated with candour. She believed him. She smiled, and placed a hand on his wrist.

'You know, we have so much in common, though my story isn't as fascinating as yours. But I too was raised in privilege. And it was discovering the logies on our plantation that first woke me up to the inhumanity of the plantations, too. And I made a similar comment about our stables to my sister: I said the labourers should be housed in the stables and the horses in the logies. Seems like we see eye to eye on this, Mr Campbell. In truth, I don't understand how anyone could not care. *I* can't not care – and Yoyo cared too, at first. But the love of profit – well, it's addictive. The moment Yoyo smelt profit, compassion fled. It turned to greed. And it was a fight, a real fight, to get our logies pulled down and replaced with proper housing. It can be done, and we did it – that is, my mother achieved this, with some help. So you won't find logies on Promised Land any more. But it's not an easy fight, Mr Campbell.'

'Jock. Please.'

'Jock. It's not easy, you'll find resistance.'

'It doesn't matter. I'm the boss, what I say goes. I've got a lot of plans, Mrs Quint.'

'Please do call me Winnie.'

He bowed slightly. 'Thank you. In fact, that's why I'm in town right now. And I'd love to discuss my plans with you, if I may. I haven't found a single person from the so-called ruling class who can even begin to understand.'

'You must come to dinner, Jock. I'd like you to meet my sons.'
'I'd love to.'

It was the most exhilarating dinner Winnie had had in years. She
didn't often entertain any more, but Jock was more than entertainment. His enthusiasm, his passion, his charisma thrilled and
elated her to the core; it brought back memories of the days of old
when she and George still had a dream, still *believed*. Believed that
change was possible, and change would come. Believed that God
cared about right and wrong and would put right a situation that
was so very, very wrong. That such a thing as karma existed, as the
Indians believed; the evil- doers would be punished, the oppressed
find justice and relief. Not after death but in the here and now, so
that all could see and know.

　None of it had materialised. She had all but given up: the dream
was dead. The plantocracy was too mighty for the ragtag rebels
who sought to overthrow it. The plantocracy had the power; all
the workers possessed was their anger, their flailing fists. They had
tried everything: strikes and revolts and marches. She had lost her
sister. George had lost his life. And nothing had changed. Yes, on
Promised Land the logies had been replaced – but that was the
extent of the reform dreams she had once entertained. She had
pulled all her energy out of politics and concentrated on domestic
harmony: the one area in which she had the power: the one area
in which she really could change the world. What could be more
satisfying than raising good strong men, who would go out into the
world and help set the tone for the generations to come? Children
were the future. Raise them right, and the world will be right. Raise
them wrong, well…

　Her boys were turning into good men, strong men. Apart from
Leo. Leo was selfish, had always been selfish, and nothing she'd
tried had been able to knock that trait out of him. She'd had to

shrug him off; sometimes inherent human nature triumphed over good nurturing. She loved him all the same.

Her boys gave her such joy, each in his own way. Now, tonight, they had as usual all gone their separate ways, so that only two remained for dinner with Jock Campbell; but the two that remained were the right ones: Charlie, because Charlie loved farming and art, and Jock had a farm, and loved art; and Rudi. Because Rudi was a fighter, and Jock's talk was fighting talk. George had passed the baton to Rudi. In Winnie's family each son played a distinct role: Will was the musician, Percy the writer and Leo the business-man; Gordon was the explorer and wildlife expert, Humphrey the philosopher, Charlie the artist and Freddy the social rebel. Like Jock, most of them were good at sport, especially cricket; even Humphrey, whose limp prevented him from running, but who was the best bowler of them all. But Rudi was the revolutionary.

Now, Rudi gazed at Jock, frowning, doubtful, as Jock elucidated his ideas for the future. 'Not just a cosmetic change,' he said. 'I want to see the workers respected for the work they do, and justly compensated. The logies have to go. Not just on Promised Land and Albion, but everywhere, everywhere in British Guiana. On every plantation. Every single worker must have access to a doctor, a hospital; must have schools for his children. Reasonable working hours, days of rest, a pension. My God, these things should be a right! I'm ashamed of my class, my race – I can't believe the things I've seen, the things we do.'

Rudi nodded in agreement. 'They kick their workers into the gutter, and then they all rush off to church on Sundays, calling themselves Christians. Treat their workers like scum. Christianity is a joke. Hypocrites, every last one of them.'

Winnie raised a restraining hand; it was an ongoing argument between herself and Rudi.

'If they don't follow the words of Christ, they aren't Christians,' she said now. 'A Christian is a person who aspires to do as Christ would: feed the poor, clothe the naked, help the needy. Going to church and hanging a cross on their walls doesn't make them Christians. By their fruits you will know them, Christ said, by their acts. So they might call themselves Christians – but if they don't act in a Christian way, they aren't. Don't throw out the baby with the bathwater. This is never Christianity.'

'I'm an atheist,' said Rudi to Jock, ignoring his mother, 'and proud of it. I can't stand the hypocrisy.'

Jock nodded. 'Everyone has his own advantage in the foreground, and that's where society falls. I'd like to see another ethic take root – an ethic of caring and compassion, of looking out for each other and ensuring that each one gets what he deserves.'

'From each according to his ability, to each according to his needs,' said Rudi. 'Karl Marx got it right.'

'So you're a Marxist as well as an atheist?' said Jock with a chuckle, and Rudi nodded.

'I actually agree with that philosophy,' said Jock, 'and I'm a capitalist – a planter, the sworn enemy of the Marxists.'

'Exactly!' said Rudi. 'And here's betting all your good intentions crumble once you get your hands on the accounts.'

'Rudi!' exclaimed Winnie. 'He's different – can't you tell?' She turned to Jock. 'If all capitalists were like you, there wouldn't be a problem.'

'It's money that causes the problems, the root of all evil – it's in the Bible,' said Rudi.

But Jock shook his head. 'Wrong. It's the *love* of money that's the root of all evil. Timothy 1. I'd say, the *worship* of money. When money becomes a god, and wipes out the notion that we must care for our neighbours.'

'Well, we'll see,' said Rudi. 'We'll see. Me, I prefer not to trust, not even you. I like to see actions. Up to now, it's just words. In a few years' time we'll see. Money corrupts, Jock. Let's see how your principles stand up to the reality of running a plantation.'

Winnie nodded. 'What you're saying makes sense, Jock. It's what we all want. But how are you going to fight it, as a lone rebel? And so young, as well. Bookers rules supreme in the colony. You know what they say: BeeGee stands for Booker's Guiana, not British Guiana. Nobody can fight Bookers – they've been here for centuries. They own everything: plantations, shops, shipyards. They've got a finger in every pie. They've been ogling us – I mean Promised Land – for decades, waiting for us to fail so they can scoop us up for a bargain. Those Booker men who head the plantocracy, they'll never take you seriously. They'll say it's all hot air, and carry on as before. They'll sweep you aside. How do you expect anyone in the Sugar Producers' Association to take you seriously? At the moment, it's just words. Tilting at windmills. You're young, and full of dreams – I'm afraid, though, that reality's a different matter. You're David, up against Goliath.'

'But David won in the end,' said Jock, turning to Winnie. 'I may be young, but I know what I'm doing and I've got plans: big plans, long-term plans. But I need allies, people on my side. I can't do it all alone. It means so much to me, this conversation. To meet you, and Rudi.'

Rudi shook his head, as if to say something less than polite, but Winnie interjected before he could speak.

'There's someone else,' she said slowly. 'His name's Jim Booker – we call him Uncle Jim. He's getting on now, retired, but he lives in the Corentyne. A very old friend and mentor of mine.'

'Booker, did you say? He's a Booker?'

'Yes, but a different breed of Booker. A renegade. He married a black woman and sided with the underdogs. He's a pariah as a result. You should go and visit him. Just go to Promised Land village and ask anyone, they'll show you the way. Tell him I sent you.'

'I certainly will. It's been wonderful getting to know you, Winnie. And you, Rudi. I hope to see a lot of you – and the others. Charlie, if you ever need a new job on a new plantation, just knock on my door. I'd better be going now – it's late, and I've got an early meeting tomorrow. Got to meet some crusty old men from the SPA.'

He scraped back his chair and rose to his feet, then hesitated.

'And – Mary Grace? Will she be back any time soon?'

'She certainly will,' said Winnie. 'She'll be back from Caracas next week, and she'll stay for all of August.'

'Wonderful! I wonder – I wonder if I'll run into her – maybe…'

Winnie patted him on the shoulder.

'That can be easily arranged, Jock.'

'I'd love to see her again.'

'I'm sure she'd love to see you again, too.'

'Well then, that's settled.' He reached for his hat on the hatstand. 'Goodbye, Winnie, Rudi, Charlie. I'll be seeing you – soon, I hope.'

When Jock had bounced down the outside staircase Winnie and Rudi looked at each other with knowing grins.

'I have a gnawing suspicion that our Grace… well, I won't jinx it by saying it out loud.'

'He'd be perfect,' Rudi agreed.

Chapter 15

1935

It was good to be back. Yes, Caracas had become a second home in the past year, and Gabriella's home a second family. And the temptations – oh, the temptations! But the moment I stepped off the ship at the Georgetown harbour I knew that this was it – this was my true home on earth, and no other place would ever replace it. I placed my bags on the ground, closed my eyes, took a deep breath and inhaled Georgetown's spirit. Even the cacophony of the dockside: the raucous cries of the dock workers, the clanging of diverse chains and motors, discordant though it was, it lifted my heart. Relatives calling to each other and crying out in glee as they fell into each other's arms: it was my own welcome home.

Nobody was at the wharf to meet and greet me. It was my choice. Had I told Mama the date of my arrival she'd have dropped everything to come to town to pick me up, but she'd have wanted to whisk me up to Promised Land immediately and would have grumbled all the way home about the massive problems she was facing and how little time she had to solve them. That's what had happened when I came for Christmas – faced a whole litany of complaints, and spent just a short while in town. I couldn't deal with Mama and Promised Land yet, that time would come. First, Georgetown: Auntie Winnie, my cousins.

Neither had I told Auntie the exact time of my arrival, so I knew that neither she nor one of the boys would be there to meet me. I signalled to one of the porters and he grabbed my bags; together we passed the immigration and customs officials and then I was out in the street. Taxis were lined up outside the dock, and I hailed one of them, tipped the porter and climbed in. Five minutes later, I was at the house I called home, in the arms of the woman who had mothered me the most, laughing and crying as she swayed me in her arms.

'Let me look at you!' she cried, and pushed me away to hold me at arm's-length. 'Yes, you've changed. More beautiful than ever – your hair! Your eyes have a sparkle they never did before; you're so strong! A little woman!'

I laughed, and hugged her once again. 'Caracas is magnificent, Auntie. I've learned so much. If you thought I was a good pianist before, well, I was just at the beginning! And there's so much still to learn. I can play the flute now as well – I brought it with me! And Gabriella sends her love and she was just wonderful, they all were. And all thanks to you!'

'Well, you must be starving. Lunch is in half an hour. Go upstairs and freshen up. The boys will be in soon – they're all in town now! No, almost all. Leo went back to America – he's got an apprentice-ship at a bank in New York, just half a year, sponsored by Bookers. Charlie stayed an extra week just to see you; so did Gordon. Will's back for good – he's a doctor now, imagine! And he still plays the violin. You and he can play for us tonight – we'll have a little concert. Freddy's got some parties planned for you – he's going to whisk you around so you can meet all his friends. The whole social whirl.'

I groaned. 'Don't tell me he's still trying to matchmake!'

'Always! You know Freddy! But—'

'Oh, Auntie! Well, he'd better stop right now. I've got more suitors than I can count on both hands. Caracas men are not at all like the English. They are so charming, I can almost take my pick! It's that Spanish heritage, I think; not all this tight-lipped snobbery. They are gay and charming and so delightful. They've swept me off my feet!'

I thought Auntie would be pleased to hear that but she actually looked a little disappointed. 'Oh, that's nice to hear!' she said. 'Is there anyone – in particular? Any proposals?'

'Masses of proposals, Auntie! Well, to be honest, only three. But parties galore! Don't worry, though – Gabriella's taught me how to play the field and keep them all at arm's-length, yearning. I haven't made any decisions, I just love being young!'

'Young and beautiful! And now, so confident. That makes all the difference, you know. It means you can bide your time and wait for the right one. There is a right one, you know. Enjoy your youth and your beauty and don't get carried away just yet. You never know what might turn up.'

'I won't! And now I'm off to wash and change. This dress is drenched in sweat. And my hair must be a perfect mess.'

'Your hair is perfect, as ever!'

'In perfect tangles!' I laughed, and skipped away to dash upstairs, grabbing the smaller of my bags as I went. My hair had grown to halfway down my back; I had taken to wearing it like the Caracas girls, loose and free, and it cascaded down my back in a waterfall of curls. But yes – it tangled easily, and sometimes I just wanted to cut it all off, to wear it short, like a boy's. But everyone I mentioned this to was horrified: my crowning glory, they all called it. Easy for them – they didn't have to brush it out every morning and evening!

Now, I longed to wash it, but that would be too much trouble and it would mean appearing for lunch with wet hair. I sufficed with a short cold shower and then in Auntie's bedroom I changed into a light cotton frock, and tied my hair up with a ribbon on the top of my head so that my shoulders were free of it. For some reason, I had developed freckles in Caracas. I had a sprinkling of them over my nose, and a few on my shoulders. Some of the Caracas ladies had said I should hide them, cover them in make-up, but Gabriella had been horrified at the suggestion. 'They are lovely on your golden skin!' she said, and I agreed. I don't know where they came from, but I loved them – they suited the new saucy me!

Yes, there was a new me. The shrinking violet had vanished in the whirl of music and dancing and wonderful people, men and women, which had been Caracas. In Caracas, I was not an outsider, a shadow who belonged between two worlds and never fitted into either. In the racial melange that was Caracas I had finally become myself; grown into my own skin, as it were – and if freckles were a part of that, well, so be it. Let them come!

And now I was back at home, in the country I loved – but a new me, ripe and filled with laughter and gorgeous music; I felt the way a rose must feel when she has just opened to reveal her inner soul, her intoxicating fragrance. People, men, told me again and again that I was beautiful, but they saw only the outside – I felt that beauty in every pore of my being and it was intoxicating, a sheer explosion of joy and the delight of being alive. I wanted to kiss and hug every single person I met. It seemed to burst forth within me – I could hardly contain it all!

Now, I heard voices from below – my cousins were arriving! Barefoot as I was, I slipped from the room and plunged down the stairs. There was Charlie, waiting for me; I leapt into his arms, laughing and almost weeping at the joy of seeing him again. He was my favourite cousin. No, Freddy. No, Gordon. They trooped in, one after the other; they whooped when they saw me, twirled me in a polka, flung me into the air as if a rag doll, hugged and kissed me. Oh, it was good to be back with my brother-cousins!

Chapter 16

After lunch Auntie came up to my room with me – actually it was her room, of course, but in typical Auntie Winnie style she had stripped the bed, changed the sheets, cleared the dressing table and a shelf in the wardrobe and told me it was mine for as long as I needed it. 'I can sleep anywhere!' she said. 'We all shuffle around in this house. I'll find a bed in one of the boys' rooms. Half of them will be gone tomorrow anyway.'

'I won't stay too long, Auntie,' I said. 'I have to go back to Promised Land – back to Mama. She'll be upset if she hears I stayed here too long.'

'You worry too much about your mother's feelings,' said Auntie, 'and not hurting them. Trust me, Yoyo's feelings are not that easily hurt. Her hide's tough as old leather. It's not her feelings you'll hurt, it's her pride.'

'Isn't that the same thing?'

Auntie shook her head. 'Not at all. But let's not talk about Yoyo and her feelings now, let's talk about you. And your music. I take it you've learned a lot?'

I beamed at her. 'Oh, Auntie, yes! So much! It's funny how I thought I was so good and everyone told me I was so good and yet I still had so much to learn. So much to improve! It's as if the goal of musical perfection has stretched way, way ahead of me and I'll never, ever be able to reach it. But it's a good feeling, it makes me work harder.'

'That's it,' said Auntie, 'never get complacent with yourself; never pat yourself on the back, thinking you've arrived. Always be on the move.'

'And yet, Auntie, sometimes I wonder…'

I paused.

'Yes?' she prompted.

'I wonder what I'm going to do with it. I mean, I can't very well become a concert pianist in BeeGee, such a thing just doesn't exist. I know that good solo musicians get invited to go on tour and earn a lot of money and become famous… But me? It's as if my talent is just wasted. What am I doing this for? People tell me I could try my luck abroad. In Britain or America. But…'

I paused again. I could feel it coming on, one of those dreadful moods that overtook me from time to time. Did growing up have to be this way: up in the clouds one minute, down in the doldrums the next?

'I'm only seventeen, Auntie. The scholarship is for three years. And I wonder, what's it all for? What good will it do me? What can I do with it? It'll all be over in two years and then I'll be nineteen and that sounds all grown-up, but I can't possibly move to Britain or America on my own to pursue some kind of musical career. I don't want to go to a country where everyone is white and looking down on me and I'm trying to make my way as a pianist. I would feel so – so lonely.'

'What are you trying to tell me, dear?'

And all of a sudden it all rose up in me in one big heaving wave. I collapsed on to the freshly made bed in a torrent of tears.

'Oh, darling! What is it? Tell me, what's the matter?' She wrapped her arms around me and pulled me close and for a minute or two I did nothing but sob.

'What is it, darling?'

'I'm so lonely, Auntie! So alone! The only place I really feel happy is here, with you all, but I can't be with you and I have to go back to Mama and she doesn't really know me, and anyway, I'm too old to cling to my mother and nobody loves me and—'

'What do you mean, nobody loves you? We all love you! You saw it today. You're part of this family, Grace, whether you're here with us or not. And Yoyo loves you, in her own way; you know she does.'

'Yes, but…'

'But it's not enough? Sweetheart, you mentioned – in Caracas. So many suitors, you said. So many proposals. Is that what you mean? Is there someone special there you love and he doesn't love you back?'

I tried to nod and shake my head at the same time.

'Yes – no. It's all of no consequence, it's all so shallow. All this flirting around – I do it too and it's a lot of fun and all the parties and everything. I'm very popular over there, you know? The very opposite of here. And I could even get married if I wanted to and in a way I do want to; I want to have someone of my very own, someone to love who loves me back and there's no question and we're like one entity, but none of them are like that. There's no love, Auntie. It's all just like a big game. All these swirling emotions and you get caught up in them but then – boom! It all comes crashing down. Because at the back of it I remember how here in BeeGee I couldn't find anyone and then it was the opposite in Caracas and I wonder why, why, why, and what is wrong with me? It just doesn't make sense. And then I think, oh, I should just marry Carlos and then I'll have love and live happily ever after.'

'Carlos? Is he…?'

I brushed it away. 'He's just someone. He proposed. He's in love with me, he claims; a good catch, Gabriella said. I could just marry him and have babies and live happily ever after. But…'

'But you don't love him enough? But, darling, sometimes love grows, you know. It's not always this big overwhelming thing that knocks you over and sets your whole world into a whirl. Sometimes that kind of love isn't love – sometimes it's something slow, that grows.'

I nodded. 'Yes, I know that. And I like Carlos a lot, but – but, Auntie, I would *know*, wouldn't I? I'd know that he's the other half of my being and I want to go through life with him at my side? I mean, people say you go mad with love but I'm not doing that at all.'

'Oh, sweetheart! You shouldn't be even thinking these thoughts right now. You're only seventeen – give it time. You've so much time! It's so easy to make mistakes when you're young and in the throes of a – a grand passion.'

She blushed then, and I knew she was thinking of herself and Uncle George.

'It's so easy to mistake turbulent emotions for love – and it isn't that at all. Be glad, be very glad, you don't feel that way about Carlos. You shouldn't even be thinking of marriage at your age.'

'All girls do, all of them. That's all they think about.'

'But you don't have to do what everyone else does. You have your music, your whole life before you.'

'But, Auntie, what am I going to do with that life? Before I went to Caracas I thought that music was my life, it was everything to me. But the thing is: what next? What's the point? What can I do with that music? It's just a dead end.'

'You underestimate your possibilities here, my dear. I must introduce you to Eleanor McGregor, my dear friend. Do you remember her? You met her when you were a child; she admired your playing. She's a very accomplished musician – she used to play the piano to accompany the silent pictures when she was very young. Anyway, she's a concert pianist and she's also a teacher and a choir leader. *And* she raised a family, all on her own. I'm sure she'll help you find your way, if that's what you want.'

'I suppose so. But still… I'm so adrift. I'm like an empty vessel waiting to be filled.'

Auntie stood up then, took my hand and pulled me to my feet.

'Right then, enough of this morose talk. You know what? We're going to have a party. Right here. Tomorrow night. The boys will organise it, invite their friends. You will stop this morose sulking and self-pity right now. Anyone would think you were a forty-year-old spinster instead of a beautiful seventeen-year-old with all her life in front of her. And you've got eight big cousin-brothers who adore you – what girl wouldn't give an arm and a leg for eight big brothers? So, my dear, you're going to snap out of it, run downstairs, beg the boys to take you out and show you some fun. And you'll come home laughing and joyful and play for us and show us what you've learned, and then we'll have a party and after a few days you will go to Promised Land and see your mother. Understood?'

I couldn't help laughing. Auntie was so good at snapping people out of their stupid old moods. I let her drag me from the bed and, hand in hand, we skipped downstairs to where my wonderful cousin-brothers were waiting for me.

After all, if no one wanted me I could always become a piano teacher. A happy piano teacher, just like Aunt Winnie's friend.

Chapter 17

'But what am I going to wear?' I cried. 'All my party dresses are in Caracas. I just brought some old cotton frocks for Promised Land. I didn't think…'

'Darling, you could wear an old rice sack and you'd still be the belle of the ball. But I see what you mean. Come with me.'

Aunt Winnie took my hand and led me upstairs, to a small room at the back of the house. I had never been in this room before; it seemed to be storage space, with a wardrobe at the back and several boxes and suitcases piled against the opposite wall. A third wall was lined with shelves, on which several smaller boxes sat gathering dust. There was a small window at the top, but it was closed and the air was stuffy and smelt vaguely of mothballs.

'When you've got such a big family you tend to – well, things start to collect. So many *things*! Usually I like to pass things on when I don't need them any more, but some things – well, some things have sentimental value.'

She opened one of the suitcases. It was filled with albums; they looked like photo albums, but she opened the top one and I saw it was filled with stamps.

'Pa's stamp collection,' she said. 'Part of it. It's so huge we had to split it up – Humphrey's got part in his room, and Pa's kept part; he's got them with him in the annexe. These are all the stamps they don't need, the albums they keep to pass on to the next generation.' She chuckled, and shook her head fondly. We all tended to make fun of Humphrey and his stamps; he and Pa, Uncle George's father, could spend hours poring over these little scraps of paper. Some were valuable, they claimed, but I could hardly believe it.

She tapped one of the boxes. I saw that it had BOOKS written across the top and I gasped. 'Books!' I said. 'Can I have a look? Can I borrow them?'

'Why, yes, of course! These are books I brought from Promised Land when I originally moved out – thank goodness, or they'd have been destroyed in the fire. You can have them all.'

I had already opened the box and was examining the titles of the top books, opening them and smelling the pages. They were books I had not yet read, and they smelt of heaven. I had not had the chance to do much reading over the past year, and anyway, all Gabrielle's books were in Spanish, and my Spanish wasn't good enough. I had all but forgotten about books in the whirlwind of music that the past year had been, but now, returning to the isolation of Promised Land, I would need friends. Books. I'd get back to reading.

'Come on, dear, don't forget your dress!'

I reluctantly closed the box and stood up, stepping across the room to where Auntie stood in front of the wardrobe. She opened the doors with a flourish.

'Here you go. The choice is yours!'

A second later we both squealed and sprang backwards, under attack by a swarm of moths.

'Oh, no!' wailed Auntie, collecting herself and swatting them away. She ran her hand along the line of hanging dresses, only to release yet another swarm. 'My best dresses! My lovely frocks! All my memories!'

She removed one by its hanger; it had obviously once been gorgeous, turquoise satin; but the fabric was now in tatters, devoured by the moths.

'That would have suited you so well – you're just the size I was.'

She replaced it in the wardrobe, and her voice became matter-of-fact. 'Right, that means a bonfire for them, and for you—'

'I've nothing to wear!' I cried again. 'We'll have to cancel it! I can't go in these rags!'

She chuckled. 'I wouldn't let you, dear! But never despair. No time to lose.'

She took me by the hand and practically pushed me down the front stairs and into the car. We drove to Bookers Universal Stores, where together we chose a suitable material – nothing too formal, Auntie said, we don't want to overdo it – and then, fabric chosen, cut and bundled in brown paper, it was back into the car and off to Kitty Village.

I had never met Auntie Dolly but I'd heard of her, another legend from Auntie's youth. She was a fixture of Kitty Village, just outside Georgetown to the east; the village seamstress and, by now, wise woman dispensing free advice and counselling to any young girl who would listen. She had played an integral part when Aunt Winnie and Uncle George had been courting and I felt honoured to finally meet her.

'She's old now,' Auntie explained on the way there, 'and her eyesight isn't too good. But her hands are as steady as ever and she has two or three young women she's trained and I'd bet anything she'll have you all sorted out for tomorrow night.'

Auntie Dolly welcomed me with a hug as huge as she was herself; it was like being embraced by an enormous, warm, soft cushion smelling of Johnson's Baby Powder and sweat.

'Leh me look at you! So dis is dat lil baby! Oh Lordy, she grow into a real beauty!'

Auntie smiled. 'And she needs a dress, urgently! Can you fix her up for tomorrow night? We brought the material – it should be enough.'

Auntie Dolly had already unpacked the fabric and was holding it up against my body; we had chosen a lovely white taffeta with a red floral design.

'Lovely, lovely!' she said. 'It will look gorgeous against your skin. What style? You brought a drawing? No? Then have a look at those magazines and see what you like. All the latest fashions in there.'

I leafed through a few of the fashion magazines piled on the table and the three of us made our choice, Auntie Dolly sketching as we talked. We finally decided on an elegant yet feminine sleeveless style, a snug, high waist and a skirt fitted through the hips, slightly flaring to mid-calf. It would have a scooped neckline with a lace collar – Auntie Dolly happened to have some leftover lace that would suit perfectly.

That done, we drove on to Bourda Market, where Auntie did some shopping for tomorrow night's food, and then home again.

Gordon greeted me the moment I stepped through the door.

'There she is! The Piano Princess!'

He grabbed me by the waist and flung me around in an impromptu polka, all the while singing:

Gracie, Gracie

We've got a surprise for you

You'll go crazy!

All in a night or two!

He let me go with an extravagant whirl, whereupon Freddy caught me and took up the dance, twirling me through the room, all the while singing:

It'll be such a stylish marriage,

For he MUST afford a carriage

And we'll all be there

So he won't dare

Bring a bicycle made for two!

Freddy spun me around, then let go of me suddenly, and I was gasping and laughing and stumbling, trying to keep my balance as my knees gave way; but Rudi caught me and steadied me, and I finally came to a halt. Breathless, laughing, I manged to chide them:

'What have you boys been up to? Not another of your match-making fiascos?'

When I came for Christmas I'd first spent a week in town with them, and they had fallen over themselves trying to get me to meet various friends of theirs, young men who, they thought, might be worthy of me. I had already, by then, been courted by a variety of Caracas boys and had gained some confidence, but I still knew, at the back of my mind, that Mama would be horrified at their suggestions. If there's one message she had indoctrinated me with it was this: I must marry up, not down. Only men are allowed to marry down. A woman preserves her social standing or improves it by setting her goals high, not settling for a poor man, or, worse yet, a man of colour.

'Don't follow in the footsteps of your foolish aunt!' she always said. 'Winnie ruined her life by marrying George. Made herself a social outcast; she was ostracised and vilified for years by society. I don't want you to endure that. A girl must choose carefully. Guard your heart and be vigilant. Make sure that any suitor is actually suitable before permitting your feelings to take over. That's the only way.'

Personally, I didn't care, and I would have liked to argue with her; in the end, Auntie Winnie had triumphed. Nobody could call her life ruined by any stretch of the imagination. Even if it had been difficult at first, she had emerged all the stronger and was now a respected icon of Georgetown society. As for Mama, she had married twice using the formula of marrying up, and both marriages had been a disaster. She was, after all, still married to her second husband, the American Geoff Burton; but what kind of marriage is it when you only see your spouse for a few months a year? Uncle Geoff, as I was supposed to call him, seemed more attached to Mama's property than to her. But then again, Mama didn't believe in love marriages. She surely had her own calculations in mind.

So yes, I could have argued, but I didn't. And though I was always open to meeting my cousins' friends, I knew in advance that entertaining them as husbands – well, it would break Mama's heart. I couldn't do that.

The suitors my darling cousins had in mind for me were coloured middle-class men, of good families, with good jobs, but nevertheless all with a touch of the tarbrush, and thus according to Mama, inappropriate.

I couldn't do that to Mama – I was all she had. I had told the boys that quite clearly at Christmastime. They had all poo-pooed my submission to Mama's marital guidance.

'Stand up for yourself, Grace!' Will had told me. 'Don't let her boss you around! Find a good man who adores you and ignore his race and social standing – who cares what a bunch of snoots think?'

But I shook my head. 'She does. And I care about her. She's my mother. Just as you care what your mother thinks about your decisions, don't you? You always ask Auntie's advice.'

'Yes, but our mother is good and wise,' said Humphrey. 'Unfortunately, Aunt Yoyo—'

'Aunt Yoyo's a hellion. Everyone knows it. Sorry, Grace, but you pulled the wrong lottery ticket there.'

'You should have been Mama's,' said Charlie. 'Then you'd have really been our little sister.'

Will glared at him. 'Shut up, Charlie. It's not a lottery. She can't help who her mother was.'

'It would have been so wonderful, though. If you were really our sister, growing up with us. It's what you would have wanted too, isn't it, Grace?'

Charlie was known for his persistence. Once he got something into his head, he stuck with it. But I had to agree with Will – such speculation was stupid.

'Well, Mama is my mother and she loves me as much as your mother loves you and I love her too and I can't possibly break her heart. And I won't. And that's all there is to it.'

That was then. But the way they were carrying on now – well, it was as if we'd never had that conversation. And I was a bit concerned. I could very well imagine the guest list – their friends from school, a few girls, probably, to make up the numbers – all, from Mama's point of view, completely inappropriate. I couldn't help it –I knew it was ridiculous, I knew my cousins were right, I knew my behaviour was racist. But it was as if Mama held me on a tight invisible leash, controlling my thoughts and feelings from behind; and even if I knew they were wrong, she tugged and pulled to steer me in the direction she wanted.

In Caracas it had been different. The men who had courted me might not be English – Mama's first choice – and not as lily-white as she preferred. But they were of Spanish stock, Venezuelan high society; they were the elite, and to marry one of them was to marry up. Oh, it was such a bother. Why couldn't I just cut that rein, as Will had advised? Why wouldn't Mama give in on this one rule? Why did I have to live with all these constraints? It was my life – why couldn't I decide for myself?

Why couldn't I? As I went up to my room to change, the words kept echoing in my mind. Why couldn't I? Why should Mama decide for me? Why did I feel guilt at the very idea of a party with unsuitable suitors? Why should I reject them all wholesale, just because of their colour or their race, just because Mama said I should? I was hot and sweaty from the day's exertions, so I took a shower and as the cold water washed over me, as the sweet smell of Lifebuoy soap soothed my spirit, it was as if I was shedding an old, used skin; as if the old ideas and the inborn deferment to Mama and her plans for me loosened their grip, and finally sloughed away.

I dried myself and put on fresh clothes and brushed my hair, then stood at the open window and gazed out to the north. Though I couldn't see the ocean from here I knew it was there, spreading out to the northern horizon, a vast endless world before me.

I smiled as I remembered Auntie's words. I was young, just seventeen, with my whole life before me. No need to think of marriage yet – not for a long time. Time was on my side, and why not make the most of it while I was young? The boys had planned this party, and, by Jove, I would enjoy it, and enjoy meeting their friends – I would dance, and laugh, and even flirt, and let my wayward hair down, quite literally.

Chapter 18

Mama had always enjoined on me to wear my hair up, neatly coiffed in elaborate creations at the back of my head, and my personal maid Katie was an expert; but Katie wasn't here now, I'd have to manage without her. The point was to conceal as much as possible the telltale kinks and crinkles of my hair. Let loose, it reached the middle of my back, but if I pulled at a strand it would actually stretch to twice that length, extending down to my waist. Wet as it now was from the shower, it hung around my shoulders in limp black corkscrews. And I wondered what it would be like to leave it that way; to let the corkscrews dry as they were, to let them hang loose and free. Why not, I thought, as I brushed them out and twisted them into two long plaits, a temporary taming.

The boys wanted me out of the way while they prepared it all. Charlie, appointed my caretaker, took me to the Empire Cinema to see *Top Hat*, the new Hollywood film with Fred Astaire and Ginger Rogers – to get me into a party mood, Charlie said, and by the time we returned home I was bursting with excitement. Charlie led me round to the back of the house, where we entered through the kitchen door. Auntie was in the throes of baking, cooking, mincing, mixing, flour all over her arms; I immediately offered to help, but she shooed me away, gesturing to a corner where Percy was mixing something in a bowl.

'Get upstairs,' she said, 'and keep away if you don't want the boys to yell.'

The stairwell was just behind the kitchen, the door to the drawing room closed, so I saw nothing, but heard the scraping of chairs and what sounded like a boisterous argument between several of the boys. I giggled and fled upstairs. By now it was almost six o'clock; I still had a few hours to kill and nothing to do. I tried reading a book and playing the flute, but I was far too excited for both. Shortly after six I realised that my dress had not yet been delivered. I had been to a fitting at Auntie Dolly's that morning and she had promised to send it over by five.

In panic, I flew downstairs to Auntie.

'My dress!' I cried, 'My dress! She's forgotten my dress!'

Auntie held me by the shoulders, turned me around and sent me packing back upstairs.

'Everything's arranged,' she said, 'nothing to worry about. Scram!'

Half an hour later Freddy and Dorothea were at my door, Freddy with a newspaper-wrapped package in his hands. He handed it to me. 'Your dress,' he said. 'Safe and sound.'

Dorothea smiled shyly. 'I thought I'd help you get ready – if you don't mind?'

I took her hand and pulled her into the room. 'Thanks, Freddy!' I said. 'I'm borrowing her for a while.'

I unpacked the dress and held it up to my shoulders. Dorothea gasped. 'Oh, it's so beautiful! Oh, I'd love to wear something like that!'

'Can't you?'

She hung her head. 'No, I can't go to parties. I can't even speak to boys. And to wear something like that – my parents would say I'm a harlot.'

'You mean – you aren't coming tonight?'

She shook her head. 'Not possible. I can sometimes escape during the day, when they're out, but at night – never.'

'Couldn't you just – sneak out? They wouldn't know, would they?'

'Believe me, they would. But it's all right – I'm used to it. It doesn't really bother me.'

Yet I was sure it did – she was just being stoical. But she had already changed the subject.

'Your hair,' she said. 'What are you going to do about it?'

I giggled then, and told her. Her eyes sparkled. 'Loose! Oh yes, you must! I'll help you.'

We spent the next hour delightfully. I tried on the dress, which fitted perfectly, and then she tried it on, and it fitted her perfectly too. Then we unplaited my hair, and wet it so that it hung well, and patted it down with a bit of coconut oil; and then we sat at Auntie's vanity table and experimented with her make-up; she never wore much, and some of the powders and creams were still untouched, but she had said I could use anything I wanted.

'It's not the right colour,' said Dorothea, disappointed, as she opened a brand-new box of powder. 'It's for a white lady.'

'They don't make powder for darker women,' I said. 'It's as if we don't exist. As if everyone's supposed to be white.'

'Well, we do exist! But you know what? You don't need any of this stuff. You've got perfect skin – all golden and silky. And those freckles – I love them! You shouldn't hide them under powder. All you really need is a touch of lipstick and something to accentuate your eyes – you're so beautiful just as you are!'

'But you are too, Dorothea! You are!'

Her face fell. 'I'm not, and I know it. Don't try to flatter me.'

'It's not flattery, Dorothea. You really are. Maybe not in a classical sense but – there's something special about you.'

She smiled then. 'That's what Freddy always says, and you know what, if Freddy's happy with me that's all I care about.'

By now my hair was almost dry and as she helped me arrange it, she talked. She said the thing to do was not to use a comb or a brush on it by any means, but to comb it with fingers and get the ringlets just so. When she had finished, we sat on my bed and talked some more, exchanging confidences. She told me, with some prompting, of her home life, which sounded dire. She was not allowed to do anything and, just like me, she was expected to marry a white man. 'A woman has to marry up – that's what my mother always says. It's what she did,' she explained.

I laughed. 'Exactly what my mother says!'

'But then, if your mother is white – how come – I mean, your father?'

I knew what she meant. If women were supposed to marry up, how come I even existed? Auntie Winnie had publicly defied that injunction – hence her family of rainbow boys – but Mama? Mama, who was strictly against intermarriage between the races?

'I'm a half-breed,' I said boldly. 'Papa had an affair with a black woman and she died in childbirth, so he brought her to Mama and she took me in. She couldn't have children of her own.'

'Oh, my goodness! That's so… strange! I'd have thought she'd be, you know, angry. Jealous.'

I shook my head. 'I think she was just desperate for a child and was ready to adopt anyway. But there aren't exactly heaps of white babies filling the orphanages in the colony. And at least I was half-white. And I suppose Papa was pleased to have his own child, his own blood, and must have persuaded her. But still – it's hard, you know. I'm an outcast. Mama loves me, I've no doubt, but she just won't accept that I'm not good enough.'

'I think it's really brave of her, somehow. She must be a remarkable woman.'

'She is… a little too remarkable. You don't know her. If you did, you'd know what I mean. Sometimes I just wish I had a perfectly ordinary mother, not a bossy-boots planter with all these ambitions for me.'

She sighed. 'You're so lucky! To have an aunt like Ma Quint and so many cousins, and so much freedom… You got to go to Caracas and play piano. Me – I'm almost a prisoner at home. They can never know about Freddy.'

Her eyes took on a dreamy quality. 'Sometimes I wish…'

I knew exactly what she wished. She didn't know about my other life; about Mama, and the invisible ropes she tied me up with. But I was escaping, and so too was Dorothea, each in our own way and at our own pace. I told her so.

'Your day will come,' I said, taking her into my arms.

'You think so?'

'I know it,' I said. 'You can't let them separate you from Freddy, Dorothea. You're so right for each other.'

She nodded. 'It's coming to that. One day, I'll have the courage to break away. I'll be old enough, too. Then there'll be no holding me back.'

'Good for you! But I still wish you could come tonight.'

'I definitely can't. It doesn't matter – I'm used to it. At least you're going. You must tell me all about it tomorrow. To hell with the English! I hear they've invited some really nice men for you – coloured men, all their friends. And not too many girls so you can take your pick.'

I nodded. 'I'm curious – and I think they've got a guest of honour. A favourite. Do you know who he is?'

She shook her head. 'Freddy didn't tell me a thing. I can't wait to hear!'

'Neither can I!' I shook my head fondly. 'They're always trying to fix me up with someone. But this is the first party they've ever thrown just for me. Can't wait to see what they've dug up.'

Just then a call came up from downstairs: a cacophony of male voices, some deep, some high, all calling out: 'Grace! Come down!' 'Time to come, tThe party's begun!' 'Grace! Grace!' 'Shall I come and get you, Grace?'

Dorothea scuttled to the door even before I could get up, that frightened-rabbit look in her eyes again. 'Oh, my goodness, I didn't notice the time – it's way past seven! I've got to rush – Papa will be furious!' And she was gone, down the stairs before me and out the back door. I had learned that she always came through back entrances: the kitchen door, or a gap in the fence at the back of the yard, like a runaway urchin.

I stood up, took a final look at myself in the mirror, gave my hair a final finger-comb – now dry, it fell across my shoulders and down my back in a glorious mane of tight black ringlets – smoothed out my dress, took a deep breath and followed her out of the room and skipped down the stairs. My cousin Gordon was waiting for me.

'What were you girls doing up there? Everyone's here and waiting for you!' he said. 'Come on, the grand entrance!' He hooked his arm through my elbow and drew me to the door.

Chapter 19

The door to the drawing room opened and I stepped through it, on Gordon's arm. My seven other cousins were gathered around the entrance, and now they parted to create a sort of passageway I had to walk down, like after a wedding, and they all scattered rose petals over me and cheered as I came. I could have died of embarrassment; I must have blushed scarlet, and I would have turned and run had not Gordon held me tightly clasped.

Beyond the familiar faces of my cousins was a swirling sea of strange, smiling faces; cheering, welcoming faces, blurred by the mist in my eyes. A cheer went up; glasses were raised, some people clapped and I almost fainted, and even now I would have turned and run, had I not now been totally blocked in by the boys – those naughty, naughty cousins of mine. They must have known that such hoopla was the last thing I wanted. Oh, I could kill them!

Someone pressed a glass into my hand and a chorus went up. Will was at the piano: 'For she's a jolly good fellow!' and everyone joined in, and Rudi grabbed my waist and swung me around, and so did all my cousins, one after the other, while the crowd sang, 'and so say all of us! And so say all of us!'

And then Gordon gave a short speech, introducing me as their little sister, a speech along the lines of 'She's been hiding away in the Corentyne all her life, until she ran off to Caracas, but we've got her for a few days now and can't keep her to ourselves.'

I laughed to hide my embarrassment; I hid my face in Gordon's chest, but he pushed me off and laid his arm around my shoulder and proclaimed, 'And now, dear Grace, it's time for you to meet the lovely young ladies and gents of Georgetown.' He took my hand then, took the glass from my other hand and handed it to Humphrey and led me through the room, introducing me to everyone. One smiling face after the other rose before my vision; I heard the names but knew I would never ever remember which one belonged to which face. Handsome men, pretty women, brown smiling faces – they were all there welcoming me; people like me who would never belong to the self-appointed higher echelons of society, but who seemed happy enough to be who they were – just as I would be, I swore. These were good people, fine people: the faces that welcomed me were open and honest and not a twitching nose or a pursed lip among them. Names, faces, hands to shake. Some of the ladies even hugged me. Some of the men pressed my hand between both of theirs; 'So pleased to meet you,' they all murmured, or, 'Delighted!' Or, 'Welcome, welcome!'

So we glided through the room, meeting them all, one by one. Some of the names I recognised: Joyce, Charlie's sweetheart, and Jane, Will's, and Agnes, Leo's, but it was the first time I had met them; they clasped my hands in theirs and drew me close and hugged me. The excitement had more or less died down now. Will was playing some popular tune on the piano. A few couples had started to dance; the attention had drifted away from me, for which I was immensely grateful. I began to breathe normally again, to relax into my true nature. Next, a popular American hit blared out from the gramophone – I remembered Leo saying he had brought all the latest records back with him.

Manoeuvring me gently into the gallery, Gordon patted me on the back. 'You did well, cousin! It's almost over. You can have your drink back and then you can dance. Just one more fellow dying to make your acquaintance – although, I believe, in this case, you already have met!'

I looked up and gasped, hand to my mouth. For this was no stranger. This was – Jock Campbell.

'So we meet again, Miss Smedley-Cox!' he said, amusement in his voice, and stretched out his right hand.

I almost fainted at the shock; instead, I froze, both hands clasped over my mouth. Gordon poked me in the waist.

'Don't be rude, Grace, darling. He's waiting!'

I finally came to my senses and placed my hand in his – he must have felt it as limp as a rag, but he took it firmly and shook it, and said again with that amused voice, 'So we meet again!' adding, as an afterthought, 'Delightful! Perfectly delightful! You've become a proper young lady!'

By this time all my cousins – as far as I could tell, for I did not count – had joined us in the gallery, leaving the other guests to entertain themselves; they all seemed to know Jock well, for they laughed and nudged and jostled each other and all seemed to be in on a huge joke – including Jock. Behind me at the gramophone, Charlie changed the record, and as the first bars struck up, I recognised the song immediately: it was 'Cheek to Cheek', the most popular song of the year and, probably not exactly coincidentally, one of the songs from the film *Top Hat* I'd been to see that day with Charlie.

Jock did not let go of my hand.

'May I have the pleasure of this dance, Grace?' he said, and as I nodded, he led me to the dance floor, where other couples were already moving to the song.

Chapter 20

In Caracas, I had been to many dances, danced with many men. But never like this. Jock's hand resting lightly on my shoulder, the other on my waist – his body moving so smoothly next to mine as we slid across the floor – how can I begin to describe the sensation of melting into him, into his very being? The warmth that enveloped me – not necessarily a physical warmth; a warmth that seemed to rise up from a place deep within me and soak into my senses, into my thoughts, dissolving them? The sensation of being perfectly at home, here in his arms, here in my skin, here next to him, the song seeping through every fibre of my soul?

He was a good dancer, and so was I, but it was not actually as if I was dancing – it was as if I was *being* danced, the song itself moving my legs, my limbs loose and free and lithely at one with his. Gently, he pulled me closer, and gave a faint chuckle; his lips were just above my ear and I felt his warm breath as he whispered the lyrics along with Fred Astaire. I knew without a doubt that everything I felt, he was feeling too. With a perfect and innate knowledge, I sensed it.

He drew his head back, and so did I, and we gazed into each other's eyes. A slight smile played on his lips. That silent gaze held us both as in a spell; I could not look away. The eyes are truly a window to the soul, and I entered into him, and he into me, through those windows, each merging into the other effortlessly, smoothly as two streams flowing one into the other without even a ripple. He smiled, so gently, and placed his right cheek to mine and held it there for a few precious seconds, and then the same with our left cheeks. It seemed the most intimate act in the world.

The song came to an end. We drew apart and he led me into the gallery; separated from the drawing room by a series of wooden columns, it was slightly apart and private, away from the glare and the chatter and general animation of the party, and filled with the pale glow of moonlight gleaming in through the row of wide-open windows. By the hand he led me over to one of these windows and there we stood, not speaking, not moving, only our two hands touching as we drank each other in.

'Grace, Grace,' he said at last, and raised one of my hands to his lips and kissed it. 'What are you doing to me? What is this?'

'I don't know,' I whispered. 'Some kind of magic?'

'No, not magic; magic would be unnatural, supernatural. Whereas this, now – you – me…'

He hesitated, as if searching for the right description. I waited; words failed me too. Words would always be inadequate. Music, I needed music – a song to fill my heart, a silent song of joy and fullness and perfect joy. I wished I could sing that song, play that song; already it echoed in my heart but no words, no instrument, could ever capture it.

He too gave up the search for words; he sighed, long and deep, and shook his head. 'It's no good,' he said. 'I give up. I don't know what it is.'

He shook his head, and then chuckled.

'Your cousins must have known – must have had some kind of premonition. When they told me you were back, and that I should come to the party: yes, I was pleased. I remembered you as a delightful little girl who played the piano as if it were an extension of herself; glorious music pouring from her fingers. Your music enthralled me, back then, and so I was only too eager to meet you again, to hear how you are getting on, to hear you play again tonight, to be enthralled once again by your music. But instead – this.'

I said nothing. Unlike him, I had no words. My eyes clung to him, and spoke with the perfect eloquence of silence. He continued,

'Instead, it is you who enthral me, Grace, not your music. And now that little girl has gone. You are a woman, full and glorious in yourself. Without your music.'

With that he seemed to have run out of words. He looked away, turning his gaze out of the window, towards the north and the faraway ocean and the night sky studded with stars. He still held my hand, and that single point of touch became the link through which our two souls flowed unencumbered: he an extension of me, I an extension of him. I knew this man. I had always known him, always longed for him. He was the reason I could not love Carlos, or any other suitor who had paid court to me in Caracas. He was the reason I had been so reluctant to follow my cousins' marital advice. He was the reason – for everything. I had known. Somehow, I had known.

While his gaze was averted I thought back to our first meeting and realised that it started even then; but I was too young, too naive, too star-struck, too lacking in self-awareness to recognise the call of the heart. I had placed him so far above me it would have been presumptuous to even contemplate that beckoning.

And now, well, I had grown up. As he had said, I was a woman, and could listen fearlessly to my own heart, and to his words; words that only echoed all that I felt. Never had a man spoken to me with such candour; but I had seen that from the start. I had been told he was a ladies' man, and my guard had been up, as I had learned from past experience. But now I knew that that reputation was something shallow, and false. I sensed that Jock was a man of utter sincerity and frankness; who did not hide behind a mask, who did not speak to please, but spoke his mind; who did not hide behind flattery or euphemisms. A man who revealed his heart, in a way I had never been able to. Until now. I was still in the grip of that silent eloquence, but I knew that the time would soon come to speak, and the words I would speak would be to him; and I would speak as never before.

Someone changed the record and the sultry first bars of 'Blue Moon' wafted through the room. 'Shall we dance again?' he said, and I nodded, and we returned to the dance floor, this time with the confidence that comes with clarity.

'It was all so obvious!' Freddy exulted as he said goodnight at my bedroom door. 'You two were made for each other. We all knew it. We're delighted for you, little sister!' And he hugged me and pecked me on the forehead, and I danced into my room and flung myself on to the bed and hugged my pillow in rapture. I thought I would not sleep a wink that night – but I did, exhausted by pure exhilaration.

Chapter 21

And so it all began: with a happy ending. No questions, no doubts, no game playing… He knew, I knew, everyone knew, and some had known even before the evening began.

My cousins had planned it all this way, and even Auntie had had her finger in the arrangement. Almost all the other guests, I found out the next day, had been couples: young men with their sweethearts and fiancées, young women with their suitors. It was ironic that the very night I had made up my mind to rebel against Mama, and open my choices to a more diverse set of young men, was the night I was to fall for the one man who would make Mama leap for joy. Jock Campbell, of course, was the crème de la crème.

Almost all of BeeGee's sugar plantations were owned by Booker Brothers, a conglomerate that owned practically all the businesses in the colony and ruled with almost equal status to the Governor. But Bookers was a company belonging to an absentee owner, and was run by managers, none of whom actually bore the name Booker. It was founded by a pair of brothers in the early nineteenth century, and had grown like a ravenous beast, gorging on failing businesses throughout the land and growing fat and unwieldy. Now there was just a handful of privately owned plantations in the colony: Promised Land, Houston, Glasgow and the two Campbell estates, Albion and Ogle. Of these, only the Campbell plantations had a young, handsome, eligible young man at the helm, and that was Jock. I could do no better; Mama would be ecstatic.

But the best thing of all was that Jock found approval with both sides of my family. The Quints were renegades; they all loathed the elitist racist hierarchy established by the British colonial rulers. Aunt Winnie had openly rebelled against it by marrying Uncle George, and their sons, every biracial last one of them, would have nothing to do with the British. Uncle George, indeed, had been killed by a British rifle during a peaceful protest, doing nothing more threatening than marching with a placard demanding Free the Workers. The Governor had called in the army to scatter the marchers, and Uncle George had been hit by a stray bullet – it was why my cousins were so very anti-British.

Until Jock came along. Jock was different. He radiated such genuine warmth and simple goodness – well, he was irresistible, to all. Everyone warmed to him immediately, and my cousins were no exception – quite the contrary. Unknown to me, over the past year while I was in Caracas, deep friendships had developed between Jock and several of my cousins. He had admired Charlie's art from the beginning, and the two of them discussed agriculture too. Humphrey was shy and soft-spoken, but Jock had coaxed him out of his shell, and engaged him as a legal advisor, and besides, they both loved reading and crossword puzzles. Leo became his business consultant and he advised young Percy on his short-story writing. As for Freddy and Will and Gordon – well, they became his close friends for no other reason but simple mutual compatibility. Almost all of my cousin-brothers enjoyed his company, had succumbed to his charm.

Except one, as I was to discover the next morning over breakfast. Rudi, the one we called The Revolutionary, Percy's twin, did not like him; or rather, still did not trust him.

'But why?' I asked. Rudi, a year older than me, was the thorniest of my cousins, the most critical. He, Humphrey and Will were the brainy ones; we trusted their assessments.

'He's English,' replied Rudi, and his eyes narrowed. 'And white. Never trust a white man.'

'That's not fair!' I said. 'What about Auntie Winnie? Your own mother! She's white, and English!'

'That's different!' said Rudi. 'She's proven herself.'

Auntie, entering with a fresh jug of coffee, said, 'As I suspect, Jock will prove himself. Everyone has to make a start somewhere. Jock, I'd like to bet, is of a different calibre. Like Uncle Jim.'

We all knew of Uncle Jim, of course, the renegade white man who lived near Promised Land and had supported the labourer movement.

'Uncle Jim was different from the start. This Jock Campbell – he's stuck right in there in the vipers' nest. He's a planter, unlike Uncle Jim. What else do you expect? In the end profit will win. It always does. Money and greed, the root of all evil. It's a treacherous combination: British, white and planter.'

'Well, I trust my instincts,' said Freddy with finality, leading me back to my chair. 'The moment I saw you again, back from Caracas, all blooming and beautiful, the penny dropped: Jock's the one.'

'It's destiny, Grace,' said Percy with a laugh. 'It's obvious. You're back from Caracas, he's back from Albion, both in Georgetown. We all knew it. Well – except for grumpy old Rudi. Even Mum – right, Mum? They're perfect for each other.'

'And it all went according to plan – better than plan, in fact,' said Gordon. '"Cheek to Cheek" – that was the finishing touch. Perfect for falling in love. We couldn't really have planned that part.'

And it was true; for who could have known that the moment Jock held me in his arms to the strains of 'Cheek to Cheek' our souls would touch and simply click into place, like the parts of a two-piece jigsaw.

Rudi pushed his plate away, excused himself from the table and left the dining room. The other boys continued to tease me relentlessly with wedding-bell noises and mischievous allusions to 'Cheek to Cheek' and playful jokes as to which of them would lead me to the altar. The ribaldry was interrupted when Jock himself knocked on the door.

Humphrey let him in.

'Hello,' he said to everyone. 'I've come to borrow Grace for the morning, if she's willing. Grace?'

I blushed and nodded, but Auntie bustled up and stood arms akimbo. 'Wait a minute, young man,' she said, 'where are you taking her? How long will you be gone for?'

'Just for a morning drive,' said Jock rather shyly as I slipped on my outdoor shoes and grabbed my wide-brimmed straw hat from the hat rack.

'Don't forget your hatpin, Grace!' called Freddy, and they all laughed. A while ago there'd been a newspaper article about the mashers, women who used everyday articles to protect themselves from male attacks. 'Just in case!' There had been a few attacks on women in Georgetown recently, and all the talk was about how we could protect ourselves. But of course, Freddy was joking; I was safe with Jock. I pulled the hat on to my head and stuck it in place with its long, pointed pin.

Jock whisked me away to a cacophony of whoops and whistles and catcalls, out of the house, down the stairs, into the waiting Bentley. And then, at last, we were alone together for the very first time – truly alone, for though last night we had been in our own little private world as we danced, still we had been surrounded by people.

Now, it was just me and him, and I felt ridiculously shy. What would I say to him? We had hardly spoken at all the night before – words had simply not been necessary, for eyes can speak every bit as eloquently, and the music and the night and the moonlight had all rendered talk redundant.

But now in the broad glare of the morning daylight, on the passenger seat next to him, I struggled to find something to say that would not sound utterly banal. In the end, though, it was he who broke the silence, and it was with something utterly banal.

'Did you sleep well, Grace?' He had taken to calling me simply Grace; he had picked it up from my cousins. Our heads turned to look at each other, our eyes met and I smiled.

'Wonderfully!' I said. 'Did you?'

'Not a wink!' He laughed. 'I was thinking of you all night. I really wanted to sleep so I could dream of you, but it didn't happen – seems thoughts are stronger than dreams!'

'Oh!' I said. 'Well, I didn't dream at all, as far as I can remember!'

'Not even of me? How disappointing!'

I giggled. 'I don't need to dream of you; you're here, right here, aren't you?'

'I am,' he said, 'and we're alone together. At last.'

'Where are we going?'

'It doesn't really matter, does it? But – I have something in mind. Nothing spectacular, and yet beautiful. A beautiful place for a beautiful lady.'

A delicious warmth spread through me, and any inhibitions I may yet have harboured, well, they melted, as an ice cube in warm water. We talked and talked and talked. I told him of my musical studies in Caracas, of my life there: playing down the partygoing, which now, in retrospect, seemed all so empty and shallow and useless. He told me of his life at Albion estate, and as he talked the mood sank palpably. I detected something else in his spirit, a deep sense of dejection, of anguish.

'Something has to change, Grace. I can't go on like this. I can't live with myself. It's as if there's a shadow cast over my entire life. You're the only bright thing in it at the moment.'

In an instant my own elan fell by several notches. I deliberately kept my nose out of plantation business. It was not only that it didn't interest me – the whole discord between the two sides of my family was rooted in the sugar business and to me, sugar was not sweet, but bitter. Sugar had engendered a massive controversy that had not only torn my own family apart, but was tearing my country apart, dividing it into two sides, the oppressed and the oppressors. My mother stood, sword aloft, on the one side. My beloved Aunt Winnie, and all my dear cousins, were on the other side. And I stood between them, refusing to choose a side, refusing to take a stand, refusing to even give a thought to the matter because giving a thought, even a little one, would plunge me into the fray and force me to engage. Engaging was the last thing I cared to do. Better to stand apart, neutral, uncommitted, apolitical.

Music was my safe haven; everyone loved music, and everyone would love me if I aligned myself with Bach, Chopin and Mozart instead of with workers' rights versus profit growth. Music united; music brought together all that was divided. Music was safe; music healed. But was I not hiding my head in the sand? Had music become, for me, an excuse not to engage, not to reflect, not to think: not to take sides? I shivered at that internal question. It was not one I cared to answer.

And now, here was Jock Campbell – an anomaly. A planter, a sugar king, an honourable member of that very class my cousins found so obnoxious; and yet, a man as passionately concerned with the plight of the labourers as any one of my cousins.

I didn't understand it. What I did understand was that it would be impossible to come close to Jock, to know him, without coming close to that knot of trouble I had so relentlessly avoided all my life by hiding behind my camouflage of music. And now, as he turned the car southward into Main Street and headed up towards the town centre, I saw with appalling clarity that I no longer had the option of non-alignment. Overnight, Jock had burst into my life, bringing with him the taste of bitter sugar. I could no longer remain the sweet girl weaving magic worlds of music with her fingers.

And so, as the only bright thing in his life, I knew my role immediately: to listen, to reflect, to be a sounding board on to which he could project and open up and, perhaps, find his way forward. And so, that Sunday morning, I spoke the words through which I would slip into his life and find my lodging there: 'Tell me about it, Jock.'

And he did. As he drove northward, past the Stabroek Market, where he stopped to buy some mangoes as well as a knife to cut them with; past the noisy docks of Sprostons Limited and then back into town, east down Brickdam and the imposing grey edifice of the cathedral, Jock talked. He told me of his life before arriving in British Guiana; a pampered life, I gathered, in which he had been the golden boy destined to lead, to conquer, to rule.

'But it was all a sham. It was like a beautiful palace in the sky whose foundations were rotten to the core. I had no idea. I believed the lie they told me: that British Guiana was some kind of planters' paradise, where we walked like kings and ruled like emperors. Then I came here and found the ugly truth. It was the shock of my life, Grace, seeing how our labourers live. The squalor, the degradation.'

As he spoke a new sense crept through me, a feeling I had never had before: shame, and guilt. I saw clearly my own position of disengagement; I had deliberately shut myself off from the very observations Jock had made. All my life I had sought comfort, and closed my eyes to any hint of discord. I had known of what Jock spoke, but unlike him I had shut my mind and my heart in order to maintain my own comfort. And now as he spoke, every word was like a knife cutting through my own cowardice, opening me up to swathes of guilt as I realised how I had hidden myself from the reality, closed myself to the foundation of human suffering on which my world was built.

Jock wielded his knife relentlessly. 'And it's not just what's happening today,' he said. 'It goes back for centuries. Slavery, Grace! The sugar plantations were built on the backs of slaves! Human beings torn from their families and forced to work for us whites; beaten and kicked and treated abominably – that's what our lives are built on! How can a house stand if the foundation is rotten? It can't!'

The wide causeway of Brickdam came to an end; before us was the hedge that sealed off the Botanic Gardens from the rest of the world. Jock relaxed visibly as he drove in through the wide gates and parked the car in front of the gatekeeper's lodge.

'All right, enough of politics,' he said, grinning at me. 'You've probably been here umpteen times before, so it's nothing special – but never with me. And it's my first time, so you can play the guide.'

The stifling feeling of being caged in, encircled by painful barbed wire, that I longed to escape, fell from me immediately; Jock, having relieved himself of the burdens pressing on his heart, was once again himself, gallant and charming and brimming with good cheer.

Across the sanded central road from the lodge was the manatee pond. I had been here umpteen times throughout my childhood, with Mama, with Aunt Winnie, and the boys, and even with Aunt Margaret and her children. I even had vague memories – and a photo or two – of coming here with Uncle George. By now it was mid-morning and the sunlight glistened on the opaque grey waters of the pond. The manatee was in hiding, deep beneath the surface. I bent down to pick a handful of grass.

'Come on!' I said to Jock, 'let's bring him up!'

Jock obediently picked his own handful, and we both threw our grass on to the water, where the green stalks spread out.

'What now?' he said, when nothing happened.

'Wait,' I said, 'and whistle. Can you whistle? I can't.'

'You can't whistle? Of course you can!' Jock laughed, and whistled a tune I didn't recognise.

'I can't!' I protested, 'I really can't.' I showed him, pursing my lips and emitting a sort of squeaky breath. 'See? That's the best I can do!'

'But whistling – it's surely the start of music? Our lips, our first instrument! Go on, try again.'

I tried, but such a feeble sound emerged that we both collapsed in laughter.

'All right – I believe you now,' said Jock, 'but I promise you one thing – I'll teach you to whistle before the year is up! A musician who can't whistle, what a ridiculous notion!'

I chuckled again, and shrugged, and then shrieked: 'Jock, look! There it is!' I pointed and Jock swung around and there indeed it was: the manatee, risen from the murky depths like some prehistoric snub-nosed monster, opening its massive jaws to devour the spikes of grass.

'Shh!' I whispered. 'Let's watch!'

The manatee rose and sank and rose again, its grey hulk breaking through the surface of the water and dipping down again, until all the grass was gone. Jock and I threw in some more, and that too was soon gone, after which the manatee also disappeared for ever.

'It's like the Loch Ness monster,' said Jock.

'What's that?' I asked, and then he told me about the aquatic being that had been reported by a visitor to the Scottish Highlands a year or two ago.

'But it was supposed to be more like a dragon than a manatee,' Jock conceded, 'with a long neck and humps. A few people claim to have seen it. But there's no proof.'

'How wonderful,' I said, 'a mythical creature!'

'Yes,' said Jock, 'and it will remain a myth until someone manages to get proof. A photograph, or something. Or shoots it dead. The Scots love their shootings.'

'Do you?' I asked, as we walked away from the pond, towards the zoo.

Jock shook his head. 'No,' he said. 'I'm afraid I'm a very untypical Scotsman. I've never wanted to hunt. I think animals should be free, left in their own habitat; pheasants should fly, and deer should roam the forests.'

'Don't you approve of zoos, then?' I asked. By now we were standing at the entrance to our own zoo.

'I don't,' Jock admitted, 'but still, I'd like to see the animals in this one. I've only seen pictures of them before. Come on, let's go.'

He approached the kiosk at the entrance, bought tickets and stood aside to let me pass through the turnstile.

We walked along the path between the cages, stopping at each one to peer inside. Jock said nothing for a while, but I felt his unease and it infected me. Parrots, monkeys, an anteater, a sloth; macaws, a harpy eagle; a boa constrictor, hardly visible, curled as it was into a corner of its naked cage. It was when we came to the jaguar that Jock exploded. The animal was trapped. Its cage measured no more than eight feet in length, and those eight feet it paced, up and down, up and down, glaring at us as if we were the ones who had put it there.

'This is sheer cruelty!' cried Jock. 'This animal should be free! It should be out in the rainforest, searching for food or for a mate, up in the trees, hiding from humans!'

His words stung for I had brought him here, and I should have known better.

'That's what my cousin Gordon says,' I offered in apology. 'He's an amateur zoologist. He's just back from a camp somewhere in the jungle, near Kaieteur, I believe. He's with a British zoologist from Cambridge University, who's here to study wildlife, and a couple of Amerindian guides who know the area and the animals.'

'You have interesting cousins,' Jock said. 'I like Rudi especially. Gordon sounds interesting, but I haven't seen much of him. And Freddy – who doesn't like Freddy?'

'Freddy's my favourite,' I agreed, 'but I love them all. They're like brothers to me. In fact, I wish…'

'You wish they were your brothers. I know what you mean. It's not easy, being an only child. And for you, out there in the Corentyne, cut off from the city and people and only your mama for company—'

'And my music!' I said. I could not allow him to feel pity for me, or to create an image of this lonely female creature moping around the plantation. By now we had seen all there was to see and were heading back to the entrance; once there, we passed through the turnstile and Jock threaded his arm through my elbow. He steered me towards the magnificent avenue of palms that led right through the gardens. I was glad to leave the zoo behind me.

'Right,' he said. 'Your music. The "Héroïque". Beyond words.' He paused and we walked on in silence for a few paces. And suddenly he broke into French. 'L'inspiration! La force! La vigueur! Il est indéniable qu'un tel esprit doit être présent dans la Révolution française. Désormais cette polonaise devrait être un symbole, un symbole héroïque!'

I stopped and pulled away. 'Jock,' I said, 'don't speak to me in French! I only took it a few years. My other language is German. Now translate!'

He laughed, and tucked his arm back into mine, and we walked on. 'The inspiration! The strength! The vigour! Such a spirit must be present in the French Revolution. From now on this polonaise should be a symbol, a symbol of heroism!'

'Who said that?' I asked, intrigued beyond measure, for I myself had felt that spirit of heroism as I played.

'George Sand – Chopin's lover,' said Jock. 'I looked it up in the encyclopaedia, soon after you played it last year. And she's right. And you know what? That music is going to be my inspiration from now on. But not for the French Revolution: for the Guiana Revolution. Grace, that's what we need here. A revolution. And you know what? I'm going to bring it about. Come with me. What's that bridge?'

He pointed then headed off fast, giving me no choice but to follow. 'It's called the Kissing Bridge,' I said, panting as I caught up. It was Georgetown's most potent symbol of romance. Bridal couples loved to pose here for photographs, which would subsequently appear on the society pages of the *Chronicle* or *Argosy*. It was a small humpbacked iron bridge spanning one of the many creeks that criss-crossed the gardens, its latticed wooden sides painted white, and very pretty against the backdrop of deep-green trees.

He chuckled. 'Then we have to cross it. Come, Grace!' And he let go of my elbow again, but only to clasp my hand and dash off, me laughing in his wake and lifting the hem of my skirt in order not to stumble. He made a beeline for the bridge.

We reached the apex of the hump, and only then did Jock stand still. He turned to me, placed his hands on my upper arms. He held his right cheek to mine, and then his left to my left; then looked me in the eye, and whispered, his hands gently touching both my cheeks, 'Guess what I'm going to do now.'

I giggled, and pretended to push him away, though we both knew it was in jest. 'Oh, Jock!' I reprimanded him, 'how *corny* can you get!'

'I like corn,' is all he replied, and then his arms were around me, drawing me close; and mine were around his, and our lips met, tentatively at first; and then with inspiration, strength and vigour.

It was my first kiss, ever.

Chapter 22

'Stay a week longer in town,' Jock said. 'I'm driving back next weekend; you can come with me. There's lots of room in the Bentley.'

I didn't need much persuasion. Mama wouldn't approve of me staying on at Aunt Winnie's, but I was slowling mastering the art of defiance. I stayed on.

It was a week I'd never forget. Jock worked hard during the days, attending meetings with the Campbell managers in town, or with the Sugar Producers' Association, or going off to visit the Demerara plantations, including the Campbell plantation at Ogle; but his evenings were reserved for me. Sometimes he simply came to visit, and we all – he and I, some of my cousins and Aunt Winnie – sat around in the gallery, sipping planters' punch or rum and soda and munching on Auntie's snacks. Invariably, the conversation would come around to plantation politics, and for the first time in my life I began to engage, to be interested, to ask questions, to be horrified at some of the answers. And invariably my own stance began to form – a stance that, in fact, I should have taken from the beginning, had it not forced me to take sides against my own mother. And I realised hard times were coming. As much as Mama would be over the moon at my having 'caught' Jock Campbell, she and he were at opposing ends of the debate on workers' rights, and both were as stubborn as they came. It could not end well. I began to dread my return for I would be living in her home, eating her food – and loving her opponent.

For, yes, I loved him. Perhaps I had loved him from the very first day, from the moment he stood up at my 'Héroïque' performance to applaud me, saving me from ignominy and humiliation, lifting me out of my pariah position and seating me at the table. I'd loved him then, but from the position of a subordinate, from the stance of an admirer gazing up, that of a devotee, one who had hitched her heart to a star outside her ordained orbit. But now I loved him as his equal; for that is how he loved me, and in that equalising love I realised just how damaged I'd been; just how deluded, just how brainwashed; and just how evil the prevailing system that allocated each person a position of inferiority or superiority, solely according to the colour of their skin or the provenance of their parents. I loved him; and in loving him, I found healing, for love destroys all differences, all hierarchies.

We walked along the Sea Wall, hand in hand. To our left, the police brass band played in the bandstand as they did every after-noon, trumpet, horn and trombone underpinning the afternoon mood of joyful relaxation. The promenade was busy, as always at this time: young couples, older couples, families, all came out in their fineries to enjoy the evening breeze and the sunset. I was hesitant at first; but Jock took my right hand and firmly intertwined our arms, and thus we walked, my arm hooked in his. A few heads turned and people stared; sometimes censoriously, but now and then, hearteningly, in approval; someone would smile and nod; someone would recognise him, or me, and greet us by name.

Now and then, too, a couple like us, of mixed race, would pass by, and we would smile and nod at each other in complicity, and we knew we were part of a deep and thorough upheaval of society. That he and I were part of a unifying wave that would sweep our country and, hopefully, one day, the world. Aunt Winnie and Uncle George had been among the very first to break the taboo, and in their wake we followed, and one day, I was sure, a girl would not come of age believing she was inferior solely because of the colour of her skin. As we walked, Jock peppered me with questions: how and where I'd grown up, what Mama was like, about my life in the Corentyne, and if I had not been lonely, the only girl in the planter's mansion of a huge estate. His curiosity was refreshingly open; there was no false coyness at the fact that Mama was white while I was coloured.

'I can see why your cousins are brown,' he said, 'most of them. Their father was a Negro. But what about your father? From what you say about your mother, I can hardly believe that her husband, too, was black? What happened?'

And because he was so frank, so was I.

'My father was English,' I explained, 'and white. But he was a bit of a – a philanderer. He ran after women on the estate. He sired a few bastards – I was one of them. But my mother died after giving birth. Mama adopted me.'

'That was liberal of her,' said Jock. 'I'd have thought—'

But I couldn't allow him to throw aspersions at Mama. 'Mama isn't really evil,' I said. 'Inside, she has a good heart. And she couldn't have children herself and so she forgave him. You see, he brought me to her and she couldn't resist. I was just a little newborn baby. She fell in love with me at once. It didn't matter that I was brown. It didn't matter that Papa had strayed. All married men do, Mama said, and women must accept it and turn a blind eye. It's normal on the plantations. She loves me just as much as if I were her birth child. She does, I know she does. She adores me!'

'Aha!' is all Jock said, and we strolled along in silence for a while. Then he spoke again. 'And do you believe that – that all married men stray?'

My cheeks turned hot – to me it was an embarrassing question, but he didn't seem in the least embarrassed and that helped. 'Well – I don't think Uncle George did,' I replied, 'but it's what they say, isn't it? That men have needs.'

'But have you ever wondered about your birth mother? And all the other mothers who had children with him? They are, after all, your half-siblings. And did you ever wonder if those women

had any choice in the matter, when your father had his *needs*? Did
he, perhaps, force himself on them? Did he force himself on your
own mother?'

But this was going too far. 'No!' I cried. 'No, and no! It's not
my business to know these things! I am Mama's child and Papa is
dead. I don't want to go digging up dirt on him! I don't want to…'

My voice faltered and became a croak. Jock stopped walking
and turned to look at me. I turned my face away; I could not let
him see the gathering tears. But he touched my chin and gently
turned it to him, and I looked up and our eyes met for a second,
before I could pull away and march on, away from him. He was
quick to catch up.

'Wait, Grace, wait! I'm sorry, it's none of my business. Those
were rude questions. Intrusive. I had no right – I'm sorry. It's my
blundering curiosity, that's all. I didn't want to get so personal.
I'm sorry I hurt you.'

Never one to bear a grudge, I forgave him immediately, and
my heart swelled all the more for having had a little tiff, and heard
his apology, and forgiven him. It brought us closer than ever. And
I loved him more than ever now, for having asked such honest
questions, for questioning the right of planters to take their subordinate women. By now evening was truly closing in. The crowd
was thinning. The band struck up 'God Save the King'. We turned
around and walked back to the Bentley, and he took me home.

On Wednesday afternoon, we went to see *Top Hat*; for me the
second viewing, for him the first, and he laughed and squeezed
my hand at 'Cheek to Cheek', leaned over and whispered to me
that we must dance again…

And on Thursday, that's what we did. It was dinner at the
Belvedere restaurant, candles and white-gloved waiters and soft
music, followed by slow dancing on the planked floor beside the

tables. Afterwards, once again seated, sipping at a delicious rum punch, I plucked up the courage to ask him some questions.

'You know all about me,' I said, holding his gaze, 'but I really know so little about you, except that you came here to run Albion, and your political opinions.'

'Albion, and Ogle, and Campbell Shipping,' he said. 'What do you want to know?'

'Well – everything, really. What books do you love? Who are your favourite artists? What are your hobbies? What do you like doing – apart from driving fast?'

'Oh, Grace! That's so boring! Really. Completely irrelevant. There's only one thing you need to know about me. And that is…'

He placed his right cheek on mine and held it there, and then the left.

And in my ear he whispered: 'I'm falling in love with you.'

Chapter 23

On Friday, it was dinner at Aunt Winnie's, with all of us cooking, including Jock himself; laughing and cracking jokes and then all sitting around the oval table, tearing off chunks of Auntie's soft puris to dip them into her delectable chicken curry.

Afterwards, most of us went to sit in the gallery. This time Rudi, who had till now avoided Jock's company, joined us, and before long he, Jock and Aunt Winnie were locked in a deep and passionate discussion about the running of the sugar estates. My attention drifted at this point.

I'd always loathed plantation talk. I loathed it mostly because invariably such talk tore me in two, which was why, on the whole, Auntie and my cousins avoided it in my presence. I knew their stance. But I was Mama's daughter, and loyal to her, and Mama had her ways and it was not my job, or in my nature, to disapprove of or condone her position. But now, Jock swept aside all deference to my compromised position, and let loose. He abhorred with every fibre of his body the system of indenture – little better than slavery, he said – and the injustice, degradation and exploitation of Indians that it fostered.

'How can it be,' he boomed, and his voice grew loud and angry, his cheeks red with passion, 'how can it be that in this day and age men and women are forced to labour in the hot sun from daybreak to dusk, never a day off? I see women who spend their days up to their waists in muddy creek water, men breaking their backs under the loads of cane. How can it be?'

But Auntie only laughed. 'It's what I always asked myself,' she said, 'since I was a young girl. It's the reason Yoyo and I fell apart. The reason I married George. The reason my father disinherited me.'

'Ma's a true heroine,' said Rudi. 'Have you heard her story?'

'No, tell me!' said Jock, and that's what Rudi did – the story of Auntie's drama with her father, Grandad Archie, and how she brought him to justice for killing an Indian labourer. It was a story I'd heard from various standpoints over the years – particularly from Mama's, but that was clearly a biased version and quite different to the one Rudi now told. Mama regarded Auntie as a traitor. And this was why I hated these conversations, and why I finally stood up and left the gallery, left them to wallow in their rage and their rebellion. I walked to the kitchen and removed the jug of lime juice we kept in the cooler, the Demerara window that jutted out on the windward side of the house, where Auntie kept the blocks of ice bought from the ice house. Breeze sweeping through the window would cool the whole house, an ingenious method developed by the Dutch. I poured myself a glass and drank it in long gulps, which helped cool the heat of my own inner turmoil.

A second later, Freddy appeared. I poured him a glass and we stood gazing at each other.

'Gracie,' he said. 'I know it's hard, but you can't run away all your life. You can't hide your head in the sand all your life. Now you've got Jock. He'll help you.'

He didn't need to clarify. I knew exactly what he meant, and he knew I knew. I nodded, and swallowed the lump in my throat. I knew I had to stop running, turn around and face the problem head-on. Face Mama. Face the facts, however disagreeable they might be.

Tears sprang into my eyes. Freddy saw those tears. He drew me close, into an embrace, and held me for the longest time. He was the brother I'd never had. All of them were. And I realised, for the umpteenth time, what a lonely life I led. Soon I would have to return. Return home: to Promised Land, to face Mama; and never had I dreaded home as much as now.

This time, Jock would be nearby, at Albion. But that made it all worse, not better.

On Saturday, he came early; he had asked me for the whole day and, imbued with a delirious sense of freedom, I had said yes. Aunt Winnie had not been so sure; after all, I was still only seventeen, and much as she liked and trusted Jock – well, she was *in loco parentis* and to let me go off for a whole day, unchaperoned, with a young man was, she said, courting not only scandal but very real temptations; especially as Jock had said he was taking me 'upcountry', and that I should bring my bathing costume.

'Upcountry – where?' asked Auntie, and he shrugged and beamed his irresistible grin, which for once only made her frown.

'Freddy!' she called up the stairs, and a second later Freddy, still a boy at heart, came bouncing down, half-sliding on the banisters.

'Yes, Ma?'

'I want you to go out with Jock and Grace.' She turned to Jock. 'It's not that I don't trust you with Grace, Jock. I do. It's just that – you are both so young. I was young once. Trust doesn't come into it. And a bathing costume? No! Freddy will go with you.'

Jock shrugged, still smiling. 'Very well, Ma'am. I understand.'

Freddy grabbed my waist and swung me around in a little polka. 'Got to take care of my little sister,' he said. 'Can't let her be ravished by the big bad planter!'

'Freddy!' cried Auntie, but she was laughing. 'If you can wait half an hour I'll make you a picnic,' she continued.

'No need,' said Jock. 'I've already got one. Enough for Freddy as well – I knew you'd send a chaperone. I know what mothers are like.'

Those last words melted Auntie completely. 'Well, I'm sure you'll have a wonderful day. Grace, run upstairs and get your bathing costume. Freddy, you too. And towels. Do you need mats to sit on? Parasols?'

Jock shook his head. 'Really – I've got everything. All I need are Grace and Freddy.'

And so, a few minutes later, there we were, in a rusty old jeep Jock said he'd borrowed from a friend: me next to him in the passenger seat, Freddy in the back, hanging out the window. Jock whisked us through the town, up the green avenue of Main Street, past the market and the dockyards and on up the East Bank Demerara. Glimpses of the brown river flashed past between coconut trees and villages made up of tiny wooden houses on rickety stilts, crooked staircases leading up to the front doors. Past Diamond estate, and Houston, to a surprise destination he would not reveal to me. Villages sped past: McDoom and Ruimveldt, Rome and Peter's Hall, Land of Canaan and Garden of Eden.

We passed the last village and now we were driving through jungle. He and Freddy kept up a lively chatter, mostly about cars and motorcycles and sports. I half-listened for a while and then switched off the sound; not following the gist of the conversation, I simply enjoyed the sound of Jock's voice, and engaged myself in creating the most heart-filling scenarios in which he and I would stroll through luscious gardens and kiss on humpbacked bridges and sit on the end of a jetty, holding hands, our feet dangling over the edge while gentle waves broke against the stone and sprinkled us with cool showers, and Jock told me he loved me...

After a while I jerked back to attention as Jock turned off to the left, leaving the main paved roadway and driving down a seriously potholed earthen road carved into the forest. The jeep bounced and bumped along this track for about half an hour.

'It's a secret place,' he said. 'I'd like to show you.'

The road came to an abrupt end. He pushed the jeep into a bush at the side of the path and parked – leaving just enough room for another vehicle to pass – climbed down, walked around to the passenger door and gave me a hand to step out. Freddy climbed out of the back. Jock looked at my shoes and laughed.

'Not terribly suitable for this terrain,' he said. 'I should have warned you; you need strong shoes.'

'I'll manage,' I said.

He did not let go of my hand, but led me to an opening between the trees, a footpath, quite worn.

'Luckily it's dry,' he said, 'just follow me.' He let go of my hand then and I walked gingerly behind him down the footpath, treading on crackling dry branches and pillows of moss and weeds. Freddy followed behind. The forest held us in a mysterious green light; the air was moist and alive with the buzz of a thousand invisible creatures. We did not walk for long. After about ten minutes the forest widened and I could not help it – I gasped. We had arrived at a clearing, and at the centre of it was a pool, fed by a creek that crawled from the jungle still and shiny and black, only the very faintest ripples at its edges revealing that it moved. The pond's water, too, was black, but it was as smooth and still as a mirror and reflected not only the trees surrounding it, but at its centre, the sun; and, as we leaned over the edge of its grassy bank, our faces. A tiny beach of white sand invited one to enter gingerly, while a high black rock at one end called out to divers. It was perfect; a sparkling black jewel set in emerald green.

'What's this place? What's it called?' I asked. 'It's magical! Breathtaking!'

'It's called Black Water Creek,' said Jock. 'I've been doing a bit of exploring in the past year, and I came up here with one of the dock workers I befriended – Sam. He's from a village nearby. He's been coming here to swim since he was a boy, all the village boys come here.'

'And all the elegant town-people don't,' said Freddy. 'What a find!' He tore off his shirt and trousers; he had on a bathing costume underneath. He did not hesitate: he clambered up to the rock and dived in head first.

'Reckless!' noted Jock. 'He didn't even test the water to see if it's deep enough to dive.'

'Freddy was always reckless,' I said. 'That's Freddy.'

'And you?' said Jock. 'Coming in?'

I shook my head. 'Not yet,' I said. 'I'll just sit for a while, you go in.'

In truth, I was suddenly shy. Taking off my dress, putting on a bathing costume, getting into that water with Jock – inviting as it seemed, the prospect also filled me with bashfulness, and all at once I was glad of Freddy's presence. It had been a daring idea of Jock's to bring me here, and no wonder he had counted on the presence of a third person. Now, he spread a straw mat on the sand at the water's edge and, taking my hand, led me over.

'You'll be all right?' he asked, and I nodded.

'You go ahead and swim. Don't bother about me.'

'I'll just put up the parasol,' he said, and went to fetch it from the jeep. It was a large and ponderous thing, its metal shaft in three pieces that needed to be screwed together; the bottommost pole was pointed, and this he stuck firmly into the sand before opening the canopy to provide a wide circle of shade.

'There you are!' he said. 'When you're ready, just come in. You can change in the jeep, or in the bushes.'

And like Freddy, he tore off his clothes, clambered up onto the rock and dived into the water.

I watched for around ten minutes as they cavorted and swam and laughed and jostled; and then I could bear it no more. I got up, fetched my bathing costume from the jeep, hid behind a bush and changed. I had deliberately worn a simple cotton frock, buttoned down the front, in the expectation of changing, and it was done in no time. A towel wrapped around my body, I emerged from the bushes; at the mat, I dropped the towel and proceeded to the water's edge; a toe, a foot, a calf, and then a forward plunge and I was in. A moment later I was cavorting with the men, laughing and splashing and ducking, and, sometimes, even swimming.

'That was maybe the best day of my life,' said Jock on the way home. 'A wonderful place, and wonderful company. Unforgettable.' His hand reached out and clasped mine for a moment; we glanced at each other, and smiled in solid unity. No more words were needed.

'I just wish Dorothea could have been with us,' said Freddy. 'She would have loved it.'

'That would have been marvellous,' I said.

Poor Dorothea. How terrible it must be, to be trapped at home with your parents as prison wardens; having to plot and plan and lie in order to occasionally escape.

'Who's Dorothea?' asked Jock, and Freddy told him.

'Next time, we have to arrange for her to come too,' said Jock. 'I'll see what I can do.'

'You could pretend to be courting her,' said Freddy, laughing. 'Nothing her parents would like more! They're desperate for a white husband.'

'Hmmm,' said Jock. 'That's an idea.'

But not an idea I liked at all; a stab of jealousy dug into me. Because what if— I stopped such thoughts immediately. What a jealous hag I was!

'Oh, Jock, do that!' I said. 'It'll give her a chance to get out. Then we could all go somewhere together.'

'Next time I'm in town,' he promised, 'we'll come back to Black Water Creek. All four of us.'

'Five,' said Freddy. 'I want to bring Ma too. It's almost better than Buxton Beach.'

'Better,' I murmured, and glanced over at Jock, whose eyes again were on the road. But I knew: every place would be better if he was with me.

Chapter 24

In between all these events, a telegram had arrived from Mama. I had sent her one to let her know that my journey home had been delayed, and that I was staying with Auntie. Her reply was curt and sharp:

COME HOME IMMEDIATELY STOP NO PERMISSION TO
STAY AT WINNIE STOP.

I wired her back:

COMING ON SUNDAY WITH JOCK CAMPBELL STOP.

I hoped that would pacify her. That Jock's name would be the open sesame for me to stay in town, at Auntie's, as long as I desired.

I also knew that the peace would be temporary. I could not put off matters for much longer. Jock and Mama would have to meet, and it would be a head-on collision. She might still be thinking of Jock as prime real estate as far as marriage was concerned; the reality of him would blow her to pieces. If she didn't already know, she soon would. And I was stuck in the middle.

We arrived at Aunt Winnie's in the late afternoon, fulfilled and contented and more than a little exhausted. Auntie invited Jock to stay for supper, but he said he needed to go home first, to bathe and to change. He was back within an hour, in which time Auntie had finished cooking and Humphrey had laid the table, and most of the boys were back from whatever they did on a Saturday. Only Leo was missing; but then, Leo was engaged and seriously involved in the home life of his future wife, Agnes, and her family. Auntie didn't often employ a maid, but sometimes, on a Saturday, she did; and that evening Maureen came in to clear away the wares, do the washing-up and clean the kitchen and dining room, leaving us all free to enjoy the evening. By general demand, I sat myself down at the piano and played some popular songs, to which we all sang: 'Daisy Daisy', 'If You Were the Only Girl in the World' and, of course, 'Cheek to Cheek'. Jock sang with the others; all of my cousins had wonderful round male voices, but so did Jock; once again he blended in perfectly – a part of the family. My heart swelled. It was simply meant to be. It *had* to be. And then I remembered Mama, and tomorrow, and dark dread banished the sense of euphoria. The entertainment over, I stood up from the piano and made my way with the others over to the gallery, where, it seemed, the evening would continue the Georgetown way: cosy and contented with drinks and conversation.

'What's the matter, Grace?' asked Jock as he took my arm to walk me over. 'You look rather gloomy.'

'Oh, nothing,' I said, and gave him a false smile, which he accepted with a nod. He plumped up a cushion for me on one of the wicker chairs, and took his seat next to me. Maureen bustled out with a tray of glasses and a bottle of rum and a jug of fruit punch.

'You're sure?' asked Jock, and I nodded, glad that he couldn't read my heart.

For I wished, oh how I wished, that Jock was just an ordinary planter, lacking all these revolutionary ideas and plans… just a normal British planter, ready to continue with life just as it had always been—

The moment the thought floated into my mind I caught it, and gasped.

Jock heard the gasp, looked at me and asked, for the third time: 'What's the matter, Grace? Something *is* the matter.'

'No, no, it's nothing,' I insisted, but it was a lie. It was a horrible, mean, deceitful lie. A lie to cover up my cowardice and my hypocrisy.

Because: why would I want Jock to be different than he was? Why did I want him to change, to be ordinary and safe and dull? Why did I not demand that it was Mama who should change, Mama who was in the wrong?

Because I was a lazy, weak-hearted coward. It was a moment of such intense clarity, of such powerful self-knowledge, a flash of such overwhelming self-revelation. Hence the gasp. For I had realised once again that I was not worthy. This time, unworthy not because of my race or my skin colour or the circumstances of my birth, but because I lacked fortitude, and moral courage, and the selfless will to right wrongs. I was selfish, just like Mama.

'Oh, Mama!' I cried out silently, 'I do love you with all my heart, I do. But you won't like where I'm going.'

I needed to be alone – I could not take an evening of light conversation, or an evening of more politics, whichever it would be. I needed to reflect. Aloud, I said to Jock: 'You're right, I don't feel well. I think I'll retire – it's been a long day, a wonderful day.'

I made to stand up. Jock too rose, but I was quicker than him. 'Goodnight – see you tomorrow!' I blabbered, and hurried away. I almost ran to the stairs and bounded up them, rushed down the upstairs corridor to my room. There, I flung myself onto the bed and pummelled the mattress, but not for long. After a while I stood up again, and made my way to the narrow spiral staircase that led up to the tower. Up in the glass-enclosed cupola, open to the night sky all around, I sat down on the bare floor in silence with only the stars for company, and all the pain and the heartache and the unbearable agony that had been my path through life till now coursed through my being and there was no music, no Chopin, no Beethoven, to hold it back and I let it come like an enormous avalanche of contemptibility; and that was me, in all my rags. I let it come. It was like an inner flood of bile. All that was cowardly and fearful, all that was base and foul and stinking; all that was me, up to now. I let it come; I could do no more than allow it all to flood through me. I put up no resistance; I simply observed it, as a witness standing apart.

How long I sat there, I do not know. I often came up here to play the flute, but tonight all I wanted was silence, and it seemed the stars, the very universe, wished to speak to me, to advise me, to guide me, and I closed my eyes and tried to listen to them, to their eloquent language of silence; and it was as if that very stillness sank into me and absorbed the inner turmoil and all that was despicable in me. For an age I sat there; I did not count the hours or the minutes, I only know that at some point during the night it ended. Then came peace. And calm. And well-being. And I knew for certain that, as of tomorrow, I would be a different girl.

Perhaps, already a woman.

I stayed up there – for hours, perhaps. I only know that I was alone with the sky and the stars and the chorus of night creatures with their backdrop of intermittent shrill and rhythmic piping. I leaned against the low wooden wall of the cupola, facing north, facing the Atlantic. Indeed, behind all the turbulence of the night noises, I could hear a distant hum of the ocean – a solid, unbroken drone, barely perceptible but pure and constant, and in its constancy somehow providing the calm I so sought. I closed my eyes and listened to it. At some point, I must have slumped to the floor and fallen asleep, but it was only a light slumber; I woke up to the sound of footsteps on the wooden stairs.

I sat up, rubbing my eyes, and a moment later Auntie's head popped up through the floorboards and then the rest of her emerged and she stepped into the cupola and sat down on the floor beside me. I slumped against her and she laid an arm around my shoulder and pulled me to her and my head fell against her shoulder. She said nothing; it was as if she knew.

She *did* know.

Another, less sensitive person, finding me up there in solitude, might have coaxed me to talk, to empty my soul and discuss whatever problems I had, and want to help me solve them. Not Auntie. She must have felt that I had found resolution on my own, because her silence was of the deeply embracing kind, communicating instead of distancing, and we sat there for a while thus connected before, at last, she spoke.

'It will be all right,' she said, gently. 'Grace, just know that there is strength within you and don't be afraid. You need not be afraid of her any longer.'

'I know,' I whispered. 'And I am no longer afraid. It's more – well, she'll be hurt. She'll be so hurt. If I were her real daughter it'd be so much easier.'

'But, darling, you *are* her real daughter.'

'Oh, Auntie, there's no need to say that. I know, you see. She told me. She told me the truth of who I really am. I know, and accept it.'

Aunt Winnie stirred, and pulled away. She was silent for a while, and then she said, slowly, as if measuring each word, 'So – she told you? The whole story?'

I nodded. Auntie couldn't see me nod, but she could feel it. She pulled me closer, and I took her hand and nestled into the crook of her shoulder.

'Yes. And I know she loves me just like a real daughter – but still, it's not the same, is it? I think deep inside she must doubt. Doubt my love, and her own. And even feeling resentment at what happened. It can't be easy. I'm trying to understand, you see. Because it's not going to be easy, now.'

'So you know what – what really happened?'

I nodded again. 'Yes. She told me I was adopted when I was a child, and a year ago she told me about Papa. Because I asked, you see. I couldn't understand how come I wasn't white, like her and

Papa. Why I was brown if they were white. Because being brown gives me a lot of problems. So I asked if I was adopted, and she told me I was but that she loved me just like a real daughter. That's what she said – a real daughter. Which means that deep inside she doesn't think I'm a real daughter.'

'I see,' said Aunt Winnie and once again dropped into silence; but it was an expectant silence, as if she were waiting for more, and indeed, I was eager to talk about these things, because I would never again talk to Mama about them, and now that I was ready to confront her on plantation matters – well, this was the next burden I needed to work my way through: the burden of my birth.

The silence grew so pregnant I had to break it. 'I really admire her, you see. Mama has many faults and I'm aware of them but this is the one thing she did right. It was awfully brave of her to accept me as her daughter. After what had happened, I mean. So brave, and so generous.'

Then, Auntie did speak. 'Darling – I'm a little bit confused. What exactly was brave and generous about what Yoyo did?'

The question surprised me – after all, Auntie was Mama's sister and she must know that Mama was racially prejudiced. Everyone knew it.

'Why… isn't it obvious? Accepting and adopting a brown baby that wasn't her own? Forgiving her husband? Taking in a bastard – a mixed-race bastard at that? Surely that's the most generous thing a wife can do – and to think she overcame her own prejudice to do it! It shows Mama isn't all bad, Auntie. Papa was a philanderer, he cheated on her. I'm not his only outside child but when my real mother died – well, Mama took me in and forgave him. She does have a good heart. She always loved me. She does love me. She loves me so much!'

The last words came out, against my will, as a cry – a forlorn cry at that. All the calmness I had acquired in the hours gone by had flown again, and my mind was once again a cauldron of boiling,

swirling emotions. How short-lived inner peace can be! Auntie
reflected that turmoil by pulling away from me, wriggling until
she sat on the floor facing me and taking both my hands in hers.

Squeezing them tightly, she said, and her voice shook with
passion: 'Grace, Grace, Grace! I'm sorry. I can't break a promise
and say more but you must, you simply must, talk to Yoyo and
ask – no, *insist* – that she tell you the truth. What she told you
is not – is not the whole story. There's a lot more to it. I can't tell
you – it's not my place and I promised – but you are old enough
now, a young woman, no longer a child. You must talk to Yoyo,
you simply must. I can't allow her to fob you off with – with half-
truths and fibs. Talk to her!'

'It's not true?' I whimpered. 'She lied to me?'

Auntie nodded, and said, 'Don't be angry with her, darling.
She must have done it to protect you. Or to protect herself – it's
hard to know what's in Yoyo's mind, what her motives are. But
one thing is true, Grace. She does love you, never doubt that. You
are her daughter. And never use the word "real" when it comes
to adoption. Children are children – they are all real, all loved.
Mothers simply love – that's all there is to it. But you deserve the
truth. And it must come from her. I shouldn't even be the one to
tell you there's more to the truth than what she told you, but I have
to. Because it's time – it's really time. Yoyo's time is up on many
fronts, it can't go on like this.'

She seemed to have a lot more to say, but she couldn't because
it had all become too much for me and I could no longer hold
it back. 'I can't, Auntie! I *can't*! I can't do this as well! I already
have to confront her about Jock and about the plantation and
all kinds of things, and take a stand and be strong – I can't do
this as well!'

Auntie patted my back as she would a baby. As she must have
patted all eight of her babies on the back when they wept. And
her voice was soothing, so soothing.

'Oh, Grace, darling. I'm sorry, I shouldn't have. It's too much for you now, isn't it? Too much to face all at once. But you are strong, I know it. And you will find that strength inside you and you will find the wisdom inside yourself to do it all. Maybe not all at once. But all these things have to be done, because it's the only way you can be free, and truthful, and happy. Don't be afraid of the truth, dear Grace. Don't be afraid. There's strength in truth and you will find it, I promise you.'

And I was soothed, and found myself nodding into her bosom, and my tears drying, and my sobs ceasing.

And there was laughter in her voice as she said, 'And now, darling – down we go! It's time for bed.'

We edged our way down the stairs by the light of a dusty bulb. She accompanied me to my bed, and as she tucked me in she said: 'Oh, by the way, I forgot to tell you: Rudi and Charlie will be going up to the Corentyne with you tomorrow. Jock has offered them both a job. They'll be staying at Albion.'

Chapter 25

My cousins, Charlie and Rudi, were opposites of each other. All they had in common were those long lanky legs – but that was a feature common to all Quint males. Physically, they in no way looked like brothers, and their personalities were as different as yams and tomatoes. Rudi was fiery, outspoken; full of political and revolutionary ardour, all set to change the world from the ground up. He courted conflict, and loved nothing more than a good argument in which he could show off his razor-sharp powers of debate and argument. He was young yet; barely out of school, and had not yet decided on a profession. This was his time off, time to find his bearings and decide on his future course, for, as Auntie said, you couldn't build a life on being a revolutionary. Along with Will and Humphrey, he was considered the brains of the family. Rudi took after Auntie: so fair-skinned he could pass for white, with soft dark-brown hair and hazel eyes; but all his friends were black.

Charlie, on the other hand, was of tamarind-brown complexion, with tight black wiry hair cut close to the scalp, revealing a noble sculpted head. High cheekbones and deep-set soulful eyes suggested a more artistic, sensitive nature, and indeed, he was the converse of Rudi: introverted, peace loving, disinclined to argue, skilled in the art of conciliation. The portrait he had painted of his father, Uncle George, showed a keen resemblance between the two of them, and according to those who had known Uncle, they were also similar in nature. Uncle had been a gentle, loving man, strong of heart and ready to sacrifice his all for the sake of justice. Charlie was a self-taught artist as well as a self-taught gardener and farmer, recently returned from working on a farm in the Essequibo region of British Guiana, to the west of the Demerara.

It was typical of Jock that, out of all of my cousins, he had found the deepest rapport with these two – revolution and agriculture seemed to be the topics he was most passionate about – and I was beyond thrilled that they would not only be sharing the journey back to the Corentyne but would be nearby, at Albion; that they would be my neighbours and I would and could see them on occasion. Not that Albion was the house next door, in urban next-door terms, it was two plantations down, beyond Dieu Merci; several miles away but still, in concrete terms, a neighbour.

It would be a half-day's journey to the Corentyne in the Bentley. To tell the truth, I had felt some trepidation regarding such a long journey alone with Jock, so I was glad of the company. The events of the past week had tumbled head over heels through my life, · climaxing in the perfection of yesterday. I felt closer to him, and more sure I loved him than ever before, but instead of relieving me of shyness such confidence rendered me more tongue-tied than ever and it was a relief that Charlie and Rudi were right there in the back seat, chatting away with Jock as easily as if he were an additional brother. My cousins, as men are wont to be, were spellbound by the car, and for the first half-hour that's all they talked about: Jock had imported his beloved Bentley from England and had, in fact, come over on the same ship. It was a dark green open-topped Tourer, his pride and joy, and for me it was amusing to witness the enthusiasm men can generate over something that, after all, is simply a box on wheels that can carry one quickly from point A to point B without the need of a horse. Men really are strange beings.

After a while, however, the conversation took a different turn. Not to the usual outrage over plantation politics, but to the situation in Europe. Rudi, especially, was intrigued to hear Jock's interpretation of events, his opinion of someone called Adolf Hitler, who, apparently, signified a very present danger across the ocean. I had, of course, heard the name before, picking it up in conversation, in the news, in newspaper headlines. But Europe was so very far away; events over there did not touch us at all, and up to now what went on over there had all seemed irrelevant to my life and my own problems.

But Rudi was to snap me out of my dreamworld.

'The thing is,' he said, 'I'm worried about my grandmother – she's half-Jewish. She writes to us regularly and downplays the danger – but I've heard other reports and it's worrying. Is it true that Jews are now officially second-class citizens in Germany? What does it mean for them? What's going on?'

Jock's answer sent chills down my spine. Oma Ruth, my grandmother, had returned to Austria three years ago to care for her ageing father, and it had broken my heart to see her go. But she wrote to me regularly, and had never even hinted of possible danger; never mentioned this Hitler, or the degradation of Jews to second-class citizens. What could it mean, in practical terms? I had always thought 'second-class citizens' referred to people perceived to be of inferior race – such as Africans and Indians in British Guiana – and I could not understand how it could also be applied to Jews. Especially since Oma was not, strictly speaking, Jewish. Well, I knew her father had been Jewish but her mother was Christian and though she had been raised Jewish, she had converted to Christianity when she married my grandfather. But, according to Jock, hatred of Jews – and Oma would be regarded as Jewish in spite of her conversion – was a fast-rising phenomenon in Germany. And this Hitler: well, he was more than troublesome.

'Do you think there might be war?' asked Rudi.

'No,' said Jock. 'It's not that bad. Hitler's dangerous, but he can't be that mad as to drive us into another war. The last one was awful enough. Europeans, Germany especially, have had enough – it won't happen.'

Charlie, who, like me, had stayed a silent listener up to now, said, 'The Great War was a lesson to the world. There won't be another. Humanity is wiser now.'

'I wouldn't be so sure,' said Rudi. 'Greed and hunger for power can obliterate all good sense, all the best inclinations. We see it right here in BeeGee.'

'Peace will prevail,' said Jock. 'I'm sure of it. Nobody in Europe wants another war.'

'But if Jews are being persecuted,' I said, 'wouldn't it be better if Oma came back to us? She'd be safe here.'

'She wouldn't leave her papa,' said Charlie at once. 'She returned to look after him, to be with him. He's old, and he needs her.'

'She could bring him too,' I said. 'We could look after him. I would look after him myself, if Oma would bring him to BeeGee.'

But Charlie shook his head. 'No, Grace, forget it. It won't happen.'

'But why not?' I persisted. 'I'm going to write to Oma and tell her to come back, to bring her papa and any other Jews who want to come. We've plenty of room for them. They could all stay at Promised Land. We could – we could open it up to anyone who wants to flee this Hitler. Why not?'

Jock said, 'It's a good idea, Grace. Excellent, in fact. You must speak to your mother about it. It's her home, after all. But if you do anything like that I can certainly help out. Getting them out of Austria might be a bit complicated but I've got connections – I know people.'

'Ha!' said Rudi. 'I can just imagine Aunt Yoyo having her beautiful mansion turned into a refugee home for fleeing Jews!'

'Mama would do it!' I cried, flaring up. Much as my eyes were open to Mama's faults, I could not bear anyone criticising her, and Rudi did it all the time. He could be really disagreeable in that way. 'She'd do it if I asked her.'

'Well, Grace, dear – if Auntie Yoyo is so amenable to all your suggestions, why not ask her to introduce fair and humane conditions for her workers?'

That silenced me. And I decided to say no more. I would write to Oma and discuss it with her. I could imagine nothing better than Oma returning to BeeGee, her papa in tow, and any other Jews who wanted to come. It seemed, in fact, a far easier task than the immediate one that lay before me.

Chapter 26

We missed the midday ferry over the Berbice River, which forced us to wait several hours at Rosignol. We arrived at Promised Land in the late afternoon, and found Mama at home.

She was not alone.

Mama was never the kind of person who enjoyed her own company or was able to entertain herself. She contained within herself a powder keg of restless energy, which was easily expended on the plantation; she was a tireless worker when it came to running the estate. But Sundays were different. It had been that way as long as I could remember, from the days when Oma lived with us. Sundays back then were days of rest and relaxation. The workers had their day off, and the family went to church. Mama disliked church, and always complained, but Oma had insisted; she would point to me and remind Mama to set a good example. Sunday afternoons, in Oma's time, were spent either visiting friends, going to the beach or the pool, or playing tennis at the senior staff compound; a pleasant, leisurely day.

Since Oma's departure the Sunday timetable had changed. The workers' free day was cancelled, which meant that Mama too worked, and I was left to entertain myself. I'd attend church without her, and after that spend several hours at the piano, or in the rose arbour, reading a novel. Now, I had been absent for a year, and more changes were to be expected – after all, Mama now lived entirely on her own and would have had to crank up her sources of entertainment. She loved to talk, and I was a good listener. I had not given a thought, up to now, of how she had filled the space

left by me, or even if she had filled that space. So caught up was I
in my own wants and needs and concerns that I had not thought
of Mama at all, except in terms of confronting her, standing up to
her, resisting her. I had not thought of her as a person in her own
right, with her own personal agenda.

Jock parked the car in the shade of the mango tree that hung
over the sandy courtyard before the mansion. We all got out; he
opened the boot of the Bentley and removed my suitcase. If the
sound of the car's approach had not been enough to alert the house
occupants of its arrival, the slamming of its doors was.

I glanced up, to the top of the entrance staircase, high above.
There she stood, on the top landing, looking down: Mama, regal
as a queen, straight-backed, imperious, unsmiling, looking down
on us as on minions come to pay tribute. She had that very quality
of superiority; it sent a chill down my spine. I smiled weakly, and
waved. She did not wave back, but only stood there, unsmiling. A
shadow appeared in the doorway behind her and she turned around
momentarily and her lips moved as she spoke some undecipherable
words, and then a figure stepped out of the house and stood next
to her, every bit as majestically. Indeed, they could not have created
more of an impression of royalty had they been wearing crowns.

The man next to her was white, tall, thin, bearded, and held a
glass in his hand. I recognised him at once, for he had visited several
times before, from time to time, over the years. Not so frequently
that I could have counted on his presence here, now, but also not so
rarely for me to forget him and his formidable influence on Mama.

He was Mama's husband, the American Geoffrey Burton.

'You'd better go,' I said faintly to Jock. 'It's a bit… awkward.'

I turned to Charlie and Rudi, both of whom, having exited
the car, had not stepped forward, apparently thrown off by the
presence of Uncle Geoff, as I had been forced to call him. Long
ago, before my own memory, it seemed, Mama had taken me to
his home in Louisiana, where we had all lived for a while, but it

had not worked out. She had fled back to BeeGee, intending to divorce him, but had changed her mind and continued her marriage from afar, with Uncle dropping in on us occasionally. I had never liked him. I had not counted on him being here – his presence complicated things no end.

'Why?' said Jock. 'It's time I met your mother. Who's that chap?'

'He's Uncle Geoff,' said Rudi. 'Interesting.' He took a step forward, while Charlie took a step back.

'I'll stay in the car,' said Charlie. 'It's more than awkward.'

'Who's Uncle Geoff?' asked Jock again. The three of us, he, Rudi and I, stood in a cluster while Charlie retreated backwards, back into the car. I felt the strange need to whisper, though plainly we could not be heard from the landing where they both still stood, unmoving, silently staring down on us.

'He's Mama's husband. He's… difficult. I can't stand him, it's not a good time.'

'Nonsense,' said Rudi. 'No time like now! Let's go on up.' He took a step towards the car. 'Come on, Charlie. No running away, let's get this behind us.' He held out a hand to Charlie, who took it reluctantly and stepped out again. I straightened my back – there was no escaping the ordeal – and led the way. The house being on high stilts, the wooden staircase was in two parts; first bifurcated, with a small landing, and then twenty more stairs leading up to the top landing and front door. Mama watched as I walked up, still unsmiling, still as a statue, radiating a grimness I had seldom seen in her. Nevertheless, I smiled and, even before I reached the first landing, called out to her.

'Mama! I'm back, as you can see! And this is our new neighbour, from Albion, Jock Campbell. And of course Rudi and Charlie, come to say hello. They're staying with Jock at Albion.' I started up the single set of stairs leading to the top landing. 'Hello, Uncle Geoff, nice to see you. Have you been here long? Mama, sorry I couldn't come earlier but— OW!'

Mama's hand had flown out and the slap she planted on my cheek sent a sharp sting all through my body. My hand flew to my cheek and I ducked away and stumbled. I tried to grab the banister, but missed, and would have fallen all the way down had not Jock, who had followed me up, leapt forward and caught me. He set me upright and cried out, 'Now, wait a minute! I don't think—'

'You shut up!' Mama seethed. A gaze of hot rage focused on him for a second before switching to me.

'I told you to come home!' she said in a low but wrathful voice, pointing at me. 'I told you to come home, immediately. How *dare* you stay in town and disobey me! How *dare* you!'

Uncle Geoff placed a calming hand on her outstretched arm and tried to pull it back.

'It's all right, dear. Let's all go inside and discuss this reasonably—'

'*You* shut up too! It's none of your business. And *you*…' pointing to Jock, '*You, you* and *you*…' stabbing the air towards him, Rudi and Charlie, 'get off my property! At once, just go! And *you*…' this, directed at me, 'get in the house at once, right away! We have some talking to do, young lady.'

But Jock's arm was still around my waist, providing the one bit of stability I could count on right now.

'Grace, are you all right? You don't have to stay. You can come with me, if you want to.'

My cheek still stung, and I was too dazed to do anything but duck my head and struggle to hold back tears of pain. My instinct was to turn, spring down the staircase once more, and I would perhaps have done so were they not blocked by the three unwelcome visitors I'd brought. But that moment of hesitation called me to my senses.

I removed my hand from my cheek, straightened my back and met Mama's gaze with a look that I hoped was as fiery as her own.

'No, Jock,' I said, without looking at him. 'You can go – please do. Thank you for bringing me. I'm staying. There are a few things Mama and I need to discuss.'

Mama and I stared at each other in silence, each willing the other to give in. And she was the one to concede. She looked at Uncle Geoff, mouthed words I could not decipher and waved towards the door. He turned and entered the house. Mama made as if to follow, but suddenly paused, and swung around again to face the four of us as we stood on the landing and the stairs, each one waiting for a cue from the others. Her gaze swept past me and Jock and landed on Rudi, moving on to Charlie.

'I said go! Why are you still here? Go now!'

That delivered, she spun around and stormed through the door.

Shocked into immobility, I could only stare at Jock and shake my head in apology and shame. He stood one step down from me, so that our eyes were level. His were soft, yielding, and held a question. He spoke it aloud.

'Will you be all right, Grace?'

I nodded. My right hand slipped along the banister to meet his left. He squeezed it, and reached for my other hand.

'Yes,' I said. 'I'll be all right. I can manage her – I know it. I'll be in touch.'

'If you're quite sure…'

'Yes.'

Rudi, behind Jock, spoke out, 'I can stay with you, if you like? If you need help? What a monster!'

'She's not a monster,' I said. 'She's my mother, I'll deal with her. Go home with Jock and I'll send a message in a few days.'

'You're sure?'

'I'm sure.'

I waved them all goodbye, then, and turned to step across the landing and through the front door. I had sought a confrontation, but in the end the confrontation had found me: it was right now, and right here.

Chapter 27

The drawing room filled almost the entire first floor of the house: one huge square room with a wooden floor polished to a beautiful honeyed sheen, sectioned off to provide little enclaves for the various activities, and around three sides, the veranda, jutting out beyond the upper storey, its walls of wood and windows. In one corner of the main room the baby grand piano at which I'd sit for hours each day, my fingers bouncing, dancing, across the keys. To the right, the oval dining table, in front of the door to the kitchen. At the back, the staircase to the upper storey; a door to the rear led to Mama's office. A reading corner, and a conversation corner, each with their respective chairs and carpets, tables decorated with framed photographs, almost all of me. On the wall, a large framed portrait of me, aged three, sitting on the jetty at the Georgetown Sea Wall, my hair a mane of curls, the sweetest smile upon my lips. It had been painted by BeeGee's leading artist, the Englishman Jonathan Soames. Mama had commissioned it; she loved it. Mama loved me. Nothing in my life, to date, had ever been so sure and so secure than this: Mama not only loved me, she adored me. She loved me so much, people said, she was wrapped around my little finger.

Today I had seen a new and terrifying side to her. Because how could you love a person, and look at them with eyes so full of hate? The way Mama had looked at me today, out there? And why? The slap still burned on my cheek, but the greatest sting was in my heart. For a moment I simply stood there, one hand on my cheek, the other on the back of a Berbice chair, trying to retrieve my bearings and recover my very self. For everything within me was a swirling mass of emotion.

I looked around for Mama but she was nowhere to be seen. She was either in the kitchen, or upstairs, or, and this was the most likely, in her office. That's where I headed. I knocked on the door.

'Come in,' she called, and I entered, hesitantly, for the bravado I had won outside on the landing had all but vanished, and now once more Mama held the trump card – as she always had. Because, in spite of everything, in spite of her adoration of me, in spite of her showering me with love and presents and being wrapped around my little finger, we both of us knew it: Mama was boss-lady, on the plantation, in the home, in the country itself. She had simply played at love, and for the first time ever, standing there at the threshold to her office, one hand still on my cheek, staring at her back as she bent over her desk beneath the far window, I knew it with the certainty of the passing seasons and the rising sun: love, for Mama, was a game. Even love for a daughter.

But you are not her daughter. The words rose unbidden to my mind. Not her real daughter. Perhaps that's why? And I remembered Auntie Winnie's words: that there was more to this story than Mama had revealed, and that I should ask her. And suddenly, that became the pressing question. Not Jock, or why she was, so suddenly, so venomous towards him. Not her treatment of my cousins, her nephews, with whom, as far as I knew, she had no quarrel. And certainly not now why she had turned on me. Yes, she was used to my obedience, my acquiescence in most matters, for I had never once abused my status as beloved only daughter of the house. I liked to please, to please her – I was a child of compromise and compliance. And I had thought, I had believed, I had been convinced not only that Jock Campbell would have met with her full approval as a suitor, but she would have burst into song at the prospect of such an alliance; for was he not perfect?

But suddenly, every one of these burning questions retreated into the background, and there was only one thing I needed to know, desperately and immediately. Why was I even born? If the great scandal of my paternity was untrue, as Aunt Winnie had hinted, then what was the truth? Auntie had planted a seed in my soul and it had grown to full strength as a weed, now strangling all other questions.

'Mama—' I began. But I could not finish, because, without turning, she commanded:

'Come in and close the door.'

I did as she had said, and walked over to her desk, coming to a halt right next to her so that all she had to do was look up and face me.

'Mama,' I began again, but again she interrupted me.

'Take a seat,' she ordered. 'Let me finish this.'

Glancing at her desk, I saw that she was bent over a ledger, fountain pen in hand, filling in numbers scribbled on a separate piece of paper. I recognised vaguely what she was doing: the workers were paid according to the weight of cane they had harvested. Each punt, before entering the factory, was first weighed and the labourers who had filled that particular punt were paid accordingly. These would be the numbers from yesterday. It was the most boring work imaginable; Mama had once taught me how to do it, and I had almost died of tedium, but it had to be done.

Now, I did as she had said, and sat down. I wondered where Uncle Geoff had disappeared to: he was nowhere to be seen, which meant he had either retired upstairs, or had gone outside again through the kitchen. From his previous visits, I knew that when he was at home, he favoured sitting in the gallery with a rum swizzler in his hand. This would take place on and off during the day until, when evening arrived, he was quite, as one would say, tipsy and sometimes even incoherent. Perhaps he had indeed left through the back door, to round up some of his friends from the senior staff compound. Or maybe Mama had sent him away – she'd said she wanted to talk to me.

As if reading my thoughts, Mama looked up then and glanced at me sitting stiff-backed on the chair next to the desk. She blotted the ledger and closed it, slipped the cover back on her fountain pen, screwed the lid back on her bottle of Quink and shifted her desk chair so that it faced me. To my astonishment, she was smiling; and, shocking me even more, she reached over now and touched my hand gently – the hand that still protectively covered the place on my cheek where she'd slapped me.

'Oh, dear!' she said, in her most contrite voice. 'Did I hurt you? Such a mean old mummy you have! You know my temper, it does fly out of hand sometimes, doesn't it? But then it's gone – pouf! Like a puff of air! Shall I ring for Daisy – she's our new maid – to bring some ice for you? Let me see, is it red? You will forgive me, won't you, darling?'

It was, indeed, Mama all over – Mama of unreliable moods, Mama who nobody could understand because nobody could read that complicated mind of hers, a mind that seemed built on shifting sands, blown this way and that by the winds, and yet powered by a will and a pride that was as immobile and unswayable as a mountain. That was the enigma of Mama.

'It's all right,' I murmured, and dropped my hand. How I longed for the fire that had momentarily engulfed me, out there on the landing, when I had actually, for the first time in my life, stared her down, stood up to her. Now, my hands played nervously with each other on my lap, twisting a corner of my skirt around my fingers.

'Oh, Mary Grace, do stop your twitching!' said Mama. 'There's nothing to be afraid of. I'm no longer angry with you – I never was, actually, it's just the fact that you brought that blackguard, that traitor Jock Campbell, over here, to my property. That's what angered me the most – seeing him on my doorstep. As for your disobedience, that's another matter but soon forgotten. You know

I don't like you to stay at that house. If you want to enjoy city life you really must stay at Aunt Margaret's in future. It's far superior company. Those Quints – I don't know what you see in them.'

'Mama! They're my cousins! And I love Aunt Winnie, you know that. And I don't know why you – I don't know why you hate them so much and I wish—'

'Hate? No, hate is too strong a word. Let's just say I despise them. They have no dignity, no sense of history, no sense of propriety, those Quints. There's nothing they can teach you – just a wild bunch of ragamuffins and a mother who disgraced her family. Keep away from them. I've always told you that but you choose to ignore me. Well, you're a big girl now but you'll learn to your cost that there's a price to pay for hobnobbing with the wrong people. You'll see. But as I said – it's that Jock Campbell I have to deal with now.'

'Mama, I don't understand. Jock – he's a planter, just like you. And English. Last year, you were so in favour of him… You liked him! You thought he'd be such a good suitor for me and he's a neighbour and – and such an important one too! You said – you said…'

Mama swiped the air. 'Oh, fiddlesticks! Forget what I said, that was last year. Since then I've found out about him. I know what he's doing, I know what he stands for. You'd think a man like that would know his place, know what side his bread is buttered on. All he's done, Mary Grace, in the past year, is sow anarchy. Yes – he's an anarchist!'

Mama rose and looked down at me in my chair, eyes bright and almost manic. She turned away and stalked to the door and back, back and forth, back and forth, hands balled into fists, hammering the air as she raged. 'Can you believe it? Betraying not only the entire planter class, but actually himself. Placed himself on the side of his own labourers – madness! Those Albion labourers, they now get favours pushed up their backsides. Sundays off, evenings off, sick leave, pregnancy leave, maternity leave, new housing, old age pensions – it's not to be believed! And when one plantation pushes through things like that, what do you think will happen on the others? Labour unrest. Everyone starts getting greedy and demanding the same. How are we planters to survive if all we do is run after our labourers, begging them to accept our largesse? So instead of Campbell strengthening our cause, he's ruining it. We have more strikes, more riots, than ever before; labourers demanding this and that. Can you believe it? I can't. What's the world coming to? If it goes on like this it means the end to everything.

'Look at the good life I've provided for you. Look at this house, Mary Grace – rebuilt out of ruins! Do you know how privileged you are? There's a reason why we're called the sugar kings. And me, sugar queen, you, sugar princess. Next thing you know, they'll be calling us sugar fools, sugar outcasts. Those coolies will be demanding to live in mansions, just like us. That's what your Jock Campbell is up to, Mary Grace! That's why I don't want him here and I don't want you hobnobbing with him. In fact, I forbid it.'

She plonked herself back into her chair and hammered the desk, glaring at me. 'I absolutely forbid it,' she repeated.

Till now silenced by her outburst, in the ensuing space I found the words I needed to say, the only words possible. I spoke them quietly, calmly; they came from a place of surety and faith.

'Mama,' I said, meeting her gaze from that sense of innate poise, 'I love him.'

If I had planted a bomb beneath her seat, I could not have released a greater explosion. She sprang up, leapt towards me, grabbed me by the shoulders and shook me so that my head waggled. My arms flew out to push her away but her grasp was far too tight, her fingers digging into my flesh, her lips drawn back as she snarled and snapped; vile words sputtered from between clenched teeth and her eyes aflame with fury.

'You little hussy! Traitor! Swine! Love? *Love*? So he's seduced you, you little harlot! The man is evil, treacherous! Now listen to me, I'll have none of it! I forbid you! I won't let him have you, do you hear? Do you understand? You stupid little child! Not a grain of sense in that brain of yours! Do you not *see*? Can you not guess? It's all a plot, a dastardly wicked plot! The man is our enemy! He doesn't want you, it's Promised Land he's after. He's a dirty communist! Are you blind? You always were stupid – this is the last straw! He's turned you, my own daughter, into a traitor – all for one purpose! I won't have it! I won't, I won't, I *won't*!'

At these last words she shook me and shook me and shook me and I yelled and tried to push her away but my arms found no leverage and so I used my legs; they kicked out and caught her in the belly and she stumbled then and fell to the floor. I used that moment to spring from my chair and run to the door, into the hallway, where I almost collided with Uncle Geoff, who, apparently, had helped himself to a long drink of something and made himself comfortable. Now, at the shouting and yelling, he had got up and was rushing, glass in hand, towards us.

'What the—' he began but I ran into him and his glass spilled and fell from his hand and on to the polished floor; too late, I swerved and leapt towards the front door and out.

Down the front stairs to the driveway, I ran. Down the drive to the gate, which the watchman opened for me; on to the road, northwards towards the village. I ran and ran until I was out of breath and then I slowed down and stopped and collapsed on to the wayside, buried my head between my knees and panted for breath and sobbed; but not for long.

Was she after me? I stood up, brushed the dust from my skirt and looked back towards the house. No vehicle approached. I should have grabbed a bicycle, I realised – my own bike, from the garage. Too late now. I would not go back, perhaps not ever. But there was no hurry. Even if she came after me, I would not return: I was not hers.

But I could not continue. Not just yet. My mind was in too much turmoil. My knees gave way and I slipped once more to the ground.

The road led between the canes, which were now almost at full height, towering above me on both sides of the road, forming a channel of green. Beside the road on one side lay an irrigation canal, on the other side a transportation canal, with several empty metal punts moored and waiting for the harvest. In just a few weeks these very fields would be a wasteland of blackened stumps, still smoking from the trash-burning that had gone before, their embers still glowing among the stumps and the felled canes. Then, once the fields had cooled enough, they would be swarming with cursing coolies loading the punts, their half-naked bodies bent low under back-breaking loads, wading in the trenches to align the punts, dark limbs and faces smeared even darker with the black soot.

This was Promised Land. This was the sugar kingdom I had known since childhood. All my life I had taken such scenes for granted, never questioning the lives of those emaciated fellow beings who broke their bodies with work, work that cushioned me in a life of luxury and privilege, a life I had never examined, never even wasted a thought upon, never wondered as to who paid its price.

Now I looked up at the green cane fronds waving above my head in the cool evening breeze of the Atlantic. Scenes I had witnessed a thousand times throughout my life flowed through my mind and I knew and I understood. All my life I had known of the friction between Mama on the one hand and Aunt Winnie on the other, and never tried to figure it out – out of loyalty to Mama. But the scene that had played out today in Mama's study – the hatefulness of her words, her face distorted into an ugly mask, her fingers digging into my shoulders like talons – all at once the layer of deliberate blindness, of not-wanting-to-see, had been ripped to shreds, and now I saw. I saw that that blindness had in fact been cowardice; that the price of my loyalty to Mama had been collaboration. Collaboration with – and now the word that Mama had used rose involuntarily into my soul – evil. I saw that there could be no compromise here. Here and now, I must take sides, and I knew with stunning clarity which side I would choose. A sense of peace, a sense of liberation, flooded through me: a sense of renewed strength, a strength that came from deep within.

It was time to move on. Once again I stood up, once again I brushed the dust from my clothes.

Where would I go? Obviously, I needed to go to Jock, and to my cousins; but they had left by car a while ago and would be halfway to Albion by now, too far for me to walk and arrive before nightfall – which was fast approaching.

I turned my thoughts to the various options, people I knew who would take me in at least for the night; tomorrow I would go on to Albion, somehow. But everyone I knew lived in the senior staff compound, and every one of them was a friend of Mama. I could not go there.

That left the village. I knew several of the village shopkeepers; every one of them friendly, polite people, who I thought would help. But would they really? Though they did not owe allegiance to Mama, she held the status of a queen around here: Queen of Sugar. Would the shopkeepers agree to shelter her daughter, once they knew I had run away? Would they risk her wrath and, no doubt, her vengeance? Mama held all the power around these parts, and though I was uncertain as to what exactly she could do to punish anyone who took sides against her, I knew beyond a doubt that she would. I did not want to put anyone in that position.

I marched on as these thoughts ran through my mind, as I eliminated one option after another. And just as I ran out of options, another thought, another name, dropped into my mind.

Uncle Jim.

Only this morning, on the way home, Rudi had mentioned that name, and not for the first time. The name had arisen again and again over the past week, during all those political discussions between Auntie and Jock and Rudi. I remembered in particular Auntie's suggestion to Jock: 'You must meet Uncle Jim – he lives at Promised Land village, a little way outside the village. He's not my real uncle, but he helped me so much when I was a girl, when George was courting me. He's on our side. He'll be an old man now, but he's the life and soul of the Corentyne worker movement.'

And today, passing through the village, Rudi had mentioned him again: 'I'd like to visit Uncle Jim soon,' he'd said, pointing to a narrow lane leading off between the houses. 'He must live down that road.'

'We'll do that,' Jock had agreed.

The name Uncle Jim quickened my spirits, my steps. I straightened my back and lifted my chin. As dusk fell, I reached the village, and turned into the dusty lane that led to his house. A horde of crows flew overhead as I left the last houses of the village, cawing and flapping their wings in a great excitement as they flew home to roost. They seemed to lead my way into a great empty unknown, away from the safe and the familiar. I hastened my stride, I did not want to be caught by night.

Chapter 28

I had walked for about fifteen minutes and darkness was already all around me as finally the rice fields to my left and right came to an end and a light flickering between the shadows of high trees told me that I had arrived. The two-storeyed white house loomed in the midst of a coppice. A typical BeeGee house, made of wood, on high stilts with a single wooden staircase leading up to a centrally placed front door. Set back within the trees, it was fenced off from the surrounding fields by tall white palings, arrow-topped. A wide double-winged gate, locked with a thick chain and padlock, prevented entry, but a large bell dangled on my side of it and I shook it. Immediately, angry barking broke out and two dogs flew snarling towards me and flung themselves against the gate so that it shook and the bell rang again.

Lights in the downstairs windows had already alerted me to life within the house, and now a black shape appeared at one of the open windows and a male voice hollered out: 'Who is it?'

'It's me,' I cried in reply. 'Mary Grace, Yoyo's daughter.'

The voice said something short and sharp I couldn't decipher and disappeared from the window, to be replaced by another form, smaller and apparently female. A few seconds later, the front door opened and the shadow of a man carrying a lamp descended the stairs leading up to the front door. The dogs scrambled towards him, grovelling and bouncing around him, squirming in time to the vigorous wagging of their tails, whimpering in delight. He uttered a few short commands and they immediately sat, becoming invisible against the black ground as he walked forward, lantern held at waist height so that all I could see was a pair of sturdy legs striding towards me.

Reaching the gate, he raised the lantern and we peered into each other's faces. Deep-set blue eyes, eyes that had seen everything, peered into mine. Around those eyes, weathered, leathered skin, creased with age, a face half-covered by a long bushy white beard, a moustache that camouflaged his mouth, and all of it framed by a shock of abundant white hair, wild like a lion's mane. Had I encountered this face on any other dark and lonely night I would have feared it, but knowing who it belonged to, I felt nothing but relief. In the eyes that now assessed me there was nothing to fear, only interest, and kindness, and welcome.

'I'm sorry,' I said. 'I had nowhere to go, so I came here…'

The beard moved as he spoke; it concealed a smile, which was all in the voice.

'Well, Uncle Jim's an open house,' he said, 'day or night. Refugees always welcome. Hold the lamp, please, Miss Smedley-Cox, lemme unlock the gate.'

He spoke with a curious accent: not quite British, not quite Creole, but definitely more the latter. It reminded me of Aunt Winnie's accent – but a male version, deeper and forceful, where hers was gentle, melodic. I did as he requested, and a moment later, the chain rattled as he pulled it through the spokes of the gate. He opened one wing of the gate, I passed through and he closed and locked the chain again.

'Yuh come to spend the night,' he said in a matter-of-fact tone.

'I'm sorry, bursting in on you like this, but—'

'No need to apologise!' he interrupted, taking the lamp from me. 'You can tell all when you get upstairs. Be my guest— SIT!'

This last to one of the dogs, which had risen from its sitting position and made as if to spring towards us. Immediately it sat again, its body still squirming in joy at the presence of its master. I followed him up the stairs to the front door. We entered the house.

An Indian woman, plump, middle-aged, grey-haired, was waiting for us, smiling, welcoming.

'Miss Smedley-Cox, nah? Yoyo's daughter? Come in, come in, and sit down. You hungry? Thirsty? Come to the dining table, leh me warm up some chicken soup for you.'

'Me wife, Bhoomie,' he said, gesturing towards her, but she was already retreating towards the back of the house and, no doubt, the kitchen, and, I guessed, that chicken soup.

Uncle Jim extinguished the lamp and led me to a large square dining table, pulled out a chair for me. I sank into it, exhausted, and, I realised, very hungry indeed.

I told my story between sips of chicken soup. Uncle Jim listened attentively, occasionally nodding or frowning, or smiling or shaking his head. When I'd finished, he said, 'I heard of this Jock Campbell, he's got quite a reputation. A good man, I hope to meet him soon. He on our side.'

I nodded. 'My cousin, too – Rudi. All of my cousins and Aunt Winnie, and that's the whole problem. Up to now I tried to keep out of it – all the politics, all the taking of sides. I wanted to appease Mama, to show her that I still support her. But – after today – after meeting Jock and realising and waking up – I can't any more, I just can't!'

Uncle Jim reached over and patted my shoulder.

'Good girl! You have to listen to your conscience and be brave enough to follow it.'

'But now – now I'm homeless!'

'No, you still got you Aunt Winnie. You always got a home wit her. An' you can stay here as long as you want. Plenty of space since the chirren move out.'

'You quite welcome!' agreed Aunt Bhoomie. 'More soup?' She held out her hands.

I nodded, and handed her my bowl. A delicious feeling spread through me – a sense of having come home, after an exile.

'What you say,' said Uncle Jim, 'tomorrow we go visit Albion? You introduce me to Jock Campbell and your cousins? I ain't see Rudi and Charlie since they was li'l boys.'

'Yes. Oh, yes!' I said.

'Leh me go an' make up a bed for you,' said Aunt Bhoomie. 'Feel right at home. An' more soup if you want.'

Yes, I did want more soup. Later, Aunt Bhoomie led me upstairs and showed me to my room: a north-facing corner room, just like my old room at Mama's, with Demerara windows and a double four-poster bed made of gleaming purpleheart. Aunt Bhoomie spread a crisp white sheet on to the mattress and handed me a second sheet to cover myself with and a fresh towel, and a nightie – 'It gon' be too big for you. You don't mind, right?'

I smiled and shook my head. I realised not only did I not have a nightdress, I didn't have clean clothes for the next day, or money, or even a toothbrush, because all my possessions were at Promised Land. I had truly left that life behind.

Aunt Bhoomie was waiting for me when I returned from the bathroom. She fluffed up a pillow for me, tucked me in, let down the mosquito net and tucked it into the mattress around all four sides.

'Goodnight, dear. See you tomorrow,' she whispered, blowing out the lamp, and through the ghostly moonlight that shone through the open window, veiled by the net, I watched her glide from the room. And then I fell asleep.

Chapter 29

In the middle of the night I woke up to the deep rumble of thunder, a gigantic sky-monster clearing its throat in the heavens, followed by a deafening crack, a flash of lightning and more thunder. And then the rains came.

It was as if an ocean in the sky had suddenly broken its dam and dropped upon the galvanised iron roof, creating a different kind of thunder, an unceasing dull pounding from above. A chill wind swept through the room. I sat up in bed and felt a cold mist surround me. Through the wide-open windows water sprayed and gushed. Wrapping my top sheet around me against the chill, I climbed under the net and walked over to the first window, closing first the louvred Demerara shutter and then the sash panel. There were four windows to be shut, and as I reached the fourth, Aunt Bhoomie entered, a white shroud in the dark.

'Ah – you done close the windows. Good,' she said. 'Rainy season come.' She waited till I was back in bed and tucked the net in again.

When she had left, I lay there, huddled under my sheet, listening to the pounding rain. I had always loved that sound. Rain on the rooftop was deeply comforting and as I lay there a sense of wholesome gladness spread through me, a sense of healing and inner warmth and peace; of floating in water, yet staying dry, safe and protected in a dry bubble of contentment where there was no past, no future, only a sense of a buoyant now; a now that would last for ever. As if outside my bubble was a solid mass of water, an ocean of rain, and here I was, complete and content for ever;

cast away from all that had held me bound, free and at home just here, within myself.

On and on the water drummed upon the roof, finally sending me to sleep. When I awoke it was morning; though the room was still dim from the closed shutters, thin strips of sunlight on the floor told me that day had long broken and it was time to get up. I did so, washed, put on yesterday's clothes and went downstairs. Even before I sat down at the table, the rain started up again; typical stop-and-start rain, unreliable, moody and uncaring of human plans and intentions.

While I was eating breakfast, my plate piled with perfectly scrambled eggs and toast, there came a hammering on the door. A second later it opened and a figure almost fell inside, accompanied by a swoosh of wind and rain, flapping an umbrella to clear it of water, cursing and stamping. The figure turned to close the door behind themselves and continued to shake and curse and stamp around near the door, creating a puddle of water where he stood. It was a man of indeterminate age, neither young nor old. Lean and wiry, in clothes that were wet and too big for him – a faded blue shirt and khaki trousers that hung on his hips, and old wellington boots – he gave the appearance of someone whose bones rattled within him. He was of that reddish complexion that denotes a person of mixed race and, indeed, is known as 'red' in BeeGee; his hair was long, stiff and wiry, partly matted; a ginger mane around a long, lean, bearded face. He tore off his boots, cursing all the while, and flung them aside.

'Damn rain!' he cried, 'It come a day too early. Nobody ain't gon' come to the meeting tonight. Gotta postpone it till nex' week.'

'It might clear up again by this afternoon,' said Uncle Jim mildly, getting up from the breakfast table to help the newcomer dispose of his soaked garments. He was now tearing off his wet shirt. The umbrella, it seemed, had not done its job, and no wonder, since half its ribs were broken and half its canopy sagged downwards.

Aunt Bhoomie bustled from the kitchen, a towel in her hand, and proceeded to rub down his hair and torso, as if he were a small child. 'I just brought up the laundry from under the house,' she said. 'Lemme get a dry shirt for you.' She bustled away while the man continued to curse.

'Damn blasted rain! How de hell we supposed to—'

In that moment he caught my eye. The sheer anger in his own changed instantly to astonishment.

'Who de hell is dat— excuse me, young lady. Pardon me language.'

'Mary Grace, may I introduce Samuel Jonkers,' said Uncle Jim. 'And Sam, this is Mary Grace Smedley-Cox, from Promised Land. She has sought refuge with us; she is our guest for the time being. I would ask you to watch your language in the presence of a lady.'

'Pleased to meet you, Mr Jonkers!' I said, placing knife and fork neatly together. He frowned, and peered at me. 'Smedley – Promised Land – you mean…'

'Yes. Yoyo's daughter.'

Instantaneously his expression changed. He smiled – but it was not a friendly, open, genuine smile. There was something crafty, sly even, about it. He came forward to the table, right hand held out.

'Ah! So we get to meet at last! My long-lost—'

'Shut you mouth, Sam!' roared Uncle Jim. 'She's new here. We can talk about all that later.'

I pricked up my ears. 'What do you mean, all that? What are we going to talk about?'

'Well,' said Uncle Jim, 'on a day like this, what else is there to do but talk? If you've finished eating, we can all retire to the drawing room and discuss matters. No going to Albion today, my dear, in this weather. And there are some things you need to know before we proceed.'

Aunt Bhoomie and I cleared away the breakfast table and, as Uncle Jim had suggested, I joined the two men in the drawing room. We spent the morning talking; or rather, they talked and I listened. There was so much I had to learn. But Uncle Jim insisted we begin from the beginning. The previous night, it seemed, he had already assessed me. He had seen that I was naive and cautious; he knew that only that day had I finally taken sides in a conflict that had been raging for decades, of which I had until now deliberately shrouded myself in ignorance. I knew very little of my country's history and thus nothing of the background of that conflict, beyond the snippets I had picked up from Aunt Winnie, Rudi and Jock. I had held back from fear of disloyalty to Mama; I had told Uncle Jim this much the night before. It was time now, he declared, to fully open my eyes. It was time to educate myself. Or, rather, it was time for him to educate me.

Chapter 30

When I had been at primary school in the senior staff quarters on the plantation and then secondary school, in New Amsterdam, history had been one of our subjects: but it was British history, about kings and queens of England and Scotland and wars in Europe and Romans and Saxons and Angles, and plots to overthrow parliament and beheadings and invasions. I knew next to nothing about my own country, because it was not taught to us. Now, Uncle Jim believed I needed to know that history.

'It was the same with Winnie and Yoyo,' he said. 'Young girls growing up in a bubble of ignorant privilege, just like you. Can't do nothing about the privilege, but you can stop the ignorance. Grow a spine. Your Aunt Winnie grew one, time for you to do the same.'

'But Mama? You don't think she has a spine?'

Spineless people were surely weak, and Mama was anything but.

Uncle Jim gave a wry chuckle. 'Yoyo ain't got a spine, she got a broomstick up she backside. Pardon me for sayin' so.'

Sam Jonkers slapped his thigh and burst out laughing. I did not like that; I did not like him. I did not like Uncle Jim criticising and mocking Mama. It was one thing for me to find fault with her, but family loyalty was hard-wired into my mind and I could not laugh at the stupid joke.

'Yes, and she would sweep you all away with one broom-stroke if she got the chance!' I cried. 'Mama's tough, she doesn't suffer fools gladly.'

They both stopped laughing and glared at me, and then at each other. They exchanged some secret sign, apparently, for Uncle Jim's next words were conciliatory.

'Yoyo know what she wants and know how to get it,' he said, serious again. 'You right about that. Trouble is, what she want come with a high price. Thousands of workers suffering bad. You have old women working in the fields till they fall over with fatigue – that's after giving birth to ten children, none of whom go to school but gotta work in the fields since small days. You ever see them women, up to they waist in the canal – the whole day in the water. I don't know why they don't turn into fish. When they get sick, left to die because they ain't got a doctor.'

I dropped my gaze. Yes, I knew. Yes, I'd seen those women, and those men, backs bent in the hot sun under loads that must be twice their own weight. They were part of the landscape. I had taken them all for granted, though I'd heard Aunt Winnie and Cousin Rudi and now, most lately, Jock Campbell complain about such conditions. But only yesterday, during my flight from home, had I unplugged my ears and my brain to truly, deeply, see these problems, digest them.

'What shall I do?' I asked, my voice meek this time, and genuinely open to suggestions. 'What can I do? I am her daughter, she raised me. She always wanted me to take over the plantation – but I can't – I can't! I never could! I'm just a girl!'

'What do you mean, just a girl? Do you know what your Aunt Winnie did, when she was about your age?'

I nodded. I had heard snippets of Aunt Winnie's story and I knew she had been brave and mature beyond her years, though Mama's version of the story was the opposite: she claimed Auntie was a coward and a traitor. But in my heart, I knew right from wrong. I knew that history's trajectory was towards right, and I knew which of the two, my mother and my aunt, represented that right, as did my cousins. As did my beloved, Jock Campbell. And now, I had made my decision: I, too, would place my life on the side of rightfulness. I now looked up at Uncle Jim. 'Tell me our history,' I said.

Both of the men relaxed visibly. 'Do you know my full name?'
Uncle Jim asked. I nodded. 'Mama calls you Mad Jim Booker.'

He nodded. 'James Booker, actually. The name Booker mean
anything to you?'

That made me indignant. 'Of course!' I cried. 'I'm not that
ignorant. Everyone knows the Bookers. Mama used to joke that
BeeGee stood not for British Guiana but for Booker Guiana. She
always cursed Booker Brothers. "They're like a huge spider in the
background, just waiting to pounce," she used to say. "They own
the colony."'

'That's one thing we can all agree on,' said Uncle Jim, nodding.

'So,' I said now, slowly. 'You're a Booker brother too? One of
those Bookers?'

There were two versions of Jim's story. Mama loathed him, and
continued to call him Mad Jim Booker. Aunt Winnie had reassured
me that he was anything but mad; that he was a friend, a good man.
I'd heard the rumours: that he was a white man who had lived in the
jungle backlands for many years with a darkie woman, with whom
he'd produced a horde of children. At some point, he'd moved to the
outskirts of Promised Land village. His first wife had died – in a fire,
it was rumoured – and he had remarried, so probably Aunt Bhoomie
was his second wife, or maybe even his third. It was well known that
Mad Jim mixed only with darkies and coolies; and that he was an
enemy of his own people, an enemy to the white plantocracy that
ruled the colony. That he was one of the organisers of the labour
rebellion and protest movement that rocked the plantations from
time to time. And I knew from Aunt Winnie that he had been a
great friend and mentor of her husband, Uncle George. I hadn't
thought much about the Booker part of his name.

He chuckled. 'Not exactly,' he replied. 'Them original brothers
died off in the nineteenth century. I'm one of the descendants,
though. One of the last, and a black sheep. Strayed from the pack,
and joined the other side, joined the enemy.'

'Only good white man in the colony,' put in Sam Jonkers. 'Only good white man on earth, if you ask me.'

But Uncle Jim raised a hand. 'No,' he said. 'There's another: Jock Campbell. Ask her.'

And he pointed to me.

'Your turn,' he said. 'Tell us about Jock Campbell. Rumours are rife in these parts.'

So I did.

I spoke primarily to Uncle Jim, with whom I'd felt a deep rapport from the very start. But Sam Jonkers exercised an extraordinary draw on me, and try as I might to fight it, my eyes kept returning to him. It was the way he was staring at me, with a penetrating, relentless gaze, sharp and critical. In the end, I could bear it no longer, and so confronted him directly.

'Why do you stare like that?' I asked. 'It's rude and distracting.'

He slapped his thigh and roared with laughter.

'Jus' curiosity,' he said. 'Nosy. Don't mind me – just talk. I gon' keep me eyes away from you, stare at the ceiling from now on. OK? Oh, look! A nice li'l lizard.'

And he obligingly rolled his eyes upwards and gazed upwards, deliberately staring at a lizard that was slowly making its way across one of the beams above our heads, stalking some small creature. As he watched, he whistled, mocking me.

I turned to Uncle Jim, helpless with annoyance. 'Why's he like that?' I asked. 'What's he doing here anyway?'

Uncle Jim chuckled and turned to him. 'Tell her, Sam. Don't tease, she might as well know.'

'You t'ink so? She not gon' be offended? Such a fine young lady, an' the likes of me?'

'Go on, tell her. If you don't, I will.'

'Sure t'ing. If is not too much of a shock—'

'Tell her!' Uncle Jim boomed out the command, but it was a pretend rage. Indeed, it was hard to be seriously angry towards

Sam Jonkers; yes, I found him irritating, but something about him made me want to laugh as well. Now he was pointing at the lizard and staring with slit eyes as if that was his only focus.

'Tell me!' I repeated. 'What's the big secret?'

'You ears are all agog, right? You ladies love secrets, right? An' scandals an' such, gossip. Well, I can give you something to gossip about. I, my dear Miss Smedley, am your uncle! Right, you can call me Uncle Sam from now on. That's me, at your service.'

'What? How? I-I don't understand… Uncle Jim? Please!'

Uncle Jim was enjoying my befuddlement. 'OK, thank you, Sam. You want to tell her the rest, or you want me to tell her?'

'Tell she, nah!'

'All right, I will. Mary Grace – is that how you like to be called? Or just Mary? Or just Grace?'

'Anything,' I said, slapping his question away in impatience. 'Just tell me.'

'Very well, I'll call you Grace. You tell her, Jim! You was there, I wasn't!'

Uncle Jim rolled his eyes and began. 'Well, it all began with your grandad, Archie Cox. Now, Archie Cox had a beautiful wife, Ruth. A wonderful, charming Austrian lady, your grandmother.'

Sam Jonkers interrupted: 'Charmed the socks right off you too, eh, Jim?'

'Quiet! Ruth didn't settle down in British Guiana very well. She was lonely and unhappy, and after a few years and a few children the marriage – well, it ran into a rocky spot.'

'And up rode Uncle Jim on a white steed! Right?'

'Shut you mouth, Sam! Anyway, I was tellin', Archie, like most planters, wasn't the most faithful of husbands. All of them used to havin' ladies from the plantation for they pleasure. Worker ladies. And it couldn't be avoided, that children was born to these ladies. Half-blood bastards!'

That, I knew. I, after all, was such a one… this was interesting.

'So,' I said, turning to Sam Jonkers. 'So, you are the result of such an affair? That's why you say you're my uncle.'

'Well, yes and no. Sam's mama wasn't a labourer, she was a housemaid. Name Iris. When Iris was fifteen, Archie Cox decide to make she his mistress. And so that's what happen. After a few months, Sam was on the way, and Archie kicked her out. Gave her some money and sent her on her way.'

'Oh, poor lady! What happened to her?'

'She lived with an auntie in the village for a few years – I knew her well. When the li'l boy was a bit older, she moved to Georgetown. I introduced she to a lady called Dolly, a seamstress in Kitty Village. You Aunt Winnie know Dolly good.'

'Yes! Auntie Dolly! Of course!'

'Yes – Auntie Dolly. By that time Dolly was getting on in years. She eyesight beginnin' to fail she. So she take in Iris and the child, made a room for them in the Bottom House, and teach Iris to be a seamstress. They lived in Kitty for a while. The li'l boy, Sam here, was very good at school and win a scholarship to Queen's College. After school, he move back to the Corentyne, get a junior clerk job on Port Mourant estate. Later, Iris move back to Promised Land village and start a dressmaking shop for the area. It doin' good so Sam move back with her.'

'And left Port Mourant for a better job, stirrin' up trouble along the coast!' Sam chuckled. He seemed to think it was all a huge joke.

'Yes,' said Jim, 'Sam here the worst troublemaker at the moment. We had a lot of them over the years, some didn't last. You must a hear of Bhim?'

'Yes, of course. The fellow that Grandad Archie killed.'

'Exactly. Sam here just like that. Don't worry 'bout all the joking around. Deep inside, he an angry man and he mean business, don't make no fun. That's why I want him to hear about this Jock Campbell.'

Sam slapped the air. 'I done hear plenty about Jock Campbell. Them labourers from Albion say he's a good master. But – end of day, is a white man, is a Massa. And, as we all say, Massa day done. Can't trust no white man.'

'Jock's different,' I said. 'He means it, he wants to reform the whole plantation.'

Sam sucked his teeth. 'And if so – what of it? Albion is one plantation. One li'l plantation. So what if they got good conditions there? The whole sugar industry is a corrupt, evil, exploitative institution. Until it's in worker hands, that's the way it's going to stay.'

I listened, fascinated, as Sam launched into an eloquent rant about the evils of the plantation system and the scourge of the racist system that kept it going: the British Empire, whose sole aim was to rape its colonies and grow fat from the labour of others. The more he spoke, the more grammatical his language became, his Queen's College education showing through, which was a strange thing since it was usually the other way around: people started off speaking 'good' English, but changed into Creole when passion took over.

One thing was certain: Sam Jonkers might enjoy playing the clown when it so pleased him, but he was smart, and his intentions were deadly serious. He meant business, and business meant revolt, and, eventually, revolution.

After about twenty minutes of this, he relaxed and turned to me. There was genuine warmth in his voice as he said, in perfectly grammatical English, 'Your Aunt Winnie is one of the good ones. I've heard so much about her, I'd like to meet her one day.'

Uncle Jim said: 'Yes, Grace. Your Aunt Winnie and Iris was best friends. You should get Winnie to come up and meet her and Sam.'

'One big happy family,' said Sam, with a smile in his voice. 'Happy to meet you, my dear little niece!'

'Though technically I'm not really your niece, am I?' I replied.

'Well, yes – your mama and your Aunt Winnie are my half-sisters. That makes you my niece.'

'Ah – but my mama isn't really my mama. So we're not actually blood relatives. Everyone thinks I'm adopted, but I'm going to tell you a secret: I'm a proper Smedley. You see, my father was well known for his debauchery. It's not easy for me to admit that but I might as well face facts and anyway, I never knew him – he died when I was a baby. But Mama knew. He has several other bastards running around on the plantation, but in my case, my birth mother died in childbirth so Mama took me in. It was an act of charity.'

Right away the fidgeting increased. Uncle Jim laid his pipe down again on the table, next to his tobacco pouch, and leaned forward, frowning. He and Sam Jonkers stared at each other, both slowly shaking their heads as if trying to come to some silent agreement without my knowing. I looked from one to the other. Their reaction was not what I'd expected; they looked confused rather than shocked by the news. Or perhaps it just wasn't so very shocking after all. It's well known that most planters took worker women whenever they wanted and sired mixed-race bastards on them. It was very common and no one raised an eyebrow over it. In my case it was just unusual that Mama had agreed to adopt one of those children – me – and raise her as her own child, especially since she was not exactly known for her maternal qualities. But, not having any children of her own, I suppose it was understandable. Perhaps it was Papa who insisted: when my biological mother died it must have been seen as an obvious solution to their predicament of childlessness. At least, this was the conclusion I had come to.

But both Uncle Jim and Sam Jonkers seemed lost in their perplexity. Perhaps it was awkward for them to have a young girl talking to them of such intimate matters, but I had long known the facts of life and accepted the implications behind my conception, and it did not embarrass me. I felt the need to reassure them on this count.

'It's all right,' I said, 'I've known for a long time, and I'm not embarrassed. I know it's a strange thing for a young girl to admit, but—'

'No,' said Uncle Jim, rudely interrupting me. 'No. Just no, it's not true.'

Sam Jonkers slapped his thigh, threw back his head and laughed. 'Tell she, man!' he cried. 'Tell she! Mout' open, story jump out.'

He seemed to find the situation hilarious, and continued to chuckle into his beard. But Uncle Jim was not joking. Picking up his pipe again, he recommenced the act of stuffing it with tobacco, even as he spoke.

'Grace, sorry, I can't let you go on believing that nonsense. I don't know why Yoyo can't talk straight with you – goodness knows, the woman di'n have no shame back then. I don' know why she feel shame 'bout it now. But to fill you up with lies – no, I can't let that happen.'

'Tell she, tell she!' goaded Sam Jonkers gleefully.

I looked from one to the other, perfectly bewildered.

'What do you mean?'

'I mean to say, you father ain't you father. But you mother is you mother.'

Sam Jonkers broke into song: 'You daddy ain't you daddy, but you daddy don' know!'

'Quiet, Sam! He *did* know. It was perfectly obvious, when the baby came out dark-skinned. He knew, and he accepted it, agreed to raise her as his own, accept paternity, even on the birth certificate. One of the few noble things Clarence Smedley ever did.'

A chill ran down my spine, and it wasn't caused by the cool breeze and spray seeping in through the closed louvres. Outside, the rain still lashed at the wooden planks of the house; Aunt Bhoomie had gone around removing all the furniture from near the windows to protect it from the wet, but a watery mist still touched us, though we sat in the middle of the room. I crossed my arms and rubbed the gooseflesh for warmth, but also for comfort. At Uncle Jim's words, I felt the first inner tremble as the certainties I'd built about myself prepared to come crashing down.

'What-what do you mean?' I whispered.

'Grace, I know it'll come as a shock, but your mother – Yoyo – had an affair with a black man. You were the result. Your putative father, Clarence, decided to ignore the matter and acknowledge you as his. I thought you knew – I thought she'd told you.'

'No – no! Not at all. I can't believe… how could she…? I mean, didn't everyone know? How could she keep a secret like that when I was… I mean, I'm dark! If she was pregnant, people must have known! When I was born! I mean – how?'

'Oh, she was clever, all right!' said Uncle Jim. 'Yes, she was pregnant. And when you was born coloured, she was shocked sheself and gave you away at first. Sent you to Georgetown. Spread the word that the baby stillborn. Then, a couple years later, she bring you back and pretend to adopt you. There was people who knew, of course. But your mother don't make no fun. Nobody don't want cross she. Somehow, she managed to keep the secret, and not let it blow into scandal. She ruthless like hell. So everybody frighten and go along with she story. But you – I thought she'd tell you at least!'

'She didn't,' I said almost under my breath. 'She never did. She fed me lies. I believed the lies. And – oh! So she's really my mother?'

'Correct!' said Sam Jonkers. 'And I'm really your uncle. Call me Uncle Sam.'

'But then – you said…' My eyes filled with tears as I turned back to Uncle Jim. 'You said she had an affair with-with a black man…'

'…and you want to know with whom, right?'

'Yes.' My lips moved with my one word but I'm not sure he heard it. I wanted to know, and at the same time I didn't. I was colder than ever, shivering, in fact; cold truth knocking at my door even as the wind and the rain rattled the house. I craved knowledge; and at the same time I wanted to barricade myself against knowing, because even at this point, the moment before the final blast, I knew, I suspected, that with that knowledge my life would never be the same again.

'No!' I said then, out loud, and my hands flew to my ears, quickly, before they could hear whatever it was Uncle Jim was about to say. As if I knew already. As if, deep inside, the knowledge had already been planted and had been growing underground, a seedling first, but edging towards the light of day from within until, from without, would come the confirmation, the word, the name. And in the split second before my hands reached my ears, the word, the name was spoken.

'Your father is you Uncle George,' said Jim. He stood up and walked away, towards the kitchen, where Auntie Bhoomie was rustling up some lunch.

Opposite me Sam Jonkers continued to chuckle into his beard. This irritated me: was he mocking me? I glared at him; he met my gaze with laughter in his eyes. Then he too stood up, gave me a wave and sauntered off towards the front door. Outside, the rain had grown even heavier and I didn't see how anyone could willingly walk out into the downpour. But Sam picked up the umbrella he had entered with, unfurled it with a snap, opened the front door and vanished into the deluge.

Chapter 31

I sat there, too stunned to move, dizzy with shock. But not for long…
My thoughts, at first totally shattered and scattered like shrapnel after
a bomb, lost no time in rearranging themselves into a recognisable
but preposterous order. I ran after Uncle Jim.

In the kitchen, Aunt Bhoomie was down on hands and knees
scrubbing the floor, while Uncle Jim had his back to me, bent
forward, filling the iron stove with kindling and wood. When I
called out to him he swiftly stood up straight and swung around.
His face was tomato red – he looked guilty.

'Look, Grace, I'm sorry. I wasn't supposed to tell you that. It's not
my secret to reveal. I should have sent you to Winnie if Yoyo won't
talk. I wish you'd forget I told you, but I don't suppose you can.'

'So it's true? It's really true? Uncle George, he's the one? My
father?'

He nodded. 'It's true.'

'But, but… does Aunt Winnie know? The boys?'

'Of course they all know. Why you think Yoyo don't like you to
visit Winnie? Why you think the two of them hardly does speak to
each other? Why Winnie never visit Promised Land, nor the boys?'

'I thought – I always thought – that Aunt Winnie had betrayed
her father and that's why…'

He shook his head vigorously. 'No, Grace, not at all. Look, is
a long story and not a nice one. You really gotta ask Winnie, not
me. Is complicated. And it really don't matter any more – is all
history now. But the hard facts is just that simple truth: George
was you father, and the boys is you half-brothers.'

It was those last words that did it – that evaporated all the shock, all the inner devastation caused by the revelation, replacing it all with a deliciously sweet sense of something extraordinary, something big, that inner truth that had finally spread open as what it was, had always been: the boys were indeed my brothers. The sense of belonging I'd always had at the Quint house, it wasn't just my imagination, it wasn't just wishful thinking, a dream I wished was real. It was real: they *were* my brothers, that house *was* my home. I'd known it; I always had. It was more home to me than Promised Land had ever been. And they all knew it, but I hadn't. When they jokingly, teasingly, lovingly called me little sister, they had meant it: I was their little sister, not just in thought but blood. It was real – and oh, how I loved that reality! A great happiness spread through me. I ran to Uncle Jim and threw my arms around him.

'Oof!' he said as I flung myself against his portly belly, winding him, but a smile was in that gasp. He hugged me back.

'So you're not too upset?' he asked after a while.

'No, not at all! I'm delighted they're my brothers! I always wanted them to be my brothers!'

'And also that Yoyo's your birth mother? Doesn't that delight you?'

I shook my head against his chest.

'No, not at all. I don't really care, I don't even want to know the details – I bet they weren't nice at all. So I don't want to know. I just know that I exist and they're my brothers, just the way I wanted them to be. They're my family – much more than she was ever my mother. And I found out at just the right time, too.'

'Yes. Well, I wasn't supposed to be the one to tell you but it happen so, and it happen at the right time. Not a minute too early.'

It was then that I realised two things. One was that my running away from Promised Land the day before was not simply a fit of pique, a temper tantrum, a quarrel between Mama and me that would eventually blow over. No, a decision had been made on my part and it was to be lasting, a parting of the ways. The very day I discovered that she was my birth mother was also the day from when I could never return to being her daughter.

The second thing I realised, or remembered, was that two of my brothers were close by: at Albion, just a few miles away. With Jock Campbell.

Jock. For the last twenty-four hours I had hardly thought of him once, so turbulent had been that time. So much had taken place since he'd left me there to deal with Mama that I could hardly consolidate it all, much less figure out his place in my life, and my future. But I did love him.

And yes, he fitted in perfectly. It was as if my body had been gripped by a giant hand and given a vigorous shake and all the elements, all the little bits and pieces, that constituted my personality had rearranged themselves, realigned to form a new person, a new me, a me that was radically different from the splintered being I had been in the lead-up to the climax. No more the conflict between Mama on the one side and the Quints on the other. No more the refusal to face the ugly reality on which Promised Land and all its glory was built. No more the split personality, the denial, the reluctance to take sides. This new me had been silently forming in the background of my being ever since that first dance with Jock. Now, with today's revelation, this new Grace had burst into life like a butterfly from a cocoon. I had been hiding all my life: this was the day of my rebirth!

Everything fitted together. All the people I was aligned with: Aunt Winnie, her sons, Uncle Jim, and most of all, Jock Campbell. Even Sam Jonkers, my new uncle. All on the one side. On the other side: Mama. Poor Mama. For a moment I felt sorry for her. But it was a sentimental kind of sorrow, easily swept aside. She had chosen her life, as I had chosen mine. For me, the only way was forward.

Right now, Albion called. I said it out loud:

'Uncle Jim, when can we go to Albion?'

'As soon as the rain stop,' he replied.

Chapter 32

But it did not, would not stop raining.

Water lashed down from heaven. It was as if an ocean in the sky had broken through and fell upon us in unbroken sheets, battering the roof so that I feared one day it would cave in. The canals flooded their banks and water covered the earth, so that the house became an island. Uncle Jim's cow and his horse stood almost knee-deep in water in their covered stall, their heads bent low in misery. The dogs were brought into the house. Sam Jonkers, who occupied a room between the stilts in the Bottom House, found himself flooded out and moved upstairs into the main house. Work on the cane fields came to a standstill. Lead-grey, growling clouds covered the sky and the sun.

I became a refugee at Uncle Jim's home, but nobody minded. It was a huge house, with six bedrooms upstairs and one small one downstairs, behind the drawing room; the latter was where Sam Jonkers now lived. Bhoomie took care of us all, but it wasn't long before her supply of fresh foods ran out and from that time onwards we lived on plain rice and rotis and sometimes cake. I had not brought clothes with me, but Bhoomie opened a wardrobe in one of the empty rooms and there I found an endless supply of dresses, many of which fitted me; they had once belonged to the daughters of the house, long since married off and moved on. Bhoomie was able to make simple alterations on the sewing machine.

The first day or so I was restless, eager to move on, to meet Jock at his own home, and my brothers – how wonderful, now, to use that word instead of cousins – but then I accepted the inevitability of a long-drawn-out rainy season and once I had made up my mind to make the best of the situation, everything fell into place.

In the past, when it rained like this at Promised Land, I would take refuge at the piano. The thundering of the rain provided a challenging backdrop to everything I played, and at such times I favoured music with which I could compete with the weather: bombastic, passionate, wild music. But Uncle Jim did not possess a piano, and I did not have my flute with me – that, too, was still at Promised Land. But in any case, music, right now, was the last thing on my mind.

I had not wanted to know. While coming of age I had closed my mind to all matters relating to the production of sugar. I knew nothing about the production of sugar, or the business of sugar, or the history of sugar. I, who loved stories of all kinds, who devoured the novels in the estate library so that, in time, I had read them all and hungered for more, had avoided at all costs the story of sugar – as absorbing and adventurous and thrilling a story as ever there was. Now, I heard about slavery and the abominable trade by which shiploads of Africans had been snatched from their home continent and sent on the perilous journey across the ocean to work on the white man's fields. Of black men dying in their hundreds on slave ships. Of African families torn apart when children were snatched from their mothers' arms and sold on. Of whipping and raping and the invisible torment suffered by those whose inalienable right to their own lives, their own destinies, had been stolen from them.

Uncle Jim did most of the talking. He had a natural gift for storytelling, a talent for bringing history to life so that I could see the horrific past in my mind's eye, hear the screams as infants were torn from their mothers' arms or men were lashed for stealing a cup of rice. I could smell the stench of clogged sewers that ran as stagnant gutters of black filth past the hovels they called homes. Uncle Jim spoke so eloquently of the forgotten agonies of that age at times I found myself sobbing, covering my ears and begging him to stop. And stop he did, but only to move on to the next horror; for after the abolition of the slave trade, and later of slavery itself, came the next abomination, that of indenture. Now it was no longer Africans shipped from their continent to ours, but Indians; and though they came with a semblance of freedom, on contracts that guaranteed them a return home after a number of years, their treatment and status was only minimally better than that of slaves. And it was these Indians who worked my mother's plantation. It was for their further mistreatment and exploitation that she fought. And now that I had found my bearings, I would be fighting against her along with Uncle Jim and the rest.

Uncle Jim would not allow me to bask in my discomfort. He forced me to dry my tears, claiming they were those of a crocodile: more to assuage my own guilt than to strengthen my resolve. For it was resolve I had lacked up to this point, and only with resolve could I move forward. 'If you are with us,' he said, 'let it be a hundred per cent. We don't want no half-baked buns, we need people ready to move.'

Sam Jonkers took over the story, the narrative of moving forward. He too was a good speaker, when he wanted to be, when he dropped the act of half-crazy ne'er-do-well. He put forward his plan for future action.

'We in the middle of a political process,' he said now. 'We forming a political party. It's to be a party across the divide of race and culture and religion. A party for all workers, whether African or Indian. A party for the oppressed and downtrodden. We starting to come together, both in town and out here on the plantations. We call it the United People's Labour Party – the UPLP. Jim here is funding it, practically alone.'

Uncle Jim nodded. 'Yep,' he said. 'I'm a Booker Brothers shareholder. It's only right that the money is put to good use – to bring down Bookers itself.'

'We still taking baby steps,' said Sam, 'finding suitable allies. Figuring out how to move forward. What we lack is a leader, someone to inspire and motivate and unite us all.'

'What about you?' I asked. Sam, it seemed to me, was eloquent enough. But he shook his head. 'I ain't got what it takes,' he said. 'I got the fire, but I ain't got the gift of passing it on. That's what we need.'

'Jock Campbell!' I said in excitement. They glared at me in horror.

'Jock Campbell, a planter?' said Uncle Jim. 'Grace, you don't understand one thing yet. It got to be someone from the workers. How could you have a planter leading a party on behalf of his workers?'

I blushed in embarrassment; it had been a stupid thing to say. I'd let my love for Jock blind me to the obvious: committed and passionate as he was about the labourer cause, he remained a planter and by definition, the enemy. Jock could care all he wanted but his conflict of interest was plain. He could never be more than a supporter, on the outside looking in. And so, despite all the new insights that now swarmed through me, despite the sudden influx of idealism, the new sense of realignment of direction – my elated sense of revolution, even – so was I. On the outside, looking in. I was, after all, Yoyo Smedley-Cox's daughter; one of the worst reputed planters in the colony. I couldn't help my parentage, but knowing that my mother was one of the main flagbearers for the old ways, that she represented the enemy – well, it was a depressing thought. But – and at this realisation I straightened my back, and raised my chin, for it filled me with renewed pride – I was also George's daughter. Famous George Quint, who had paid the ultimate price for the labourer cause. The blood of a stalwart ran in my veins. I came from hero stock; but so did someone else.

'My cousin— my brother Rudi's got lots of fire,' I offered, hesitantly now. Rudi, after all, followed in the footsteps of the famous George, his father. I could well see him as a political leader of the future. Highly intelligent, a brilliant orator, fired with the need to right the wrongs of society, I could think of none better.

But Uncle Jim shook his head. 'Rudi too young,' he said. 'He just a year older than you. We can't have no eighteen-year-old as party leader.'

This seemed patently unfair to me. 'Why not?' I said. 'If he's capable?'

'Because he not only too young, is the same problem as Jock Campbell: Rudi come from privilege, from a sugar-planter family. A white mother, a grandfather who was a sugar king. Rudi might be the best leader in the world – and maybe one day when he more mature he will be – but we need someone from the bottom, from the workers.'

I tried to argue; I was positive that once Rudi was given the reins of a tangible project, he would excel – George Quint, after all, was his father. But the more I spoke, the more my inexperience, my ignorance, became obvious and in the end I learned to hold my tongue and just listen.

And so we talked. The three of us, Uncle Jim, Sam Jonkers and I, huddled together in the gallery or the drawing room, and with endless patience for my deliberately cultivated ignorance the two men filled in the gaps in my education. Sometimes we drank, too, especially in the evenings when the rain's tattoo upon the roof provided the bass percussion for the croaking of amphibians and the soprano song of night creatures not defeated by a little water. Uncle Jim liked his rum, and so did Sam Jonkers, and sometimes they tipped a bit of rum into my own glasses, and sometimes, her domestic tasks for the day done, Auntie Bhoomie joined us and we would talk into the night, and laugh, and tell stories.

Aunt Bhoomie revealed herself to be a talented storyteller; she brought with her a gift of observation, especially of men. She knew the foibles and weaknesses of men, the men who passed through this house at her husband's calling, men who fancied themselves fighters and warriors of truth but whom, as Auntie Bhoomie could attest, were made of cotton. 'Matchstick men,' she called them. 'All talk an' no backbone.'

Aunt Bhoomie had taken me under her wing; her daughters having flown the nest, I was, for her, a hatchling who had escaped the mother coop to find refuge with her, to be pampered and disciplined and moulded in the right way. She believed staunchly in the superior but covert strength of women, a strength that expressed itself not in cocksure violence but in steady and crafty manipulation from behind. Women, she said, were good at this; she was Uncle Jim's boss, though she'd never let him know it. Hearing of my budding romance with Jock Campbell, she determined that I should be the subtle power behind the throne; winning him first, then guiding him shrewdly along the surreptitious path that would lead, eventually, to the overthrow of the planter class. Men were beholden to women, she declared, when her man and his friend were out of earshot; ours was the ultimate power. We were the backbone of society; invisible, yet holding up the entire edifice.

'We is like water,' she told me, 'soft and pliable; but remember, water does wear away stone.'

And so I listened and I learned; from Uncle Jim and Sam Jonkers and Auntie Bhoomie, exiled as we were in our dry bubble of refuge from the tempest. Two, three, four days passed. And on the fifth day, the sun came out. On the sixth day, the floodwaters were several inches lower. On the seventh day, land revealed itself; not dry land, by any means, but land, green-covered or moist red or brown or black earth; inviting us back into the world.

It was time to visit Jock.

Chapter 33

Uncle Jim, it turned out, possessed a jalopy, hidden away in a garage in the village, raised up on blocks as a precaution against just such flooding as we had recently survived: his pride and joy from the early days when he was still a promising heir to the Booker fortunes. It was a Morris Oxford Bullnose, he declared, beaming with pride as he stroked the red bonnet with the tenderness of a lover for his sweetheart.

The car had obviously seen better days. The bodywork had several dents, and more than a few scratches, and the upholstery was ripped, revealing woolly innards; but like an old man still in love with his boyhood sweetheart now bent and wrinkled, his eyes betrayed a deep and lasting love. As if expecting me to equal his ardour, he related to me some of her qualities – yes, he spoke of it as 'her' – such as fiscal horsepower and engine size. I nodded enthusiastically as if I knew what he was talking about, or even cared. As long as a car had five wheels (four for rolling on and one for steering), upholstered seats and a brake I was perfectly indifferent to its other seemingly magical properties – unlike Mama, who loved cars, especially new ones, and was always eager to purchase the latest model to be imported to the colony.

This car was a four-seater. The garage owner, a burly black fellow introduced to me as 'Car' (I never quite ascertained if that was his real name, or a nickname derived from his profession), carefully lowered the vehicle down to street level via a rickety ramp made up of planks that seemed, to my unschooled eye, half rotted away by wood ants. That done without incident, the men fiddled about for a while, lifting the bonnet and tinkering with spanners and

screwdrivers and a small canister of oil. Finally, Car declared it
ready to drive, and we all piled in: me on the front passenger seat
next to Uncle Jim and Sam Jonkers in the back. Uncle Jim pressed
the ignition button, and we were off.

The coastal road down to Albion was not a smooth one, and
even less so now, after the rains. We rocked and bounced along
and splashed through water-filled potholes. Uncle Jim seemed,
though, to revel in the wild ride; he enjoyed every excuse to drive,
he said, for such opportunities came rarely. Due to the difficulty
of obtaining petrol one needed a truly valid reason to use the car,
such as, like today, passengers. Now, he laughed and joked all the
way down, and coaxed the car to its full speed. But even at thirty
miles per hour, which to my mind was a race against death, it
took us an hour and a half to reach the turn-off to Albion estate.
When I saw the sign, I took a deep and satisfied breath; the very
name Albion by now had become synonymous with the beloved
name Jock Campbell, and though I had not consciously thought
of him much during the last few days of inner turbulence, he was
always there, at the back of my mind, etched into my heart, into
my very consciousness. If this wasn't true love, then what? Now,
my soul soared – I was going to see him again.

Normally it was only good manners between planters to send
a message via a courier to indicate a visit to a neighbour; this gave
the visited planter the chance to prepare, to plan meals and make
other domestic arrangements for the visitor. Due to the sodden
days we had just lived through, though, this had not been possible;
today we would be surprise visitors. This meant that Jock would
most probably be out on the fields, or in the factory, or in his
plantation office. We'd have to find him.

But that proved easy enough, as the first person we ran into once
past the wide-open gate into the estate was my cousin (my brother!

When would I stop thinking *cousin!*) Charlie, whom we found with a group of Indian men near the gate, digging a flowerbed. Uncle Jim stopped the car and I waved Charlie over. He was such a beautiful young man – in every way. Charlie brought beauty into the world. Aunt Winnie's wondrous rose garden beside her entrance staircase was all his doing, and by the looks of it he was up to his usual tricks right here. The Indians, their bare-chested brown bodies glistening in the morning sun, were all armed with spades and forks and were digging up the earth beside the roadway.

'It's too early,' said Charlie now as he leaned forward through the open car window to kiss me on my cheek, 'the earth's too wet. I wanted to get this done so I can leave tomorrow but I suppose I'll have to stay a few days longer. Jock wants a flower garden right here – roses, roses, roses. To welcome visitors. Nice to see you, Grace. You must be Uncle Jim – good morning.' He stretched out his arm past me to shake hands with Uncle Jim, then looked past me to the back of the car, and raised his eyebrows.

'This is Sam Jonkers, Charlie,' I said. 'Uncle Sam.'

'Pleased to meet you,' said Charlie, and, turning back to me, 'I suppose you want to see Jock? He's over in the estate office, with Rudi. I'll take you there. I'm going to dismiss these chaps – it's no good working while the ground's still so wet. Wait a minute.'

Charlie bounded back over to the gardeners and spoke a few words with them. He watched as they marched off, spades and forks across their shoulders, then returned to the car. He opened the rear door and slid on to the back seat, Sam Jonkers edging away from the window to make room for him.

Albion's offices were housed in a long one-storey building of white-painted wood, and like every other building on every other estate set on high stilts as protection from the ever-recurring floods, with an outside staircase. Several bicycles were parked in the shade beneath the house. A few trees in the forecourt provided further shade, and Uncle Jim parked the car beneath a tall tamarind. We all left the car, walked across to the front stairs and up to the open door at the top.

There we found ourselves in a large open room furnished with several desks at which men were hard at work, sitting behind piles of paper or jabbing away at typewriters. At least, I assumed they were all men, until I saw in the far corner two women. Another thing that struck me was that at least half the men, and both of the women, were coloured. It was a well-known fact that coloured people on the estate were not allowed office work; could not even rise up to be foremen. These advanced jobs were reserved for white men. Certainly, that was the case on Promised Land, and I had assumed on every other estate – but not, apparently, on Albion. A man at one of the front desks looked up as we entered and asked if he could help.

'Hello, Mr Foster, we're looking for Mr Campbell,' said Charlie, and the man turned and pointed to a door at the far end of the room. 'He's in his private office,' said Mr Foster before returning to his files. We crossed the room; Charlie opened the door and we went through into a corridor that stretched through the centre of the building to an open door at the far end. He led the way into the corridor; we followed. The corridor was lined with closed doors on both sides, but one door stood open and that was the one Charlie entered with a perfunctory rap. Again, we followed, and this time found ourselves in a large, light, airy room, the wooden walls painted a pleasant light green. In the middle of the room was a large desk, at which, his back to us, sat Rudi. Next to him, pointing to something written on a large ledger, stood Jock.

Hearing the knock and our footsteps, he swung around as we entered, and his face stretched into the most welcoming smile I'd ever seen. We stepped forward to greet each other and fell into an embrace as if it were the most ordinary thing in the world; his arms around me belonged exactly there, his slightly scratchy cheek against mine was the dearest touch I'd ever known, like dancing. He pulled away again, and looked down at me, holding my gaze as if we were alone in the room, and then he looked up with twinkling eyes, pulled away and greeted his visitors, whom Charlie introduced.

Meanwhile, Rudi stood up from the desk and another round of introductions followed; then Jock, hooking my arm into his, announced, 'Enough work for one day, let's go over to the house. I assume you'll all be stopping for lunch? Let's see what Bhamini can put together. A fowl will see paradise today, I believe. Come on, or would you like to see the plantation first?'

Back we walked through the main office, Jock's arm linked in mine. Now and again he stopped to introduce one clerk or another, and their smiles betrayed that he was well liked by each one of them.

Uncle Jim, Uncle Sam and I all wanted to see the changes Jock had made at Albion, and so he took us on a tour of the plantation. He was especially proud of the new housing, an innovation he had thought up and set in motion himself.

He led us into what looked like a village, a neat and tidy area at the back of the plantation, where row upon row of white-painted, one-storey cottages stood amid neat flower beds and rows of well-tended patches for provisions.

'I was horrified to see the logies they lived in,' said Jock, 'and one of my first ambitions was – this.'

'How did you do it?' I asked. 'Didn't you have trouble persuading sour business managers? I know that we had the same problem on Promised Land. New housing for all the workers – it was one of the things my grandma was able to bring about – though against the wishes of my mother, because of the cost. How does it work here? I mean, our workers still complain. Mama just kept increasing the rent, so our workers still aren't happy because they can't afford the nice houses.'

I had learned this from Uncle Jim; when Oma took over the running of Promised Land, she had appointed him plantation manager and new housing was the first thing on their list for change. The rent had at first been minimal, but when Oma left us to return to Austria, Mama had immediately hiked it. I was genuinely curious: Albion's manager, Mr Foot, was known for his mercenary ways, and I wondered how Jock had worked this miracle.

'We lease them the land, they pay a peppercorn rental of twenty-four cents per month,' Jock explained. 'We lent them money to build their homes: they can borrow up to a thousand dollars interest-free, repayable in weekly instalments of two dollars. You wouldn't believe how regular they are with their payments. Many of them have completely repaid their debt. They own their homes.'

'What an ingenious plan!' Uncle Jim exclaimed and Uncle Sam, obviously impressed, nodded in agreement. I said nothing, but as we walked to one area of the plantation, then the next, I noticed again and again the rapport between Jock and his labourers. They obviously liked him; there seemed no hierarchy at all, no sense of him as the big white boss, the Massa. I asked him how he did it. He shrugged.

'I've got a certain Irish blarney about me. Somehow, I get on with people, no matter what their status. It helps with the workers – I like them and they know that. I've made great friends with some of them.

'But that blarney of mine, it's also how I get my own way with the people above me. I tend to be a good chairman in an argument. I might be young but somehow, people listen to me. I dominate at meetings.'

He stopped, and I saw a bit of a blush. 'That sounds awful, I know. Boastful. But it's good to dominate at meetings if you're up against the terrible, terrible bigotry at play in this country. It's a culture of cruel domination. Mr Foot rules here with a rod of iron. I'm trying to change that with – well, I suppose you can call it domination in the cause of benevolence. The main thing is, it's working.'

*

The main house was through another gate at the back of the compound. Jock led us up the stairs into the main mansion; a grand two-storey building not unlike Promised Land – a typical planter's home, on high stilts, built for a big family.

The tour of the plantation had made so very clear to me that this was what I wanted. I wanted him, I wanted to be part of what he was doing; I wanted this home. A sense of rightness, of belonging, settled into me; yes, I belonged here, in Jock's arms, in this house. Now, I looked around, and I couldn't help exclaiming.

'Oh, this is delightful!'

Mama had never been one to pay much attention to the beauty of her home's interior; no curtains graced the windows of Promised Land's gallery, and the furniture had been chosen for practicality rather than aesthetics. This room was quite different.

Jock laughed at my surprise.

'Yes – but a little too feminine for a bachelor, don't you think? Rather, for three bachelors, what with Charlie and Rudi here living with me. It's all Mrs Foot's handiwork; she has an eye for interiors, it seems, and spent many days at the sewing machine. Thus the matching cushions and curtains. She and Mr Foot have moved out into rather less grand quarters on the estate. I feel bad for displacing them, and in fact I had offered to take the smaller house, but Mr Foot would not hear of it. I try to make it up to him; he and his wife, by the way, are coming to lunch today.'

At the mention of Mr Foot's name again I jumped, and probably blushed; I had forgotten all about him. It was over a year since he had masterminded my debut performance at the Georgetown Club, the evening that had changed my life, turned it around, introduced me to a whole new world, set my life on a whole new course, given me the man I loved. Yet a debt was still unpaid. I had long forgotten the deal I had so carelessly made with him, but he had surely not. And if he was coming to lunch today – well, it would be awkward. But it was too late to do anything about it; we had accepted the invitation and couldn't uninvite ourselves now. I would have to face the consequences of my rash actions; Mr Foot needed to know that his good work would go unrewarded. I was no longer the sweet and innocent little girl who needed his intervention. Here I was, on the arm of his master, and, if all went well, the mistress of this very house. Surely he would not dare be rude to me.

Chapter 34

It was an awkward lunch: Mrs Foot was garrulous and sycophantic towards Jock, Mr Foot was silent and took every opportunity he could to glare at me. On such occasions I kept my eyes modestly lowered, but I knew he had not forgotten. I vowed to myself to avoid him in future, which might of course prove difficult, should I ever become lady of this house. Perhaps I could manipulate a removal. There were other estates where he could find a better job, now that Jock had come to take over. I remembered Bhoomie's advice on the covert strengths of a woman, but right now I had other goals in my sight: I was dying to talk to my brothers, and after lunch I managed to pry them away from the others.

The conversation, by this time, had drifted around to cars. Uncle Jim had seen and admired Jock's Bentley, parked in the shade beneath the house; his own old Morris Oxford appeared quite shabby beside it, but Jock was gracious and asked some genuinely interested questions, and promised to take Uncle Jim for a spin later that day. Indeed, he and Uncle Jim had formed an immediate rapport, not only on the subject of cars but also on labour politics, plantation reform and sugar production. I had to stifle a yawn as they talked about the Bentley and the Morris Oxford.

After lunch, Mrs Foot seemed to want to engage me in conversation, but luckily her husband noticed and ushered her away with a hasty excuse. Once they were gone I approached Charlie and Rudi, who stood together at the open window, smoking. Linking my arms through theirs simultaneously, I interrupted their conversation. 'Boys,' I said, 'I need to talk to you – urgently!'

Charlie looked down fondly at me. 'At your service, little sister! What's it about?'

I looked from one to the other, unable to contain my grin. 'It's about just that – I'm your sister, your real sister, not just a pretend one! I just found out – I really am! Uncle Jim told me. And you've known all this time and never said a word.'

That silenced them, but only for a moment as their eyes met, first in consternation, then in glee. Their smiles of relief were all I could have wished for. They hugged me, both together. We'd always been a hugging family, but this hug contained the deepest warmth I'd ever known – what can compare with the hug of a brother, and now I had two, with more waiting for me down in Georgetown! By this time Uncle Jim and Jock were downstairs with the cars, Sam Jonkers in tow; standing at the gallery window I watched as the car backed out from beneath the house, turned on the red-sand driveway and then careened off towards the coast road. Surprisingly, Uncle Jim was at the steering wheel, Jock beside him and Sam in the back seat. We had all the time in the world, me and my new-found brothers. I turned to face them.

'It was so naughty of you, not to tell me! All these years I've known you were my brothers. I knew it! And you let me think we were just cousins! How *could* you?'

I smiled as I said this to let them know I wasn't really annoyed; that I was happy, jubilant, at the revelation. Rudi looked sheepish.

'Ma made us promise not to tell. She said it wasn't our place – that it was Aunt Yoyo's big secret and we had to respect it.'

'We'd have loved to tell you,' agreed Charlie. 'I for one was bursting – whenever you joked about being our sister, I wanted to say, but you *are* our sister! But we'd promised.'

He drew me close and hugged me again.

'And you've always known?'

'Always!' said Rudi. 'Of course, we don't remember – we were much too small, Charlie and I and Freddy. But the others – well, they remember when you were in the family, and—'

'I was in the family? I lived with you?'

'Yes – when you were very small. Before you went to Aunt Yoyo.'

'And – and Uncle George, my father… Was still alive? He knew me? He loved me?'

'He adored you!'

'He'd have given his life for you. He almost did.'

My eyes grew moist. I knew Uncle George – my father! – really only as a mythological hero. There were a few photos of him in an album, and of course the wonderful portrait, painted by Charlie, hanging in the Lamaha Street drawing room. But a dead uncle from toddler days, even a hero uncle, never seems as close or as important as a father. A precious father, one who loved me; an empty hole in my life I needed to fill.

'You must tell me,' I said then, and there were tears in my voice as well as in my eyes. 'Tell me everything.'

And for the remainder of that afternoon, that's what they did. They told me everything, and I learned the details of how he had saved my life, and how he had died a hero, marching for what he believed in.

It became an afternoon of secrets revealed, because in return I told them about Sam Jonkers, that he was our uncle, one of us. They were incredulous, but only moderately so. 'I bet we have a whole army of uncles and aunts and cousins out there,' said Rudi. 'Those planters took women whenever they wanted, and then abandoned them when they'd had their pleasure or when they gave birth. Disgusting animals!'

'I always thought I was one of them – Clarence's daughter. I'm glad I'm not,' I observed.

'Sam does look a bit like us,' said Charlie.

'He's got Uncle Jim's complete trust,' I said, 'but he unnerves me a bit. He's so – wild. So undomesticated.'

Rudi laughed. 'That might be a good thing,' he said, 'must be awful, growing up knowing your mother was raped by her boss.'

'He's very smart,' I said. 'He speaks little, but listens intently and seems to think everything's funny, even if it isn't, chuckling to himself when there's no joke.'

Sam often broke into a conversation with an inappropriate remark, perhaps just a word or two, which made you stop and look at him with furrowed brow, but only for a second until he would grin and wave and say, 'Carry on,' as if it had been nothing; but it had been something. It had been this way all through lunch, but Jock seemed to like him and that was recommendation enough for me, and for my brothers too.

'We'll have to invite him and his mother to town,' said Charlie, 'to meet Ma and the others.'

'Of course,' I said. 'Aunt Winnie will be delighted – his mother was her friend before she was thrown out.'

Jock, Uncle Jim and Uncle Sam returned from their jaunt and, as men do, they all gathered in the gallery and the conversation drifted back to cars.

I excused myself; I would go for a walk, I said. There was just too much to take in. The last week had reduced me to emotional mush, and now the stories my brothers had told me of my father… It was all too much to digest. I needed to be alone, to absorb it all.

I grabbed my hat from the stand next to the door, stuck it on my hair with its pin and walked out down the driveway and into the fields. By now the stifling heat of the early afternoon had diminished somewhat. I took a path in the opposite direction to the one we had arrived on, a route that led through fully grown canes higher than a grown man, tall and straight on both sides of the unpaved path, like walking through a tunnel of succulent green, blue-roofed by the sky.

One sugar plantation is very much like another. There is monotony to a cane field, a familiarity to the grid-like layout, and walking off my emotional upheaval in such a recognisable setting turned out to be just what I needed. The rhythm of walking, the monotony of the upright canes at either side… gradually a sense of ease, of acceptance of unchangeable facts became part of me. The story my brothers had told, upsetting though it was, settled naturally into my consciousness: it was what it was, could not be changed, and therefore it was I who had to change, allow it to be part of me. And slowly, sadness gave way to gladness.

After all, in spite of some of the more harrowing details, it was all good. I had a new father! No longer the debauched drunkard Clarence Smedley, but George Quint, a hero! Eventually, my heart swelled, embracing the element of new love. George had progressed from a legendary hero-uncle to the status of hero-father, the dearest male being in my world – how could I not be engulfed by love? How could that love not be bittersweet, yet the sweet gradually overtake the bitterness? For he had known me, he had loved me! He was part of me and I of him, and nothing could change that. Now I surrendered to the love that chased away the sadness completely and made me want to sing in ecstasy, and I did. I had glimpsed a piano in Jock's house: I would play as soon as I could, something joyful, something that echoed this new-found elation. With that thought my fingers began to itch for the keys – it was a long time since that had happened. It was time to go home – I turned to go back the way I had come.

The paths through a sugar estate are long and straight, laid out in a regular gridwork. I had walked directly away from the house down one of them and not turned off, so there was no question of getting lost. I simply turned and walked back the way I had come. However, there were several crossroads, and at the next one I walked straight into a person coming from the right. Lost in my thoughts as I was, almost skipping along in delight and giggling away to myself, I had not seen him, but he had seen me, run to catch up, and sprang forward so that he stood directly in front of me, arms and legs akimbo. It was Mr Foot.

'So, Miss Smedley-Cox. We meet again, sooner than you thought, eh?'

Chapter 35

My feet stopped skipping; instead, my heart skipped a beat. My laughter turned to a cry of shock. He had appeared so suddenly; it surely wasn't by accident. No – he must have followed me, and then hidden here at the crossroads until I returned; there was after all only the one straight road back. I skidded to a halt, but immediately walked on again, swerving to avoid and walk past him. He fell into step beside me.

'Isn't it rather rude, not to return my greeting? But then, you are rather uncouth, aren't you – brought up by a whore as you were.'

My blood boiled; I wanted to snarl at him, but thought better of it. Instead I said nothing but just quickened my pace. So did he.

He reached out to grab my elbow. I shook him off.

'Leave me alone!' I cried. 'Go away!'

'But why should I? I think the time and the place are quite conducive, don't you, to the paying off old debts?'

'If you don't leave me alone I'll tell Mr Campbell!'

His fingers only tightened around my arm.

'Aha – Mr Campbell! You'll run to him telling tales, is that it? Well, don't forget that I'm his trusted manager. It's your story against mine, isn't it? We all know about women and how they lie, just to get men into trouble!'

He yanked at my arm, pulling me back, and I stumbled and screamed. But there was no one to hear – out here in the fields we were alone except for miles and miles of towering canes, like high green curtains hiding us away from the world. We stood in the middle of the intersection, and in all four directions an empty road led away through the fields. It was just the two of us on an empty crossroads, in a lonely world.

'No use screaming out here,' he said. 'Because no one will hear you.'

At those words, I surreptitiously raised my right hand to my head and, remembering the mashers' advice, slid the hatpin out of my hat. Regaining my balance, I tried to run forward. But he kept pace with me; he had not let go of my arm.

He held me in a vice-like grip, his fingers digging into my flesh, and then yanked me towards him so that he faced me, his face, fleshy and red, pushed forward near to mine. I kicked his shin; he winced, but then gripped all the harder. One of my arms was free – I waved it backwards, away from him. But he was not interested in that arm.

'You sly little vixen!' he growled. 'Using me to needle your way into Mr Campbell's favour! Is that what I get for giving you a leg-up into society, eh? You worthless little hussy! Playing all innocent, right you are. Thinking you could get away with it. Who got you into the club? Who introduced you?'

'Let me go, Mr Foot! I'm not – I didn't—'

'You didn't what? We had an understanding. A promise. You led me on, you did. You and your bulging…' He didn't finish the sentence. Instead, he snatched at the bodice of my dress, tearing it away from my body. As usual, I wore only a light cotton frock; it was the only thing suitable for the tropical heat. I never wore a corset; why would I want to torture myself with armoured undergarments? Beneath my dress, all I wore was a camisole; I had not yet advanced to a brassière. Under the skirt I wore a half-petticoat, it was all I needed. Now, the camisole lay bare for him to see; his eyes bulged and he tore at that, too, exposing my breasts.

Mr Foot laughed; he stared at my now naked breasts. He still held my left arm; now, he struggled to grab my right as well, all the while pushing against me, trying to shove me to the ground, lusting eyes bulging as they stared at my exposed privacy.

'So, you think you've got Mr Campbell around your little finger, do you? Think you can catch him with your sluttish wiles? With those pert little breasts? Think he's going to marry the likes of you, a man like that, just a step away from royalty? Think again, my dear. And even if you were to ensnare him, think he'd want you after I've finished with you? Men want virgins, you know. That's why I want you. I want you first. I'll—'

'Don't you dare! I'll tell him! I'll tell him all about you!' I screamed the words even as I fought to wrench my arm out of his grip. He was stronger than he looked; though his body was quite flabby, beneath the flesh were muscles of steel. He held me at bay, laughing. My hat fell to the ground. My arm felt weak under his grip. I kicked, and hit him in his shin again, and for a moment he grimaced, but the pain was soon gone and so was his grin. His face transformed into an ugly mask.

'You little…'

It was plain what he was trying to do: wrestle me to the ground. I could not let that happen. That was when I attacked. Quick as lightning I slashed forward with my right fist, and with the hatpin struck him on his cheek. He yelled in pain and let go of my arm to cradle his cheek. Blood seeped from between his fingers.

All of a sudden, I was gripped by an overwhelming power, outrage transmuting into physical brawn whirling up from somewhere within me, electrifying my limbs and commandeering them. I kicked. Not his shin this time, but his crotch. My foot, flying forth with the force of a maddened animal, registered a bulging softness and, in that instant, he yelled out and seized his pain with both hands, his face an agonised grimace; and in that moment I ran.

*

On, on, on, in the direction of the house, back the way I had come. I did not stop to look behind me, I only knew I must flee and every ounce of self-preservation entered into my legs as I raced onwards, away from the beast, towards safety, tearing down the red-sand road as if a chased by an army in full charge.

After a while I began to tire; I could hardly breathe. Sweat poured down my forehead, and my bodice – what was left of it – was soaked through. I slowed down and listened; I could hear no footsteps behind me, no cries of wrath. I stopped, panting, and finally looked behind me. The road was empty; I had escaped. So I moved on again, this time walking. I could hear my racing heart as it struggled to slow down to keep pace with my footsteps. Then I stopped again, bent over; wiped my face with the hem of my petticoat. I adjusted my camisole and the bodice of my dress as best I could, but they were badly ripped and all I could do was pull the cloth across my chest and hope it would hold. My plaits had escaped their fastenings and hung now over my shoulders, loose and wild. I must have looked a sight, but worst of all was how I felt: besmirched, belittled, abused.

Tears of outrage gathered in my eyes but I brushed them away impatiently: no, I would not cry! Nothing had happened. Mr Foot had tried his best but I had escaped and apart from a glimpse of my breasts he had won nothing. I would NOT cry. Yet still the sense of panic tore at my being, and I could not beat it away, safe as I now was. I kept looking behind me, and though no one followed, I could not dispel the feeling of an evil presence lurking at my heels; a malevolent invisible entity, waiting to grab me again and finish off what it had started, the vile ghost of Mr Foot. All this manifested in a sudden sense of relief, accompanied by physical weakness, the need to simply collapse. My legs hurt from all the running, muscles protesting. I started to limp. There was still a distance to go.

Dusk had fallen by the time I arrived at the gate to Albion's plantation house. I entered it with relief, ignoring the gateboy's curious stare. Trying my best to cover my breasts with the torn remains of my dress, my hair all dishevelled, I hobbled towards the house and it was then that Jock rushed forward towards me. I stumbled to meet him.

'Oh, Jock!' was all I could say as I finally, gratefully, collapsed. The last thing I was aware of before fainting were Jock's arms reaching out to catch me. I let go, and fell into them.

Chapter 36

The first face I saw on awakening was Jock's. I blinked, and moved my head, and saw Rudi and Charlie on either side of him, all three perched on my bed. I was in a bedroom, and it was dark, the room lit only by flickering lamplight.

Jock smiled. 'Well, hello!' he said. 'Awake at last!'

'What-what happened?' I muttered, struggling to sit up in bed, and then I remembered. Horror shuddered through me at the memory. 'Oh!' I said, falling back against the puffed-up pillow behind my head.

'That's for you to tell us,' said Jock, wiping my forehead with a wet cloth. I liked that. I had a splitting headache. I looked down discreetly, lifting the sheet that covered me, and saw that I was wearing a nightdress, a clean one. Jock chuckled as he saw my glance.

'It's all right, Bhamini changed you, not me. Your dress can't be saved, I'm afraid. That's what she said.'

'Grace – what on earth happened?' asked Charlie. 'You were in a state. Someone must have attacked you. Who was it?'

'Did they – did they do anything?' That was Rudi.

I looked from one face to the other, each one etched with worry, and nodded, still mute from memory, and then shook my head. He hadn't actually *done* anything, had he? But he had tried to do the worst, and the attempt was bad enough. Tears gathered in my eyes.

'Who was it?' repeated Jock.

I sniffed, trying to hold back the tears, and shook my head.

'I'll go now,' said Jock fiercely. 'I need to know who it was. I think I'd better go now – you can talk to your brothers. I understand. But – I need to know.'

I nodded, and he got up and walked away, into the darkness. I was glad – I would talk, but not to him.

Rudi and Charlie were the ones I told my story to. I told them everything, right from the beginning: my delight when offered the chance to play for Jock and Mr Foot's understanding that there would be a price to pay, his sleazy aspirations, my rejection of him.

'It was all my fault,' I said, flooded with relief. It was an unburdening; I had finally liberated myself from a dirty secret. 'I must have teased him, make him think that—'

'No, Grace, it's not your fault at all! It was awful of him to bargain with you in that way, so disrespectful. He'd never have done it to a white girl. And you were right to grab at the chance offered.'

'But maybe I led him on? Make him think that—'

'No matter what he thought you were offering, no matter what he thought the deal was, he was about to rape you,' said Charlie. 'There's no excuse for that.'

'But I let him believe—'

'No matter what you let him believe, he was wrong. And there'll be consequences.'

'You're going to tell Jock? Because – because I can't.'

'Of course we will,' said Charlie. 'Mr Foot won't get away with this. You've nothing to fear from him again. Jock thought it was one of the labourers; he'll be surprised to hear it was one of the senior staff, a white man. His manager, in fact. But I can guarantee the consequences will be the same – Jock's a fair man.'

Rudi nodded, and stroked my face, pushing my hair behind my ears.

'It's all right, Grace. It'll never happen again. We're going to report it to the police, and Mr Foot will be charged with attempted rape.'

I sat up, alarmed. 'No!' I cried. 'No police! I don't want to talk to anyone else about it – just you. Not even Jock. I can't tell the police.'

Charlie and Rudi exchanged a meaningful look, and seemed to agree.

'Don't worry about it, little sister,' said Charlie then. 'Look, it's getting late. Time to sleep. You'll feel better tomorrow. Uncle Jim and Sam have gone home – you're here with us, and tomorrow's another day. Would you like a glass of water? Are you hungry?'

I said yes to the water, no to food – I really only wanted sleep. Tomorrow, indeed, was another day.

Tomorrow and tomorrow, and tomorrow… I gradually recovered from Mr Foot's attack, and he indeed paid the price – Jock dismissed him without notice and, having nowhere else to go without a reference, he returned to England whence he had come, and good riddance. On my insistence – I did not want the terrible hullabaloo an attempted rape charge would cause – I did not report the attack to the police. Losing his job, being sent home in disgrace, his mortified wife in tow, was surely punishment enough.

Charlie's duties at Albion had been expanded: he was now deputy field manager, swiftly learning the ropes, and was given his own cottage in the senior staff compound. Rudi, meanwhile, moved to Uncle Jim's house, where we both stayed for the rest of that glorious season. We became a family: Uncle Jim and Aunt Bhoomie as the grandparents, Sam Jonkers as the father, myself and Rudi the adult children, all moulded together, all of one mind. Sam took Rudi under his wing. He had potential, said Sam, and though too young to be the leader the movement so desperately needed, he had the intellect and the oratory skills to grow into that function. He only needed training, and here, at Uncle Jim's, he was right in the centre of things.

And so I became part of a wonderful movement, the formation of the labourer party Sam Jonkers so desperately wanted. I went to the meetings, held at Uncle Jim's house, attendance growing by the week. By the end of the summer, Uncle Jim's huge yard filled to overflowing at those meetings.

Once a week we all visited Jock, and spent the night at Albion, a household of men and me. I learned to think like a man, a revolutionary in the making. But with Jock, I was all woman.

We were in love. When I was with Jock, time stood still and my heart soared. Whether it was a walk through the cane fields, hand in hand, or a swim at the beach; whether I played the piano for him, or we played tennis together, or went out riding, that was the summer of pure delight, unforgettable, unrepeatable.

Then there was the social life – balls and parties held by the managers of plantations up and down the Corentyne. Jock escorted me to all these events, danced with me, encouraged me to play the piano and to sing I would walk in on his arm, greeted and courted by all. How proud I felt, driven to these balls in his shining Bentley, escorted up the front stairs to those magnificent mansions, on Jock Campbell's arm! Jock was still one of only a handful of owner-managers in the colony; most of the managers were Booker employees, so his status was impeccable, and some of that glow fell on me and finally I found the acceptance I had longed for, at least in the Corentyne. In Georgetown it would be different; but we were here, in a world of our own. I half expected I'd run into Mama at some of these functions, but I never did. It seemed almost that she had retired from the social round, and perhaps she had, because of me. She must surely have heard the gossip; perhaps she was sulking. But I did not care.

The great paradox was that though everyone knew of his radical views on plantation reform, they still loved him, courted his favour and ignored his politics. Jock emitted such charisma that he found acceptance on both sides of the divide. The labourers respected him, but so too did the elite. How long could he maintain that balance? How long, indeed, could I – attending the revolutionary meetings of Sam Jonkers at the one end, attending, and enjoying, the parties of the snobbish upper class at the other? Was I a hypocrite, two-faced, dancing at two weddings (but never, let it be said, at my own)? Was Jock? Where was all this leading?

But I cast aside such nagging doubts. I was young, and in love, and my time here was limited. There was no Mama to rein me in and tell me what I should think or whom I should love. I would never compromise my conscience, but in the meantime, I would enjoy myself. This was my first season of love: my summer of love.

But it was over too soon. The second year of my musical studies would begin that September, and I had to go. I didn't want to. Given the choice I would have married Jock on the spot. But marriage now was out of the question: he was still too young, he said, too unstable in his position. We should wait a year or two. He was working towards higher ends; he did not tell me what. Aunt Winnie came up to visit us all, once, and she insisted I return to Caracas. 'A woman should strive for her highest potential,' she said. 'I never got the chance, but you must. Be the best musician you can be. You never know when you'll need that resource.'

And so, at the end of that magical summer, I returned to Georgetown, and then to Caracas. Reluctantly, it was true, but with a sense of the inevitable. My future was as bright as could be: our future; the future of my country, dear beloved BeeGee. With such splendid minds united and fighting for justice, what could ever go wrong?

Chapter 37

* 1936

My second year in Caracas finally came to an end; this time, I had not returned for Christmas due to strike action on Georgetown's wharfs, so the wait had seemed endless – mitigated only by the fact that Jock and I wrote each other long letters almost every week. I now felt I knew every corner of his soul, and that he knew mine. I returned to the Corentyne and what I hoped would be a repeat of that wonderful summer before. And indeed, there had been few changes, and all to the good. The United People's Labour Party was stronger than ever; Rudi was in his element as an eloquent and passionate apprentice leader under the mentorship of Sam Jonkers. The crowds at Uncle Jim's meetings were larger than ever. We were moving forward! And yet there was disgruntlement.

'We're still too small,' said Rudi. 'It's just a few hundred workers from a handful of plantations from one corner of the colony. We aren't loud enough, important enough, to make a difference.'

Jock had similar complaints. He had continued with the reforms on his own plantations: better housing, schools and medical care for the labourers, more friendly working hours, pregnancy and maternity protection. But what were one or two plantations against the entire sugar industry? Booker Brothers was the enemy, and Booker Brothers held the whole industry in its grip. They made no concessions: Bookers was about profit and profit alone, and nobody gave a hoot about workers and their living conditions and their complaints.

'It's David and Goliath,' said Jock. 'If I'm going to fight Bookers, I need a magic slingshot and a stone to hit them where it hurts. In the meantime, the workers live in unimaginable conditions. And I'm David without that magic slingshot.'

I cuddled up to him; we were sitting on a fallen log on the Atlantic foreshore, at sunset. Behind us, a flock of crows flew home to nest, cawing and croaking as they flapped their way home. The tide was out; the last crabs scuttled into their sandy caves. Fishermen had already brought in their boats, turned them over in case it rained, covered them with nets and gone home. The western sky was a riot of red and yellow, the setting sun invisible behind a vividly gleaming bank of clouds. Behind us, coconut palms waved in the evening breeze, which was cool but not cold. Best of all, Jock's arm was around me.

'Sometimes,' I said, somewhat hesitantly, 'sometimes I have the feeling you love your workers more than you love me.'

He pulled me closer, turned my face towards him with gentle fingers.

'Gracie, how could you think that? I love you, you know it!'

'But you love your workers more, don't you?'

His answer didn't come immediately, which should have given me warning.

'Gracie,' he said, 'It's different. The workers, their liberty, their rights – it's a big thing. It's history in the making. It's bigger than you and me. Our love – it's big, of course it's big. But don't you see, it fades in comparison. People are suffering, and I'm one of the few people with influence who can fight for them. Of course, I'm putting them first!'

'Last year,' I said, and this time the hesitation was longer, a cloud clamped over my heart, for no girl likes to put herself forward, 'last year you said we'd be married in a year – this year. I mean, I don't want to rush you, but…'

He squeezed my hand and I felt something in that squeeze: a sort of apology.

His next words confirmed it. 'Don't worry, Gracie. Don't worry about a thing, it'll be all right.'

I pulled away – something was definitely wrong.

'Why do you say that? Why should I worry? I wasn't worried – just wondering!'

Silence followed, confirming my doubts.

'Jock, what's the matter? Don't tell me nothing because I know something's wrong. Tell me.'

'Well, I'm sure it will eventually all work out. I can straighten it out.'

'Straighten what out? Jock, tell me!'

I pulled away from him, sprang to my feet. 'What's going on, Jock? Have you stopped loving me? Have you found someone else?'

He too stood up, clasped me in his arms. He felt so strong, so grand. All I wanted was to melt into him, to be his for ever. He clasped me all the tighter, and said, 'Grace, of course not. I love you just the same as last year. More, even. It's just that – well, yes, there's a small problem. But we can overcome it. Come, sit down again, I'll tell you.'

My heart fluttered with fear as he pulled me back down to settle next to him on the log. It was all to perfect. I couldn't help it, I felt fear: fear for our future, fear for our love, my love. The love that had been so long in coming; that I had waited longer and longer for, and finally found; and it was drifting out of my hands like mist, insubstantial.

'You see,' said Jock, 'Mr Foot – you remember Mr Foot? Mr Foot's been up to no good again. When he returned to England, he visited my parents. He knew them via correspondence, of course – he'd been manager before I came, keeping my father informed of estate business, and in charge of my welcome and initiation into the running of Albion. So he and Father were on friendly terms, terms of trust. But when I dismissed him, he was furious, and vengeful – with me, and especially with you. So he went to my father and told stories. About you. Lies, of course. I'm afraid my father, my parents, believed him.'

A lump rose in my throat. 'What did he tell them?'

'Grace, it doesn't matter. A pack of lies – about your reputation, your race. Something about you being out for my money, turning my head, seducing me. That sort of thing, but in such language, that – well, I won't repeat it. He told them I want to marry you, which is true. And they've forbidden me.'

'Forbidden you! But how could they? You're an adult!'

'I am, indeed. But I am here in the colony, in my position, only at my father's behest. I'm not independent – yet. And word has reached them that I'm not exactly – well, not exactly acting in the company's best interests. Of course, Mr Foot has elaborated on that; told Papa and my uncles – the board of Campbell Company – that I'm a renegade, bringing down the business, that I'm siding with Communists. My status here is precarious – Papa could recall me at any time. Bring me back to England, if I go against his wishes.'

'You mean, if we were to marry, he'd force you out of Albion, and we'd be on our own?'

Jock nodded. 'That's about it. And I can't give up this fight, Gracie. I can't. I'm far too deeply entrenched here. My work has only just begun! I've a mission – a calling.'

I pulled away. 'So I was right. You *do* love your workers more than you love me.'

He sighed, and tried to pull me back.

'Don't be like that, Gracie. Please! Try to understand.'

'I understand perfectly well, Jock. Let's go home.'

As I stood up again, so did he. I turned to walk back to the car, dejection pulling my shoulders down. So Mr Foot had, in the end, won. I said it out loud.

'I hate Mr Foot! He's a horrible, spiteful, beast of a man!'

'He is,' Jock agreed, walking beside me and taking my hand. 'But you have to understand – even without Mr Foot there would have been problems eventually. My parents are – well, they're snobs. Even without Mr Foot's character assassination of you, they'd have found out about your – your race, your colour – and objected. Even my coming here in the first place was an attempt to break me up with a woman they thought unsuitable. In their class, these things are important. It was always going to be a problem; Mr Foot just poured oil on to a potential fire with his attack against your honour.'

'But you still love me?'

'I do, Grace. I really do. And we can work this out. Together.'

'But – how?'

'Just wait. Wait for me. It might take a few years, but you're young – we're both young. We have time. I have a plan – a long-term plan. And if you wait I think it can work. It's in its infancy yet and I don't want to talk about it, but if things go according to plan we can be together – in a few years. And I can be David, and find that magic slingshot. Just trust me – and wait.'

'I suppose I have no choice.'

'The time will fly, I promise you that. If you want, we can get engaged but it will have to be secret.'

I shook my head. What was the point of a secret engagement? 'No, we'll wait, and do it properly and openly and joyfully when the time comes. I love you, I love the Corentyne, I love BeeGee – this is home.'

'BeeGee's my home, too, now. I'll work it out. I promise to do my best.'

He'd called it BeeGee – that intimate name shared only by those who knew the warm, soft richness of our country, who could feel the motherly embrace of our homeland; those who knew her as heart, as home, with all the comfort and sheer contentment that implies. Even with all the strife and all the conflict and all the problems that undoubtedly lay ahead, to speak that name meant that you were committed, and that you belonged.

I squeezed his hand to show him I understood. He said nothing but stopped and turned me around and hugged me. Then we walked back to the car and drove home.

Many other circumstances changed in that second summer. Charlie had recently been promoted to senior field manager at Albion. It was the first time a 'native' – that is, a dark-skinned employee – had been promoted to that position in the entire colony. He was the second darkest of his brothers after Freddy, not a man who could pass for white and thus managed to slip through the cracks in a disintegrating system. It was a blatantly provocative move on Jock's part, and it ruffled several white feathers, for two or three Englishmen had been passed over.

The first thing Charlie did was to marry his sweetheart, Joyce; it was the first wedding among my brothers and they waited for me, as I was to be a bridesmaid. It was a beautiful wedding, at Brickdam Cathedral. Aunt Winnie was there, of course, and all the boys, and even Dorothea managed to attend. I believe she lied to her parents, pretending to be a good friend of the bride.

At his marriage, Jock awarded Charlie one of the pretty white family cottages at Albion's senior staff compound – another first, since all the other families there were lily-white. When I came for the holidays it was now with Charlie I stayed, and no longer Uncle Jim. Charlie and I grew closer than ever; he was such a gentle, sensitive soul.

During my second year at music school, I had gained much proficiency on my second instrument, the transverse flute; and, because Charlie did not have a piano, the flute was the instrument I played that summer and I learned to love it almost as much as the piano. The flute, it seemed to me, produced a sound that aligned itself perfectly to the higher flights of the mind; it let you sail up to the heavens on smooth and blissful waves. The violin is similar, and the violin was Charlie's instrument. Aunt Winnie, being a gifted violinist herself, had taught him personally, just as her mother, Oma Ruth, had taught me piano. And now, as the two of us played our duets of an evening, we fell into a beautiful accord, a meeting of souls that needed no words.

Charlie was something of an all-rounder, and very good at tennis; he brought me back into form, for I had loved the game as a child and had been good at it. He and I played every evening once the sun had lost its heat, and at the weekends we played mixed doubles: Jock and I against Charlie and Joyce. That is, until she became too pregnant to play.

I loved Joyce. Charlie had made a good choice: from an East Bank Demerara plantation, Joyce adapted well to Albion life. We became friends; I told her my secrets, and she told me hers. I knew that she was expecting a baby before anyone else but Charlie; it had to be kept secret because she was already three months gone at the time of the wedding. Not even Aunt Winnie knew.

'I'm a bit scared of her, actually!' Joyce confessed. 'She told Charlie not to touch me before we were married. Well, not in *that* way. She tells it to all her boys – to respect women and not to compromise them before marriage. And now look what we've done!'

'Don't be scared,' I said. 'Aunt Winnie doesn't bite. It's just a precaution, to make sure no one gets into trouble. Now you're married, it's all right. Aunt Winnie understands people.'

'I love her – but I'm so in awe of her!'

'Everyone is – especially her sons, my brothers. They might all be strapping men, but Aunt Winnie only has to raise her little finger, and they're like boys again.'

That was the reason why this year Rudi was absent from the Corentyne. After a year of revolutionary training – as we teasingly called it – under Sam Jonkers, Aunt Winnie had declared a year was enough: Rudi had to put his brains to good use, to learn a sensible profession. Rudi, Will and Humphrey were the most academic of the Quint boys. Humphrey had studied law in England and Will medicine, and now it was Rudi's turn. He could choose the subject, Aunt Winnie said, but he must go – no more flapping around, trying to change the world. So Rudi had chosen engineering, and two weeks after I arrived back from Caracas, a week after Charlie's wedding, he had set sail for Southampton.

'But I'll be back,' he promised as he kissed me goodbye. 'I'll be back with a vengeance. I love my country and I'll be fighting for its freedom. In England, I'll learn how.'

Sam Jonkers, too, had taken a break from political activity. The UPLP had, in my absence, slowly disintegrated through lack of leadership – neither Sam nor Rudi had had the skills to take the labourer movement forward. Sam had disappeared from the scene – taken himself off to the interior to become a pork-knocker, a freelance prospector mining for diamonds and gold on the alluvial plains far away from civilisation. I did not see him for that whole season.

And so that second summer passed, with me closer to Charlie but further from Uncle Jim, without Sam and Rudi, and playing a distant role as far as Jock was concerned. It lacked the heady promise of the year before: the euphoria, the elation of first love. But I loved Jock, and I trusted him, and love and trust sank down from the giddy heights of rapture into a deeper place in my being, a quiet, steady, stable place, where the roots were strong and held fast to their foundation. Nothing fickle and reckless about this love, no passing infatuation: it was real, and it was true. I believed in it, with all my heart. And that belief gave me patience. I would wait for it, for ever.

According to Jock's plan, we should be less public about our love. And so the balls and the parties ceased. We visited each other, but took care not to be seen together as a couple in public – easy enough when one did not live in Georgetown but in remote homes in the countryside, with no spies about, but only allies and workers and staff. There would be no salacious rumours spread about us, no whispers of an unsuitable romance drifting back to Jock's parents on the wings of upper-class gossip. Utter discretion was our watchword. And if anything, it lent a frisson of danger to our love; and that frisson led to a deepening. This was no more a light-headed romance; it was serious – a thing we were working on, together, even while he worked on a greater plan, his big-but-secret David-versus-Goliath scheme.

During that summer I corresponded with Aunt Winnie; she was the only person who could possibly understand and give me unbiased advice. Aunt Winnie never minced words, always gave her forthright opinion, and I thought she would advise me to step away, to let Jock go if he could not commit, if he did not love me enough to defy his parents. But I could not have been more wrong. As ever, Aunt Winnie was understanding; not just of me but him too.

'He reminds me so much of George,' she wrote after my first rather disappointed letter outlining the situation. *These hero men who want to save the world, to throw away the old order and bring in the new, they are so full of passion, so full of selfless goodness! George and Jock have the very same mettle; and I'm afraid, dear Grace, that we women do take second place in their hierarchy of needs. They need us and our love, but they need to invest their passion, their energy, their beings in something bigger, greater, more permanent than romance and its domestic consequences.*

George was exactly the same when we first met. 'This is bigger than us!' he told me then. 'Bigger than our love!' Just the way Jock is telling you now. And they're right: a hundred years from now our little love will be all forgotten, the world will have moved on without us, without me marrying George or you marrying Jock, if that's how things turn out. But you know what? Once George finally did settle down he became the best husband and father the world has ever known. He adored me and our children. He would give his life for any one of us – and he proved it, didn't he? And even as he was sounding off about needing to make this great choice, even while he dreamed dreams of being the hero and the revolutionary, and what have you I always knew, and I always trusted I could forgive him – well, anything. And I think, dear Grace, that trust in him is what gave our marriage its foundation. I was never jealous of his calling, don't you be jealous of Jock's. I believed in him; I was his partner, for a time, fighting for justice at his side.

'That's what I am,' I replied by return of post. *His partner. Jock has opened my eyes to that higher cause – through him I've been able to see through my dependence on Mama, and sever myself from her. I haven't seen her for over a year now; I've really cut that cord. I understand this thing, this greater cause we must fight for. I realise it's noble and heroic and all that. But sometimes – well, I suppose it's selfish of me. I just want to be his completely: his wife, the mother of his children. Is that so very wrong?*

Aunt Winnie's next letter was encouraging but cautionary at the same time. *It's not wrong, sweetheart. It's only natural. But don't try to force it; there is time – you are both so young! Let it be, let him be, wait; love him, yet leave your heart open for whatever may come. If it is meant to be, the distance and the waiting and the separation and his parents' disapproval will solder the love between you and eventually fuse you into one. If not, you will both move on. Like George, Jock has a calling – can't you see the fire in his eyes when he speaks of it? Don't be a bucket of water, insisting on instant decisions. He's a man of integrity, that should be enough for you right now. You are so young, so much is waiting for you. Finish your studies, become a musician; go your own way, while nourishing your love and believing in it.*

I sighed, knowing she was right. At the end of that summer I returned to Caracas for my third and final year of musical studies.

Chapter 38

1937

That third year sped by. This time, I did manage to come home for a short break at Christmas, but I stayed in Georgetown for the festivities, for Jock was there and we were able to meet at Auntie's house, if not publicly. Rudi had stayed in England, deep in his engineering studies; he was staying with Aunt Kathleen, Mama's eldest sister, in London, and told us frightening stories of the possibility of war. But I dismissed such tales as fearmongering; I refused to believe in something as ghastly as war. It just could not happen. I worried about Oma Ruth, and the dreadful things going on in Austria, as reported by Rudi; but Rudi seemed to have a plan to evacuate both her and her father to England, and I had faith in him. It was going to be all right.

When I returned to Georgetown that summer, I was surprised to find a letter waiting for me at Aunt Winnie's. I recognised the handwriting immediately: it was from Mama.

The rift between Mama and me was wider than ever – I had not seen her, not communicated with her for two years now – and, it had seemed up to now, permanent. Whenever I came to spend my summers in the Corentyne she must have surely known; the rumour mill is as active there as it is in Georgetown, and certainly the first year, when Jock and I had been actively courting, the gossip must have reached her ears. The very fact that she had not been at any of the balls or parties we'd been invited to was proof enough – Mama was a social butterfly, and if she stayed away from these events it must have been for a reason, and the most likely reason was not to bump into me. My hosts had now and then dropped hints, and I had put two and two together. I was not in the least afraid of bumping into Mama at some ball or the other; but she was clearly avoiding me. But I shrugged it off – I had made my decision, shoved Mama into the past. Until she changed her ways, until she repented her past and turned over a new leaf, I wanted nothing more to do with her. I had made my choice. I could not appease her by being her obedient daughter and at the same time stay true to my own principles.

And so, when Aunt Winnie handed me the letter, I took it with a shudder of trepidation and hesitated a moment before opening it.

'What on earth does she want?' I said.

'Well, there's only one way to find out!'

I turned the envelope over. Yes, there it was, her name and address on the back in her large, right-sloping handwriting. It was a thin envelope; it couldn't contain more than a sheet of paper. Curious as I was, I still could not break the seal.

'Go on, Grace. I've been dying of curiosity for the last two weeks – open it, read it!'

'I suppose I'd better.'

So I broke the seal, removed the single page of paper, flapped it open. There was not much written on it – just two lines, in fact, cold and stark. I read them aloud:

Dear Mary Grace,

Please come to Promised Land as soon as possible. There's an important matter I need to discuss with you. It's very urgent.

Mama

'What on earth can it be?' I said, handing the page to Aunt Winnie. 'How mysterious! She could at least have given a hint.'

'Yoyo likes to be mysterious and secretive, as well as blunt and direct when she chooses. This time she's chosen mystery. You'll have to go.'

'Really? Do I have to? I don't want to.'

'I'm afraid you have to, Grace,' said Aunt Winnie. 'Yoyo's a proud person. She wouldn't have written to you if it wasn't serious.'

'What on earth can it be?'

'Go. Find out. Go tomorrow.'

'But I wanted to spend some time with you!' I wailed. 'I've so much to tell you.'

She laughed. 'But I bet you're also dying to get back to the Corentyne, and Jock! You can't fool me.'

'Come with me, Auntie! Why not? We can all stay at Charlie's then you can find out what it's all about sooner. And – oh, the baby!' Lilian, or Lily as we called her, had been born in October the previous year, soon after my return to Caracas. I had missed her birth by just a month; now she was ten months old. 'I can't wait to see her! And I bet you don't need an excuse to see her either – your first grandchild, and a girl. Your first little girl!'

Auntie gave a wry smile, and hugged me. 'No – *you* were my first little girl, Grace! I will never forget the first time George handed you to me. I may not have given birth to you, but you were in every way my daughter. You still are.'

A lump rose in my throat. We had never discussed the matter of George being my father; for me it was far too invasive and intimate a subject to discuss with an older person, and she – well, this was actually the first time she'd even hinted at the matter.

'Even though...?' I was still reluctant to talk about it. I felt bad, guilty. But Auntie dismissed the awkwardness immediately.

'I forgave him right away,' she said, 'because you were the most beautiful baby in the world.' And with those words the subject was closed, there was nothing more to say. She swiftly changed the subject:

'But you're right. I haven't seen Lily for four months and it's time. I'll come with you, we'll take the car.'

Chapter 39

Aunt Winnie and I arrived at Albion the next evening. Charlie and Joyce were delighted; there had been no advance warning, as a telegram would not have arrived in time. Aunt Winnie swept little Lily into her arms and cuddled her, then handed her to me. I buried my nose in her soft baby neck; an intoxicating sweet baby scent sank into me and with it came an unexpected and visceral reaction; a deep and overpowering yearning, a hunger, almost, but a love-infused hunger that swelled from the depths of my heart. Lily struggled and held out her arms to her mother, and I laughed and handed her back.

'I want one of those!' I said.

'Your turn will come,' said Charlie. They both knew, of course, of the situation between Jock and me, and though they offered no advice I knew they would be there for me whatever happened. I had a home with them, and always would. Joyce was my sister.

Joyce warmed up the leftovers from lunch and we sat on the balcony long into the night, exchanging news. Albion, Charlie said, was still the colony's most progressive sugar plantation, the only one in which native Guianese – that is to say, Guianese of African and Indian blood – were allowed to rise to the hallowed heights of senior staff. Charlie had been the first; he had been followed by several more.

'It's brave of Jock,' he said. 'It leads to a lot of disgruntlement among the white staff. They can't bear to see a coloured man promoted over their heads, brought in as newcomers for a position they thought was theirs.'

'They'll get used to it,' Aunt Winnie said. 'The world is moving on. One day there'll be not only black senior staff but directors and chairmen and governors and presidents. Just wait and see.'

'A hundred years from now,' said Charlie, 'if we're lucky.'

Aunt Winnie was more positive. 'In my lifetime,' she declared, 'but if not, definitely in Grace's. And Lily's. And black men will marry white women and vice versa, and no one will turn a hair.'

'Wishful thinking!' said Charlie.

'Pessimist!'

'No, just a realist. Not in my lifetime,' he said with a stamp of finality, and a good deal of prescience.

The next morning, Aunt Winnie drove me to Promised Land. She did not enter the mansion compound; instead, she let me out and turned the car. We had left early, so as to catch Mama before she went off to work.

'I'll go and visit Uncle Jim, and wait for you there,' she said. 'You can take a bike and cycle over when you've had your talk with Yoyo. You do still have a bicycle here?'

'Yes, probably,' I said. 'There've always been tons of old bikes in the garage. But I don't expect I'll be here long. Why not just wait for me?'

'No, take your time. I don't want Yoyo to peer out of the window and see me waiting outside her gate.'

So I walked away from her, down the sandy driveway leading to the house and up the bifurcated front stairs, and rapped at the door. I had to wait some time before it was opened, by a maid I did not recognise, but after all, it had been two years since my last visit.

'I'm Mrs Smedley-Cox's daughter, Miss Mary Grace,' I said.

She curtseyed and stood aside to let me in.

'Madam upstairs,' she said, and seemed about to lead the way.

'It's all right – you needn't escort me. I know the way,' I said to her, and she scuttled off in the direction of the kitchen.

The drawing room looked somehow unfamiliar, but I couldn't quite grasp what had changed as I walked across to the staircase leading to the upper storey. It was more a sensation – or maybe it was just me, for the sensation was of sadness. Neglect, maybe. Neglected relationships? Unresolved conflict? Whatever it was, I felt distinctly nervous as I walked up the wooden stairs, but it was only as I reached the top landing that it clicked – the change was physical. All the chairs in the gallery were covered with white protective sheets, as if they had not been used for many months. A sense of foreboding gripped me. There was also a certain smell, unfamiliar: something pungent, medical, but also with a slight undertone of – vomit. A chill ran through me. A premonition. I knocked on Mama's bedroom door and, without waiting for a reply, opened it and walked in.

She was lying on her bed, propped up by a few thick pillows. But it wasn't Mama. It was a ghost of Mama. An ethereal shroud wrapped around a skeleton, a fragile, lost thing diminished by the huge bed and bundled bedclothes.

'Mama!' I cried and rushed to her side. 'What's the matter? What-what…'

She tried to smile but it was a smile of agony. Then she raised an arm, reached out for me.

'Mary! Oh, Mary Grace! You came. I didn't think you'd come. I thought – you hated me so much—'

'Oh, Mama, I don't hate you, I never did! Why didn't you send for me before? Why didn't you – why aren't you in hospital? Oh, Mama!'

I bent down to gather her in my arms but drew back at the last moment – she was so fragile, I feared she would disintegrate if I so much as touched her. Instead I took the proffered hand – hovering, trembling – above the white sheet that covered her. Pale, so pale.

Mama had always had a golden glow to her skin; not perhaps very fashionable, as the pale look was favoured in Georgetown, but she liked it, for she said it showed she was a hard-working woman, out in the fields all day. Now, she was the colour of a ghost. The colour of— no, I would not say the word.

I couldn't believe that this was my mama. This shadow of a human being, who had been a paragon of health and bursting strength, blooming. Where was her glow, her verve, her fire? All extinguished.

'You were in Venezuela. I didn't want to – to disturb you. I was in hospital. For a month. I came back – they sent me back – last month.'

'Oh, Mama! What is it? Why didn't you stay in hospital? Do you have a doctor? I want you to go back to town – the best treatment, the best doctors! What is it – what do you have?'

But I already knew, even before she answered. 'Cancer,' she whispered. 'Breast cancer. They've done all they can, Mary Grace. No doctor can help me now. No hospital. Mary Grace, I'm so scared! I'm going to die!'

'No, you're not!' I cried. 'I won't let you! I'll – I'll fight for you – we'll fight together! You have to fight it, Mama; you can't give up! You should have sent for me much earlier. Why didn't you?'

'I did fight it, Mary Grace. I did – I didn't want to let it win. I fought it, I tried, but then – then I saw it was winning. They all said so… the doctors.'

'Well, maybe you needed someone to fight it with you? Me! You can't be expected to struggle all alone. Oh, Mama! You should have called me. If only I'd known! You should have told Aunt Winnie – I can't bear to think of you all alone here with this horrible, horrible disease…'

'Geoff was here,' she whispered. 'He was here – at the start. He said he'd stand by me.'

'Where is he, then?' I looked up and around as if I expected to see Geoff Burton materialise out of the curtains, or the cupboards. It was only then I noticed the second person in the room – a woman in a pale blue dress under a white apron, with a white cap on her head. The uniform told me everything: she was a nurse. She sat quietly on a rocking chair in a far corner of the room. I had not seen her at first as she was partially hidden by a clothes horse placed between her and the bed.

'He – he came with me to town. To hospital. But then when they said I wouldn't recover, they wouldn't operate, he… he said goodbye. He couldn't manage, he said. He had to get back – to America. To his plantation there. I don't think he's coming back.'

'Well then, good riddance! We don't need him. But Mama, you should have called for Aunt Winnie then. Why didn't you?'

'Winnie – Winnie hates me.'

'Mama! Of course she doesn't hate you!'

'Oh, she does, she does. You don't know the story, but she does. I'm wicked and she hates me. You don't know how wicked I am.'

Up to now her eyes had been fixed on mine, holding my gaze. Unlike the rest of her, her eyes were bright, alive, eloquent, but now they turned away from me towards the window, and brimmed with tears.

I gently squeezed the hand I still held – that thin, fragile wren of a hand. 'Mama – look at me.'

She shook her head and the tears spilled out, down her pale papery cheeks. I reached out, softly touched her chin and turned her face towards me so that once again our eyes met. Hers were filled with an expression I'd never before seen in her – one I had thought she was incapable of. Where was my tough, unrelenting, proud mother? Where had she gone? This was a woman whose innards were as water – pliant, soft, flowing. Humble. Pleading.

'I'm awful,' she whispered. 'You don't know how awful. I'm a liar. I'm—'

'Mama,' I said, and now I was the forceful one, the one in charge. 'I *do* know, I know everything. I know you lied. I know

I'm really your daughter. I know Uncle George is my father. I know what you did. And—'

'You know? Who told you?'

'It doesn't matter, I can't remember. My brothers – no, Uncle Jim – but it doesn't matter. Nothing matters except getting you well again. I don't care what you did a hundred years ago; what matters is what you do now, and you need to fight, Mama. We need to get you back on your feet. I need to tell Aunt Winnie and get her over here. We'll take you back to Georgetown. Find a good private hospital, with the best treatment. If need be we'll send you to Europe. To Oma, in Salzburg! Or to Aunt Kathleen, in England. I'll travel with you. We'll do everything – everything! You're not going to die, Mama! You *can't* die! I love you, Mama, I do! I'm so sorry I wasn't here – when – when…'

By now I was weeping, overwhelmed by regrets and guilt. Whatever happened between us in the past, she'd needed me and I had failed her, and I was desperate to put things right.

We spoke for a further hour. I learned more of the details. Geoff had been with her when she first suspected something was wrong, and had accompanied her to St Joseph's Mercy Hospital in Georgetown. After several tests, breast cancer had been diagnosed. There was no cure, the doctor had said, and no treatment that promised success. She would die within the year; the best she could do was arrange for palliative care. On hearing the grim news, Geoff had backed away.

'He said I should tell my family, let them deal with it,' Mama told me.

'And why didn't you? You should have gone straight to Aunt Winnie, she's your sister! You know she would help.'

Mama nodded. 'I was just too ashamed. And besides, I had to get back here. I have a plantation to run.' She paused. 'Though there's not much I can do from my bed. I've neglected things over the past weeks, it all happened so quickly.'

'So who's running it now?'

'My estate manager, Mr Bond, but he can't do it alone. There has to be someone, a supervisor – someone in charge – to take my place.'

'I'll take care of that,' I said. 'Or-or Uncle Jim, he'll do it.'

Once again, tears brimmed in Mama's eyes.

'Uncle Jim's another one who hates me,' she said. 'He worked here before and I gave him the sack. Why would he come back to help?'

'Because he's a good man. And because it's a good job and you'll pay him well.'

She was silent then; she knew it was the truth. Uncle Jim's integrity was undeniable – even Mama must have seen that, even if it was to her disadvantage.

Now and then as I spoke, the nurse came over to wipe Mama's face with a rag dipped in cool water. She held up a glass of water, and Mama sipped slowly at it. At midday, the maid brought up a tray with lunch: chicken broth, and two slices of bread. Mama instructed me to tear the bread into bits and immerse them in the soup, and then to hold the bowl while she fed herself. Even the act of raising the spoon to her mouth seemed to exhaust her, and I realised she needed to rest.

'Mama, I'm going now, but I'll be back.'

And I was – with reinforcement.

Chapter 40

In the end Mama had no choice in the matter, and neither did I. There was no question: she came first. I didn't even have a chance to see Jock. No holiday for me this year. The very next day Aunt Winnie and I held my mama between us, her arms linked over our shoulders, ours around her waist, and helped her to the car. It was frightening to see how very weak she was.

Then it was off to Georgetown, leaving Uncle Jim in charge of the plantation, just as I had promised Mama. I think she was relieved and even seemed to gather strength from the knowledge that she had that burden off her hands. The burden of her health, too, she finally passed on to Aunt Winnie and myself. Simply the fact that she was no longer alone with her devastating illness, that she was in good caring hands, brought colour to her cheeks and some strength back to her body. The past was no longer a burden; it was irrelevant. There was just the present moment, the needed reprieve.

What I had expected to be a well-deserved holiday for me turned into an open-ended period of amateur nursing. Mama was given the annexe where once Uncle George's father – no, not Uncle George, *Papa's* father, my grandfather! – when would I learn to think of Uncle George as 'Father'? – had lived until his passing a year ago. It was a large square room with windows on all sides, linked to the main house through a short passage. So Mama had her peace and quiet away from the hustle and bustle of Aunt Winnie's household, while the bulk of caring for her comfort and well-being lay firmly on my shoulders. I shared the room with Mama, for it was a day and night duty, though, of course, I had help.

Aunt Winnie was a constant background presence, always there to relieve me or offer a word or two of encouragement or advice. And then there were my brothers, those who still lived at home: Humphrey and Freddy, Percy and occasionally Gordon. All helped whenever they could. My brother Will was now a fully-fledged and working doctor in the private practice of Dr D'Andrade. He had moved out of Aunt Winnie's home a few months ago, for he had married and established his own home in Queenstown, just a ten-minute bicycle ride from us, but he came daily to visit and check on Mama. We employed a nurse to come for two hours each morning to provide more expert assistance – injections for pain relief, measuring Mama's blood pressure – and Sister Martha taught me several of the tricks of her trade. I learned to turn Mama every now and then to prevent bedsores and when they did appear, to treat them with a tincture that, Sister Martha said, was a secret but sure-fire recipe made of herbs from the interior, provided by an Amerindian medicine woman she knew and trusted. An ancient and time-tested cure, she claimed, and indeed, it did seem to help.

The emphasis was on keeping Mama and her linens clean, and, as Will advised, stimulating blood flow; that is, using heat and massage to induce blood to flow to the tumour, a hard hot lump on one side of Mama's breast. It was the hottest of seasons, and she suffered greatly from that alone. She needed to be regularly sponged with alcohol, for cooling down and when the occasional fever took over. The advantage of living in town was that unlike in the backward Corentyne, there was an ice factory in Water Street. I would chip ice from the large block Auntie kept in the Demerara window cooler in Mama's room, mix the chips with water and wipe down Mama's entire body with cool flannels, or place them folded on her forehead. Mama's great shame was that she was often incontinent. I learned to fold cotton sheets into nappies for protection and pin them together around her emaciated form. A rubberised sheet protected the mattress, with rolled blankets beneath its edges.

Aunt Winnie provided meals. Soft eggs, almost raw, custard, porridge, gruel, rice cooked into a watery mush, and of course the cure-all, chicken broth. I held the bowl while Mama fed herself, but sometimes she was too weak even to hold the spoon, and I feared the end was near.

Sometimes, Will sent me to the pharmacy on Water Street to pick up medicines for Mama. The pharmacist was a mixed-race man called Mr van Groenwedel, who began to take an interest in Mama's progress, asking which medicines worked and which didn't.

'Call me Michael,' he said after my third visit, and I suspected his interest in Mama was a cover for an interest in me. At my fourth visit he asked if he could come to my home 'to see for himself'; I told him Mama didn't like to meet strangers and with that ended whatever designs he had been cultivating. After that I went to a pharmacy on Regent Street for Mama's needs.

When I told Aunt Winnie she rebuked me gently. 'I know Mr van Groenwedel,' she said, 'he's from an old Dutch family, mostly planters from the Essequibo and the Canje region. He's a good man, a bachelor with good prospects. Is it wise, dear, to cut yourself off from all your – alternatives? After all…'

She didn't finish the sentence; she didn't need to. I knew exactly what she meant. What if it didn't work out with Jock? Was it wise to bind myself so adamantly to a man who was already married to a cause? As much as she believed in supporting a man with a higher calling, I knew that my own doubts and insecurities had transmitted themselves to her. The reality of our relationship did nothing to bolster my hopes of marriage.

Jock came to town for a week. He still had his family home, Colgrain House, just around the corner, and he came to visit me every night. Sometimes he took me out, but our relationship was now officially secret, so we went to small private restaurants where the English upper class would not see us, or to the cinema, where we would slip into a private box once the film had started, and hold hands in the dark and kiss where no one could see us. The rumour mill had to be closed down: his parents must be appeased, for otherwise his big plan would be in jeopardy. History had to be made, and our love must take second place. He could not risk the future for a private, selfish desire.

'I'll be returning to England soon,' he told me. 'And I'll tell my parents what you're really like. I'll sort it all out. I have a plan – a big plan.' And I had to be content with that. Yet still I doubted.

'He's so much like George used to be,' Winnie sighed after one of Jock's visits. 'Their entire person, all their passion, surrendered to a cause bigger than themselves. Once that cause is realised, once they are ready, then they are ready to love, and they love deeply and strongly. But George was not ready when I first met him, and Jock's not ready now. You can wait, dear, if you have the patience, but Jock's cause is a mighty one and you could very well be waiting in vain. Don't cut yourself off from the world, from marriage and a family. One day it might be too late.'

But I only shook my head. 'I love him,' I said simply. 'I'll always love him. No other man can compare.' And with that I firmly quashed my doubts.

'Mr van Groenwedel asked about you the other day when I stopped in at the pharmacy,' said Aunt Winnie. 'He's still interested – very interested.'

'I love Jock,' I said. 'It wouldn't be fair to encourage anyone else. I can wait.'

And so Jock returned to Albion, and several months slipped by; sometimes they passed so slowly it seemed like years, but looking back, they seemed like days.

Four months after Mama joined us in town, we had a surprise visitor: Sam Jonkers, back from his pork-knocking gold-seeking adventure in the jungle. He looked a mess; his brittle hair was matted and long, giving him a wild and disreputable appearance that would have been shocking to more conventional society. And he stank.

But Aunt Winnie welcomed him with open arms. Quite literally, she hugged him, which even I was reluctant to do, given his ragged looks. But Aunt Winnie was delighted to meet him.

'Iris was such a good friend when I was a young girl,' she said. 'I never thought of her as my maid, I just loved her, and missed her so much when Papa sent her away. I didn't realise what had happened – how could I? I was just a young girl at the time, unaware of the facts of life. What did I know about rape, and the disgraceful way plantation owners, my own father, treated their female servants! I remember seeing her once, in the village, when you were just a toddler, and greeting her with rapture – and she just ignored me. I was so hurt. It was a snub. But now I understand. Do give her my love, when you return to her; tell her I know the truth and it shames and hurts me, and if she would like to renew our friendship – well, here I am!'

Aunt Winnie offered Sam a bed for the night or for as long as he cared to stay. He showered and went to the barber and put on some of my brothers' clean clothes – and ended up looking very smart indeed. But Sam Jonkers had another surprise, held in the dirty, battered canvas bag that contained all his possessions. After hearing about Mama's illness – from Uncle Jim – he had come straight down to town without even stopping to wash. Now, he opened the filthy bag and removed another, even dirtier, cloth pouch. 'Dis for your mother,' he said to me. 'Corilla. Cut it up, boil it, give it to she. It gon' cure she cancer.'

He held the pouch open for me to peer inside, then passed it to Aunt Winnie so she could see. It was filled with a strange green fruit – a few inches long, oval in shape and completely covered with plump spikes, like small prickly cucumbers.

Aunt Winnie removed one and held it up. 'I've seen this vegetable at the market,' she said. 'I even bought it once to try out. It was horrible, really bitter! I never bought it again.'

'Very powerful medicine,' said Sam. 'Bitter melon. The Amerindians use it for all kinda ailments. See, I live in an Amerindian village now more than a year – them people does know things doctors don't know. This corilla, bitter melon – it does cure cancer.'

Aunt Winnie smiled, and replaced the corilla in the bag.

'Well, I don't know about that. Yoyo isn't a guinea pig, Sam. I don't want to poison her, or give her food that tastes as nasty as this.'

But Sam ignored her and thrust the bag at me.

'Try it, Grace. I promise, is good. Don't mind it taste bad – all good medicine taste bad, castor oil and so. You must cut it up and boil it and mash it up and give she, make she eat it even if she don' like. It gon' cure the cancer.'

I looked at Aunt Winnie. 'I've heard those Amerindian doctors do have herbal cures,' I said. 'Uncle Jim told me. It can't hurt, can it? Why don't we try?'

'Well, it *can* hurt – the taste alone!' said Aunt Winnie, yet she took the bag from me. 'But I'm not going to reject anything that might help. I'll try it out, but if she refuses to eat it, don't blame me! I would too.'

Mama did refuse it – at first. But I persuaded her, and fed it to her, a teaspoon at a time, washed down with some sweet-tasting pineapple juice or crushed ripe mango. She ate it. And then, miracle of miracles, her strength began to return. Little by little, she began to recover, to return to her former self – her former self, but without the sting. She sat up in bed, read the newspaper, commented on the news, read novels, talked to us about local goings-on. She even asked for visitors, and her friend Margaret dropped by. I was not present at their meeting, but something seemed to have gone wrong, for it was extremely short and Margaret never came again.

The next person Mama asked for was a lawyer. 'I need to write my will,' she declared.

But I didn't want to know. She was making such progress – I had placed all my hopes in the corilla. 'But Mama – you're not going to die!'

'Some day, I will,' she said, 'and I need to put things straight. If I don't, that false husband of mine will get everything, or try to – I want Promised Land to come to you, Mary Grace.'

'Oh, but Mama! I know nothing about running a plantation. I don't want it!'

'You're going to marry that Jock Campbell, aren't you? He'll know how to run it. It'll be like your dowry.'

'I don't need a dowry, Mama! You should leave it to Charlie, he's the farmer in the family.'

'When I'm dead and gone you're welcome to pass it on to Charlie. I don't care. But I need to leave it to you.'

Humphrey came up to her room and prepared the paperwork, and the deed was done: I was to inherit Promised Land, even against my will.

The next thing Mama did was to set in motion the process of divorcing Geoff Burton, which was to prove difficult since he had absconded back to America. She would divorce him on grounds of desertion.

'In sickness and in health, my arse!' she said, and I smiled to hear her curse again. Mama had never been too delicate for curse words, but her illness had cowed her in that respect. To hear her use such a word was an enormous sign of hope. And so that too was done: the wheels were set in motion for divorce from a husband who had been so only in name.

Chapter 41

Mama's recovery proved short-lived. The cancer's forces were by then too mighty, and it won the war against the corilla. In early 1938, it returned with a vengeance. I stood or sat at her bedside night and day, mopping her face, her whole body, with rags cooled by ice chips, holding her hands as she moaned in agony, holding a water glass to her lips to keep her hydrated – for she could hardly eat any more – holding pans for her as she vomited bile. Aunt Winnie and the boys took over from time to time, to give me respite. And then, in February, during a violent storm, she was gone. Gone out with thunder and lightning, just the way she had lived – she would have liked that.

Her going was, on the one hand, a relief – her life had become agony, and dying was an escape, and once she was gone her face, so often distorted with pain, sank into a pale slack mien of utter peace, all tension and struggle evaporated. On the other hand, I was left with a vacuum. Though I had cut her out of my life for two years, still she had been a background presence, unacknowledged, but still a constant in my life, and now I was left with this: an empty body. I cried bitter tears, yet I had to be grateful that towards the end there had been reconciliation, and peace between us.

And now I was free to go my own way, but that freedom felt like a prison. I could return to Promised Land, which was now mine, and run it with Charlie and Uncle Jim, but I found no impetus to do so. I could, perhaps, align myself more snugly to Jock. Seek a job at Albion, and help in its transformation into the most advanced and successful plantation in the country. Yet by now a little seed of resentment had sprouted in me, for Albion was my rival; Jock's big plan, whatever it was, had stolen my love from me. I had started out as his partner in a wonderful cause, but we had never been side by side, equal partners in a lofty mission, simply because I had neither the status, the background nor the knowledge to be such. Instead I had been in competition; and Albion had won. I could support Jock only from a far distance. So, no, I could not return to the Corentyne.

'Well, dear,' said Aunt Winnie, 'now you know why I encouraged you to take that musical scholarship. A woman must always have options. Some of us don't ever marry, and then what? A woman needs to be independent – just in case.'

She herself exemplified that advice. Long before Uncle George – oh, when would I stop thinking of him as Uncle! – died, she had set up a business of home-made jams, jellies, chutneys and dried fruit, and Quintessentials, as it was called, was still thriving, bringing her a healthy income long after her husband's life insurance was spent.

Now, she introduced me to her friend, Eleanor McGregor, who already worked as a music teacher. Mrs McGregor told me that musicians of my calibre and my qualifications were in great demand in all the leading schools; she could not possibly do it all. And indeed, I was snapped up. I was offered jobs in all four leading schools: Bishops' High School and St Rose's for girls, Queen's College and St Stanislaus for boys. In one case to teach the subject of music, in two cases to lead the school choirs and in a fourth to work as a pianist for assemblies and dance classes. I chose the teaching job at Queen's College and the choir job at Bishops' and St Stanislaus, and answered several letters from parents who wanted me to teach their child piano. By the end of March 1938, I had a full programme of activity, and launched into it with enthusiasm.

Jock returned to town. We met, and the news was bad.

'I'll be leaving for England at the end of this week,' he told me. 'But I'll be back, I have a plan.'

'Am I part of that plan, Jock?' I asked him, and my voice was cold.

'Of course you are! You're a big part of it. I'm going to have a long talk with my parents. I'll tell them why you're exactly the right woman for me. Just wait! Wait for me, I'll be back.'

But somehow I doubted it. I doubted that I was the right woman for him; though I knew he was the right man for me. This big plan of his, it sounded like a pipe dream. Once he realised how hopeless it all was, how small the chances of David against Goliath, he'd give up.

Doubt is like a little weed that can crack through stone. My own doubt began as a tiny seed lodged beneath the huge and immobile boulder of my love; a love I had thought indestructible. The seed was invisible to the eyes, but it was there nevertheless, doing its work. As it began to sprout, so did the very substance of my love; cracks appeared through the boulder, cracks of excruciating pain. Just as I had wept at Mama's death, so now I wept for something indefinable as the cracks filled with the poison of doubt. Love, something so beautiful, defiled by doubt and fear and insecurity. At night I hugged my pillow and pretended it was him; I called for him in my dreams. I saw his face last thing before I went to sleep and first thing when I woke up. The last three years I had taken this wonderful thing called love for granted; it had been as a sun, shining within me. Now, there was nothing but a dark and moody cloud. And though I worked hard during the day to dispel it, at night I could not hide and a deep sadness crept through me; and just as faith can indeed move mountains, so can doubt manifest in just the thing it fears: it springs from heart to heart to become a self-fulfilling prophecy.

It didn't happen immediately. Jock's first two letters from England were full of hope and optimism. He was *working on* his parents. Explaining his big vision to them. Telling them that I was perfect for the function of his wife exactly *because* I was mixed race. This fact would endear me to all Guianese, who would see that he meant well, that he was not the usual kind of racist Englishman. And then came a long pause. A pause lasting several months, months in which I agonised, fearing the worst, months in which the seedling of doubt, having wilted slightly as a result of renewed hope, refreshed itself with renewed vigour. After that third letter there was no more doubt. The rock of my love crumbled into a million pieces.

My dearest Grace,

I'm sorry for the long silence. I'm sorry for so much. Mostly I'm sorry for planting such hope in your heart only to crush it, and so cruelly. It breaks my heart to tell you this, but it's no good. My parents are adamant. I may not marry you; and if I do, against their wishes, I may no longer return to my beloved BeeGee, may not fulfil my plan. You know I have always said that history must come first, before our personal dreams! And I'm afraid that is the choice I was given.

I am to be married soon, to an eminently suitable woman, chosen by my parents. I need not tell you how I feel about this but I will do my best to be a good husband, and a good father if that is to be.

I know you have waited many years for me. I am sorry for keeping you so tied down. I can only say that you are young enough, and beautiful enough, both in appearance and in character, to find someone far worthier of your love than me.

There are no words to describe how I feel. I cannot begin to imagine how you must feel. I will say no more, except that I hope you can forgive me one day.

I truly am not worthy of you…

Even while reading the letter tears clouded my eyes. As I read the final words my fist closed on it and I thrust it away from me. I escaped to the piano, where I poured my anguish into music, mutating it into melancholic beauty.

As always, Aunt Winnie was my rock in the following days and weeks, lifting me up when I fell into the depths of despair, pouring hope into my heart, and the will to move on. It was she who showed me the announcement of Jock's wedding in *The Sunday Times*, borrowed from the public library. After that it was easy. A full stop placed at the end of my heartbreak, and a way forward, my emotional footing restored. That done, she invited Mr van Groenwedel to tea.

'Call me Michael,' he repeated.

Michael asked me to go to the cinema with him, and I agreed. We saw *Carefree*, with Ginger Rogers and Fred Astaire, but I could only think of *Top Hat* and dancing 'Cheek to Cheek' – with Jock. In the middle of the film Michael reached out and took my hand, but I pulled it away, for which I earned a rebuke from Aunt Winnie.

'You're walled in, Grace!' she said. 'This is all sentimental nonsense now, not love. Let go of the past, embrace the future.'

The next film we went to was *Holiday*, with Katharine Hepburn and Cary Grant, and this time I was slightly friendlier. I allowed him to hold my hand. When Sunday came around we went for a walk on the promenade, and as we strolled among the other couples, arm in arm, a sense of rightness overcame me. Michael, so dapper in his Sunday best and top hat, so chivalrous. So very much in love with me.

A month later, he asked me to marry him. I said yes.

Michael was a good man, and he adored me. He had no ambition to change the course of history. He had no Big Plan, to which his love for me must take second place. No shining city in the sky lit up his eyes. Michael liked tennis, and so did I. He liked music and reading, and so did I. We were well suited. It felt good to be adored by the man I had promised myself to. It felt good to look forward to a home of my own, since I would never move back to Promised Land.

A year later, in July 1939, we were married.

Chapter 42

In the year between our engagement and our wedding Michael worked hard to lay the groundwork for our life together. Together we sought out a home; together we decided on a three-bedroom house on Peter Rose Street, Queenstown. High up on its stilts, it gleamed white in the sunshine; its doors and Demerara windows were dark green, and so too was the galvanised iron roof. It had a large garden with a swing hanging from a mango tree, left behind by the previous owners. My brother Will lived around the corner, in Crown Street. It was perfect; Michael paid the down payment and took out a mortgage for the rest.

After a quiet wedding at the Sacred Heart church in Main Street, he whisked me away to a short honeymoon in Barbados, and there we spent our wedding night. I did not let him see my tears. This was supposed to be my gift to Jock; and Michael, I was determined, was never to feel second best. I refused to grieve for what could not be. I refused to submit to the sense of failure that threatened me from within. No, I was Michael's wife now, and I would pour my heart into our journey together, just as he did; I would learn to love him as he deserved.

We stayed with relatives, a Great-Uncle Don and his wife, Aunt Jane, whom Auntie Winnie knew well from her youth, for she had spent a year there to cool off from Uncle George – unsuccessfully, as it happened. We even met a former suitor of hers, a certain Thomas, now happily married to a beautiful Englishwoman and settled in a majestic house on the beach. Aunt Jane whispered to me that this could have been Aunt Winnie's life, for he had offered it to her first.

'I'm glad she didn't accept,' I said, and I was.

The sea in Barbados was soft and soothing, pale aqua in colour, transparent in substance. It lapped sweetly, gently, at our calves as we walked in the frothing surf, hand in hand. Happiness, too, lapped at my soul. The struggle, the doubt, the anguish was over. I had brought my flute, and played it for Michael, on the beach; and people stopped by to listen, and life was good. Not what I had imagined, but it was good; and goodness heals wounds.

Aunt Winnie gave me her piano for my wedding present. 'I hardly ever play any more,' she said, 'and our musician Will has moved out, and has his own. It's yours.'

I continued my various jobs at various schools, and now that I had not only my own household but also my own piano I taught children, and one or two adults, at home. I made friends with our neighbours; I visited Will and his wife almost every afternoon, became an aunty to their little children. I looked forward to children of my own. I loved my new home, especially the garden, and that became my new focus. I would make it beautiful, a little paradise with bougainvillea and oleander and hibiscus and, of course, roses everywhere, climbing up the outside staircase and up the stilts almost to the windows, mingled with the abundance of bougainvillea. Every evening Michael and I sat together in our rose arbour and I played the flute for him and all was well in our little world.

It was a sunny, beautiful life; so sunny I did not notice the dark clouds gathering, for they were far, far away. Of course I picked up on the talk of war; I saw the headlines in the newspapers, I heard the news on the radio, but it did not concern me. That was all far away, in Europe. I had worried about Oma in Salzburg, who was half-Jewish, but her letters soothed me. 'We are safe,' she wrote, 'we have friends who are helping us to get to England. We will go to Kathleen.'

Kathleen was her eldest daughter; and Kathleen herself wrote to reassure us that Oma and her father would be joining her. She'd be safe.

Here, in British Guiana, we too were all safe. Here, in my little idyll, war could not touch me.

Until it did.

On the fourth of September I woke up to find Michael sitting next to the radio, his face a mask drained of blood.

'It's happened,' he said. 'Britain has declared war on Germany.'

Even then I was too naive to understand. Perhaps because I did not fully understand the male need for heroism – you would think my time with Jock would have warned me, but it hadn't.

The telephone rang; it was Aunt Winnie. We should both come, immediately, she said.

All my brothers were gathered in the drawing room, all the ones who were in the country, which meant all except Rudi, who was still at his studies in England. Even Charlie, who was supposed to be at Promised Land, was there.

'What are you doing here, Charlie?' I asked. He replied only by shaking his head. He looked bad – pale, and stricken.

Rudi had sent a telegram, which was why Aunt Winnie had summoned us all.

'Rudi has volunteered to fight for Britain,' she said. Her voice shook and so did her hand holding the telegram. I gasped; how could that be? What did Rudi have to do with Germany? I couldn't even point to Germany on the map; I was confused.

'Why, Auntie, why? Why should he?'

'Because we're British,' said Charlie. 'It's our duty. And I'm sorry, Ma, I can't help it. I knew this was coming, I came to town to tell you: I'm going to do the same. There's no question.'

Humphrey nodded, and so did Percy and Leo. Will hesitated then he nodded. 'Me too,' he said.

We all looked at Freddy. Barely twenty, Freddy was a happy-go-lucky non-conformist and social rebel who had not yet found his way in life – he couldn't possibly go off to war. Deathly pale, he stared at the ground, saying nothing. Auntie reached out for him; took his hand.

'Freddy's too young to go,' she said with a semblance of sternness, but I still detected a slight tremble in her voice. 'You know that, Freddy. You're underage. You can't sign up without my permission – and I won't give it.'

Freddy continued to stare at the floor, and then he stood up and walked out.

By now the realisation had reached my blood. An awful numbness and cold shuddered through me; I could not speak but only stare. I held fast to Michael's hand. All my brothers, except Freddy. All of them. Off to war. Across the ocean, to fight a nation they had nothing to do with, for a nation they belonged to only nominally. We were British, yes, but British *Guianese* – why did they have to rush off across the ocean? Why? Why? Why?

It was only when Michael and I were home again that he delivered the final blow: 'Darling, I'm sorry. I'm so, so sorry. I'm going to have to sign up too.'

I screamed: 'No! No, no, no! You can't go, you can't leave me!'

'I have to,' he said. 'I couldn't live with myself otherwise. I'm sorry, my darling. I'll make sure you're all right. Don't worry, I think it will soon be over and I'll come back to you. Please don't worry! Please don't—'

'I won't let you go!'

I was crying now, clinging to him. Hammering his shoulders with my fists. Because now, only now, when I was about to lose him, I realised: I loved him, I did love him. Just as I had hoped, in a silent, stealthy way, love had crept into my heart and taken hold. Not with the passionate, overpowering turbulence of what I'd felt for Jock but with a quiet, unobtrusive, peaceful love – and strong. How could he even think of leaving me, now that this miracle of love had happened?

He pushed me away, held me at arm's-length, tried to talk to me.

'Darling – I have to. I can't explain it. It's something, well… beyond me. Bigger than me, bigger than us and our needs… That would be selfish. It's my duty, my calling. I have to go.'

There it was again: this 'bigger than our private needs' excuse for a man to neglect his personal love. How could I accept it? And yet I had no choice; he did not give me a choice.

'What if I'm pregnant?' I wept after I had calmed down somewhat. 'What if, after you've gone, I find out a baby is coming? What if – what if…' But I could not give expression to the fear that clamped my heart. If I did not say it, the worst could not happen. I could not even think it. If I did not think it, I would be protected.

'If you have a baby when I'm gone,' said Michael, mopping my tears with a handkerchief, smoothing my hair with his gentle hands, 'that will make my homecoming all the more wonderful. You'll be taken care of. There's your Aunt Winnie, and my parents, and my brother and his family. Everyone will be there for you. You can even move in with my parents, if you want to.'

But I didn't want to. I would stay right here in my home; distract myself with my work and my music. I would not run away.

In the end Freddy too went off to war, in defiance of his mother; but he married his sweetheart, Dorothea, first, and she moved in with Aunt Winnie, in defiance of her parents. Auntie wanted me to move in as well, but I couldn't, and wouldn't; a house full of wives and mothers, comforting each other, wouldn't work for me. It would only make me sadder. Joyce came to town with her two children, moved back in with her parents. Uncle Jim continued to run Promised Land, with the help, now, of Sam Jonkers, who moved into the main house.

As for me: from a material point of view I thrived. I had an income from the plantation, but I kept up my music teaching, to keep my mind off war, to distract me from fear. But it didn't work. The very earth had moved from under my feet. From under *our* feet, for we all lived under that dreadful shadow, all we women, wives and mothers.

Our only comfort was that Humphrey would not be going. He failed his medical exam on account of his clubfoot, a disability he had had from birth, the reason for Aunt Winnie's first sojourn in Caracas. He was disappointed; he thought he could have done administrative work, but the rejection was final.

Poor dear Humphrey, the kindest man alive, gentle and softly-spoken and desperately in love with Dorothea; we all saw it, the melting of his eyes whenever they set on her. Humphrey deserved a woman of his own to love; but Dorothea was taken by Freddy, and he accepted it. And now he was left behind, to his great chagrin and even shame.

Auntie was ecstatic; at least one of her sons was at home, safe. But seven had gone off to war, and we had no idea how many would return – seven sons and, with Michael, a son-in-law. For now, more than ever since Mama's death, Winnie was my mother and I her daughter.

It had always been that way, she told me: 'You *are* my daughter.'

I was not pregnant, and neither was Dorothea, to her disappointment and my relief. When I did have a baby I wanted Michael to be at my side from the start. I would wait for him to return; the war would surely soon be over, and then we could start our family.

But it wasn't. On and on it dragged, year after year. When my brothers or Michael had leave, they stayed with Aunt Kathleen, in London. Letters came, with words blacked out. We did not know where any of our men were. We clung to the notion that no news was good news. As long as we heard nothing to the contrary, they were all alive, all eight of our men. But now we followed the war's progress avidly; we heard of bombs and devastating defeats and hundreds of men killed, and we shuddered and gave thanks to God none of our loved ones were among the dead.

But wasn't that selfish? How many women, just like us, living in dread, would wake one morning to find their worlds had ended; their sons, their husbands, their sweethearts, had been torn from life? We hoped, we prayed, but we all knew: with eight men gone, how high were the chances that all would come home safe and sound? It would be a miracle; we knew it was unlikely. We lived beneath the shadow of fear, which, coupled with the lack of knowing what was happening to our loved ones, and where, meant that anguish was our constant bedfellow, the radio our lifeline. Each day that a telegram did not arrive we breathed out; every morning again we breathed in and held our breath. Bad news would come, one day; we knew it. One of our boys would never come back. We did not know which one.

One – or even more.

'It's Russian roulette, with eight targets, and we don't know how many bullets are in the gun,' said Aunt Winnie, and her words filled me with dread. 'All we can do is pray. It will keep us strong,' she added.

And so I prayed. It was all I could do. *Keep him safe, oh Lord. Keep him safe. Keep them all safe!* And though I knew that other women also prayed thus and yet their men would die, still prayer helped. It was an anchor in a stormy ocean, a rope to cling to in the tempest of terror.

Eight men of ours were over there. *Bring them all back safe and sound*, we prayed. Yet we all knew with devastating certainty: when the war was over there would be a hole in our family.

Which of our boys would be ripped from our midst? Only God knew that.

We women clung together, deriving strength from one another: Auntie, Dorothea, Aunt Winnie. Sometimes Joyce came for dinner, and it was on 2 February 1942, while we were seated around the dining table, that it happened.

Aunt Winnie had had many photos taken of all her sons before they left, or sent from England; all together, in groups of two and three and alone, some in their uniforms, some in their Sunday best. She had had those photos framed and they hung on the wall behind the dining table, before them a small table with a candle that always burned: a shrine constantly alive. Michael's photo was among them, of course.

On that fateful evening, Auntie was just dishing out her mulligatawny soup when one of the photos crashed to the ground. A chill went round the table. We stopped in the middle of whatever we were saying or doing, and Aunt Winnie spoke the fatal words: *Charlie is dead.*

She knew it. Yes, it was Charlie's photo that had fallen. My darling brother Charlie, so sensitive, so caring; a husband, a father, a son, a brother. An artist, a farmer. The last man, you would think, equipped to be a soldier, for Charlie was peaceful and never argued but always found a mediating word when there was strife and always a smile when others felt low. Always a hug when you needed one. And now that dreaded hole opened in our hearts and Charlie fell in. We looked at each other in anguish; we sensed it, but refused to believe; we would cling to a spark of hope up to the last moment, the moment of confirmation.

It came, a few days later, the confirming telegram: Corporal Charles Douglas Quint of the Royal Corps of Signals Unit, reported killed as a result of enemy bombing action when his ship was torpedoed by the Japanese off the coast of Singapore.

All our preparation, all our prayers, all our clinging to each other for strength, did not at that moment relieve the utter devastation that Charlie's loss wrought upon our family. And yet, too, that crippling sense of *not knowing* had been taken from us. Now we knew. So it was Charlie, *he* was the one. Now we could only hope that he'd remain the only one. Seven of our men were left. We prayed, oh, how we prayed, that they would all come home safely; that this terrible war across the ocean would soon be over. Aunt Winnie often said that she wished she lived in England because then she'd be closer to it all, closer to them all, exposed to a similar danger; for in England women, too, were killed for London was under siege and the war was closer to home than ever – if your home was England. Here, across the Atlantic, we were all safe, but that did not make us feel better – on the contrary. We were too far away from our men. We wanted to be near them, physically, as well as holding them in our hearts and minds. But we had no choice: we could only hope that it would soon have an end, one way or the other, that the killing would stop; that our precious seven could be spared.

We waited and waited. The months dragged by with no hope of an end. And the years – another one, and another… But no more photos fell from the wall. And then, on 6 June 1944, we heard it over the radio: Eisenhower had successfully masterminded the invasion of Normandy. We would win the war, our men would all return! This dreadful war would soon be over! Oh, how we celebrated!

But we rejoiced too soon.

On 8 June I was just preparing to go off to school for choir practice when a telegram was delivered. At that moment everything within me turned to ice.

No, no, no, screamed a voice within me. It can't be! The war's almost over! The invasion was successful!

I could not open it.

I stuffed it into my pocket and cycled over to Aunt Winnie's, where we opened it together, but by then I knew.

The word *Deeply* had been placed, in handwriting, before the printed word *regret*, followed, at intervals, by: to – inform – you – that Corporal Michael John van Groenwedel died of wounds on 7 June 1944.

My wail of anguish must have been heard from the beginning to the end of Lamaha Street – so different from the silence that had accompanied the falling of Charlie's photo!

We later heard that Michael, a member of the 5th Parachute Brigade, had died when his battalion had tried to cross the River Toques in France. But the details meant nothing to me. All I knew was that my husband, my beloved, was dead, and would never return to me.

That was enough.

Chapter 43

Aunt Winnie had suffered many deaths and other losses in her lifetime and recovered from them; she was a professional at getting back on to her feet, and helping others to do so, no matter if they lay in scattered bits across the floor, as I did. She raised me up, and life continued. One by one her boys returned – or didn't, as was the case with Leo, who stayed in England and sent for his bride and married her there.

Slowly I grew used to my life as a grieving widow. There was a hole in my heart, in my life, but I filled it, as always, with music. Again, as in my youth, music was my lifeline. I had my daily routine – getting up, going off on my bike to the various schools where I was employed, visiting my pupils in their homes, visiting Aunt Winnie, and my brothers, and their growing families. I missed Michael dreadfully. And I missed something else, something only Jock had given me, something only he could give me: a higher purpose, a goal, a something. Something bigger than the two of us, as he had put it. And then, out of nowhere, that something happened.

One morning soon after breakfast the telephone rang. It was Sam Jonkers, whom I had not seen for a year.

'Hello, Sam! Are you in town? How are you?'

Sam didn't like the phone, and so he came straight to the point.

'Good. Look, there's someone I'd like you to meet – you and Rudi. Meet me at Winnie's at six this evening. Bring your bike.'

'Who?'

'You'll find out.'

Obediently, I rode over to Aunt Winnie's house at five. As always, she was pleased to see me and plied me with one of her home-made drinks and all the latest family news.

'Do you know what Sam's got up his sleeve? Who's this person he wants me to meet?'

'I have an idea,' said Winnie, 'but you better see for yourself.'

Mystified, I let her change the subject. Rudi arrived soon after, and he, too, hedged when I asked him if he knew where we were going and who we would meet. 'I think I know,' was all he would say, but there was a certain gleam in his eyes that told me the evening would be interesting.

Sam arrived on time, which was unusual. He rode a rickety old bicycle no doubt borrowed from a friend. He simply stopped outside the gate, signalled for us to follow and rode away with us in pursuit, pedalling swiftly to catch up. He led us up Camp Street and after a few blocks came to a stop, got off his bike, wheeled it over the bridge and leaned it against the fence outside the property. There was a modest sign on the building: Dental Surgery.

He led the way up an outside staircase. At the top, he knocked at a door. 'Is me, Sam!' he called out, and a voice called out in reply, 'Come in, Sam!'

I found myself in a small living room that merged into a dining room. At the far end stood a wooden table, around which sat four people. One of them was a young white woman. Another was an East Indian man, also young. Of the two other men, one was black and the other was of an indeterminate racial mix. The East Indian man jumped to his feet as we entered and strode over to shake Sam's hand vigorously. He looked at me with kind eyes, saying, 'Welcome, welcome to my home, Mrs van Groenwedel. Sam has told me all about you. Pleased to meet you. And you must be Rudi Quint? Yes, I heard about you too.'

'Grace, let me introduce: Cheddi Jagan,' said Sam, 'and this is his wife, Janet.'

The white woman had also left her seat and walked over to meet us. She held out her hand.

'Pleased to meet you,' she said, with a strong American accent. I greeted them both in return, still wondering what was going on, why Sam had brought me there. He introduced the other two men as Vincent and Catfish, no surnames.

'Come, come, take a seat. You are welcome,' said the man named Cheddi Jagan. He pulled out chairs for Sam, Rudi and myself, and we sat down.

'Dhal puri?' he asked, and without waiting for a reply pushed a large pot over to me and removed the lid. It was filled with steaming, soft, hot puris, obviously fresh from the griddle. I nodded and took one and held it carefully, the folded puri in my right hand and my left cupped below to catch the inevitable falling crumbs of the dhal filling. I didn't know what to say, and eating seemed an adequate alternative. Sam, meanwhile, was grinning from ear to ear, obviously delighted at my expression of befuddlement. The others were chattering among themselves, small talk about food. But now, Sam turned to me and said, 'Grace, Cheddi is the leader we all been waiting for. He de sugar messiah.'

Cheddi turned to me now, graced me with a winning smile and said, 'Don't worry with Sam, I not leading no one to the Promised Land. But I might lead you out of it.'

Sam burst out laughing, and slammed the table with his hand. 'Tell she, tell she, brother!' he cried, and Cheddi told me, me and Rudi.

'We're going to turn things around in this colony,' said Cheddi. 'We'll do it through the workers.' And he proceeded to tell us how. Cheddi's vision, in a nutshell, was one I was not only already familiar with, but had lived and breathed since the age of sixteen, since falling in love with Jock. All of Jock's idealism, all of Sam Jonkers' fervour and Rudi's passion, underpinned by Aunt Winnie's sense of justice, all rolled into one and expressed with such intelligence, such zeal and determination and palpable sincerity it gave me gooseflesh. Sam and Rudi peppered him with questions, and he parried them all with quick-witted eloquence. The man was a genius. A firebrand.

'A saviour!' cried Sam.

Later, much later, after the puris had all been eaten and the mauby all been drunk, Cheddi told us of his background, and the forces that had brought him to this particular juncture in BeeGee's history.

In 1901, a ship arrived in Demerara from India, bringing a new set of indentured servants. Among them was a family called Jagan, from Uttar Pradesh.

'My grandparents,' said Cheddi.

They were allocated to the Campbell family estate at Albion. 'The Jagans were labourers of the Kurmi caste, known for its thrift and industry,' said Cheddi, 'and their children worked as hard as the parents. Their son, Bharrat, was a child-labourer on the estate. He married when he was ten years old, as was the custom, and his wife a bit younger; but they lived separately until they were about sixteen and then moved in together, to the neighbouring estate, Port Mourant. They had eleven children and I was the eldest.'

From a very young age, Cheddi observed his world and found it flawed. Between the estate managers and the workers he saw an unbridgeable gulf.

'I saw the white masters striding through the estate in their short pants and white pith helmets, so confident, so assured, giving orders, cracking whips, the entire world at their feet. I saw my own people, slaving all day in the broiling sun. I saw the cane-cutters, their skin glistening with sweat, their cutlasses slashing through the fields of cane. I saw the loaders, semi-submerged in water, pulling the laden punts, their muscles bulging under the strain; their faces distorted with agony.

'I knew about cane-cutting. I'd seen what happened to my parents. It's back-breaking, soul-destroying work; it demands the last ounce of strength from a man. At the end of the day every taxed muscle screams, every crushed joint moans. Night comes like a blessed angel with soothing hands to ease the pain for a few hours, until the next dawn breaks with the agony of the new day. My mother worked for eight cents a day, from 7 a.m. to 6 p.m. My father rose at 4 a.m. and had to trek five miles on foot to work. It was awful.'

Cheddi's future lay bare before him. As a member of the child-labour gang his career as a cane-cutter was preordained. His father, despite starting as a menial cane-cutter, rose on merit to the position of driver, the foreman of a cane-cutter gang. That was as high as a coolie could rise; the next higher position, that of overseer, was reserved for the white ruling class, the British. Cheddi coined a name for them: the sugar kings.

'Those sugar kings,' Cheddi said, 'they lived in palatial mansions, behind white picket fences and beautifully mowed lawns.'

The labourers lived in hovels little better than pigsties, surrounded by filth and sewage, infested by vermin, with floors of mud and walls of rotting wood. I knew all this; though I had not seen the logies with my own eyes, Aunt Winnie had told me about them, and so had Jock. But hearing it from Cheddi, from someone who had actually lived there, who knew the conditions first hand – well, his story gave me gooseflesh.

The paths to those mansions and the paths to the logies never intersected. Two worlds, heaven and hell, a bottomless gulf between them and no bridge across it. No white man stepped into hell; no coolie could ever rise into heaven.

Cheddi's parents were industrious, and thrifty. His father supplemented his earnings with rice growing, some cattle and a kitchen garden. There were thirteen mouths to feed, and pay was a pittance. And yet like all parents the Jagans were ambitious for their offspring, determined they should do better, that their lives should be one step higher. The only way out of the estates was education, and for that they worked themselves to the bone.

'My people are Hindus,' said Cheddi, 'a patient people, who accept life as it comes. "It's karma," said my mother. "There's nothing we can do. It's God's will." But not for me. For me it was simply wrong. Let me tell you a story. This happened when I was about ten.'

Cheddi was a born orator. When he told a story he brought it to life, with every detail. As he spoke I felt that I was right there with him, in the logies.

'Cheddi! Cheddi! Have you heard?'

It was Cheddi's friend, Ravi – wild with excitement, at the door of Cheddi's hut.

'Heard what?'

'Mistress Gibson! She say all ah-we boys to come to she house!'

'What for?'

'Is Christmas, man! She want give ah-we a present!'

A Christmas present, from the Lady of the Mansion! Mrs Gibson was known as formidable, something of a dragon – why, suddenly, a Christmas present? Cheddi was sceptical; he was intrigued.

'With the other boys from the child-labour gang I walked, barefoot, up the sanded path that cut through the mansion's lawns. Our mothers, excited as we were, had dressed us in our very best clothes; rags still, yet clean. And they had scrubbed us down to remove the ingrained grime from our skin, and combed our hair and slicked it with coconut oil, and warned us to be on our very best behaviour.'

The boys stood before the mansion and looked up in awe; never had they been so close to paradise. Their hearts rattled with excitement; Cheddi's too. What went on inside those palaces, what was it like? The universe of the white man was a thing beyond his wildest imagination, hidden from him by those pristine white walls. Would they be invited in? Would they know paradise, if even for a while? He had heard tales of shining wooden tables, laden with food, at which these white gods ate – would he partake of such a feast? Or *should* he?

'I was aware of a nagging feeling, a sort of resentment, a feeling that all this, somehow, was just not right. But I couldn't put my finger on it. I was too young.'

Mrs Gibson appeared at an upstairs window. She looked down at the boys and smiled; she waved. Quivering with anticipation, the boys waved back, even Cheddi; but despite everything the nagging at his heart grew stronger, a vague, restless thing he could not define.

'Merry Christmas, boys!' cried Mrs Gibson gaily, and flung out her hand, bestowing her largesse like a great goddess sprinkling her devotees with divine blossoms, beaming in her magnanimity, bestowing her blessing. Spontaneously the boys all raised their arms, as if in adulation.

But these were no divine blossoms falling on them. It was… money. Coins fell about the boys, pennies from heaven! At once they dropped to hands and knees, grovelling in the sand, crying out with glee and gratitude, snatching the coins from each other, shoving them into their pockets. Mrs Gibson stood at the window, a smile of smug satisfaction on her face, watching the wild scramble down below. Cheddi looked up, and saw that smile.

'I never forgot it,' he said.

Cheddi, the eldest child, was sent to school in Georgetown. 'My father saw that the only escape was education,' he said now. 'And I escaped. My parents sent me to Queen's College, in Georgetown.'

'How did you get in?' I asked. All my brothers had attended the prestigious Queen's College, the government's selective boys' secondary school, an institution reserved for the elite of society, and the most brilliant. Even for them it had been hard to win a place – but for a cane-cutter's son?

'On merit alone,' said Cheddi. 'I did well at primary school and secondary school. I had a good headmaster who recommended me for Queen's College when I was fifteen. I was breaking the mould. I was the only boy from my whole area to attend that school, one of the very few to attend any school at all. Still, they put me in Form II, where I had to learn baby lessons. I protested and they advanced me to Form III and then I skipped a whole year of school.

'And I studied hard. I had no concept of pleasure for the sake of pleasure, culture for the sake of culture. Rum flowed freely in Georgetown, and was cheap, and real men drank; but I never did. I didn't read for pleasure, either. She does.' He gestured towards his wife, Janet, who smiled and nodded.

'The world of literature and the imagination was a foreign one for Cheddi,' she said, speaking for the first time since our introduction. 'It was useless for his purpose, and thus of no interest. He read his school books, that was all. All he wanted to do was pass exams.'

'And I did,' said Cheddi, somewhat proudly.

'Where did you stay in Georgetown?' I asked.

'I was a lodger,' he replied. 'I stayed with other Hindus who treated me like a servant, forcing me to do menial chores. So I moved to the home of a high-caste Kshatriya Hindu, but that was hardly better. He made sure I knew my place as a Kurmi – an agricultural worker. I had to sleep on the floor, even though there was a spare room in the house. Finally I moved to a Christian family and that was actually the best place. But the humiliations added up, cutting notches into my soul. Little drops of fuel to a fire smouldering underground.'

After graduating with an Oxford and Cambridge School Certificate, Cheddi's indignities continued. He wanted a civil service job in Georgetown but could not get one. He wanted to be a teacher, but was told he had to convert to Christianity. A brilliant School Certificate was not enough: one needed a 'Godfather' to get in, a sponsor, the right connections, the right skin colour, the right family, the right religion. Cheddi was from the wrong side of the tracks.

'In 1936, I left the colony for Howard University, Washington, to study dentistry. My father sent me with every penny he had, which was $500, and had to pay for my second-class cabin and two years at university. To complete my course I'd have to work as well as study. By that time rage burned in my heart. By then I had already somehow resolved, maybe not yet consciously, to change everything. It was the embryo of a vow to right ancient wrongs. I was still so young, but I had the instinct, an innate knowledge, that if things were to change, I had to do it.'

As he spoke those words, a chill ran down my spine. Because Jock Campbell had said the same, spoken almost exactly the same words. Jock and Cheddi: their backgrounds the polar opposites of each other, and yet both coming to the same conclusion, the same realisation, that they were to be agents of the very same change. How fortuitous was that?

'Go on,' I prompted, 'what happened then? How did you meet your wife?' I smiled at Janet; she seemed so relaxed, so at home here, even though she was American. How had that come about?

'Howard University was good for me,' said Cheddi. 'It was the best black university in America; it had a beautiful campus and the finest professors. And I loved being in a place where black people were recognised and supported. I was surprised to find that the word coloured had a completely different connotation in America; in BeeGee it meant mixed race between African and white and even had a certain social status; in America it meant black and was a derogatory term; there was a clean cut between whites and anyone with a drop of black blood, whereas at home racism was more subtle, stratified. Anyway – I'm rambling, sorry. I won a free tuition scholarship for my second year there, then a tuition scholarship to Northwestern University Dental School; only the very best students were accepted there, so it was a move up. So I moved to Chicago. That's where we met.'

He smiled at his wife; she smiled back. Between the two of them an unmistakable rapport seemed to flow, a connection that was more than romantic, more than intellectual.

'I was a nurse, but already involved in radical politics when we met,' said Janet. 'In fact, it was I who gave him his first Marxist tracts. You could say I seduced him.' She laughed, and they exchanged another fond glance. 'We had an instant connection. My parents – my father – was of course furious. My family was of middle-class Jewish stock – Rosenberg was my maiden name. My father tried to prevent our marriage – what was I doing with the son of agricultural workers from some remote British colony? It didn't work. We married anyway.'

'My parents were just as opposed,' said Cheddi. 'I was supposed to marry a good Hindu bride they'd choose for me. But Janet and I – well, we just became a team.'

'We married in 1942, and he came back here to set up his dental practice. I came a year later. We've been working together ever since,' added Janet.

'The entire Corentyne coast, all the workers, stand behind Cheddi,' said Sam. 'Every last one. He is the leader we've been waiting for. It's going to be a revolution.'

When he spoke those words something within me seemed to burst open. It sounded wonderful – too good to be true, even. But just one word, one name resonated inside me: Jock. What would he think, what would he do? Jock and Cheddi; Cheddi and Jock; Jock versus Cheddi?

I had to know.

'Have you heard of Jock Campbell?' I asked, tentatively.

'I have, indeed. He sounds like a good man. But don't fool yourself, he's on their side, he's one of them. He's a planter, a sugar king.'

'And anyway,' said Rudi. 'Jock's given up. He's gone back to England and he won't be back. He dreamed an impossible dream. Cheddi's our man. The movement must come from below, not above.'

And Rudi was right.

Jock was in England. He hadn't been heard of for years. He'd plainly given up his pipe dream of reform in BeeGee; he had his wife and, no doubt, children too. He would, by now, be distracted by the trappings of domesticity. He would never return. Rudi was right: the revolution, if and when it came, would be from below, from the people, and not from above. Jock's dream had been usurped, by a man of the people, and it was better that way.

Jock was in the past: my past, and my country's past.

Chapter 44

Sam Jonkers came to visit me the next day, and we discussed plantation business. I had planned to give half of Promised Land to Charlie after the war, but that plan now thwarted, it continued as before, in the capable hands of an ageing Uncle Jim. Sam was the manager.

Following the lead in the reforms that Jock had initiated at Albion, Promised Land was thriving; it turned out that happy workers made for efficient workers, and profits rose. After discussing matters – really, there was not much I had to say; I might own the plantation but I left the running of it entirely to Uncle Jim and Sam – our conversation returned to yesterday's meeting with Cheddi and Janet Jagan.

I was surprised at the change in Sam: from down-and-out pork-knocker living from hand to mouth and stirring up revolution where he could, to responsible and hard-working planter. In the past year he had married one of Uncle Jim's daughters, and had settled in the senior staff compound of Promised Land. But now, something else had taken over; a new verve, a new spirit, and I knew the cause.

'He got the gift,' said Sam. 'He the leader. The one we was waiting for.'

Cheddi and his wife Janet had been busy on the plantations, Sam told me. Cheddi had a voice, and a charisma; I had seen that yesterday, and I could well imagine how inspiring such a speaker must be for the workers. When Cheddi spoke, people would listen. I had listened to him for hours yesterday, never bored for a second. Janet, I learned, was more than his wife. She was his partner, in every way, equally involved, equally passionate.

For now, she worked with him in his Camp Street practice as a dental hygienist and office assistant. His fees were low, Sam told me – he did not want to exploit his patients. Sam chuckled. 'The Dental Association trying to get him to raise he fees – they don't want the competition. But nothing doing, Cheddi and Janet work for the people.'

'He strikes me as very sincere,' I said. 'I liked him. And her. Somehow, I trust them.'

'They is the revolution,' said Sam. And I believed him.

The following years proved Sam's prophecy was correct. Cheddi was the messiah the workers had yearned for. In no time, the dental surgery on Camp Street became a hive of activity, for the poor, ordinary rural and urban workers chose him as their dentist. A movement began to build. His name and reputation spread along the sugar belt, to the very estates where he had grown up. He was a son of the soil who had made good: how could his people not be proud, and turn to him as a leader? They invited him to speak and advise them on industrial matters. Cheddi was well educated; he believed wholeheartedly in the Marxist idea: from each according to his ability, to each according to his need, and preached it far and wide. The idea took root – the idea of a movement from below, a movement from the workers. He became their spokesman, their champion. Up and down the coast Cheddi and Janet travelled; Janet, by this time, as outspoken and angry as he. She wore a sari; she, a white woman, found reluctant acceptance when the people learned to trust her. She was on their side, fighting for their rights.

In 1945, Cheddi became treasurer of that sugar workers' union, the Man Power Citizens' Association, but was removed after a year; he objected to the glaring reluctance of the union to defend the interests of the sugar workers. And no wonder: it was, he discovered, a company union.

In 1947, the first elections since World War II were held. Janet and Cheddi Jagan ran as candidates for the British Guiana

Labour Party, calling for the introduction of universal_suffrage, self-government, fair wage rules and land reform. Janet ran in Georgetown, but lost to John Fernandes, a businessman and a Catholic, who invoked the dreaded bogeyman of communism against her. Cheddi ran on the East Coast Demerara, where he fought against some well-established politicians, including John D'Aguiar, not only a powerful rival but a man of great wealth and enormous influence. At the end of the count, Cheddi was declared the winner by a landslide.

The revolution had truly begun.

Chapter 45

I did not need to work, but I did, continuing with my teaching, though empty at heart. I now wished that Michael had indeed left me with a baby; for without someone to care for in my everyday life, what joy could that life bring? I needed to care, to share myself with others; but remarrying was out of the question. I had loved twice in my life, lost twice, and it would not happen again.

I spent most of my evenings now with Aunt Winnie, whose house was once again full as family members returned from war, married and had babies, and she fulfilled her role as living core and beating heart of the Quint family; and I too, of course, was now truly a Quint, part of her wide network of love. It was that network that kept me going. Aunt Winnie was like an electrical socket, a constant source of stable energy. Whenever we, her family members, ran low, we only had to return to her and plug into that source – feel her arms around us, hear a word of encouragement – for that inner strength of hers to enter into our own hearts, become part of our own beings. And so we grew from strength to strength, but all connected to that one heartbeat at our core. She was, indeed, a matriarch, coaxing us gently but discreetly in the right direction, helping us all to find the right path we did not yet know ourselves.

And then one evening, Rudi, now a marine engineer at Sprostons Dockyard, bounded through the door.

'Ma! Grace! You'll never guess the news!'

'What? Good or bad?'

'Depends on how you see it, but – Jock's back!'

I gulped, and sat down.

'Are you all right, Grace?'

'Yes, yes, I'm fine. He's back? Back at Albion? How – what…?'

Auntie, hearing the commotion, stood up from the table, where she was mixing dried fruit and rum for a Christmas black cake; prepared months in advance, it would be black and moist by December and so rich you could almost get drunk on it; children were not allowed to eat it.

'You won't believe it,' said Rudi. 'You just won't. Jock's now a director at Bookers! Bookers has taken over the Campbell estates – a friendly takeover – and Jock's on the board. He did it! He's manoeuvred himself right into the seat of power! Bookers! Do you realise what that means?'

I did indeed. Booker Brothers was the most powerful entity in the entire colony, higher even than the Governor, who represented the King. If Jock was on the board…

And now I knew exactly what his Big Plan was; his great idea, his castle in the sky… How impossible it must have seemed for a neophyte young man in his twenties! How huge an ambition! Bookers' administration was riddled with crusty old men who wielded great power, who said what was to be done, and how. But now he had another force to contend with; a force, perhaps, yet more powerful than the cranky old men of the Booker board. He had to contend with Cheddi Jagan.

Jock had left BeeGee with his mission half-completed, his big dream a pie in the sky, his love life in jeopardy. Now he was back, and everything had changed dramatically. Cheddi Jagan was a potential ally, holding the very same dream as he did, the goal of a humane life for the workers. But Cheddi was also a potential enemy. How on earth would it all work out? How could it?

Over the following years, I sought out all the news about Jock as well as all the news about Cheddi; their careers developed in tandem. I heard it second or third hand from Rudi and Sam and Aunt Winnie. I read it in the newspapers. I followed it on the radio.

I discussed it – discreetly, never letting on about my past relationship with Jock – with friends, people who worked at Bookers. I knew many of those; everyone knew Bookers' employees, so ubiquitous was the company. I was riveted, distressed, fascinated, all at once.

Booker had been run by a senior management of antediluvian old men, entrenched in their ways, confined in their thinking; men rooted in a framework of self-interest intrinsically opposed to change. Jock dismissed them all as hopeless. A new broom sweeping clean, he ran rings around them.

'He's whirling through the company like a hurricane,' one friend told me. 'He exhausts us – such energy!' Exhausted maybe, but also exhilarated, his staff rallied to keep up as he removed the old and replaced it with new.

The company was in complete disarray; so splintered nobody knew what was making a profit and what was making a loss. The machinery was old and derelict after the war years, and a serious fire had destroyed several Booker buildings. Worst of all, Bookers was universally hated, both inside and outside the colony, and even by the colonial authorities. It was the textbook example of an arrogant, imperialist juggernaut grown obese and unwieldy off the fat of the land, except that it was now making a loss.

'Everything's changing!' exulted another friend. 'I love working there now, I just got a promotion!'

I knew it so well, and I thrilled to think of it happening: Jock's unique vision, centred on people. 'No person is ever redundant, only jobs,' was his motto – one of them – and his staff were never to forget that. 'People are more important than ships, shops and sugar estates,' was another motto, not just words, but practice. I'd heard it from his lips so many times, in these very words or similar.

With his whole being Jock believed that people came first; that there should be values other than money in a civilised society. He believed in truth, beauty and goodness. He believed that business-men had to set an example to the rest of society; for if they made money, profit, greed and acquisition their highest values so too would nurses, teachers and ambulance men. As the greatest power in the country it was up to Bookers to lead the way. Now I could see it happening, if only from afar.

Bookers, once a synonym for greed, day by day transformed into a model of benevolence. And the process began with people. The company began to recruit new managers, efficient managers, ethical, hand-picked managers; a difficult task, which Jock solved by breaking it down into small and manageable units.

Most important of all, the new people were Guianese; qualified, home-grown individuals who had caught the infectious spirit of their leader. I saw personal friends of mine, coloured people, black people, Indians, promoted into positions of responsibility. If they lacked the skills for the job, they were sent abroad for training. The glass ceiling of skin colour cracked and crumbled; and it fell apart not through protest by the workers, not through rebellion or revolution, but through a decree from above. It was all Jock's doing. In 1947, aged thirty-five, Jock became Booker's vice-chairman, the youngest ever in such a position.

I watched and marvelled as he lifted the archaic company right off its hinges, gave it a vigorous shake, and set it on course to run in an entirely new direction. I watched and cheered from afar as he created a miracle: the bully Bookers, that cruel and cumbersome giant we all hated, turning from ugly to almost beautiful. Changing direction, discarding the habits of the past, it transformed itself into a fresh, forceful and benevolent friend of the people, modern, successful and social. It was the dawn of Bookers' glory days. Jock moved back and forth between BeeGee and England, managing the process of change, working his unique magic. Now that there were regular BOAC flights between Georgetown and London travel between the countries was so much easier.

One of the most gratifying – for me – symbols of that change was the creation of the Booker Arts Foundation, through which all the arts were encouraged and particularly talented artists sponsored for overseas training. The emphasis was on painting and writing, with prizes and scholarships abroad set up. Music, I noticed, had as yet received no support, and I wondered if this neglect was deliberate and personal. But then, Jock had always loved painting and literature and had admitted to me early on that he simply did not understand music. Only in that sense was it personal. It surely had nothing to do with me; Jock had clearly forgotten me.

From afar I rejoiced with Jock. I followed the news, indeed. But I avoided Jock himself.

Chapter 46

1950

For years, I went out of my way to sidestep an encounter with Jock. I never attended any function, any party, any gathering where there was even a remote chance that he might be there. Georgetown is a small city, British Guiana a tiny world, but I knew how to carve out a social niche for myself, one in which he was unlikely to appear. And so I went my solitary, and sometimes lonely, way.

By 1950 I had built up my reputation, both as a musician in my own right and as a teacher of music. Auntie's friend, Mrs McGregor, had helped me at every stage, and by now I had a foothold in every single secondary school in the country, both in an advisory function and in some cases as a choirmistress, or as a teacher of particularly promising music students.

My big vision was to create a home-grown orchestra: how wonderful that would be! But I soon realised that that dream was as good as impossible. The country lacked teachers of the less popular instruments necessary for an orchestra; it lacked the instruments themselves. The best I could do was to organise two ensembles: a string quartet, to be directed by Aunt Winnie, and a woodwind quintet, directed by me. Both groups had already had one or two bookings for chamber music. Jock did not move in such circles.

I had the feeling that the avoidance scheme was mutual. Why had he not gone to visit Aunt Winnie, for instance, when they had once been so close? And Uncle Jim? Why had he not sought contact with Rudi, his one-time employee? I assumed that Jock was suffering from a bad conscience, as well he might. And to tell the truth, and being quite honest with myself, I was wounded that he had not sought me out. He had discarded me by letter, and I had never heard from him again. Surely the polite, the caring thing to do was to seek me out and apologise in person? A little seed of hurt nestled deep within. I tried to ignore it, but it was there all the same.

And so I continued to follow Jock's rise from afar, watched him leap from strength to strength, but with mixed feelings. I rejoiced at the benefits he brought, but ached from his rejection, so complete, so final. For a while I tried to purge him from my mind, but it was impossible, for hardly a day passed without a mention of him in the *Daily Argosy* or on the radio. And his story was just beginning to get interesting. Jock's power within the colony was no longer unassailable; for Cheddi Jagan was on the rise, more vocal than ever, storming up and down the East Coast and the East Bank Demerara. More than intrigued, I was also, in a mild way, involved.

Cheddi and Janet remained my friends, though I saw them seldom now, and I knew Cheddi's opinions well. Having grown up on a Booker estate, he hated the very name Booker with a particular loathing; and in spite of the company's complete volte-face under Jock's leadership, Cheddi refused to be appeased, refused any suggestion that management and labourers could actually work together; there was no way on earth that the inherent conflict of interest could be overcome.

Bookers, according to Cheddi, was a capitalist imperialist power; evil incarnate. It must be resisted with every breath of a worker's body. Jock Campbell came from privilege, from a class known for its hypocrisy and deception. He was not to be trusted. People took sides; I was astonished when even Rudi, who had once been so taken with Jock, now sided unequivocally with Cheddi. I read with fascination as snippets of Cheddi's objection to the new Bookers ethos came to light; and I couldn't help a sense of *Schadenfreude*.

Good for Cheddi! I sometimes thought. Good that not everyone
falls at Jock's feet, as I once did, as we all had done. But deep inside
I knew that such reactions were personal and unfair. Deep inside
I knew he was good; deep inside I knew I still loved him. And the
more I read of the mounting tension between him and Cheddi,
the more I became aware of a little inner itch I could not scratch.

It made itself known as a pinprick of pain I felt each time I
rode past Jock's house. Jock lived mostly in town, now, in the
Campbell home, Colgrain House on Camp Street. The very fact
that I knew this was proof of my ongoing interest. I visited Aunt
Winnie frequently, riding my bike from Peter Rose Street down
Church Street and Camp; I could have chosen a different route,
but I didn't. I enjoyed that frisson of pain, mingled with longing,
granted by those few yards of street outside his property. They
were all I had left of him. And though I avoided every possibility
of meeting him face to face, I would not deny myself this flight
of sentiment. It was an emotional luxury in a well-regulated life
by no means devoid of affection: I had the love of Aunt Winnie
and my brothers, the friendship of Dorothea and Joyce, as well as
many other women I had met through my work over the years.
But this was different. In it was a quiver of danger. And I not only
enjoyed it, I courted it.

I suppose, then, what followed was inevitable. It was the last
piece missing from the mosaic of my life, without which I would
never be complete. A loose end that needed to be tied; a full stop
to a story that had not yet come to its designated end.

For one day: there he was.

I had seen the Bentley before, parked beneath the house,
hardly visible behind the lush foliage that filled the front garden,
or sometimes even in full view on the front drive. And yes, I had
taken to peeping in to see if the car was there or not. Sometimes,
as recently, it was locked away in the garage next to the house,
though still visible behind the latticeworked walls: a clear sign

that he was in England. But now, suddenly, here it was again: not in the yard, not on the drive, not in the garage, but on the bridge over the gutter outside the house. A great shining grey Bentley, a brand new model, and a man polishing it to an even greater shine. And the man was Jock.

I saw him from a considerable distance, and my heart turned somersaults. I had the option, at this point, to quickly leap from my bike, cross the road to the central walkway and turn away to ride in the opposite direction, southwards, on the other side of Camp Street. I wanted to do that; I commanded myself to do that. But I didn't, and then it was too late, and I was just yards away, and he looked up. And our eyes met. And then I was right beside him and I could have smiled and ridden on with a curt 'Good day,' but I didn't do that either. I braked and jumped off my bike and there we stood, facing each other, at first silently. And then he said, 'Grace.' And I replied, 'Jock.'

That was all that was needed.

I had thought I was so strong, so independent, so armoured against heightened emotion. I thought I could fight back any show of weakness, should I ever be confronted by this man who had broken my heart. I was wrong.

I wrestled with those tears. I would not let them fall; but they gathered in my eyes and oh, what could I do? They were running down my cheeks now, and I had no words and I urged myself to get back on my bike and ride away, and indeed, I must have made some move to do so but I could not because he had left the car, polishing rag still in his hand, to stand just next to me, one hand on my handlebars, holding the bike still. His eyes locked on to mine; and his, too, grew moist and then wet and I wasn't sure if that made it worse or better.

'I'd better go,' I snivelled, and made to move on once more, but he grabbed hold of my handlebars now with both hands, and he spoke too.

'Grace – please. Come inside. Let's talk.'

I shook my head, no. And I wished I had a hanky but I didn't. But he did; he looked at the polishing rag in his hand, chucked it to the ground and removed a huge white handkerchief from his pocket and dabbed at my eyes, and I sniffed and laughed and so did he.

'I need to go,' I said, and again tried to push the bicycle away, but he held it fast, and turned the handlebars to face towards the house, and proceeded to wheel it over the bridge, narrowly avoiding his precious car; and he held out a hand to me and said, again, 'Come, Grace! Please! Just come!' And as in a trance I followed him over the bridge; he set my bicycle on its stand and took my hand and led me up the stairs and through the front door, and then into the gallery, where he pulled out a wicker chair for me and I sat down.

'Are you thirsty?' he asked, and I nodded.

'Wait there!' He walked past the enormous polished dining table to a Frigidaire, and I watched as he prepared for me a glass of lime water with ice, and brought it to me. And I drank.

I set the glass down and we looked at each other. He still looked the same – almost. The eyes were the same greeny-brown, liquid, eloquent, but they now seemed even deeper than before. His hair was as black as ever. Everything about him had matured, to his advantage. I tried to look away, look down, but couldn't. I didn't want him to see the tears pooling in my eyes, escaping down my cheeks. I wiped them with his handkerchief, which I clung to. He spoke again:

'Grace. I'm sorry, I'm so sorry. What I did – it was inexcusable.'

I shook my head vigorously.

'No, Jock. I know now – it had to be this way. You had… a calling. You were right. It was bigger than us. We had to go our separate ways.'

'But it was horrible, the way it happened. I should have known. Not kept you hanging on like that.'

'I married, Jock. Michael was a good man, a good husband. We were happy.'

He nodded. 'I heard about your husband, what happened to him. I'm so sorry. He was a hero.'

I nodded. 'He was.'

We were both silent for a moment. Then I said:

'Your wife – she stayed in England?'

'Yes. She's a good woman – suitable in every way. We have four children.'

'Michael and I had none, unfortunately.'

'You're young. How old are you now?'

'Thirty-three,' I said. 'Practically ancient!' I managed to chuckle.

'No, you're young and beautiful. You'll find someone else in time. And anyway, you're doing well, I heard…'

I smiled at that. 'You heard? So you keep track of me?'

'Indeed I do. Sometimes I drive past your house, you know. Hoping for a glimpse of you. I've never quite found the courage to, you know – actually stop and knock on your door.'

'It wouldn't have been – appropriate.'

'I suppose not.'

'I thought you'd forgotten me. Completely.'

'Grace, how could I ever forget you?'

There was no answer. We gazed silently at each other for a while. I took several deep breaths and pushed back the tears and drained my glass. Somehow my emotions calmed down and I felt capable of normal conversation. We both relaxed into our chairs, placed at a decorous distance from each other. I felt it necessary to steer the conversation on to safer ground, and I was relieved when Jock asked me about my life. I told him about my work. I told him how desperately we needed instruments, how much I wanted, at least, to introduce recorders in the primary schools and transverse flutes in secondary schools, and the difficulty of obtaining instruments for the poorer pupils. He listened attentively, nodding, and at last I felt it was safe to talk about him.

'I've been following your career,' I said, in a perfectly normal voice. 'Congratulations, you've performed a miracle!'

'Well – it's what I always had in mind. I always had my eyes on the Booker throne.'

'We thought you weren't coming back, once you'd left and married. What happened? How did you do it?'

'Well – it was quite straightforward, really. Back in England, I worked in the Colonial Office and prepared the groundwork. My plans were always quite clear: the Booker empire. My father and uncle owned the company Curtis Campbell, but I'd seen how useless it was to own two estates and a dock. Structural and social changes had to encompass the entire sugar industry, and that could only mean Bookers. So I convinced my father and uncle that a merger between Curtis Campbell and Booker Brothers was necessary for the survival of the family concern. Those two were on the board of Bookers, and helped negotiate a takeover of our own company in 1939. Shares were exchanged. I was appointed a director and moved into the Booker stronghold. That's it in a nutshell.'

'And how do you feel about Cheddi Jagan? Is he an ally or an enemy?'

'I've met Cheddi, I've talked to him. I like him, actually. But – I have to admit – he's a thorn in my side, my nemesis, maybe. I don't agree with Cheddi's ideology; I'm not a Marxist. But I understand his motivation. It's almost identical to mine. I feel almost a – a symbiotic link to Cheddi. We both grew up in king sugar's shadow, I as master, Cheddi as servant. But though I'm from capitalist stock my leanings are entirely left wing, which makes me something of a renegade. But Cheddi won't have it. He won't believe I'm on the side of the workers; that I'm as radical as he is. Cheddi's extremism, in fact, drives me even more to the left. The truth is that Cheddi's pressure and demands force the pace, and enable me to gain acceptance for reforms that the Booker board and the shareholders never would have accepted in a quiescent colony.'

'I've met him too,' I said. 'And Janet. She's remarkable. She makes me realise it would never have worked between us. She's a true and equal partner in his fight. I never was. I could never have been a Janet to you.'

He leaned over, placed a hand on mine, resting on the chair's armrest.

'Grace – you were – you are – perfect the way you are. I loved you for yourself.'

He added, beneath his breath but loud enough for me to hear: '…and I still do.'

The silence hung once more between us.

And then I said it, the thing that was taboo. The thing that would either break down the wall between us, or make it inviolable.

'And me – us – was that the price you paid for your position in Bookers? Was I your bargaining chip?' I paused. 'You can be honest with me, Jock. I can take it.'

He was silent for a long time. I waited. I knew how awkward this must be for him. I knew he cared, and didn't want to hurt me. He knew how hurtful words could be. I knew he was choosing them carefully – Jock was always good with words.

'Grace,' he said finally, resignation in his voice, 'I know how terrible this sounds, but it was a huge sacrifice on my part. And I accept blame. It was my choice to make that sacrifice, and it was simply served to you, cold, and you had no choice. That was wrong of me. I'm sorry, so sorry.'

'You haven't answered my question, Jock. Was I your bargaining chip?'

He hesitated again, and then said, slowly, 'Yes, you're right. By going along with my family's choice of wife I secured the ground to make demands of them elsewhere. So yes, I gave you up in order to realise my vision. It was selfish.'

'Or unselfish, from a different vantage point. After all, your vision was for the greater good – for humanity. Something bigger than the two of us, as you always used to say.'

He nodded. 'And yet, even that vision was personal, Grace. I had this deep-seated guilt I needed to appease. I had to do it. But I also wanted you. I really did, Grace. That was sincere. I thought I could have both – you and my vision.'

'But, Jock, you must have known from the start that your parents would object! Why did you encourage me? Why did you let me hope? Why did you not warn me from the start?'

He shook his head. 'I didn't know, Grace. As far as I was concerned you were an upper-class girl, from aristocratic stock, even. An impeccable English family background. The only child of a planter family; really, a most suitable alliance under normal circumstances. I thought they'd been pleased! I'd never considered your skin colour. It just didn't matter to me. I had never encountered racism before. I was just – naïve. I loved you Grace. I'm sorry.'

Our eyes met, and I realised that his were moist and full of unshed tears. I felt the need to reassure him, to comfort him.

'It's all right, Jock. I understand now.'

Another moment of silence. And then I hastily stood up, and said in a rush:

'Jock – it's not appropriate for me to be here. Not at all appropriate. I'm sorry, I'll go now. I shouldn't have come. I—'

But he too was on his feet. He took me in his arms. Held his right cheek to mine, and then his left to my left; and then… I don't know how it happened. It was as if we were in a magnetic field, so powerful we could not resist. I was in his arms. They were around me, holding me tight; my face pressed against his shoulder and my eyes leaking tears, soaking into his shirt; and then strong arms lifted me up and he was carrying me up the stairs.

'No,' I said, 'no'; but it was a weak and wavering no and we both knew it was a lie, for love was palpable in every cell of my body, love yearning for him, a yawning reception in my very soul, and my body was simply the physical expression of a need to become one, to unite with him, completely and utterly. There was no sin, no betrayal in the intimacy of that union, for love had brought us together; and love is pure and perfect.

I wept when it was over, and so did he. Bittersweet tears that contained the love of a lifetime, lost and found and lost again.

Later, when I retrieved my bicycle, I said, 'I'm sorry, Jock.'

'I'm not. I'm glad.'

'It won't happen again.'

'I know.'

And it never did. I never saw him again. Our story had come to an end.

Chapter 47

Two months later I found out I was expecting a baby. Of course, there was only one person I could tell.

'We'll find a solution,' Aunt Winnie said.

'He must never know,' I told her.

'That's why we must find a solution. A good one. And we will.'

'I can't stay here, in BeeGee. He's sure to find out, to know. And the scandal…'

'Don't worry, I have an idea.'

A few weeks later the solution was clear, and it was a good one. Aunt Winnie's sister, my Aunt Kathleen, whom I had never met as she had lived most of her life in England, had married a man much older than herself. He was now retired, and the two of them lived in a mansion in Eastbourne, on the south coast of England. Kathleen, Winnie said, would be happy to take me in. All of my brothers had stayed with her during their studies or in the war years. Her house was open for family.

'But what will I say to people? How will I explain to people in England that as a single woman – a baby—'

'You are a widow. It's all very respectable.'

'But my husband died in the war! So long ago!'

'They know that in BeeGee, which is why you can't stay here. This society can be vicious if you don't play by the rules. But in England, no one need know when he died. They won't know if you don't tell them, and you won't. You are Grace van Groenwedel, a respectable widow, come to stay with your aunt, who is helping you out in your time of mourning.'

'And if they ask, I should lie about it?'

'Sometimes a white lie is necessary.'

'But, Auntie, I'll miss you!'

'And I'll miss you. But it need not be for ever.'

'It won't be.'

Before I left I had to make arrangements for Promised Land; but I had always known what I would eventually do. I summoned Sam Jonkers, and told him I was giving it to him.

'No,' he said, 'I'll buy it from you, at a fair price.'

I laughed. 'Sam, don't be silly! If you like I'll sell it to you for a dollar, if that makes you happy and satisfies your pride. But I want you to have it. You are the rightful heir – my grandfather's son. It should go to you.'

'You think I don't have money, nah? Well, I do. I said a fair price, and that's what I'll pay. You gon' need all the money you can get, raisin' a child in England.'

'Oh, Sam! I can always get a job as a music mistress. And I'm selling the house on Peter Rose Street, so I'll be well off – and anyway, where did you get money from? They always said you were a bit of a gangster, don't tell me...'

'I earn this money fair and square!'

And he pushed his hand into that ubiquitous, dirty, ancient canvas bag. And again removed a pouch. He handed it to me. 'Look inside,' he said. I laughed as I took it; the last time he had done this, the pouch had been full of corilla pods. But this time it was hard and heavy, and crackled as I took it. I raised my eyebrows and looked inside – and gasped.

'Gold!' I cried. 'Gold nuggets!'

Sam laughed, took back the pouch and emptied it on the floor. The nuggets were of varying sizes, one or two as big as peanuts, some the size of peas. And every one solid and real and...

'Precious,' said Sam. 'I work hard for these things. Pork-knocker life is hard, but sometimes it does pay out. These are all mine, but now they are yours.'

I bent over to gather up the nuggets, return them to their pouch.

'And Promised Land is yours, Sam Jonkers. That's how it should be.'

*

Two days before I set sail for England a delivery was made to my home – two huge boxes, postmarked Liverpool, so heavy two strapping men had to carry them into the house. In bemusement I opened the first box. On top of the contents was a card, which, when I opened it, said quite simply, 'With the compliments of Booker Arts Foundation'. Underneath the note were countless long thin boxes: recorders. I counted them later: one hundred. One hundred recorders, enough for every single primary school pupil in the country who wanted to learn.

The second box was smaller, but heavier. It contained a similar card, but the boxes inside it were longer and thinner: transverse flutes. Tears pooled in my eyes; tears of gratitude, but also of regret. I would never be able to teach the children on these flutes, but I was not irreplaceable. Mrs McGregor would be here, and she would ensure that every child who so wished would receive a flute. And so, in the end, they were tears of gratitude.

Chapter 48

I was excited when Cheddi Jagan's newly established party, the People's Progressive Party, won the 1957 election in British Guiana hands down, and from my new home in Eastbourne paid close attention to what would happen now that he stood at the colony's helm. What would happen to Jock? Could they work together at last?

Aunt Winnie continued to send me news clippings, and I followed events avidly. She and Rudi kept me duly informed.

'We're all worried,' wrote Rudi, 'Britain is scared stiff of Cheddi, they call him a damned communist. They're backing Forbes Burnham.' Burnham was a brilliant lawyer of African descent, who, like Cheddi, had attended the elite Queen's College in Georgetown. Now he was in politics, initially as Cheddi's ally and, with Britain's backing, as his opponent.

'The next election's crucial,' Rudi continued; 'whoever wins that will lead the colony to independence. Burnham's formed a new party, the People's National Congress, a new opposition political party to race against the elected PPP. It's dangerous.'

Aunt Winnie, in the meantime, wrote: 'Jock detests Burnham; the idea of him as the country's leader is a nightmare. He's the epitome of the wily politician with no greater aim than his own advancement. There's only one way to prevent this: Cheddi has to reassure both the USA and Britain that he's willing to compromise, to work with the benevolent capitalist force that Bookers has now become.'

'But how can Jock do that?' I wrote back. 'Cheddi's so stubborn, he'll never work with Bookers!'

'Jock has an idea,' Aunt Winnie replied in her next letter. 'It's a big gamble, but it might work.'

Aunt Winnie had become something of a confidante to Jock; he came to tell her his thoughts and to unload his frustrations; they would sit in her gallery talking into the night. And so Aunt Winnie was among the first, and the few, to know the details when Jock played his last and final card, his ace.

Even in writing, she sounded breathless when she related the extraordinary scene. 'You'll never believe this,' she said. 'Cheddi must be out of his mind!'

Jock invited Cheddi to a private talk in the chairman's office of Booker Sugar Estates. It was time to get down to the nuts and bolts of Bookers' future in British Guiana. The two men spoke alone for two hours but made little progress.

'They talked around and around in circles,' Aunt Winnie wrote. 'You know how annoying Cheddi can be, how stubborn? Well, here he was, playing the mule. Jock couldn't make any headway. So he played that precious ace. You won't believe it, Grace.'

'Listen,' he said slowly. 'I'll make you an offer. A once-in-a-lifetime offer.'

Cheddi said nothing. He only watched. He was speaking to a quintessential capitalist, a breed not to be trusted.

'I have an idea,' said Jock. 'I know it's daring, I know it sounds ridiculous, but it could change everything. I'll give you fifty-one per cent of Booker shares. You, the government, holds those shares in trust with the unions. Bookers retain forty-nine per cent of the shares and manage the whole enterprise. We'd have a two-tier board. I envision a shareholders' board consisting of sugar workers, political parties, unions and individual Guianese: that board would have a controlling interest and lay down the policy. Then there would be the practical management board, on which the top board, the shareholders' board, would also be represented – that's us, Bookers. We'd…'

Jock spoke on, lit by an inner fire, carried away by the beauty of his idea. It was perfect; it was the very solution.

Cheddi interrupted. 'Have you discussed this with the Booker board of directors?'

Jock shook his head.

'No, but I can convince them. I know I can.'

'What about Follet-Smith? Does he know, at least?'

Follet-Smith was the chairman of Booker Sugar Estates; they were sitting in his office, Jock sat in his very chair. A man of the old guard, a man of encrusted concepts and inflexible notions, he was one of the hopeless old men Jock had been struggling against ever since he'd headed Booker.

Again, Jock shook his head.

'I'll take care of that – once I get your approval.'

'It was an outlandish scheme,' Aunt Winnie wrote. 'Unheard of, really. It was revolutionary. Jock was, in effect, handing him Bookers on a plate, while guaranteeing the expert management and foreign capital needed to keep the concern going. Furthermore, it would convince both the USA and Britain that Cheddi Jagan was flexible; that he was not a Soviet pawn, and would work with Western forces. It was a way out of the morass, and, as far as Jock could see, the only way. His last chance; if this failed, he had no choice but to give up, return to England.'

But Cheddi was silent, his eyes on Jock.

*

'Despite himself, he likes Jock,' Aunt Winnie wrote, 'but in the end Jock's a capitalist; and Bookers the quintessential imperialist concern. What Jock offered made no sense whatsoever, neither from a Marxist nor from a capitalist point of view. It couldn't be done. Finally, Cheddi got up, and all he said was:

"You're joking, of course."'

Chapter 49

Grace van Groenwedel

Holywell Priory Cottage

88 Meads Street

Eastbourne

5 August 1957

Dear Aunt Winnie,

At last, good news! I got the job! Yes! Yesterday I received the letter – my application for the position of music teacher at Moira House School has been successful! It's an all-girls independent school here in Eastbourne with a stellar reputation and I'm beyond ecstatic! And as you can see from the address – the purchase of Holywell Priory Cottage has been completed, and Joanna and I have moved in. It's a darling cottage, right on the edge of town. The seafront is just a short walk down the pavement, and the South Downs is practically on our back door: all we have to do is cross the road behind the house and there we are – glorious miles and miles of rolling windswept hills. In fact, I could right now break out in song, 'Jerusalem', to be specific, for this is the quintessential England's green and pleasant land.

Jo is such a big girl now, as you can see from the enclosed photo. Do you also think she resembles Jock, with her curly black hair? Her eyes are also his – greeny-brown. Whenever I see her, I think of him – it's awful, but comforting at the same time. I've told her all about you and she sends her love and she hopes to meet you one day – and she will. We'll definitely come when she's a bit older. Maybe next year?

*Moira House has accepted her as a pupil in their primary depart-
ment, and as the daughter of a staff member I'll be paying reduced
fees, so that's more good news – we both start next month, and
though she'll have to say goodbye to her old class, she'll still keep
her friends. She's terribly excited, chattering away about it all the
time. It was lovely living with Aunt Kathleen but I feel it's time to
be on my own, stand on my own two feet, and now with this job
everything has fallen into place.*

*I enjoy your letters. Enjoy hearing all about the family and what
they're up to – everyone seems to be having such adventures! And
I can just imagine you surrounded by all your grandchildren,
your expanding family; the matriarch in her element. I will miss
Christmas, I always do. I miss black cake and pepperpot. I miss
you all. But one day – I'm sure of this now – we'll be there. Give
my love to everyone. You are all in my heart.*

Grace

The Aftermath

British Guiana became independent Guyana in 1966, and that's when Jock Campbell finally left the country for good. Back in Scotland, he was playing golf with his good friend Ian Fleming, author of the James Bond books, when the latter revealed a secret to him: he had cancer, and did not expect to live beyond a year. The inheritance tax at his death, he feared, would be tantamount to a confiscation; he wanted to do something to protect his assets for his heirs, and asked Jock for advice.

Jock had always loved literature. And if there was money to be made in fiction, then – why not? He arranged for Bookers to buy Fleming's interest in the James Bond books; and to this end he created the Booker Author Division. That division soon purchased the copyrights to many writers' works, including Agatha Christie.

Meanwhile, Tom Maschler, a publishing director at Jonathan Cape, impressed by the French enthusiasm for its great literary prize, the Prix Goncourt, began to campaign for a comparable English literature prize. And thus it was that Jonathan Cape came together with Bookers, a company already deeply involved with literature. Bookers agreed to sponsor the Booker Prize; and so the company, once a synonym for greed and exploitation, became the benevolent champion of excellent fiction.

In 1969, two years after Jock had resigned the Booker chairmanship, the Booker Prize was awarded for the very first time, and from that moment on there was no stopping it. And thus the Booker name – linked first to entrepreneurship, then to slavery and exploitation, then to social reform – found its final cause in fiction. It would never have happened without Jock.

A Letter from Sharon Maas

First of all, I want to say a huge thank you for choosing to read *The Girl from the Sugar Plantation*. I hope you enjoyed reading Grace's story just as much as I loved writing it. This novel has been brewing in me for a long time, and I'm so glad that it's finally 'Out There' with readers.

The Girl from the Sugar Plantation is the last book in the trilogy, The Quint Chronicles; although a standalone novel, it wraps up the central story of the Quints, and you can find out what went before in the novels *The Secret Life of Winnie Cox* and *The Sugar Planter's Daughter*. The story has now come to an end.

If you'd like to **keep up to date with all my latest releases**, just sign up here:

www.bookouture.com/sharon-maas

Yet as with all family sagas it branches off, and you can read more about how it continues in my novel, *The Small Fortune of Dorothea Q*. You have of course met the title figure, Dorothea, in *The Girl from the Sugar Plantation*. *The Small Fortune of Dorothea Q* is her story, but you'll also meet Freddy and Humphrey Quint again, as well as members of the following generation. So if you are curious as to what happens next, I invite you to move on to that book – which is already published, so no waiting!

As a writer, I always feel a deep connection to my unseen, unknown readers, and I'd love to hear from you, know your reactions to this book, either through a review, through my website or through my Facebook or Twitter pages.

Thank you so much for your support – until next time.

Sharon Maas

www.bookouture.com/sharonmaas

 @sharon_maas

sharonmaasauthor

www.sharonmaas.com

Historical Notes

As you may have guessed, Jock Campbell was a real person, as was Cheddi Jagan.

John 'Jock' Middleton Campbell, Baron Campbell of Eskan, died in December 1994, but remains very much alive in the minds of those who knew him. I am lucky enough to have direct contact with some of these people: Clem Seecharan, author of the book *Sweetening Bitter Sugar*, and Ian McDonald, a friend and fellow Guyanese writer, whose article on Jock first made me aware of the charismatic effect he had on his staff, and in fact on everyone he came in contact with. No wonder Grace fell in love with him! That article is available to view on my website.

It's not an easy matter, weaving historical fact and fiction together, especially if the era concerned is not so very long ago. In a nutshell, I'll say this: Jock's public story as recounted in this novel is true, give or take some flexibility with dates. He had a galvanising effect on British Guiana's sugar industry in that he turned an oppressive power – Booker Brothers – into a force for humanistic values. That part is fact.

The fictional part is of course the story of his relationship with Grace, the love that grew between them. And yet, even that romance is based on truth: Jock did fall desperately in love with a Guyanese girl. Her name was Philomena D'Aguiar. Philomena was the sister of Peter D'Aguiar, the business magnate and politician, and, later, leader of the conservative and economically liberal political party United Force. As in the story with Grace, Jock's parents would not countenance a marriage between them: Philomena was Catholic

– the Campbells were Presbyterian – and of Madeiran Portuguese stock, descended from indentured servants, and so not the right class. The family found a suitable bride for Jock; he accepted their choice, and he and Barbara had four children, three of whom survive today.

When I first discovered Jock I was astonished that I had never heard of this extraordinary figure from Guyana's history; he seemed in danger of disappearing into obscurity, despite Clem Seecharan's wonderful book. There wasn't even a Wikipedia article on him at that time – so I created one! Since then, that first entry has been expanded upon, but I was the originator, back in 2007. I hope this novel brings more awareness to him; he deserves it.

I've always regarded Jock as an unsung hero, not only relevant to the history of Guyana but the kind of leader with moral backbone we in the West so yearn for today. I've tried to capture the charisma of his personality; but in particular, his philosophy that 'people matter'; that the well-being of workers should be at the forefront of every business enterprise; that profit should not be the only driving force in business or leadership. We urgently need this wisdom in our day and age.

As for Cheddi Jagan: even his political enemies conceded that he was a man of high integrity, genuinely concerned for the underdog and the rights of those who had no rights. Both my father, David Westmaas, and my Uncle Rory were huge supporters, and in fact my father was his press secretary in his later years, so I would often run into Cheddi when visiting Dad at work.

In the end Cheddi won the 1953 elections in British Guiana. However, Winston Churchill, fearing that Cheddi was a Marxist-Leninist and could allow the Soviet Union a foothold in Latin America, ordered military intervention only days after his victory, forcing his resignation after only 133 days in power. Accusations of voter fraud came with all subsequent elections, which Cheddi lost. In 1992, however, he won the presidency in independent

Guyana, this time monitored by former US President Jimmy Carter's team of election observers. After Cheddi's death his wife, Janet Jagan, took over the presidency, and was later herself elected as Guyana's president.

Guyanese politics have always been volatile, with controversial leaders, often beset by racial divisions and violence, often descending into the usual political finger pointing. Yet it's still possible to identify those whose hearts are in the right place, and Cheddi was one of them, as was Jock. Such a pity they could not work as one!

The 51 per cent shares offer Jock made to Cheddi is true, and recounted in *Sweetening Bitter Sugar*. Had Cheddi accepted that offer history would have taken a completely different course. Instead, disaster followed disaster, and Guyana still has not recovered from the chaos.

If you would like to know more about either one of these lesser-known historical figures, I recommend the following books:

Sweetening Bitter Sugar: Jock Campbell – The Booker Reformer in British Guiana 1934–1966 by Clem Seecharan

The West on Trial: My Fight for Guyana's Freedom by Cheddi Jagan.

Acknowledgements

My first thanks go to John and Peter Campbell. They are the sons of Jock Campbell, who, thanks to the magic of Google and the help of their cousin, Mark, I was able to track down. They have been tremendously supportive during the writing of this book, always answering my questions and providing further information, even such small details as the colour of his hair and eyes. I hope I have done their father justice! (Ironically, I could have saved myself a lot of googling, had I known that one of my pre-existing Facebook friends, the acclaimed children's writer Anthony McGowan, was John Campbell's son-in-law!) So, my first thanks go to the Campbell children, John, Peter and Lou.

But no less, many thanks to Clem Seecharan, whose book, *Sweetening Bitter Sugar*, has been my Bible of Guyanese history as it pertains to the sugar industry; as well as to Ian McDonald, who wrote the preface to that book and who, as a Booker employee, knew Jock personally through work and experienced his extraordinary effect on people from all walks of life. Both Clem and Ian have been most helpful with my persistent questions via email. It was a very personal article by Ian in the Guyanese press that first alerted me to Jock's significance. Thank you both for your help and patience.

Thanks to my cousins, Susan Conliffe, Nancy Westmaas and Mark Westmaas, who grew up on Albion estate. Their father, my Uncle Bill, was one of the first beneficiaries of 'Jock's policy of 'Guianisation' – allowing qualified non-white employees into senior positions. I once spent a holiday with them at Albion, and it was one of the most enjoyable holidays of my childhood. I remember well that neat white house on stilts on the estate, the swimming pool, the fun we had. This was during Jock's heyday; he would have been in charge at the time, and I might even have run into him without knowing. Uncle Bill and his wife, my Aunt Trixie, were sure to have known him personally.

Thanks also to my cousin, Peta Westmaas, granddaughter of Eleanor Ruby Julia McGregor, MBE, OBE, GAA; accomplished musician, concert pianist, teacher, choir director, and tough single parent after her husband died, who makes a cameo appearance in this novel. Thanks for your valued input regarding music as practised by that outstanding generation. I think we can learn a lot from women, real and fictional, like Ruby, Grace and Aunt Winnie. Peta's dad, Rory Westmaas, was the inspiration for Rudi Quint: Peta, Storm, Blaise and Wylde, I'm sure you'll recognise him immediately!

Friends, both in real life and virtual, are right there behind me when I am writing my books; I need them. So thanks go to Gisela Oess-Langford, Rita Coughlan, Elke Neukum, Renate Boy, Ulrike Mack, Regine Elsässer, Helen Zettler, Ann Claypole, Angelika Frank, Diane Reichart, Gisela Baldwin, Ulrike Böhm in Germany. Guyanese readers have always been a support on the home front: Sarah Mair Morgan, Andrea and Salvador deCaires, Elizabeth Alleyne, Su Bayne, Jocelyn Dow, Michael Wight, Tiffany Westmaas-Futral, Sharena Annamunthodoo, Jennifer Young, Maggie Cheek and many others. Thanks to Lloyd Austin of Austin's Book Store in Georgetown, for always stocking my books, in spite of the bother involved. To Vanda Radzig, and her sister Danuta, for organising launches and readings of my books at Moray House when I'm in Guyana. Gloria Austin, for being a friend in need, as well as Marilyn Clark and Pratima Nath-Willard. Thanks too to my cousin, Rod Westmaas, and his wonderful wife, Juanita Westmaas-Cox, for their unending support, and Juanita, an extra thank you for lending me your precious signed copy of *Sweetening Bitter Sugar* while my own copy is in storage in a box of books in Eastbourne! You can have it back now, hopefully none the worse for wear!

I'd also like to thank my fellow Bookouture authors, Rebecca Stonehill, Renita D'Silva and Debbie Rix, as well as all the other members of The Lounge (you know who you are!) and members of Toytown Germany, who prevent me from becoming quite the hermit. Thanks to AbsoluteWrite members, who have been there for me with expert advice and writerly suggestions when I needed it: in particular, Lisa Spangenberg and MacAllister Stone, but also Jane Smith, James Macdonald (another wise Uncle Jim!), Rob McCreery, Jamie Mason and Laurie Ashton Farook. Not to forget each and every one of the bloggers who have taken the time to read and review my books in the past, as well as the online book club administrators who help promote them – what would we writers do without you! Huge thanks to you all.

Thanks of course to my children-friends, Saskia and Miro. It's so easy to fly off into a fictional world and never return; thanks to you all for helping to keep me grounded! To my dear husband, Jürgen: you may not be aware of all this, but in a way it's for you.

Last, but not least, thanks to my super-editor, Natasha Harding, for her help in moulding this book into its proper shape. Also, huge thanks to Claire Bord, Jacqui Lewis, Lauren Finger, Kim Nash, Jane Donovan, Ellen Gleeson and to everyone else on the Bookouture team – and of course to Oliver Rhodes for making this all happen.

Sharon

Lightning Source UK Ltd.
Milton Keynes UK
UKHW020614111219
355129UK00015B/431/P